TEED OFF

It was the great detective himself who unlocked my memory. I lay, feet up, on my brother's old corduroy couch and watched my favourite television program *Sherlock Holmes' Mysteries*. While watching Holmes enthrall his buddy Watson, I had been going through Pitts's condominium in my mind. Something hadn't been right.

"Is there any other point to which you would wish to draw my attention?" one of the characters asked.

"To the curious incident of the dog in the night-time," Holmes replied.

"The dog did nothing in the night-time."

"That was the curious incident," remarked Sherlock Holmes.

I snapped my fingers. "Elementary, my dear Watson," I said aloud while chewing a chocolate. In my mind I could see the surface of Pitts's writing desk. It was clear.

"So," I said to the television, "where was the envelope?

Teed Off

by

Nicola Furlong

Mes,

Thanks for
coming !
Keep in touch
via Dorothy.

Nicola

**Commonwealth
Publications**

A Commonwealth Publications Paperback
TEED OFF

This edition published 1996
by Commonwealth Publications
9764 - 45th Avenue,
Edmonton, AB, CANADA T6E 5C5
All rights reserved
Copyright © 1995 by Nicola Furlong

ISBN: 1-55197-091-0

This work is a novel and any similarity to actual persons or events
is purely coincidental.

Designed by: Jennifer Brolsma

Printed in Canada

Dedicated, with love,
to my trinity of inspiration.
Mary Eileen (Pat O'Brien) Furlong,
Glynne Turner and Carla Furlong.

Acknowledgements

Special thanks to:

Glynne Turner, Jennifer Wyatt, Roseline Ménard, Joan Rickard, The Ladies Professional Golf Association, Caroline Keggi, Martha Figueras-Dotti, Lori West, Tina Barrett, Alison Munt, Cherie Smith, Dr. Walter Harris, Dr. Bob Steveson, Jocelyn Bourassa, Jim Ritts, Patty Sheehan, Karen Davies, Cindy Mackay, Elaine Crosby, Sandra Post, Rita Tettenburn, Chuck Strong, John Hamie, Jim Haley, Jennifer Dobson, Kurt Thuemmel, Judy Collins, Lanie Cahill, Ellynne Dickson, Don Noseworthy, Hilary Pearson, Robert Pohl, Everett Beemer, Merle Lemon, Charles Gross, Cindy Kenjerska, Muffin Spencer-Devlin, Colleen Walker and Michelle McGann.

One

Rubbing too little sleep from my eyes, I flipped the fax's cover sheet and stared.

> *Stop the killing!*
> *You have until July 28 or you will regret it.*
> *Golf can be dangerous!*

The terse message was a shock but I have to admit, after seven years as a member of the Ladies Pro Tour and almost 18 months as a teaching pro, I had no quarrel with the last line. Some of these rich yahoos may sport the latest boron-graphite shafts with high kick points and modified hosels, but look out for the ubiquitous banana slice!

The cover sheet read:

> *Riley,*
> *Look into this, will you? It's the third I've received in the past few months. Probably some nut, but with the Classic in ten days...? See you at the ferry terminal.*
>
> > *Pitts.*

I shook my head. So typical of Peter 'Pitts' Wyndamere, the man who is my best friend, my brother-in-law and, most recently, my boss. The guy waits months to tell me he's got trouble, then faxes his problem to me only hours before he arrives.

I flipped back to the fax. Centred, near the top of the plain white paper was a small globe with an outline of North America visible. BioAction was printed in a semi-circle above and a thick, fat arrow curved along the Canadian-U.S. border. The words below were obviously cut and pasted from various newspapers. Though the letter size and fonts were different, the collage message was clear. Somebody was threatening Pitts.

Though early morning, the cinder track buzzed with golfers. Tee off time for the First Annual Sea Blush Charity Pro-Am was in twenty minutes. Not enough time to deal with the facsimile, but enough to check The Witch. Lately, the ol' gal had been yelping when struck. I yanked her out of my bag and peered at her stainless steel noggin. Poor thing, she had a lot of nasty nicks.

In Delaware, at the McDonald's Championship, Jennifer Wyatt, my best friend on Tour, had dubbed my club a sorceress. The McDonald's was the first time I used a Callaway Big Bertha driver and the first time I won a Ladies Professional Golf Event. Jenny's nickname was right on. I found my Callaway witchy 'cause she had tons of power but gave it capriciously. The former I learned early in the first round, upping my driving average by five yards to 250; the latter late in the second. The Witch had a mind of her own and, on the eleventh and fourteenth holes, my ball hooked violently, air-mailing into stunned galleries.

I blinked back to reality. My touring days were over. All I had left were memories and a teaching job I never wanted. Thank God for my new part-time job. Moonlighting as a coroner with the province of British Columbia restores life to my days. Rubbing a thumb along her ribbed grey face, I gently placed my magician, scuffed head up, against the Pro Shop wall.

If British Columbia is a golf bag, and sometimes I think it is, then the new Sea Blush Golf Club in Nanoose-a tiny hamlet on Vancouver Island-is its most important club: the putter. Now some of you mainlanders may argue that the venerable Vancouver Golf Club or even the upstart Arnold Palmer-designed course at the Chateau Whistler Resort deserve this accolade. Interesting thought, but...naah. Maybe the sand wedge, perhaps even the driver, but Sea Blush is the ol' flatstick. It's a 6,208 yard course which works with local topography, slicing through 150 acres of lush hard and softwood forest, and snaking around eight natural ponds. Of course, being the Head Pro, I may be accused of prejudice.

The pièce de resistance is my Pro Shop. The Hut, as I call it, is a single story miniature version of the 12,000 square foot, two-level, window-choked clubhouse which sprawls 200 yards to the west. The Hut's mine. Well, not literally, but who else's moniker is burned into a rough-hewn chunk of dogwood nailed above the entrance? I used to think it odd to see my name, in lights so to speak, on a building. It was embarrassing enough on a golf bag, but now *Riley Quinn, Canadian Professional Golf Association Member* is part of the Nanoose landscape. The life's not what I'd planned, but I guess it's better'n kick in the head.

The sky was a pale, cloudless blue and though the temperature of twenty degrees Celsius was cool for mid-July, all but a couple of wimps were dressed in shorts. Not a breath of wind; A-1 conditions for golf. Groups of twos and fours gathered outside the side door, impatiently waiting for their clubs in storage. Two of my guys were lugging bag after bag through the double doors, yet 20 or so members still waited, their bright colours clashing. The whir and squeak of golf carts punctuated excited bits of conversation. Most teams wore matching sweaters or shirts. Thank God, my group had more sense.

Today we were playing a shotgun Pro-Am: thus,

a teaching pro and three amateurs wait at each hole. When the gun sounds at 8 o'clock a.m., each group plays 18 holes, finishing one hole behind the one on which they started. My group, the Frequent Flyers, was to tee off from Number 6, a dogleg right which finished a hundred yards beyond the practice putting green. I stuffed the fax into the junk drawer pocket of my bag.

"Yo, Riley!"

Stifling a yawn, I turned. Thomas Kent, Pitts's son-in-law and minority owner in Sea Blush—thus by definition another boss—was striding towards me. A tightly knit white golf sweater and crisp black shorts draped his filament-thin body.

"We've got, like, fifteen minutes," the young estate lawyer said, running long fingers through his sleek, cap-like black hair. Though not attractive, Thomas's angular features, strong jaw and sleek body are fascinating. Like the golden sea lions slithering through the Pacific surf, Thomas is quick and fluid. "Where's Joel?"

"Don't know. Juet coming to see us off?"

Thomas stiffened. The ever-present Ray-Bans shielded his dark eyes. "No," he said brusquely. "Too busy."

"Oh." I fiddled with my clubs. Sea Blush's Assistant Club Manager, Juet Wyndamere, always managed to nip out of the clubhouse when Thomas was playing. Something amiss in newlywed heaven? "Is everything...?"

"Fine," he snapped. "Just fine."

I nodded and concentrated on sliding The Witch's protective sock over her head. When I looked up, I had to grin. Thomas bristled then looked behind, following my eyes. Struggling up the path was our new Course Superintendent, David Deugo. Though a course super for years, David, or Dai as he's called, was a neophyte golfer. Why he wanted to play in our foursome was beyond me. Both Thomas and Joel are 4 handicappers.

Dai was battling with one of my old ten-inch leather bags, filled with rental clubs. I'd offered to lend him a smaller one free of charge but he wouldn't have it. Fortunately for him, we were using power carts.

Thomas glanced at me with uplifted eyebrows, made a steering motion with his hands then moved on around to the back of the Hut. Dai stepped beside me and, with a supreme effort, carefully lowered the red and white bag. He rubbed his right shoulder, then yanked off a ball cap and ruffled his black hair. At 5'10", Dai is a whisker taller than I am. But with my busby-like curls, I'll bet we look the same height. Of course, at a slightly soft 195, he's got 50 pounds on me.

I don't know about you, but I look at hair and eyes first. Then, if they make the grade, my eyes'll travel further down. I've glanced at Dai a couple of times and made it past his head.

"Man, that weighs a ton! Don't know how you carried it."

He caught my quick look. His dark blue eyes widened, sparkling in the sun. Dai scrambled to recover. "I'm sorry, I didn't mean to insult you. It'd be heavy for anybody."

Looking into his round, weathered face is like looking into the face of my high school counsellor, open, attentive, eyes soft with concern. The guy's awfully nice, but he always says the wrong thing. "It's heavy, all right. It's why I don't use it any more."

I tapped my smaller, canary-yellow nylon bag. "This baby's the latest, lightweight, waterproof and enough Velcro pockets to do the Pacific Rim Trail.

Sure you don't want one like it?"

"No," Dai replied, suddenly flashing a wide grin. Much better looking than my counsellor. "Can't play worth crap, but at least I'll look the part."

"Don't know about that," a deep voice said. We turned to find Joel Sanderson, the last of our foursome, strolling toward us.

Joel epitomizes two ridiculous male symbols, the Ken doll and the hyper-fit TV aerobic evangelist. The twit is what the gals on the Tour call a "nice piece." Deeply tanned, despite the latest craze of ultra-violet warnings, Joel's chest and arm muscles nudged through a turquoise Cardin shirt—so chosen to match his eyes. It did. He was one of the few players wearing pants. In fact, I've never seen the new owner of the Island's largest car dealership in shorts—some rumour about weak calves. Never understood it. I'm a shorts person, not skirt and not bloody likely a dress; I live and die in shorts. Can't breathe properly otherwise.

Joel put his thick, hairy arm around my shoulder and squeezed. Almost too hard but not quite. His hair and eyes are so unreal, I've never bothered to looked much lower. "You're going to have to do a lot more than carry a big bag to impress this lady, Dai. Ol' Riley's the best, you know." Joel spoke quickly, sharply hissing the s's and h's.

The creep bugged me. Had I known him better, I'd have ripped his arm off. Pitts's partner for many years, Joel had just returned from 20 or so months sojourning in eastern Canada. For Pitts's sake, I was going slowly but one of these days, Mr. Business was going to push his handsome mug and 35 per cent ownership in Sea Blush too far.

Patches of red bled through the tan on Dai's cheeks. I deliberately picked Joel's arm off my shoulder. "Nobody needs to impress me."

Thomas whizzed around the corner in an open golf cart. He jerked to a stop, leapt out, grabbed my bag, all the while shouting, "Get a move on! We've less than five minutes. Dai, get the other cart—Number 17."

The group ready and waiting at the first tee hooted at us as we raced by. Thomas slammed the pedal to the floorboards and thrust his thin body forward, urging on the little electric motor. His left leg twitched impatiently.

His anxiety made me think of my first time at Qualifying School. Now, there's a place where officials are sticklers for time. What a misnomer! There's no actual schooling at Q-School. Instead, there you are, in Palm Springs, California, playing golf in the rain against some of the best women in the world. All 200-plus wannabees with the same goal, to play on the Ladies Professional Golf Tour. But first you've got to make it through one of two regional qualifying rounds. Then it's onto the finals in Daytona Beach, Florida, scrambling to be one of the dozen or so top scorers who are invited to join the Ladies Professional Golf Tour.

It didn't help that I had been a dew-sweeper, first off with no time to practice. Never got the feel for the putter. The wet weather had dampened my nerve as well as my spirit and I was three over par on the front nine. Got back some concentration and birdied two then parred the next four holes. Sitting pretty, I think, only one over. Then my playing partner jumped in the cart and scooted over to the porta-john.

So I'm standing there, on the next tee, putter in my hand, waiting. The official sitting to my right starts looking at his watch. We've got 14 minutes to play each hole but from his pained expression, you'd think I was Rip Van Winkle. I panicked and

sprinted the 50 yards to the cart to snatch my
three wood. My partner comes out of the john—a
little breathless, still tucking in her golf shirt—
sees the club in my hand and says accusingly, "I
was coming, Riley." I tried to slow my breathing as
we raced up to the tee and I concentrated hard on
that little white sucker but cold-topped the ball
anyway. Missed the cut by two. Another year down
the drain.

Of course, today was just a Pro-Am, with 54 of
the Island's bitchin' business best doing the fairway shuffle with the local pros. So I was the only
female pro...what else was new? There are only a
handful in all of Canada. Recently, I read a study
which claimed that a million females play golf in
Canada and are a nudge over fifty percent of the
total new player population. So where are they?
Toronto?

We heard a distant crack. The Eagle Beagles,
at the first tee, let out a joyous whoop. The scramble was on!

The sixth hole wrenches right around a flat
pond. Despite the stand of arbutus which guards
the fairway left about a third of the way down,
there's little doubt about which club one pulls to
initiate this 359 yard par four.

Roughly, a scramble format works like this,
throughout the round, each team plays the best
shot of all four players. So every player drives a
ball. The team then chooses the best shot and marks
its location, often using a wooden tee. The players
collect their respective balls and take their second
shot from the tee marker-no more than a club length
away and no closer to the hole. The game continues in the same fashion, hole after hole. Each player
attempts to putt out. If all four miss the putt, a
stroke is added to the team's score. The team

continues to putt until a ball drops into the hole.

Usually in a scramble, you tee off worst player to best. That meant Dai was up first. I felt a little badly for him. We've been practising but he hadn't even played a full 18 holes yet. Carefully, methodically, he set his stance then waggled his driver back and forth as I'd taught him. He took the club head back well but, like most rookies, broke his left wrist early and chopped down. The ball squirted off the tee and trickled about 150 yards to plunk into the little lake on the right. We three remained silent but a capped-tooth smile split Joel's face.

"Pig!" Dai said, under his breath. He marched off the tee, studiously avoiding my eyes.

"Don't worry about it, man," Thomas said. "Next time."

Thomas and Joel flipped a loonie to see who teed off second. Joel lost and grudgingly stepped into position. A strong, compact man, he does everything the same way, punching with grace, power and a lot of flourish. No one on the Tour waggles the club quite like Mr. Business. Joel slammed his drive dead straight, about 255 yards and stood posing for an extra second, pretending to watch the Wilson ball leap forward. I knew he was eyeing our reaction. For Joel, an audience is essential.

Dai responded in kind. He loped over and clapped the proud Papa on the back—just what Mr. Business craved.

Thomas cocked an eyebrow and stepped into position. No time wasted, no lengthy pre-shot routine. Thomas Kent's delivery is quick. He's wire—thin but wire—strong, using a high kick point on his graphite shaft and every ounce of his 165 pounds to control it. His drive rolled a few feet short and to the left of Joel's.

Dai shook his head and whistled softly.

I took a deep breath but got caught in a yawn. Shaking my shoulders lightly, I walked to the middle of the tee and looked down toward the hidden flag. Pitts's fax dashed into my thoughts. I've been in a ton of tournaments, seen some right disasters, usually due to weather. Tournament organizers bust their butts for an entire year for seven days of golf. Everything's organized just so...but no one controls Ma Nature. I'd done a lot of fretting about the next couple of weeks but never dreamed about a glitch like a threat to Pitts. Who or what was BioAction?

"Hey, Riley! Gonna play or pose?" Joel snapped.

I flushed, and quickly nudged the little mystery into a holding slot. No time now. Using my ball—a Titleist 3—I shoved an extra long tee halfway down into the firm grass. I rotated my left wrist; a little stiff but no pain. Then, as always, I went through my pre-shot routine; walk behind the ball, pick out a target, grip the club and visualize the shot, align the club face with the target, step into stance, waggle the club three times and let 'er rip.

The Witch's extra-large sweet spot's hard to miss. Especially with the swing my Dad taught me. It's so classic, that early in my pro career, I earned the nickname the lefty Patty Sheehan. To be compared with one of today's best had been awesome. I was thrilled; my father less so. "You're Riley Quinn," he'd said sharply, "not some clone of Patty Sheehan."

The Titleist flew past Thomas' yellow Pro-light and bounded yards beyond the Wilson.

Man, golf's a gas!

Then Joel chipped a nine iron within five feet of the pin and Thomas neatly stroked it in for a birdie. To put it simply, golf's a game of par. The goal is to hole the ball in as few strokes as possible.

We were one under par.

We combined some great shots to birdie 7 and 8, two short holes.

Three under.

Then we parred 9, 10 and 11. Shooting par's a snap when you can choose between four shots. Even so, I had a tough chip in on 9, but though the wrist tweaked, I managed to keep my hands and weight just right. The ball jumped high and danced back to within two feet of the pin. There are advantages to being a lefty.

We ran into a bit of trouble on 12, a notoriously tough hole, when both Joel and I sliced our drives. Mine, of course, spun left. His careened right and landed in the middle of the thirteenth fairway. The fool kicked at the grass and pounded his driver into the ground. We watched quietly. Not a good sign.

Thomas's drive wasn't much better, hooking left. The ball hit a clump of evergreens and dropped from the sky, a piddly 130 yards out. Dai surprised us with a dead straight worm burner and beamed for the next five minutes when the group chose to take his shot. Unfortunately, we blew a chance at an eagle when Joel followed our lead and his five foot putt became the fourth victim of a nasty patch of winter kill.

Joel swore. "What's this, Dai?" he demanded angrily, jamming the head of his putter into the dead grass. Another expletive. "This green's a joke! What d'ya water it with, gasoline?"

Thomas and I exchanged a quick glance. Dai pulled himself up to his full height, at least four inches shy of Joel's, and calmly regarded his antagonist. A small pulse beat in his left temple but his voice was soft and controlled. "You know as well as I do that the winter was bad. I've worked fourteen hours a day since I got here in April but there's only so much you can do."

I punched Joel in the shoulder and laughed. "Don't blame Dai or the bloody grass for that putt. The green's the same for everybody. Face it, you blew it just like the rest of us."

Joel jerked back as though struck, his aquamarine eyes blazing. Thomas and Dai moved beside me. We stood there, with the sun warming our backs, throwing fat shadows over the green. Joel squinted at us, perspiring heavily. Finally, Thomas broke free, grabbed his putter and tapped the ball in for a bird. With a nod toward the carts, he said, "Let's move!"

By the time Dai and I reached Number 13, Joel was smiling and laughing. Our luck changed and we had three birdies on a trot.

Seven under at 16.

By 10:40 a.m., it was getting warmer; Thomas and I pulled off our sweaters. We parred 16 and birdied 17. On 18, the last to attempt a 20 foot uphill putt, I kissed the cup's edge and blew a bird. My wrist was aching continuously now. Joel stroked the ball in for par.

Eight under.

As Joel and I rolled past the club house heading for the first hole, we were stopped by the Balls Up foursome, led by Doug Carlisle, a Nanaimo stockbroker. "Well, if it isn't the effin' Flyers," Carlisle said, his heavy jaw tightening.

Joel's body tensed. Carlisle's partner piped in hurriedly, "He's just joking, guys. How ya doin'?"

"Ten under!" Joel shouted, the 't' hissing loudly. I kicked his shin but he ignored me.

"No kiddin'!" the little guy squeaked. "We're only seven."

Carlisle was momentarily speechless. No small feat for the man they call The Mouth. His jaw worked for a few seconds then he spat, "Ten under. Bull!" The veins on Joel's forehead popped out. "The sonofabitch'll lie about anything, eh, Joel?" Carlisle's watery eyes washed across my face. "G'ahead, Riley. Ask the bastard 'bout the soft costs."

Joel grunted and flew out of the cart. Startled, I lurched after him. In seconds, Joel's hands gripped the stockbroker's fleshy throat. Carlisle's partner frantically pushed Joel back while Carlisle clawed for freedom. Thomas was beside me as I yanked on one of Joel's shoulders. Together, we wrenched the two men apart. Thomas ducked and used his shoulder to butt Joel back toward our golf cart. Dai dashed in to help. With a howl, Carlisle clambered out of his cart. The little guy dove after him and hung onto his back.

"Sonofabitch!" Carlisle roared, twisting his passenger loose as though he were a scarf. Dai turned and blocked his path.

Slammed against the golf cart, Joel shook Thomas free and grinned back at Carlisle. "Don't blame me, sucker. A fool's born every minute."

Carlisle howled. Thomas shoved Joel into the seat, jumped alongside and punched the gas. I leapt in the other, Dai dove in and we shot forward. A couple of hundred yards later, we jerked to a halt.

"What was that all about?!" Dai and I yelled in unison.

"Forget it," Thomas said, anxiously looking behind. Joel grinned but his veins still pulsed blue.

"Are you kidding?" I said. "The idiot attacked one of my mem..."

"Drop it!" Joel snapped.

I stared at him. "Out of the blue, you jump a guy..."

"It's none of your business," he said, gaining some control. Turning to Thomas, Joel ordered, "Let's go!" Their cart leapt forward. Dai rolled his eyes and I hit the gas.

Studiously quiet, we birdied the first, a long dogleg left par five, to drop to nine under.

Numbers 2 and 3 are both par four's, generously lined with bunkers and water. At 2, Thomas's drive went for a swim. Joel bailed out and underclubbed to lay up in front of the water at 205 yards. As usual, Dai's drive found the right rough. My wrist had eased a little and, though the water was on the left, I pounded The Witch. The ball soared past the pond, smacking down in the middle of the fairway. A good shot but I paid for it: the wrist pulsed dully.

Dai took a deep breath and neatly chipped with a nine iron. The ball landed dead centre, six feet uphill from the flagstick. Joel fiddled, knelt, cleaned leaves and imaginary dirt from the lie, then drained the downhill putt. Another bird, 10 under!

We waited on the third as the Swinging Singles putted out ahead of us. I wondered what the fisticuffs had been about. Knowing what slimebuckets Carlisle and Joel were, it had to be juicy. The Swinging Singles' pro shouted that the top score was 10 under. We were tied!

The sloping green on Number 3 tricked us for another par. The fourth hole is a long, straight par three. Thomas, after his usual half-second study of the hole, blasted a five iron shot. It struck the pin! Joel let out a whoop. Dai danced a jig and grabbed me for a quick spin. Birdie. 11 under.

Number 5, our last, was a medium length par five but dotted with bunkers left and right. The tee area, smothered by thick Douglas firs, gives me claustrophobia. The pin's just visible, despite the snake's back fairway. The rookie's drive was weak but the rest of us avoided the rough. All three balls landed at about 240 yards.

We followed with fairway woods; Dai fell 100 yards short, Joel shanked to the left and Thomas and I found the green. My shot had too little spin and quickly died. Thomas's ball caught the speed of the green and rolled uphill past the hole. That left two 40 foot putts, one uphill, the other down. With the slick green and steep front slope, we nabbed my spot. A missed hit ball from above would dance off the bottom apron.

Dai tried first. For a beginner, his putting stroke is strong, soft, firm hands and a nice free shoulder swing. Must be his teacher! But he has no sense of touch yet, the ball braked halfway to the hole.

Joel was up next. He plumbed the line with his putter, walked up and beyond the hole, returned, took three practice strokes and laced into his Wilson. His go-for-the-gusto style reminds me of Caroline Robbin, a Tour friend. An aggressive putter, she rarely falls short. Too bad Joel doesn't have Caroliune's feel. The Wilson screamed wide and chugged uphill.

Thomas chuckled, wiped the head of his putter, quickly took his stance and stroked. Good hands, but a shade too soft for the lie. The ball broke slowly to the right, stopping inches from the target.

I grinned at them. "Now, gentlemen, stand back and weep." This is the stuff I love, and mourn; being in contention, under the gun, making putts worth $30,000. I'd already checked the line, so I stood over the ball and brought myself to focus on its very white dimples. This's what separates golf from other sports; the ball is stationary, taunting, waiting, the player is completely proactive, never reactive.

I glanced at the hole, pulled my eyes back to the ball, saw only the ball—huge now and glowing—and stroked. The Titleist flew up the hill, hit the back of the four and one-quarter inch cup and dropped in. Eagle! 13 under!

"All right!" Thomas yelled. "A slam dunk!" Much hugging and slapping of backs followed.

I didn't want to leave. For a delicious instant, I'd found my playing zone again, that quiet, intimate space where nothing intrudes...where the ball, the swing and time are one. It's like you're watching, you're not stressing, you're just doing it, no big deal. Tears stung my eyes. Since the accident which had forced me to abandon the Tour a couple of seasons ago, I thought I'd never find that zone again. Dai mistook my reaction and gently asked me about my wrist.

His voice shattered the moment. I laughed a little too harshly and wiped my eyes. "Nothing a little ice won't cure."

Two

By twenty to two, I had showered, changed, iced
the wrist for twenty minutes and was watching
Vivian Graves hold court in the Club's cavernous
lounge. The rustic, honey-coloured log walls are
dotted with paintings—oils and waters—by British Columbian artists. Vivian, the Tournament
Director for the Classic, was admiring Pitts's most
recent purchase, a huge watercolour by a little-
known local Salish Indian.

The highly stylized rocky shoreline was unusually dark and moody for a watercolour. I said
so. Vivian flicked me a sharp frown. It was gone in
a blink and her perfect, doll-like features relaxed.
She laughed loudly, flashing cherry lips and
quickly regained the room's attention.

The lounge was filled, mostly with middle-aged
men who were patrons of the arts, so long as the
arts were female. These businessmen either openly
gazed at Vivian or covertly cocked their heads for
a quick glimpse. It all depended on whether their
spouse had arrived. Vivian, looking thin in a sleek
emerald green dress, absorbed the attention with
a model's assured grace and confidence.

Gazing down at my wide-spread, silk trousered
legs, I self-consciously crossed them. Perfect teeth,
complexion and petite figure were bad enough, but
Ms. Vivian Graves was a natural strawberry blonde
to boot. I felt, as always in her presence, like a
gangly filly.

"You okay?" Dai asked, sitting down beside me.

I choked off the tail end of a whinny and nodded.

"Lemme get you another drink. Diet Coke?"

"Ah, yes. The nectar of champions," Vivian said,
turning golden eyes in my direction. In the dap-

pled light, her eyes and hair were the same colour. "Tell me about the round. Understand you're to be congratulated."

"She played brilliantly," Dai said. "Didn't she, Thomas?"

Thomas Kent had just entered the room and was quietly eyeing Vivian.

"He said you were wonderful," a woman's voice called from behind him.

Thomas turned and quickly held out his arm to his plump, dark-haired wife. Juet slid past the outstretched arm and walked over to the painting. Thomas' face coloured, then he forced a smile. "Yep," he said dully. "We were the greatest out there."

I sidled over to Juet. "Hey," I asked Pitts's daughter, "everything okay?" She tried to nod but her eyes were too bright. "Wanna talk?"

Juet bit her lower lip. "No," she whispered.

Thomas stepped beside his wife and handed her a glass of water. She took it but stiffened when her hand touched his. I flicked a glance across their faces. Both were tense, eyes filled with unspoken words. I backed off.

"So," Dai asked Thomas, "what was the fight all about?"

"Fight?" Both Vivian and Juet responded.

Thomas flushed. "It's nothing, really."

"What d'you mean, nothing?" I asked. "Joel almost took Carlisle's head off!"

"Joel!" Vivian said, her voice filled with concern. "Joel was in a fight? Is he hurt?"

"No," I replied. "But he outta be. Man, he was crazy! Carlisle alm..."

"Carlisle's an ass!" Vivian snapped.

I raised my eyebrows at Dai. "Uh-huh," I agreed. "But..."

"Enough already!" Thomas said, throwing me

a dark look. "It was nothing. Just bad blood, that's all. Let's just drop it, okay?"

He meant it. Silence followed. Since we weren't getting anywhere, I broke away. As the head pro, I'm always on duty so I wandered about socializing, wishing I'd had more sleep. Last night's emergency call had come just after midnight and the sheets and I didn't meet again 'til quarter to four. Fortunately, it took little cerebral effort to mix with this crowd —most of whom I knew by name or, at the very least, by golf swing.

This was a choice time for a teaching professional to do a little schmoozing. Mostly you're dealing with men. So you've got to sidle in, joke with a guy, flatter him silly, ask about the kids and exit quickly, hinting at lessons. Although successful, I find this one of the toughest parts of the new job. As a touring pro, especially a winner, you're the magnet. Everyone runs to you. It's hard to drop that coy wait-and-see posture and replace it with a cheery, non-sexual you-need-lessons-so-come-see-me-in-my-hut smile.

After discussing the merits of perimeter club head weighting with several equipmentophiles, I spotted Dai chatting with one of the Eagle Beagles. I bet he was talking turf stuff.

"The greens're fast," Dai replied, nodding vigorously. "The LPGA has strict requirements for their speed. We're double-cutting today, taking off more grass to get to tournament level."

"How d'you measure speed?" the Beagle asked, keenly interested.

"Well, we've been bringing the height down all spring. It's kinda trial and error for us but I'll have a better idea next week when the Tour's advance official arrives."

I suppressed a yawn and looked around. From

across the room, Carlisle and I suddenly locked eyes, but he quickly jerked his bushy eyebrows free. No matter, I thought. There'll be other opportunities.

To the Beagle's displeasure, Dai stopped his dissertation on turf grass to question me.

"Just heard you were called out last night."

"Yeah, Dr. O'Brien was on another case." I told him briefly about the motor vehicle accident.

"Ugh, woken up in the middle of the night to see a dead body." He shivered. "Don't know how you do it."

I didn't say anything. A lot of people didn't understand my part-time job. It didn't matter, I thought, being a coroner was the bee's knees. You see, in lotus land even a golfer can be a coroner. No medical experience required; instead, take one keener, spice 'er up with a heavy dose of instruction, add qualified help to taste, and voila, an investigator of unusual deaths extraordinaire!

"Anyway, why didn't you tell us? Four o'clock in the morning, you must be beat!"

I stifled another yawn. "No reason. Nothin' you could've done."

During lunch, the comparisons finally came. As I knew they would. It was almost a relief.

"She just won last week, didn't she?" Good ol' Viv, so quick with the obvious.

I nodded, chewed my carrots and waited.

"She's some golfer, Ril," Thomas added. He glanced anxiously at his wife. "Isn't she, Juet?" Juet nodded slightly. Eyes hardening, Thomas continued. "Pitts damn near blew my ear off watching. That last putt, what a beauty!" He stabbed the air with a fork. "I thought Sheehan had 'er. That it'd be sudden death but man, that Hal, she's got iron in her veins."

I studied my mushy peas and slowly shuffled

them onto my fork. After all, I'd won a few tournaments, too.

Thomas swallowed and then asked the killer
question. "How many more for the Hall of Fame?
Two?"

"One," Vivian answered loudly, again espous-
ing the obvious. I threw her a withering look.

Thomas dropped his knife and fork, shoved
back his chair and looked me squarely in the eyes.
"Imagine! Your sister's one measly win away from
the Hall of Fame!"

The rest of the group nodded and murmured
appropriately.

A tap on the shoulder saved me from shouting, *Enough about my bloody, wonderful sister!* The
freckled young waiter whispered that I had a phone
call.

"Who is it?" I asked, tossing my napkin beside
my plate.

"Halliday Quinn."

"Well, I'll be damned," Thomas said.

Damned. Yep, that's the word all right.

Three

2:45 p.m., Sunday, July 19.

"Riley? It's Hal." My sister's voice was hesitant. That made me feel guilty and that made me feel angry. So I waited an extra heartbeat.

"I know. I'm in a bit of a hurry, in the middle of lunch." I was sitting at Pitts's huge mahogany desk in his office one flight up from the dining hall.

"Hey! I understand congratulations are in order! Hear you—what'd Thomas call your foursome? The Frequent Flyers?—just won." She was, as always since the accident, trying too hard.

I studied the gold framed picture near the phone. It was of the three of us, Pitts, Hal and myself—all smiling. When was that? "Yep. Mucho big time."

There was a small gold trophy sitting by Pitts's blotter. The tiny plaque read, *Winner, First Annual Sea Blush Charity Pro-Am.* Our prize. Whoop dee doo.

"You're playing again. That's what matters."

"Yeah. First the Sea Blush Classic, next the Phar-Mor."

There was several seconds of silence then Halliday exhaled heavily. "You heard. I wasn't sure you still paid any attention."

"Even in the wilds of lotus land, we heard about the Great Halliday Quinn's victory at Youngstown. Three round total of 207: six birdies, one eagle, winner of seventy-five thousand American bucks." I dropped the trophy on its head. "That must put you at the top of the money list with Sheehan."

Hal cleared her throat. The connection faded then her voice burst in. "—I know it's been a while."

I waited.

"Riley, you there?"

"I'm here. Just a little busy."

"Oh," she said, an edge entering her voice, "no time for your own sister. Still mad aren't ya? How many times can I say I'm sorry? That I wished it could've been me who got hurt."

There was nothing I could say.

"Look," she sighed, "I'm not calling about me. It's about Pitts."

"What about him?"

"Well, we spoke and..."

"And what?"

Her voice dropped to a whisper. "He's upset."

Carrie, Pitts's young secretary walked into the room. I looked up. She shrugged an apology and handed me a note. She'd written in large, childish writing that the lab had called. I took the note, nodded and she left.

"What? Sorry, I got interrupted."

"Dammit—he's upset!"

"Your husband? Well, let's be real, Hal. You've hurt him. Badly."

"All right, all right. I'm to blame." She sighed again. "Just tell me, will you pick him up?"

"What, now you care?"

"Dammit, Riley! Is this never gonna end? It's been two years."

Don't I know it, sister. Two years since the accident—years not of living dangerously but of living angrily.

Halliday was talking. "Just do me a favour. No. Forget that. Do him a favour. Get 'im at the ferry, okay?"

"Don't worry 'bout it. Picking Pitts up's no favour." I looked at my watch. The Rolex said 2:55 p.m. I was late. "I've gotta go."

"But..."

"See you Sunday."

I stared at the phone. Damn. I grabbed the

trophy and tried to rip the tiny gold golfer off his base. My palm split along a rough edge running up the back. I watched the sliver of blood.

Shiiit! Seventy-five thousand dollars!

* * * *

Ten minutes later, I was booting it south along the Island Highway to Nanaimo. Though late for my three o'clock with Dr. O'Brien, I thought I might catch him. I had to go to town anyway to meet Pitts's ferry at Departure Bay.

The Highway reminds me of the line *ribbon of darkness over me* in the Gordon Lightfoot song. I've always liked its haunting image. Our dark ribbon winds its way mostly along the eastern edge of Vancouver Island, ending eventually in Victoria, Canada's best bloomin' city and the capital of British Columbia. What is it about Canadians always living near the edge? Ninety percent of our population straddles the southern border of the country and most Vancouver Islanders live within sight of the choppy, blue Strait of Georgia which separates us from the mainland. Geography and proximity to the commercial gods of the U.S., I guess we do live near the edge.

With the top down on Emily—my tiny, yellow convertible—my lungs, hair and eyes were quickly awash with salt-water wind. My anger at Halliday tugged free, words and phrases best forgotten ripped into harmless letters and fluttered along the tree-lined coast. Didn't even flinch while edging through the latest construction zone. I grinned and waved at a bald eagle, wheeling slowly above a rocky ridge ahead. Damn, I played well! My left wrist, now deliciously sore, gripped harder at the wheel. The Tour was coming and with it, old friends. I made a mental note to thank Pitts for bringing professional women's golf to the Island, although his caddieing idea twitched at me like a tired eye muscle.

As the rooftops of the small tourist and residential retreat of Lantzville flashed by on my left, my thoughts slid back to tournament disasters like the Hawaiian washout in '88 when it rained ten to twelve inches in two days and the course disappeared under water. We lost the Pro-Am, didn't even tee off a ball. Then the next year, we had the stalker incident. The tournament was delayed while police searched the grounds for a nutcase with a hit list. Huddled in the locker room, nervously anticipating gun shots, we made bets as to who headed his list. Fortunately, the cops quickly caught the loonie. They wouldn't show us the list so nobody won the bet. I don't know who was on it but I had a couple of nominees.

Ten minutes from Nanaimo, the highway ducks inland a few kilometres, providing peek-a-boo ocean views. At least that's the cutsie term the local real estate hacks employ to sell properties where water views might be possible—if MacMillan Bloedel clear cut straight to the ocean. Sometimes, I wouldn't put it past the logging giant. I slapped my right wrist—Dad would never allow MacBlo— bashing. After all, they're the largest custodian of Island forests.

Yeah, right.

As always, the parking lot at the Woodgrove Centre sparkled with chrome. The Island's largest shopping mall is retail heaven for the 75,000-plus inhabitants of Nanaimo and surrounding communities. When pressed, I admit to a visit or two.

I leaned over and blew a loud raspberry as I whizzed by one of our arch rivals, the Nanaimo

Golf and Country Club. Then the highway cut into suburbia, meandering through the chunks of houses that wrap the city.

Nanaimo is an Indian word for The Great And Mighty People. A bit grandiose for a waterfront community built on the dirt, sweat and danger of coal mining. Nowadays, the hard hats are worn by 12,000 blue collar lumberjacks-and-jills working for MacBlo. Though situated out of sight, the company's flagship Harmac Pulp Mill is never out of scent.

I turned left onto Comox Road, then a quick right onto Front Street with its view of the harbour. Banners for the Annual Nanaimo to Vancouver International Bathtub Race still fluttered from the lightposts. I parked on Church and entered number 16. I've always thought Church is an appropriate name for the Coroner's office. Both the Church and the Coroner's office have a long history; both are tranquil, both deal with death. Though the former is largely spiritual and the latter completely physical.

"You're late."

"I know, I know, Wheez. Couldn't be avoided. O'Brien in?"

"You missed 'im," Louise said with a tight smile. She tugged at her too-impossible-to-be-true black hair then checked her long purple nails. "'E wasn't appy."

I sighed and sat on the edge of her immaculate desk. We don't have much in common. Louise Ménard was a woman in battle. My guess, she was on the dark side of 45 but fighting back with every weapon known to Avon. At 33, my battle was just starting. Having never had the bone structure nor the interest to launch a defense, I'm certain it'll be a massacre.

I'd known O'Brien's moody secretary as long

as I'd known O'Brien, a little over 10 months, and still was not comfortable with either. She's a transplanted Parisian; he a wayward Englishman. Add me, the token Canadian, and you don't get the U.N..

One thing I had learned with Louise. A little French goes a long way. As does a nickname. So, I started over. In my high school dialect, I asked Wheez how she was. There must be something about my accent 'cause she grinned, as she always does, then replied with one of my favourites, "Pas pire."

I like the sound of that, whole lot more punch than saying not bad. It's an expression I use a lot at the Hut, often with hysterical results. I have, I've been told, my mother's raw voice—Dad used to call it smokin' spoken—and foreign jargon sharpens its edge.

"Why so all dressed?" she said.

I looked at her to see if she was teasing. When it comes to discussions on looks or clothes or women's things, I never know how to react to Louise. I usually stumble along with humour.

"You make me sound like a hamburger. It's dressed up. I just came from the Pro-Am luncheon." Speaking quickly to avoid any further discussion on my obvious lack of style, I asked, "When'll O'Brien be back?"

She frowned. The tiny lines around her eyes and forehead cracked and deepened. Not a pretty sight. "Don't know. E's assisting at a p.m. this afternoon."

I enjoy the way the French use the verb assisting in place of attending. So much more action-oriented. The truth be known, O'Brien wouldn't be much help at the post mortem. Instead, he'd be watching, light brown eyes soaking it all in.

"Well, I'll just use the phone, okay?"

She shrugged her slight shoulders and turned back to a violet-coloured computer screen.

O'Brien's telephone has the numbers for the Nanaimo Regional General Hospital's laboratory and the local detachment of the Royal Canadian Mounted Police stored in memory. I punched the button marked LAB and was soon speaking to the soft-spoken technician, Barb Jenkins.

"Just got back the blood alcohol test, Riley. The Fowler boy was legally impaired, about 160."

"160!" Twice the legal limit. The kid must have been flying. "That's about six drinks, isn't it?"

"About. This guy's small, could've been less. Doesn't really matter, anyway, case closed."

"For you, maybe," I sighed.

"What d'you mean?"

"When the officer told the parents, the father was adamant. He wants to know if the kid was drinking."

"Oh," Barb said in a small voice. "Doesn't seem much point, does there?"

"Nope." I took a deep breath. "I hate telling parents their child was driving under the influence. It's bad enough the kid's dead."

"Sure glad you're the coroner 'n not me."

While listening to the phone ring at the RCMP detachment, I mentally rehearsed the familiar scenario of talking to bereaved parents. It starts and ends the same; me apologizing, them crying. Worst part of the job. I could just imagine the conversation with the Fowlers, *I'm terribly sorry for your loss, Mr. and Mrs. Fowler.*

Thank you. A hesitation, then it comes. *There, there's something I...* An exchange of glances, *We need to know. We just can't believe that Roddy...the road was...*

I know, sir. You've suffered a great shock. I don't want to make it worse.

We want to know.

Yes. Roddy was legally impaired.

Silence. Heavy—into the pit of despair—silence. The mother's red, puffy eyes flood with more tears. The father's glazed look of shock sharpens. His voice, very small. *Thank you.*

Both bodies will seem to shrink and age visibly. It's a good sign when couples hold each other closely. When I see them start apart and stay apart, I know they're in for a long-term struggle...

I detest these so-called visits. After one of 'em, I've got to exercise. To breathe. To sweat. To touch life. So I rollerblade around Nanoose Bay, through West Bay Estates to Schooner Cove and back down to the highway. I skate until my lungs thicken, my thighs shriek and I can no longer control the fat, blue wheels. Still the parents' glassy stares, the kid's lifeless eyes, haunt me. I skate on, muscles screaming, mind whirling. Gratefully alive.

"Royal Canadian Mounted Police, Parksville Detachment. May I help you?" The disembodied voice shocked me back to reality. I blinked a couple of times and found my tongue.

"Yes, Constable Dickson, please. It's Riley Quinn."

The phone crackled, seemed to go dead and then Dickson's disc-jockey voice filled my head.

"Riley? Hey, pard, congrats on the Pro-Am!"

Small town, big news. I'd known Walter Dickson since elementary school. He wanted to be a cop, me a pro golfer. We both got our wish, but he's still living his. "Thanks Walt. How're you doing?"

"Same old stuff, chasin' nosepickers...uh," he stopped. Walt knows that I hate that generic term for lawbreakers but it's common lingo on the Force. "Sorry, I mean perps. Hey," he hastily changed the subject, "Mom says she saw you last week."

"Yes, the old gal looks great."

"Yeah, she's adjusting to the home not bad. It's awfully good of you to still visit."

"What d'you mean? I'd go nuts without my monthly fix of cribbage."

"Means a lot to her. And me. She's not the only one who's glad you're permanently back in town." The boom dropped slightly from his voice. "You calling in an official capacity?"

"Yes. Sorry, no golf tonight. Pitts's coming in. Remember?"

I could just see his linebacker figure slump down in the too small regulation chair.

Walt exhaled. "I forgot. So what can I do you for?"

"It's about Pitts. He's been receiving threats."

"Threats? Wyndamere? How? What'd they say?"

"I'll fax you one inna minute. Have you ever heard of a group called BioAction?"

He paused for a moment. "Nope."

"Okay. Well, whoever they are, they've threatened him three times."

"Three? Why the hell didn't he tell you earlier?"

"Question of the hour. Don't worry, I'll ask him. You know Pitts. Guess he didn't take it seriously."

"Send it through, Ril. I'll get back to you when I get something."

"Okay. Thanks."

"See you at hockey?"

"Not this week."

I grabbed a photocopy of the BioAction letter and gave it to Louise to fax. I could hear the high pitched dialling tones of the machine as I ran out. The ferry would be docking.

Four

Five minutes later, I was waiting in the small, glass-enclosed B.C. Ferry anteroom as the first foot passengers trickled out. The staccato roar of engines and clanging of metal ramps reverberated outside as hundreds of automobiles fled the gaping hull of the Spirit of Esquimalt. Pitts was a slow walker so I was certain I hadn't missed him. I couldn't wait to see the old bugger. Because of him, there were two weeks to go to pro golf and I was so excited, I could spit.

"Riley!" a guttural voice shouted. I waved and looked beyond a mother struggling to hold a howling infant and control an impatient toddler. Pitts's ruddy face, partially hidden by a yellow baseball cap and bushy grey eyebrows, burst into a smile. He waved exaggeratedly. A tiny warning signal beeped in my head. I watched his careful stride and was certain. He had been drinking. B.C. Ferries doesn't serve booze so he must've looped it up before travelling. Damn him. Damn Halliday.

Pitts gave me a massive bear hug. Though a couple of inches shy of six feet, the former Floridian makes this up with bulk. Peter Wyndamere, a crude, uneducated son of a southern fruit grower, had a remarkable horticultural touch and marketing savvy. His first wife's family grew money the way Pitts grew citrus. From a net worth perspective, the marriage was an astounding success. Too bad the relationship withered on the vine.

Selling millions of oranges earned him his distinctive nickname. For their fifth anniversary, Halliday gave him a specially designed Rolex watch. In place of the usual teeny square magnifying the date window, Pitts's window was shaped like an orange. He loved the watch, forever shoving it into every available face.

The acrid smell of alcohol mixed with smoke sickened me and I held my breath against his chest. I've seen the signs before, but his tolerance is exceptional. He must have felt me stiffen for the big guy rocked back, arms outstretched, square hands still on my shoulders and said, "Let's have a look at you."

Pitts's pale, rheumy eyes stared at me for a long moment. His huge ears, which stuck out more than ever beneath the ball cap, rose sharply as he smiled again. "You look great!"

I wish I could say the same for him. I was shocked. I hadn't seen him for three weeks and suddenly it seemed that the ravages of five and a half decades of extremes had enveloped him. It had become harder the last few years to look at the growing pot belly and slackening chin and see a former golden gloves boxer. Pitts has always been a chronic workaholic and continually mocked my regular workouts, preferring to exercise his jaw and elbow muscles. But for the first time, I began to fear for my brother-in-law's health.

"Oh! Almost forgot," he said and reached into his suitcase. His thick fingers grabbed a huge, red-wrapped, rectangular box of Roger's chocolates. "Five pounds! All cherry and peach. Your faves."

Pitts handed the cache to me. Before I could thank him he grabbed me again to his chest and whispered into my ear, "Sorry 'bout the booze."

An apology dipped in chocolate. What could I say?

As I manoeuvred the cap's peak out of my eye, I noticed a short, immensely obese Oriental man watching us with expressionless black eyes. He caught my glance and nodded slightly. I pulled away from Pitts.

Pitts looked momentarily bewildered until I cocked my head towards the round man. Then he turned, saw him, and shouted, "Beg your pardon, K." Pitts turned back to me and introduced me to Kim Karatsu, a Japanese real estate developer.

Recently, Pitts had been doing a lot of travel throughout the Orient—fly fishing, as he called it— for possible real estate investors. Obviously, he'd hooked a biggie.

The foreigner with the bone-yellow face offered a limp, cotton-ball hand. Then, in perfect English, Karatsu inquired about my wrist.

Surprised both by the question and by his American accent, I hesitated then spit out that it was fine, thank you.

Pitts looked at me with a glint in his eye. "The guy knows golf. Ol' K's here for the Classic." He handed me the baseball cap. The word "AKU" was emblazoned in purple on the front. "He's got a company introducing this new line of clubs and he's hoping Halliday'll use them."

His voice thickened and he ran his fingers through flattened silver hair. The dense hair seemed dulled by a yellow sheen. "What d'ya think? Have you talked to her lately?"

I groaned inwardly. *Yeah, I've spoken to her. It's over, my friend, only you won't accept it.* Then, pursing my lips, I looked down at Karatsu's middle-aged face, not a line visible. The black-haired guy was disconcerting. Everything about him seemed hidden, except his appetite. His expression never changed, his posture was perfect and so, it seemed, were his manners. The catch from Japan wore a nondescript dark suit, crisp white shirt and solid red tie-all too tight.

I shoved the yellow cap on my head. "We've

talked briefly. Don't know if Hal'll want to change before the event but she may try 'em in the Pro-Am." I hesitated. "Pitts, about the fax..."

He cut me off. "Later. Come on, let's not stand around here all day. Take us to the club, my dear pro, and don't spare the horses."

Us? Shit. My convertible's a two-seater. A sober Pitts would've remembered that.

I shoved the heavy box of chocolates under my left arm, grabbed Pitts's briefcase and reached for Karatsu's but he surprised me with a quick, smooth movement to pick it up. I shrugged and headed to the parking lot, calling over my shoulder, "We'll have to call a cab."

"What? Where's Emily?" Pitts asked, now talking and walking with great care.

"Emily?" Karatsu said.

Pitts grinned. "Tell 'im."

"Emily's my car."

"Tell 'im why you call it Emily," Pitts said with a grin.

"I named her after one of British Columbia's greatest artists: Emily Carr."

"Car—get it?" Pitts chortled.

Karatsu's lips moved slightly but I wouldn't have called it a smile.

"She's right over there but she's a two-seater, remember?"

"No problem," Pitts said heartily, avoiding my eyes. "I'll get in the back."

Karatsu and I looked at the small rectangular space behind the two seats. The newcomer's expression didn't change but his shoulders seemed to droop. "No way, brother-in-law. First, it's against the law and second, you couldn't fit even if we pried you in with a sand wedge."

Pitts spat an expletive then quickly apologized

to Karatsu. "You stuff the bags in the trunk and I'll get in."

I sighed. I learned early in life not to argue with someone under the influence. Pitts struggled over the seats and with a great deal of grunting and moaning, wedged himself in. Karatsu actually smiled, albeit thinly.

As we headed north up the Island Highway, Pitts pointed out area landmarks, shouting from the back. He gets motor mouth when his tongue's lubricated and nothing'll stop him. Karatsu looked impassive, maybe he just couldn't hear above the din. At a traffic light at Hammond Bay Road, Pitts began to describe French Creek's Morningstar community, one of his earlier real estate developments. Suddenly, Karatsu was like a mongoose, listening intently. As I geared up, he strained against the seat belt trying to hear.

"400 acres of prime land," Pitts shouted from the back. Karatsu shook his head. Couldn't hear. Pitts slumped dejectedly until the next stop light. Then he spoke rapidly, eyeing the red light. "Like I said, 400 acres, most of 'em adjacent to agricultural tracts. The 7,000 yard championship golf course has been open for several years and we're completing Phase Three, another 100 single family homes."

"Who's involved?" Karatsu asked.

"Practically everyone. That's the problem, too many cooks for my taste." Pitts clapped me on the back. "That's why we're concentrating on Sea Blush."

Surprised, Karatsu turned to me. "You're an investor?"

I laughed. "Nope, just an employee." I started to pull away. We got dragged down by a little traffic so I dropped into second, leaned toward the fat man and continued, "I put all my money into the world's greatest view."

"Don't you believe her," Pitts added. "Riley's the heart and soul of Sea Blush. Without her, I'd be sunk."

He shifted uncomfortably, grabbed at my head rest as I cornered hard, then continued, "You see, even though there's a tremendous market for golf in Canada, there's a lot of competition. Somebody like Riley gives us the edge."

The traffic started to move so I hit the gas, a little too hard and Pitts rocked back. "Sorry!" I shouted and sneaked a few kilometres above the speed limit.

At Lantzville, traffic was heavy due to a tortoise-like road crew. They'd been at this stretch for weeks and I'd never seen more than one guy working and five others watching. Why is multiple close supervision essential in the laying of asphalt? While we millimetred forward, Pitts's mouth ran on.

"We've done our homework. Golf's a two billion-a-year industry, with about three million duffers participating. That's 18 per cent of Canadians, the highest in the world."

He poked Karatsu's shoulder. "Compare that with 13 per cent in America! But now there are over 1800 courses, up 75 percent since the '80s. You know the old story. Despite continuing growth, you've gotta be different."

Karatsu coughed as a dump truck rolled by along the shoulder. He swallowed and asked with his tight smile, "What's your secret?"

I shot Pitts a warning look in the rear view mirror. He ignored me. "No real secret, just common sense."

We were dead in the water now, my view

blocked by a black van. I'd had enough of the clutch and gas tango so put the car in neutral and yanked up the emergency brake. Then I turned and gave Pitts my full attention.

Beaming, he counted off the fingers on his right hand. "One: Riley; two: a great course; three: location, location, location. You've seen yourself how easy it is to get here. We've got spectacular views, wide-open spaces and enough nature to choke a horse."

He moved onto his index finger. "Four: possibility of equity memberships; five: custom-designed homes to suit all needs—seniors, families, everybody."

"Equity memberships? I thought it was privately owned."

The jeep behind me honked and I realized the milk train had left the station. I inched up ten whole feet then rolled to a stop.

"It is, now," Pitts said. "There're three of us, but I've got the lion's share and I'll decide when to sell. And six," Pitts dramatically changed hands and grabbed his right pinkie, "we've got the LPGA And seven," he added with great glee, "we've got North American TV rights."

Karatsu shook his head, obviously impressed. I honked the horn for good measure and the guy in the van ahead gave me the finger.

Finally, the great tortoise up ahead moved and we were once again sailing along.

The uninterrupted speed was heavenly and we sat back and sucked in fresh air. I glanced over at Karatsu. He seemed entranced by the scenery. I've lived here most of my life and am still caught breathless. *Beautiful* isn't on our licence plates for nothing.

I've never been far outside Tokyo but I doubt the island of Japan has the rugged cliffs, towering evergreens and lush undergrowth of my island.

Just as I pointed out the mud flats of Nanoose Bay, Karatsu leaned over and shouted, "Where'd you get the name, Sea Blush?"

Pitts and I laughed. I pointed over my left shoulder, up a cliff opposite the Bay. "Up there," I yelled. "It's the name of my street."

Minutes later we pulled into the club's jammed parking lot and I tucked the convertible into my spot near the clubhouse. "Home sweet home," I said, jumping out. I pulled the luggage from the trunk as Karatsu stepped neatly out of the car. We both stood and watched Pitts yank himself free. He was sweating a little and the back of his suit was crushed, but his eyes were clearer and his face shone with pride.

I snagged Sandy, a sunburned groundskeeper who was trundling by in a golf cart. Though a little vexed at the interruption, he took their bags and left with instructions to put Pitts's in his condo and Karatsu's in the club.

"Let's walk a bit before dinner, show you the place. Afterwards, I'll take you in, introduce you to my daughter, Juet. She's Assistant Club Manager. Sound good?"

"Wait a sec," I said, touching Pitts's arm. I glanced at Karatsu. "Excuse us for a sec?" I asked, herding my brother-in-law aside.

"Not now, Ril!" Pitts whispered urgently.

"But we've gotta talk." I lowered my voice. "That fax could be real trouble."

Pitts's eyes widened. "Later!" he hissed. Then, beaming broadly, he strode back to Karatsu. "Come, come," he said heartily, "lots to see."

We strolled past the clubhouse, perched high on a rocky outcrop which overlooks the practice green and the undulating, pond-choked front nine.

Stopping briefly, we watched while James, Dai's

assistant superintendent, cut holes in the huge, kidney-shaped putting green. Using an auger with a T-shaped handle, the young man expertly sliced into the green and pulled out a plug of dirt. He walked a couple of steps then carefully dropped the plug into an old hole. Dissatisfied with the depth, he pulled the plug out, reached into a bucket at his side and dropped a little dirt into the hole. Down went the auger, down went the handle, up came the auger, down stayed the plug. A quick stamp, a thorough soaking and the newly filled hole was almost invisible. Then Shelley, a young, fair-haired woman, dropped a white plastic cup into the fresh hole.

"That the way they do it in Japan?" Pitts asked. Karatsu hesitated then shook his head reluctantly.

"What's different?" I asked.

His black eyes searched my face. "Not a job for women," he said, without a trace of embarrassment.

I bristled. Business or not, I don't take crap from anybody. Before I could answer, Pitts jumped between us and took both our shoulders. "Come on, lots more to see."

We walked apart, with Pitts chatting in the middle, regurgitating the sales litany he knew so well. I'd heard his spiel a thousand times, yet like a great Broadway actor, Pitts Wyndamere replayed each performance as enthusiastically as the first.

"We've got 1,500 acres, give or take. Everything in nature you could possible want. You want waterfront? We've got waterfront. Hillsides? Forests? All those and more—meadows, bald eagles, even deer, views of the Strait of Georgia and the Coastal Mountain Range on the mainland."

We strolled past the Hut and I glanced inside. Brenda was at the cash, two eager players handing over the second-most important green in golf, money.

Pitts and I waved hello to a couple of members.

"We developed this course hands-on, right, Riley?" I nodded. "A lot of people think our business is just playing golf but we were out there with the architect-up to our pitts, if you'll excuse the pun-with the snakes and toads and ticks. Right now, the course is two-thirds complete. It'll be 27 holes by next fall."

He stopped and stared at the mountains, just visible above the horizon. "I'll show you the blueprints later but as I mentioned to you on the ferry, we're developing in four phases: the first was the course; Phase Two we've just completed. Fifty developed lots located immediately off the back nine. One of 'em's mine, you'll see that later."

"And Phase Three?"

"Three and Four are the final housing developments, one hundred homes apiece. They're scheduled for next summer and the following spring, but we may put them together."

Karatsu allowed himself a slight look of surprise. "200 units at the same time? Is that feasible?"

Pitts shrugged. "Don't know, but if things don't pick up after the Classic, we're going to be a little tight."

"What are your development and land costs?" Karatsu asked.

"Nothing like they are in Japan. Still, expensive enough. Just over $13 million so far."

"Yeah," I added, "that's a lot of green fees."

Karatsu looked at me as if I were deranged. "Thirteen million? Why some of our initiation fees exceed that." My jaw dropped. He looked at me with disdain. "It costs hundreds of millions of dollars to build a golf course in Japan."

Well, I knew a good exit line when I heard one. I had some Hut stuff to attend to before dinner so

I said my goodbyes and watched them head up the incline to the Clubhouse. I was disappointed. I needed some time to talk to Pitts alone. We hadn't discussed the fax and I was curious to know why Mr. K was getting the red carpet treatment. Pitts told me he'd never sell Sea Blush. It was in my personal contract.

Five

By the time I stepped into the dimly lit dining room that evening, Pitts, Karatsu and Dai were already there. Obviously for some time, judging from the empty glasses around the circular table.

The dining hall, all glass, is huge and shaped like an upside down capital T. The stem of the T, jutting out about twenty feet, rests on a raised rock base. The room was half full, with most members sitting along the glassed walls. A low murmur of conversation beckoned me.

Pitts and Dai smiled, but Karatsu did not, from their table at the T's apex and all three stood as I approached. Was I imagining it, or had Karatsu hesitated? Dai beat Pitts and pulled back my chair. Now when it suits me, I'm a fervent feminist but I never object to common courtesies. A sucker not only for dark chocolates but also for the occasional tea rose.

Dinner was a semi-casual affair so I wore the same black silk pants but had changed into a dark green blouse and a soft, cream sweater, colours Wheez informed me, that compliment my auburn hair. Pitts and Karatsu wore the same suits. David had changed from his ever-present grey dungarees and thick workshirt to tan slacks, dark mauve shirt and black tie. I'd never seen him in non-work clothes and found myself studying the new man. I had to admit he didn't look half bad, brown wavy hair under control, tanned, round cheeks freshly shaved. Somehow, the mauve shirt enhanced the darkness of his blue eyes. His wife probably bought it.

"We were just discussing some tournament basics," Pitts said and turned to Karatsu. "It's been a rush, we've had to do stuff in nine months that should take a year. Fortunately, Viv and her crew are fantastic."

"Oh, yes," Karatsu said quietly. "Vivian Graves."

There was an awkward silence. Dai jumped in. "That's right! She's from Japan. You know her?"

Karatsu's head nodded slightly.

Pitts gave us an odd look. "Viv originally worked with K, where she got her tournament experience." Again, silence.

Dai fingered his glass. The waiter brought me a Diet Coke. It's nice when you're so well known that you don't have to order. The men hurriedly asked for refills and we watched the waiter leave. What was the problem?

Finally, Karatsu asked, "Tell me, I've never started an event from scratch, where did you begin?"

"Well," Pitts said, "Since Viv was new to North America, we first went to the Safeco Classic in Washington. You know, talked to their organizers, saw how they set up. 'Course," he said suddenly smiling in my direction, "with Riley and Halliday, I've been to dozens of events, but it's different as a spectator. When we got back, I got some names from Vancouver."

"Ah, thank-you," he said, interrupted by the delivery of a fresh Scotch. He took a large gulp and continued. "Viv deserves the credit, though. She's a wonder! In about three weeks, she'd hired a crack team, several with experience in pro soccer. A couple of 'em suggested TSO, a tournament services group from Washington. Viv and her group do the marketing, fund raising, logistics and so on, and TSO will handle the on-site set up stuff, like scoreboards and roping. They arrive next week, so we'll see."

"Pitts's done an amazing job," I said, not wanting Vivian to get all the credit. After all, she was just a hired hand. "It's a huge risk, running one of these tournaments." I looked at him apologetically. "I, for one, was pretty doubtful, didn't think he could pull it off but..." I raised my glass. Dai followed suit. "Thanks to you, bro-in-law, professional women's golf is coming to Nanoose."

We all took a hefty swig.

"Yeah," Dai added, "it's been a lot of work but I never thought I'd get the chance. There's what, thirty five women's events?" He glanced at me. I nodded. "Maybe forty or so on the men's Tour, 'bout the same on the senior's?"

"Close enough."

Dai nodded. "Out of thousands of Course Superintendents, I'm one of a lucky hundred getting professional tournament experience. It's unbelievable."

"What is?"

We turned to see Thomas and Juet waiting. "Daddy!" Juet cried and moved to give her father a kiss on the cheek. The men stood and Juet slid into the chair beside me. Pitts made the introductions. Thomas gave Pitts a fleeting glance as he shook Karatsu's hand. Pitts didn't notice. The young man slipped down quickly beside his wife.

"Don't tell me, lemme guess," Juet said dramatically. "You're talking tournament." The 24 year-old smiled. "All anyone talks about these days. You'd think there was nothing else to Sea Blush but the Classic. Of course, if you spoke to Daddy or Riley, that's all you'd hear." Pitts and I grinned. "What these two fanatics seem to forget is that when the last porta-john's picked up in two weeks, the club'll still be here."

"Now, wait a sec..." Pitts sputtered.

Juet laughed and reached across the table to

touch her father's hand. Pitts gave hers a squeeze.

"Your father tells me that you're his assistant manager," Karatsu said.

Juet smiled.

"You bet," Thomas jumped in. "Damn good one, too. Juet can do anything." He shot a dark glance towards his father-in-law. "If given a chance."

Pitts's eyes opened wide. I thought he might shout but instead, he reached for his glass and tossed the contents down his throat. Juet turned deliberately and looked coldly at her husband. Her face was suddenly very pale and she looked very much like her mother. Thomas dropped his eyes and fingered his fork.

"Things must be pretty quiet up here, eh, Juet?" I said into the following silence.

"A bit," she said quietly. Then Juet laid her napkin across a too-tight blue dress, fluttered long, black lashes at Karatsu and asked the question we all wanted answered. "Tell me, Mr. Kar...atsu, is it? Right. Mister Karatsu, is Daddy selling you Sea Blush? Do tell, Thomas is dying to know."

There was quite a response. Pitts reddened. A look of surprise flashed across Thomas's thin face only to be immediately replaced by anger. Karatsu leaned forward in his chair. Juet sat back, pleased at the reaction.

"Now, Juet, honey," Pitts sputtered. He switched to his father-knows-best voice, "You know better than to discuss business like this. You stick to learning about managing the club. Lemme handle the rest." He glanced at Karatsu. "Don't know where you get these ideas. 'Course there's no talk of selling." He looked hard at Thomas who was staring at his wife. "None."

"That's too bad," Juet said coyly. "I might be interested myself."

"What?!" Thomas exploded.

Juet looked uncertain, as if her joke had failed. "Well, I, I thought...with my inheritance... What are you all staring at? Everyone else is in on it." She looked around the table accusingly. "Even Riley."

Pitts started to laugh. The man has a great laugh. His shoulders shake, he grabs a lot of air then he finally releases it with soft, whimpering sobs. It's so ridiculous, it's hysterical.

Juet and I howled. Even Karatsu smiled. Eventually, Thomas forced a grin.

Finally, Pitts caught his breath. "That's rich! You're about to turn twenty-five, get your mother's trust fund and the first thing you want to do is buy the old man out!"

"Why not?" Juet asked, her confidence returning. "Then I'd have control over Thomas!"

Pitts and I roared but Thomas' face darkened. "What's so funny?"

Still laughing, we turned to the voice. Vivian was walking toward the table. Our tournament director arrived in, surprise, surprise, a different dress, this one a deep red slinky number, left side cut up the ying yang. Everyone in the dining hall watched her entrance. She knew it, expected it and made the most of it. How could any woman be taken seriously in those heels? I felt an uncontrollable urge to whinny and was relieved to see Juet looking a little peeved.

The men scrambled to their feet; the chubby Karatsu quicker than the rest.

"Please, gentlemen," Vivian said loudly and waved at them with her bare right arm. "Sit down."

A bit of a commotion followed as chairs were pulled out and places shuffled. Vivian slid into the now vacant chair between Pitts and Karatsu and

Dai moved next to Thomas.

"You're looking well," Karatsu said neutrally. "Canada agrees with you?"

"Oh, yes, K," Vivian said loudly, patting her long, strawberry hair. "The climate is much nicer than in Tokyo. Don't you think?"

"I don't know," he answered with grave politeness. "It's a little soon."

"Give it some time, you'll see." Her gold eyes bored into his. "Of course some things never change. Even in Canada." Karatsu looked more white than yellow. Vivian's teeth gleamed as she shouted at the waiter.

The young man hustled over and scribbled down her order for a very dry martini. Thomas and Juet requested the same.

"So, Viv. Tell us how it's going." Juet asked. "Everything on schedule?"

"I think it's going real well. The floor for the media tent was a bit of a shock, six thousand dollars!" Pitts rolled his eyes. "And we sure don't have a thirteen million dollar budget like the Dinah Shore, but," she glanced at Pitts. He nodded and she continued, "the quote, unquote, problems have been real minor things, like the tickets."

"Tickets?" Dai asked.

"Yeah. Organizing a tournament's a lot bigger than people think." She glanced around the table, solidifying her audience. "It's like setting up any event, there's just a lot of steps between setting the schedule for game day and the actual playing of the game."

She paused, reached into her purse and pulled out a slip of thick, pink paper. "Like something as simple as tickets." A red taloned hand waved the paper. "Somebody has to decide what it's going to look like, what it's going to say, what weight the paper's going to be, who's going to print it, what day it's going to be delivered...all those things."

"I mean, it's not just one phone call and poof..." she said, snapping the paper. "Tickets arrive. It's eight or ten or twelve steps. The whole event's like that. There's a lot more to it than even I thought and I've been doing this kinda thing a long time."

Pitts cut in. "You wouldn't believe the stuff she's involved in, committees up the wazoo, transportation, security-can you believe it, we're actually hiring cops-marketing, concessions. It's effin' incredible!"

"And then you get bombarded with all kinds of unpredictable crap," Vivian said, turning her gold eyes to Pitts. "Hear 'bout McNaugton?" Pitts shook his head. "Not coming. Supposedly needs a rest but rumour has it she's boycotting."

"Boycotting!" Pitts took another mouthful. His face was flushed and sweat glistened on his forehead. "What for?"

"Something about too much development, not enough forests."

Pitts swore rapidly. "The number three on the money list and she's complaining about development! Who's she thinks pays the purses?" His voice rose. "Shit! We walked and staked the course, restaked it around the firs, kept the bloody arbutus. We even moved tees to save existing ponds!"

"Now, Pitts," Vivian said soothingly. "Don't make your blood pressure any worse than it is. Remember what the doctor said about your heart." She snorted. "You know Kitty." Vivian glanced around the table and explained. "They call her the Cause Queen." She laughed heartily at her joke. "She's even got Save the Whales painted on her bag and, Riley," she looked at me, "doesn't she have fuzzy, pink sharks as club booties?"

I liked Kitty. Yeah, she was a bit strange, ate some pretty weird stuff, but she had some great reincarnation stories. Anyway, I admired her conviction. There were times when I stood looking at a new, oh-so-manicured golf course and wondered where all the little creatures had gone. This was one area where Pitts and I disagreed. I was thankful for the job and consoled by the familiar rhythms of golf over the last hurtful months, but I still wondered. Where are the little creatures?

"Her beliefs are her own," I replied, a little too huffily. I tried again. "There're over 140 excellent players coming next week. I don't think she'll be missed."

"She's very popular in Japan," Karatsu said.

"Really?" Juet asked. She frowned. "I'd have thought she'd be run out of town."

Puzzled, Karatsu looked at her.

Thomas started to speak, but Juet cut him off. "You know, the whale hunt and all that. You guys still go after 'em, don't you?"

There was a moment's silence. Then Karatsu replied, "You are correct. Japan treats whales like other marine species, to be managed and hunted."

Thank heaven the waiter arrived with more drinks. Everyone busily handed them around. Pitts grabbed the opportunity to change the subject to one of his favourites. "Wine, anyone?"

Six

"Hey, Bren. How's the puzzle this morning?"

Brenda stood up from kneeling behind the cash and dropped two handfuls of golf balls into the bright yellow plastic bucket placed in front. She grinned toothily. "King Tut's grave robbers would give up."

I grinned back. Same question, same answer, practically every day of our lives. I looked down at the 20-by-25 inch tee off booking form spread out on the wooden counter beside the phone. It was only five after seven and already penciled names and erased smudges almost covered the pink and white surface. July's hairy anyway but members and guests were frantically calling to get their licks in before the club was turned over to the LPGA on Sunday afternoon.

The phone rang. Brenda answered on the first ring. "Sea Blush, may I help you?" Her freckled young face scowled at me as she listened. She ran her finger down the middle booking column and jabbed at a name. "Jameson? Yeah, okay, we'll switch you for 12:30. You'll be playing with a couple named Fredericks, okay?" She paused then erased the two names in the 11:53 slot and scribbled them into the new time slot. "Right, bye."

I nodded approval. We sell time on the golf course, so we maximize it at every turn. Twosomes have no priority in golf etiquette and are commonly slotted together. Makes for a more efficient business from our perspective and a social opportunity from that of the players'. "Any messages?" I asked.

Brenda shuffled through some yellow slips near the phone. "Not yet."

"Nobody loves me."

She grinned. The phone rang again. Brenda chatted into the receiver while I turned away and rapidly inspected the public side of my Hut.

Our motto, burned into a wooden plaque which hangs behind the cash, is 'The Hut's got it'. Within a 300 square foot rectangle, we manage to squeeze in a product to meet every golfing request. Racks of club sets line both the front glass wall and the back wall adjacent to storage. Tucked into each of the three corners is a circular, multi-levelled rack, one filled with books and magazines, another stacked with videos, and the third-where I have to admit Kitty McNaughton could find her clubs some new animal booties-stuffed with miscellaneous trinkets, like golf spikes, brushes, grips, cart name tags, personal shoe shines, etc.

In the middle, thus creating an aisle on both sides, are two large, rectangular shelving units separated by a small circle of golf bags. Oddly enough, I'd found bag sales to run in three-year cycles. This was the second, so I didn't expect to move many until next year.

I ran my fingers down the first shelving unit, quickly rearranging the golf shirts, sweaters, shorts, rain suits, hats, socks, all of varying sizes and colours. The second unit has box upon box of golf shoes, three brands, one completely waterproof. I removed two empties and realigned the remainder.

Near the cash, which is snuggled in a corner along one of the side walls, are two circular racks, one lined with putters, the other with sand and pitching wedges. I gave them each a good twist and watched them rotate soundlessly. The drivers hang out nearby, wooden and metal heads up, stuffed into an oversized Wilson golf bag. I fingered a Big Bertha, remembering I'd probably have to replace mine.

Brenda headed down the small hallway into the back room. I ducked behind the counter, grabbed a handful of bags full of tees and threw them into the miniature Maxfli golf bag standing at the base of the cash. The phone rang. I grabbed it and gave the basic spiel. "Yeah, twenty five a day." I nodded. "We rent both clubs and carts, clubs are nine a day, pull-carts ten and power carts twenty. Uh-huh. You're welcome." I hung up as Brenda returned from the back, a bucket of balls in each hand.

She laid these last two buckets alongside thirty-eight others on the four shelves which lined the narrow hallway. As usual, when Brenda's working, the place's ship shape. I just wish all my staff were as diligent.

I nodded to her but her thin back was turned as she rifled through the glove rack near the door. So I quietly ducked into my tiny office for forty-five minutes of hopefully uninterrupted work. The life of a pro; paper before putting.

"Imagine you're standing on the edge of a swimming pool, gripping the pool edge with your toes, crouched, ready to jump in."

Dai Deugo straightened up and stared at me.

"No, really," I said. "That's what Palmer says. If it's good enough for Arnie, it's good enough for you. The idea is to get the weight off the back of your heels, get it evenly distributed. Try."

He did and looked as foolish as he must have felt.

"I know it feels stupid but it works. That's it! Now, bend your knees towards one another, pretend you're gripping a soccer ball. Good. Now, take an easy swing."

Dai swung and fell forward, pitching face down on the grass. I grinned down at him. "Not bad."

His face flushed. "No, really."

He scrambled up and looked around. "I feel like an idiot." It was 8:30, the sky was clearing and a slight breeze joined us. We were alone on the driving range except for two senior members. They quickly looked away.

"Don't worry. It's going to feel weird for a while," I assured him, rubbing the dampness out of my left wrist. "Good balance's essential. One of golf's fundamentals. Try again."

Dai took his swimmer's position, pulled in his knees, inhaled deeply and swung. This time, he lunged forward with his right leg only.

"See! Better already. But don't hold your breath. It'll just come out while you swing and throw you off."

We worked on it for 10 minutes and slowly he looked less like a scared non-swimmer and more like an Olympian.

"It's funny," he said, eyes following a hooked ball. "We work at the same place, during the same crazy hours and we hardly ever seen one another."

"Not so surprising. You're all over the course and I'm either in the Hut or out here. Hey, slow it down a little."

He complied and swung a few more times. "Feels better already. Think I'm ready for the Tour?"

"Don't quit your day job."

He swung more.

"Tell me, how'd you get the nickname Dai?"

He concentrated on his set up. "It's Welsh. My Mom's from Wales."

"I like it, whole lot more interesting than Dave."

He hesitated, started over then, with a grunt, swung perfectly. "How 'bout you? Riley's an unusual first name."

"It's a last name, really. We were all given last

names as first. My brother's called SinJin-short for St. John, which is my Mom's maiden name. My older sister Halliday and I were named after our grandmothers. Now you've got the rhythm! That's good but your grip needs a little work. Another fundamental. I know we've gone through it before but lemme review."

Being left-handed is a real advantage when you're teaching. I can give a right-handed student an exact mirror image of what they should be doing. Like most lefties, I'm also ambidextrous, so I can show 'em with right-handed clubs as well. Using The Witch, I demonstrated the overlapping grip that Dai was using.

"No matter which grip you use-overlapping, interlocking or even the ten finger-there're common elements, the top or left hand should hold the club across the base of your fingers, not your palm, with the thumb straight down and slightly right of centre." I showed him. "You want the V made by the thumb and forefinger to point between your right ear and shoulder. See? Okay, you try."

Dai gripped his club with his left hand. I tugged his hand a little further to the right and turned it over. His hand was warm and a bit rough. "See those knuckles? That's what you want, two or three visible. Now, the lower hand. Grip the club with the fingers, not the palm. See?"

He tried it.

"Good. The left thumb fits into the palm of your right hand. Yeah, that's it. Now, here's the difference with the overlapping grip. The little finger on the right overlaps between the first two fingers of the left. The V made by the thumb and forefinger points in the same direction as the left. No, not straight down. That'll shovel the ball off to the right. That's better. Give it a try."

Dai swung awkwardly, forgetting all about his swimmer's position. I let him swing a couple more times. "You're gripping too tight. Just try and keep the fingers tight, the wrists loose...yeah, that's better."

Fred Willcock, one of the guys down the range, sauntered over. I smiled. David looked a little self-conscious.

"You listen to this lady," Fred said, his narrow chin jutting forward. "She's the best goldarn teacher this side'a the Rockies, maybe the Atlantic."

I cleared my throat. David looked at the elderly man, then slowly at me and replied seriously, "You don't have to convince me, sir."

Fred clapped me hard on the back and I almost choked. "See you on Sunday, 3:30, right?" I nodded, catching my breath. "Eileen all right?" I sputtered. "How'd the surgery go?"

"She's fine, came through with flying colours."

"Give 'er my regards. Tell 'er I expect to see her out here in a couple 'a weeks."

His pale eyes shone. "I'll tell her." Fred insisted on shaking Dai's hand and then slowly walked away. I nodded to Dai and let him swing for a few more minutes, watching the tall, gaunt figure disappear. I shivered. Cancer's a horrible disease.

I found Dai looking at me. "Now," I said sharply, "swimmers take your marks."

Surprise filled his round face. Then he smiled. "Palmer's position, right?" I nodded. "Forgot all about it. Okay, here goes."

The first few times were pretty ugly but, despite his non-athletic look, Dai's a quick study and by the end of our half hour, he was positioned and swinging the ball with a lot more confidence.

"So, tell me about life on the Tour."

"What do you want to know?"

He paused and checked his club's head. "What's it like?"

I sighed and looked out at the mountains. "A dream. I couldn't believe I could make money doing it. The travel gets old, the days are long, but..." I hesitated, swallowed then continued fiercely, "I loved every single second of it."

Dai was quiet, fiddling with his grip. He looked up at me with such tenderness, I felt tears develop. Blinking frantically, I said harshly, "Stop fooling around and swing."

His face hardened and he swung, without thinking, again and again.

"That's good," I said quietly. "Very good."

A couple of minutes later, he spoke. "I'd like your help in buying some clubs," he said, watching the ball sail dead straight.

"Glad to help you, Dai, but why don't you wait 'til the tournament?"

He stopped swinging and looked at me.

"Well," I said, hoping I'd wiped away all the tears, "I don't usually tell people this but...the average person's using junk. Clubs that're just thrown through the production line. You know, attention to detail's non-existent, weights and flexes are different. Next week a couple of good manufacturers will be here. Maybe I can get you a deal."

Dai's face beamed but he answered softly, "That'd be great. If you're sure it wouldn't put you in an awkward position."

"Don't worry, I still have a little pull out there." I glanced at my watch. "Next time, we'll deal with that chicken winging."

"Excuse me?" Dai asked, wiping his brow.

"Another term for a flying right elbow on the backswing."

Still the dark eyes looked puzzled.

"Don't worry, nothing a handkerchief under the right pit won't cure."

His puzzled look deepened. I shoved my left hand under my right armpit and flapped my right arm wildly.

Dai hesitated. "Oh!" he exclaimed then burst into a smile. I grinned back.

By ten o'clock I'd called a couple of individuals to schedule lessons—I average about six, half-hour sessions per day—and placated a disgruntled renter who trudged back from the first tee and insisted on shoving one of our green golf bags in my face. Can't blame the guy, the bloody bag was missing a putter. I made a mental note to jaw with the guy in rental and apologized profusely. Then, much to Brenda's astonishment, I gave him an expensive Daiwa graphite as a replacement. Gotta keep those customers happy.

Hadn't heard anything from Walt on BioAction. Not much to do but wait. I hoofed it outside, waved a quick hello to Juet as she trotted into the clubhouse and ran across our course marshal in the middle of the first of his three daily rounds. John Stevenson smiled, tucked his cart under a tree, stuck his size 13 hightops on the dash and gave me a blow-by-blow of the holes.

A marshal's job is to make sure that the rules of etiquette are met and that play is moving as quickly as possible. This is one of our busiest times of the year, therefore the toughest for him. John's a good herder though—probably a border collie in another life—and he assured me in his slow, careful delivery that everything was peachy keen. Just the usual dawdling old farts, lost balls, that sort of thing. Nothing, thank god, like the epileptic seizure on the fifteenth green last week.

"Well," I said cheerily, "next week you're on holiday."

"Nope," he replied with a slow smile. "I'm a volunteer."

"That's right! I forgot. What're your duties?"

"Standard bearer," he replied, shaking his curly pony tail. "Can't wait."

I watched him roll off to greener pastures and tried to envision his tall figure marching down the middle of the fairway. Yep, he'd hoist his pairings' scoreboard with pride.

As a player, I had never realized one tenth of what's involved in running a tournament. Now behind the scenes for the first time, I was agog at the year-long preparation involved, the full time team, the expenses and the hours. But mostly I was flabbergasted by the number of women and men who, by paying fifty bucks for the privilege of four days' work, actually nurture the tournament to life.

Pondering those thousand volunteer souls, I went into my little office to attend to one of the more distasteful sides of my job. I waited for Carlisle. I knew what tack I had to take, but that made it worse.

The Mouth was, as expected, 20 minutes late-enough time to schedule two more lessons. Then he burst into my domain, as contrite as a puppy who's had a toilet-training accident. "Don't kill me," he begged, his square jaw drooping below his clavicle. "I know the payment's late but...it's been a slow month. You know how it is."

"Yeah," I nodded, summoning courage, "I do know how it is. But it's been four months now and I'm in business too, you know."

He shifted uncomfortably in my spare chair but The Mouth remained quiet.

I hadn't been a teaching pro for a month before I'd encountered my first unpaid bill. I didn't handle it at all well. It ended up in a shouting match, the cheapskate claiming the lessons were of no help. What could I say? We parted on icy terms; he still plays, but avoids the Hut like the plague.

Welcome to the school of hard hearts.

Since then, I'd developed a little strategy for those nasty no-payers. Nothing special, just the usual verbal and written reminders, but I carefully document the product sold, both equipment and lessons, and the efforts I go to collect. Then I meet with them, owee to ower. I look 'em flush in the eye and walk 'em through it. So far, it's worked like a favourite putter, though thankfully I've only had to resort to it a couple of times.

I sighed. My neat little strategy was of no help with Carlisle. He'd already conceded to being an ower, admitted I was the owee, but just wouldn't deliver the doughee.

I looked directly into his dull brown eyes. "Look, Mr. Carlisle. I've been patient, more than fair, I think, but something's got to give. I can't just forget about twelve hundred bucks. You've got to start paying, maybe a third each month."

He shook his head and spoke in a remarkably humble tone. "I'm broke. The wife's taking me to the cleaners, kids are in university. I just can't do it."

"No?" I asked, still staring. The guy didn't even flinch. "Then who paid for the new boat?"

That got 'im. His heavy face flushed, his eyes flashed and he started to speak but I cut him off.

"Small world, Mr. Carlisle. Look, I'm in a bind. You know the rules. I report to the Board of Directors. It's my job to balance the Hut's books, to immediately inform them of any irregularities. I've already broken that commitment, I don't want to break any more."

"So what're going to do?"

"The Board meets the middle of next month. I have to give a quarterly report." I shook my head. "This irregularity will be in it unless a large chunk is paid."

"You wouldn't," The Mouth said in a small, mean voice.

"You're right," I replied cheerfully, "I wouldn't, but it just so happens the books are being audited as we speak. You know Pitts, everything always done to the nth degree."

"Bitch," The Mouth whispered.

I stood up. "That's enough. I'll expect payment by end of the week. Now, if you'll excuse me, I've work to do."

Carlisle stood for a moment, jaw clenched, staring. I stared back. He turned and left, slamming the door behind him. Too bad, I wanted to quiz him about Joel.

It took over 30 minutes of fresh air to clear The Mouth from my mind. I desperately needed exercise or a change of scene but there wasn't enough time before I was to meet Pitts for lunch. I found myself staring at the white tournament trailers which lined the back of the parking lot. So I did the next best thing and visited the one marked Tournament Operations. Vivian's maroon Audi was parked nearby.

All six trailers are the same size: 25 feet long and 12 feet wide. Out of curiosity, I'd ducked my head into most of 'em and found little of interest. Inside usually stood a large table, chairs, boxes, papers, signs and phones, lots of phones. And, in the case of the temporary home of the LPGA reps, a sleek black computer stand. Of course, it was early days yet for most of the committees. Their duties churned into overdrive on Sunday.

By contrast, the Ops trailer hummed at me like a printing press.

"Now I've ran this through the copier, where would I find my copies?" asked Jake McNall, a transportation volunteer.

I closed the trailer's door, shook my head and stared with him at the massive, grey photocopier. There were so many side trays, it looked as if it could serve lunch.

I looked around. Four adults were busily working, squeezed among a desk covered in plastic-wrapped golf shirts, two long narrow tables littered with paper, Styrofoam cups and half-eaten donuts, and a small fridge topped by a coffee maker. Boxes of all shapes and sizes peaked out from under and over everything. I felt a little claustrophobic and walked near the small front window.

"I think it's actually, 'I've run', Jake," Vivian said, nose buried in a pile of flyers.

Unoffended, the fifty-year old grinned. "I've been runnin' and rannin' all week. How can I get these stapled?"

"The machine staples, Jake," another volunteer wearily replied while reaching to answer the ringing phone.

"I've got to tell you...that machine scares me. I'm afraid if I hit the wrong button, I might end up in East Samoa."

"You are in East Samoa, Jake," Vivian said with a smile.

I grinned. Just the change the doctor ordered.

"So," I asked Vivian, "how's it going?"

She looked up at me, her small face suddenly serious. "Signage costs are going to exceed sixty grand. That's 'bout fifteen percent more than we budgeted, but," she sighed, "overall, I think it's all right. We might even make it. Excuse me for a sec?"

She picked up the walkie talkie at her side and punched a thick button. "Come in, Gil?"

She waited a moment then the walkie talkie squawked. "Gil here. Go ahead."

"It's Vivian. We need to move the Aku sign on the ninth green."

The black machine crackled. "Shit! That baby's in the ground."

"Maybe so, but it's gotta come out. TV wants to put a tower there."

Another pause. "Okay, where d'ya wan it?"

"Give me five on that. I've gotta check with TSO 'bout roping."

"Right."

Vivian looked back up at me, brown eyes distant. Then she shrugged, "Sorry, Riley. But you can see," she said, fluttering her arm, "we're under the gun here. I thought it was busy in Japan. This's ridiculous! We've got to get the electrical and phone wiring finished, the LPGA advance official just arrived with four golfers who're-believe it or not-going salmon fishing up north, bleachers and TV scaffolding's sitting on a truck in the parking lot and the tents are somewhere between Vancouver and here."

"Maybe they're in East Samoa," Jake said with a smile.

"Well," Vivian replied wearily, "then you'll know just where to find 'em."

"Who's going fishing?"

"Oh," she said, ticking off last names on a scrap of paper in front of her, "Milroy, Agnew, Muny and Robinson.

I nodded. The mid-West crowd, not my kind.

The beige door swung open. I moved out of the

way. A tall guy with a handlebar mustache and a tan that would make Joel Sanderson look like he'd come from the Yukon strode in.

"Charlie!" Vivian exclaimed and slid out of her chair.

They hugged like old lovers-don't think I didn't wonder-and immediately started jabbering about some tournament in Tokyo.

I waited politely, as did the other three inhabitants, until Charlie took a breath and looked around. "Riley! Wow! Hey, good to see ya," he drawled, giving me a hug. "That's right, this's your tournament."

"Riley's not really involved in tournament setup, Charlie," Vivian said crisply. "She was just going, weren't you, Riley?"

I looked into her terribly sincere eyes. "Are you nuts? And leave Charlie just when he got here? No way. This guy's a good buddy of mine, helped me out a lot." I laughed and turned to the three wide-eyed volunteers. "Charlie's one of the best rules guys there is, always fair. Just ask Elaine Johnson." Charlie snorted. "When needed, Charlie'll give a good ruling, eh guy?" I said, punching him on the shoulder.

"Yeah, haven't had too many like hers. Didn't really know what to do."

"You're never gonna believe this," I said to our captive audience, "but Elaine actually had a ball ricochet off a tree and land in her bra!"

Charlie threw his head back and hooted. Then, with tears in his eyes, he tried to demonstrate exactly where the ball had landed.

We all broke up.

"Yeah," he said, between gasps, "but you should've heard her. Man, it was classic. She looks me in the eye see, the ball still," he pointed a finger at his chest, "you-know-where, and she says," he almost lost it but bit his lip and continued, "'I'll take a two-stroke penalty, but I'll be damned if I'm going to play the ball where it lies'."

We roared until our stomachs hurt and our faces streamed with tears. The phone rang and it took one of the volunteers several seconds to produce words. When she did, she sputtered a reply, broken by hoots of laughter.

We laughed even harder.

"True story, honest to goodness," Charlie whispered breathlessly.

Seven

"Basically, it comes down to this, d'you want to bring in the galleries to watch people shoot twenty under or not?" My question was a toughie, but one I truly believed essential to the future of the LPGA I was sitting at the lounge with Pitts and Charlie and grabbed probably my last opportunity to put my three cents into the future of professional women's golf. A player has official and unofficial ways of getting ideas to the Commissioner but those avenues were blocked from me forever. "Heck, ninety nine percent of the players could walk into any public place and not be recognized. We play for less than half the men's purses, even less than the seniors. We call ourselves the Tour of the nineties and yet we're on TV less often than the Queen of England! Something like sixty eight men's' tournaments were televised last year to maybe fifteen of ours. I don't think it's going to improve unless we set up golf courses for women pros."

"Wait a sec," Charlie Gregg replied. "We set about 2,500 to 3,000 hole locations a year and I'll bet our percentage of error's less than one. We can tell by the complaints. You've gotta take into consideration the player who's complaining. Now, you an' I both know the one who shot sixty-five isn't and the one who shot eighty is."

"Yeah, but that's not what I mean." I looked across at Pitts, whose dark eyes were watching us intently. I sipped my Diet Coke. "We all know they set up the men's Tour courses easy, so they shoot twenty under. The seniors, same thing, they shoot twenty under. Tons of people go out and watch 'em."

"I don't know about that," Charlie said, suddenly regaining his corporate composure.

I brushed his officialdom away. "Sure you do! That's business, smart business. All I'm saying is, people don't show up to watch somebody shooting eighty."

Charlie looked at me and then at Pitts. He sighed and fingered his mustache. Then he took three packets of sugar, pinched them together in his right hand and shook. He carefully tore off the tops, poured and then stirred violently. "You might be right but...we're in a bind. If we set the courses up easy, the top players bitch." He raised his voice a couple of notches and stirred a little harder. "Too easy, it's a putting contest."

He dropped back to his baritone drawl. "You can't blame 'em. They want it to be tough, so the cream rises to the top. See?" he asked, squirting some into his coffee. "Plus which, the courses aren't set up for women pros. You know that, Pitts. What've you got here at Sea Blush? Three sets of tees, right?" Pitts nodded, fingering an almost empty glass of Scotch. "Yeah, the women's, the men's and the blues. Well, we don't play the women's and we can't play the blues. So we're tryin' to modify the men's tees so they still play tough or hard but you can't always move 'em and get that."

Pitts replied a little stiffly, "I think you'll find, when you go to mark the course and set the holes, that this course'll challenge anybody, male or female, amateur or pro."

"Sure it's a good course, Pitts," I said smoothly. "It's just the point I want to get across."

He finished his drink and wagged a finger at the waiter. "Since we're on the topic of the woes of the LPGA, answer me something, Charlie?"

Charlie nodded and finally sipped his coffee.

"Why're the press beatin' us into the ground

every chance they get? Last year, the men's Tour lost four tournament sponsors and it barely got written up in any of the golf publications. If we lose one tournament, it's national headlines."

Charlie rocked back in his chair, a look of surprise frozen on his face.

"What's wrong?" I asked.

He shook his head and carefully wiped the handlebar. "You don't know how right you are," he answered in a whisper. He glanced around the now crowded room. "Phar-Mor's given us the boot."

"What!" we blurted. Phar-Mor, an American discount drug chain, sponsors two tournaments with hefty purses plus a bonus purse for combined performances.

"But Hal just won it!" Pitts exclaimed.

"Sssh!" Charlie hissed frantically. "She'll be the last. It's not public yet. Bell's gonna make the announcement tomorrow."

Pitts swore. "That calls for a double," he said, downing his drink. I shot him a glance which he avoided. He turned and ordered. The waiter took his glance then looked at Charlie and me. We both shook our heads.

"Sure don't envy Harold Bell," Pitts said. "Ever since he became Commissioner, he's been fighting fires.

"What happened?" I asked Charlie.

"They're in deep financial doo-doo, something about hundreds of millions embezzled."

Pitts's face brightened. "Of course! The new basketball league. Thank God, I stayed outta that."

"We'll be okay," Charlie said. "Our Tour's locally involved. We may not have sponsors locked up for ten years like the men, but still, we'll do okay. I figure we're a generation behind the men..."

I snorted. "No surprise. Welcome to women's'

world." He nodded and continued, "The men've been playing longer. They're more established. They've had the advantage of television a lot longer than we have. But we do well, historically, in smaller communities. Just look out there," he said, waving toward the huge windows. "We've got Nanoose as a new stop. We'll get others."

He turned back to Pitts. "You'll soon know what it's like. Not many tournaments make mega bucks early on."

Pitts nodded, taking the drink offered by the waiter. "We're treating it like a business. It'll take a while to build," he said. "We've got some smaller sponsors, hole and leaderboard stuff. They'll generate some income, a little profit for our charity."

"Well," Charlie said, getting to his feet. "Gotta get cracking. Great to see you again, Ril." He walked around and gave my shoulders a squeeze. "Good to see you, too, Pitts." They shook hands. Charlie started to walk away.

After a couple of steps, he turned and the mustache rose in a grin. "If there's some, you know, grandfather around who wants to give us two million dollars, tell 'im, yes, we'll play."

"So," I asked, "what's the scoop on Karatsu?"

Pitts stopped in mid-chew and looked at me strangely. His jaw and ears worked as he swallowed a hunk of bread. "What'd you mean, scoop?"

It was my turn to look a little strange. "You know, are you going to sell?"

Pitts's shoulders dropped. "Sell?" he replied, a little weakly. "Don't really know, yet."

"What d'you mean?" I almost shouted. "You promised m..."

"I know what I promised!" he snapped. Then Pitts took a deep breath. "I'm sorry, my dear pro," he said with a heavy sigh. "Right now, it's just talk. Offer's bloody attractive, though. The guy's worth billions. We'd be a piss in his bucket, that's all."

"Maybe, but the club's mine, too. I'd just like to know what's going on, 'kay?" Pitts nodded while his lips pulled at his glass. "Hey, slow down. It's still early, right?"

"Don't worry, everything's under control," he said carefully, smiling at a couple at the next table. He tapped the menu. "Let's order. I've got to go to the bank, get those bloody BioAction letters for you."

It was twenty-five after one and the lounge was slowly emptying. I didn't have a lesson until three, so I was trying to enjoy our time together. It shouldn't have been an effort but, as usual, the great spirit of alcohol danced in our way.

"By the way, I won't be able to make dinner tonight."

"Oh," I said with a laugh. "Rendezvous with any one I know?"

His face coloured. "Business," he finally stammered.

"Oh, sure," I said, mockingly. "What'm I, chopped liver?"

"It's not that." He looked down at his drink. "Someone I've got to meet, that's all. I'll try to call you later. All right?"

He looked so uncomfortable, I pitied him and tried another subject, one guaranteed to re-light his fire. "So, have you solved the day care issue?"

He winced. "No, the whole thing's a pain in the ass. I know, we're supposed to be enlightened and everything but, dammit, children don't belong at a golf tournament."

"Oh, yeah? And where should they be? At home with their mothers? For God's sake, even the men's

Tour provides day care so that the little wives and kiddies can come along."

His brown eyes flashed, but he caught the trap before he loosened his tongue. "All right, all right. I see your point. It's just that it's one more thing to contend with, one more hassle. Some of 'em are even worried about kidnapping. What's that got to do with golf?" He downed the last of his drink as our food arrived and quickly re-ordered.

I counted three so far but decided to hold my breath. Maybe a little food would slow him down. "What's with Joel?"

Pitts looked at me sharply. "What d'you mean?"

I shrugged. "Just that he almost tore Carlisle apart yesterday. The Mouth said something 'bout 'soft cost's'. Mean anything?"

"Don't know anything about it, 'cept that Carlisle's an ass."

That surprised me. Almost the same reaction as Vivian. "That's what Vivian said." His eyes widened. "I've had problems with the guy but I can't imagine pro shop bills are anyone else's problem. So why d'you think he's an ass?"

Pitts eyes darkened. "Don't want to talk 'bout him. Or Joel. Got that?"

I reared back, only partially in mock injury. "Okay, okay! You don't have to snap my head off. Jeez, I was only asking." We sat without speaking for a couple of minutes. Then I suddenly remembered something. "Still taking those anti-depressants?"

"Now an' then," Pitts said, fingering a glass. "Bottle's 'bout full." He smiled lazily. "Didn't need 'em in Tokyo."

"Remember the promise?"

He nodded.

"Say it."

"Here? Oh, for heaven's sake..." I stared him down. "All right, all right." He stopped, swallowed and looked me in the eye. He raised his right hand, palm up and open. "I, Peter Wyndamere, do solemnly swear never to mix the demon drink with the devil's drugs."

"And?"

"Oh, yeah. And never to drink alone. Amen."

We laughed. It was great to watch his body shake, to hear the soft whimpers of glee.

"So," Pitts said when he finally stopped. "What's Walt got to say?"

"Nothing so far. Only gave it to him yesterday." I paused, holding my fork in mid-air. "Why didn't you let me know sooner?"

He waved that question away, sloshing vinegar on his fries. "Didn't take it seriously 'til the third one. Still don't."

"Well, Walt'd never heard of BioAction, so it can't be too big a group. He said he'd call me as soon as he gets something. Hopefully by tomorrow."

"I should think so," Pitts raised his voice a notch. "The tournament's in a week."

"Yeah. Well, I'm not the one who waited 'til the last minute."

"All right, already!" His new drink arrived and he immediately tasted it.

"Pitts..."

"So, any better with Michael?" he asked, deftly changing the subject.

I paused, a little thrown. "Uh, no." He waited. "Haven't spoken to him since you left."

Pitts crinkled his heavy eyebrows. "But that's over three weeks..." He shot me a sharp glance. "Something's wrong, isn't it?"

I could feel the tears pinch the backs of my eyes. I looked down and angrily stabbed a French fry.

"I'm sorry, kid." His voice was soft. "Neither of us has much luck in that department."

"Yeah. Well, at least you know what happened. With Michael, I've no idea."

"What d'you mean," he asked, his face suddenly the colour of tomato juice, "I know what happened?"

"Don't pull that innocent face." I put my fork down. "Look at yourself." I shook my head. "Hal's fifteen years younger than you. You don't take care of yourself, you're overweight and you drink too damn much."

"It's none of your Goddamned business!" he suddenly shouted. Startled, I looked around. People at the other tables were staring, beginning to whisper. "Keep your voice down! You want the whole place to know?"

"Know what? That I'm a cuckold?" His words shot at me like bullets. "That my wife can't stand the sight of me?"

"No!" I looked at him, horrified. "Halliday cares for you. I know she does."

He sighed and rubbed his eyes. "Maybe you're right." His roller coaster moods when drinking throw me off. "I've blown it. She never really loved me as a man, more like a father."

The last words were spoken with such bitterness, I didn't know what to say. It was the truth. There was an uncomfortable silence. The other guests stopped paying any attention and turned back to their own little lives.

Pitts looked through me with unfocused eyes. "Y'know? Sometimes, I don't think it's worth living without her."

"Don't say that! It's just...well, you don't make it any easier." I pointed to his glass. "And that makes it practically impossible."

He swore loudly and knocked the glass off the table. The woman at the table beside us threw down her serviette and left.

"Calm down," I said urgently. "You're making a scene."

"I own this effing place and I'll make a scene any time I damn well want to!" he shouted.

The waiter looked apoplectic. The whispers grew and there was much pshawing and tsk-tsking.

"Who're you to talk? Can't keep a relationship going to save your soul, and you're still whining 'bout not being on the Tour."

That hurt. A waiter caught my eye and anxiously raised his eyebrows. I glared at him.

"That's not fair," I hissed at Pitts. "You don't have a clue about Michael nor any idea what it's like not to play."

He was suddenly quiet, a little shaken. "Maybe not, but I do know it wasn't your sister's fault and yet you make her suffer."

"Suffer?" I surprised myself. Words, anger, built up over a lifetime spilled out. "She doesn't know the meaning of the word. My big sister got everything she ever wanted. Why," I said, sitting back in my chair, "she even had you buy her way on the Tour. She wouldn't have survived a week without you." I laughed bitterly. "I got the scholarship, I won the NCAA two years running and look who's heading for the bloody Hall of Fame."

He sighed, then spoke, his voice raw with resignation. "You drive me crazy, the pair of you. The point of my getting this whole bloody tournament's to force you together, to make you deal with it and then get on with it. Listen to yourself," Pitts said suddenly urgent. "You don't mean it. You can't. When was the last time you spoke? Last year, right?

At the funeral."

I almost responded without thinking. Horrified, I stopped. He was right. Except for the call about picking Pitts up at the ferry, my sister and I hadn't spoken since we laid our father's ashes into the moist earth over eight months ago.

He shook his head. "You two're great together. Before the car accident, nothing could've come between you. Halliday adores you. She brought you up. Did everything for you."

I wasn't thinking. Too mad. Words spilled out. I felt like I was bleeding. "Why'd she leave? I was only sixteen and she left."

"She married me," Pitts replied, surprised. "You'd gone to college. SinJin was already working. She'd missed her scholarship. I loved her, wanted her to have her chance."

"Wait! What do you mean, missed her scholarship?"

"Holy Mother!" Pitts eyes flew open. "Oh my God, I swore I'd never tell. Riley," he reached across and grabbed my right hand, "promise you won't tell. Hal'll kill me."

"Tell what? What're you talking about?"

He looked down. Then he raised his head, hair glinting in the sun. "Maybe it's about time you knew." He nodded to himself. "She did get a scholarship. Your father made her turn it down."

"What!? But she never...when?"

"Offer arrived the day of your mother's funeral."

Suddenly, I felt faint. An image slammed into my consciousness. I was thirteen, lying on my bed, still in my one and only dress, listening to Dad and Hal's muffled voices. SinJin was still at the cemetery, saying goodbye. For a few moments, I couldn't make out words. Then suddenly, Halliday's voice rose and I caught a single phrase,

"Then the scholarship's over?" My father murmured something. I heard footsteps, then he called out, "Hal! Halliday!" The front door slammed.

A minute later, Dad knocked and came into my room. He stood over my bed, his grey eyes dark with pain. "Riley, honey, it's been a bad day." He took my hand and patted it. "It'll get better, I promise. There's just the four of us now. We've gotta stick together."

I nodded.

"Your sister got some bad news about the scholarship. She's really upset. We've got to be strong and help her out. Okay? Promise me you'll never ask her about it?"

I nodded again...

Pitts's face came suddenly into view.

"Riley? You okay? You're as white as a sheet."

I nodded, blinking, unable to comprehend.

My turn to shout. "You knew all this time and never told me? Damn you! Let me be a fool for most my life."

I stood up, tears hot on my cheeks and shook my head. "I thought we were friends. Now I don't even know who you are."

I walked away and never looked back.

Eight

"No, no, shorter backswing, Mr. Miller. Try and remember the rhythm; one, backswing, two, forward through the ball and three, bring the club back."

"Rhythm, smythm," the old guy said, standing motionless over his putter. "Never had enough to dance, why'd I have any for golf?"

I sighed and looked at my watch. My head was pounding. I couldn't get my conversation with Pitts out of my mind. It was ten to five. Ten minutes to go. "Just try it one more time."

I was using a common drill; two irons laid down about six inches apart acted as a runway for his putter. For the fiftieth time, I placed the ball near where the two clubfaces crossed.

"Now, as I said, when you swing too far back, your sub-conscious knows that if you follow through with the same tempo and distance, the ball'll be hit too hard. So, you automatically decelerate to compensate. That throws everything off."

He peered up at me through thick, polarized lenses. "I told you I can't concentrate with these clubs in the way."

"They're not..." I stopped, suddenly realizing I was shouting. "I'm sorry, Mr. Miller. What say we pick it up next time? Thanks." I forced a smile. "Any hey, don't forget, ninety five percent of golfers shoot over one hundred."

I wanted to talk to Pitts, I even thought of having him paged, but then I remembered he was going to the bank. I'm no good at arguing. Almost immediately I want things back the way they used to be and am willing to apologize, even when not at fault, to succeed. It had been a tough job, keeping angry at Halliday all these months. What had worried me plenty was that it seemed to be getting easier.

A car honked and I swerved left, narrowly missing its high right fender.

"Hey! Watch where you're going," a familiar voice shouted back.

I braked gently and slid to a stop, hugging a small tree. Joel's head poked out of a dark sedan. I gave him a half-hearted smile. He shook his head and hit the gas. I rolled forward and backward on my Rollerblades as the tournament background came to life in bits and pieces.

The parking lot was like an ant hill; pickup trucks and vans weaved slowly around several eighteen wheelers, men scrambling, unloading equipment of all shapes and sizes. Two guys levered a Go Hut onto the pavement while a woman lugged scoreboards from the back of her van. One guy stood, looking puzzled, in the middle of huge spools of black wire. Two golf carts darted in and out like angry drones. There was an air of confusion tainted with frustration, but the crack of excitement undercut it all.

I snapped shut the strap on my helmet and dug the rubber wheels into the pavement. Within ten minutes, my head was filled with air rather than pain and I felt the familiar tingle of sweat on the insides of my elbows.

This was my other zone. The one I could always find.

"The temp's 107. I know the cut's going be 224 or 225. Going to have ta shoot even par or one under," I said. "Told myself don't put pressure on, try to relax. Started out, par, par, birdie. Staying relaxed. Parred the next hole. Then hit a long seven iron, bad chip shot, bogeyed. Back to even par. Started getting ahead of myself, make a birdie and think I can finish at one under. Caught myself doing it a couple of times, brought myself out of it, seemed to work. Eighth hole, par three. Land on the green, three putt. Bogey, back to even. Ninth hole-really the eighteenth, as I'm on the back nine-is a par five. Good, slopey green. Hit above the pin about 25 feet. Downhiller, slick putt, drained it for par! Made the turn at one under."

"The turn?" Dai asked.

Startled, I looked at him. In the cadence of my walk and talk memory, I'd forgotten he was there. A few minutes ago, I had left the clubhouse after my shower and practically bowled him over skipping down the front steps. After the poor guy checked for injuries, he asked if I wanted to go for a walk. Well, my hair stuck out in wet curls and I wore a baggy Vancouver Canucks T-shirt and neon yellow shorts, but I thought, *What the hay?* The night was calm, the wind thick and warm.

I blinked the tenth hole out of my mind and stopped walking. "Uh, the turn's when you move from the first nine to the back nine." My face felt hot and I moved on. "I'm sorry, I just seemed to run on. Stop me next time. It's boring."

"No," he replied, blue eyes serious. "I find it fascinating."

My face felt even hotter.

"It's hard to imagine. You know, most professional sports, you travel with your team, so you've got somebody to be with who's on your side. How's it work?" he asked. "Dog eat dog, cut throat kinda stuff?"

"No, not really. It's kinda like being in high school, where everybody knows everybody. Yeah, ultimately you're by yourself out there, but you have a select group of friends. 'Course, fifty per-cent of the people don't care what you shoot and fifty percent wish you'd shot higher. I was lucky, with Halliday and being Canadian and all. The Canadians look out for one another."

We walked silently for a while, exactly in step. It felt natural.

"You stay in hotels all the time?"

"No, that's the nice thing about the women's Tour. You often get to stay in people's houses. It's great, like having a family at every event. They come and watch, cheer you on. 'Course, sometimes it gets a little embarrassing."

"Oh, yeah?" Dai asked with a smile. "How?"

"Well, I don't mean sound ungrateful or any-thing, but like sometimes they hover over you so much, they want to pour your cereal in your bowl."

He burst out laughing. A nice rolling sound.

"And then," I added, laughing as well, "you come home and feel like, *Moi? Clean the toilet?*"

Dai laughed so hard he crumpled at the knees and couldn't continue walking. Instinctively, I grabbed his shoulders. He tensed and turned. I pulled back.

We stood motionless-face to face-in the moon-light. A couple of seconds without breathing, then we both whirled and hoofed back at a faster pace.

"So," I said, eyes firmly ahead, voice deliber-ately light, "what about you? You arrived in April. Where from?"

"Richmond. Was the assistant super for twelve years. Then somebody mentioned Sea Blush. I applied, had a great interview with Pitts and here I am."

"Family?"

"Um, sort of. Divorced. Two daughters, eighteen and sixteen. They live with their mother."

"Eighteen!" I glanced at his face, now sheathed in dusky shadows. "Don't look old enough."

"Oh, I am. Don't worry 'bout that."

The lights of the clubhouse glowed ahead.

"So, how old?"

"Forty." He didn't hesitate. I liked that.

"Oh."

"And you?"

"Thirty three."

"Oh.

I glanced up. We stood where we had started, at the foot of the clubhouse stairs.

"Join me for a drink?"

"I don't know, gotta get up early..."

"No earlier than the Superintendent," he replied, taking my arm. "Come on."

"Your first professional tournament, what was it like?"

"Veeery intimidating." I sipped on my second cup of tea. "I was still an amateur and was just plain star struck. Patty Sheehan, Candy Lovenzo, they were like TV superstars to me. When I first drove into the parking lot, I was practically hyperventilating."

Dai laughed.

"No kidding, my heart was beating so loud... Couldn't hear anything, barely heard my name called at tee off. I didn't play with any superstars but just being there, playing with people who were so calm." I leaned back. "Missed the cut by nine shots, but it was a great experience, being there, in the locker room, having all the freedom and attention. Just being one of 'em for a week."

His eyes shone and I couldn't tell if it was the alcohol or something else. He took another drink of Courvoisier. I always thought you sipped brandy but Dai chugged it back like mineral water.

"My ex hates golf." The words slid together. "Doesn't understand it. Never came to the course." He looked down and rolled his glass, the reddish gold liquid sloshing against the sides. "I used to bring the girls when they were younger." His face beamed. "They had a great time, you know, scooting around in the carts, riding the mowers..." He stopped abruptly and took another drink.

"What happened?"

"Hard to say. Probably my fault. This job's sixteen hours a day during the summer and not a whole lot less in the winter. Tough on the family life."

"I'm sorry," I said, surprising myself with a lie.

"It's over now, doesn't much matter." He finished his second brandy. His round face was flushed, eyes glassy, a little on the edge.

"Don't drink much, do you?"

He looked directly at me with puppy dog expression then looked down and fumbled with his serviette. "Not very often. You?"

I shook my head. "Rather spend my calories on chocolate."

Dai laughed. "Sometimes, I find, it's helps me to relax." He looked up, blue eyes burning like propane. Suddenly, he reached across and touched my hand.

I drew back, as though burned. "No, I...I can't," I stammered. I stood up, almost tripping over the long table cloth. Dai's face turned pasty then flushed a patchy red. I turned and fled.

"Michael loves me..." I whispered then swung. Thunk! The ball whistled into the inky sky. I reached down and laid another on the tee. Whack! A tiny white comet streaked left. "He loves me not."

Hitting a golf ball, or anything inanimate, is great therapy. I should've gone home to bed but knew I couldn't sleep. My days on the Tour gave me enough crummy sleep to last me a lifetime. Now, no longer stuck in some two star hotel in a mid-western American city desperately watching the hours tick by before tee off, I don't lie prone unless my eyes mean business.

I like the driving range at night. The blackness and still air envelopes me, protects me. Reminds me of being a kid. Of the sheets Mom used to throw over our heads, straight from the dryer. I don't have many images of my Mom but I can see her thin figure clearly, outlined in the harsh light of the bare basement bulb. She's laughing and pulling soft white sheets free while Halliday and I look on, giggling, waiting for their warm cover. I'm never afraid of the dark, for I know she's watching me and I imagine her hidden behind a bright star.

I put another ball on the tee and changed victims. "Halliday, you're up next." Whack! Another ball, another victim. And so, for over half an hour, I pulverized every violent emotion surrounding my sister, my brother-in-law, my bloody are-you-or-are-you-not? boyfriend Michael and now, for the first time on the tee off release, Dai Deugo.

It was ugly, but I slept like a baby.

Nine

Walking on walking on broken glass...

Annie Lennox's powerful voice had blasted my ears since my Walkman and I started our daily double, nine holes played as a twosome. Contrary to popular belief, only fifteen percent of a teaching pro's job actually entails playing golf. I up that percentage with early rounds.

I punch a pink Titleist and, switching to Hall of Famer Candy Lovenzo—today's opponent— smack a neon green Spalding. I never play against men; I don't find their conversation particularly interesting. Exceptions are Hogan and Nicklaus. What's small talk when you're competing against the best?

I'm living in an empty room...

Up ahead, I caught a glimpse of a mower criss-crossing the end of the pale, undulating fairway, trailing an emerald green swath. Waiting, I glanced at my watch. The Rolex Lady-a gift to all first-time LPGA winners-read twenty-five after seven. I'd been whacking pink and green balls since just before dawn and was 10 minutes ahead of schedule. Candy Lovenzo's a quick player. Unfortunately, she was winning, hitting 22 to my 24. I must have played Sea Blush a couple of hundred times, yet now with my trick wrist, every shot's different. It's the reason I'm no longer a touring pro.

The Walkman jammed. Damn! For the millionth time, I swore I'd get it fixed. A bang of crashing metal, followed by a rippling of laughter echoed at my back-groundskeepers on Number 15. A wriggle or two with the casing and *Diva* erupted once again in my ears.

The sixteenth's a bugger of a par 4. Course

management is critical as the fairway, which starts off straight and flat, banks sharply left and develops deeply cut valleys. Hit further than 240 yards and you're poking about in a toad pond. Hit less than 220 and you need a boomerang instead of a ball to skirt the tree-blocked angle. Either way, add another stroke, sucker.

I'd just cracked a 225 footer with my trusty three wood. Candy responded with a smooth swing and her green ball hopped up the first valley and sat posing on top of a ridge.

By the time I reached my shot, the mower had trundled on. I punched a nine iron that dropped two feet from the pin. Hugging the club to my chest, I danced the Yellowknife Hop. I could grab a stroke at least. Birdie this one, maybe the next?

'Cause if you really want to hurt me you're doing really well my dear...

CAndy's turn. I took a deep breath, exhaled, then swung at the green orb. Just as the nine iron made contact, my left wrist cracked. I crumpled, suppressing a yelp. Swing broken, the ball skittered off to the right. Sheeitt.

Walking on walking on broken glass...

Rubbing my wrist, I watched the green spot disappear into the woods which separated the course from the condominiums, built as part of Sea Blush's second phase. I saw a splash of yellow and used it as a marker. I flicked a glance around. Great. No witness in my world of green. Yanking a wedge out of my bag, I trotted into the tangled shadows.

With the morning light scattering through the tiny conifer forest, I caught the flash of yellow. Edging closer, I whacked at the thick underbrush with my club. Up ahead, Candy's ball glowed beneath a thick bush.

Lunging forward, I tripped over a stump and crashed headfirst into the spongy forest floor. The music stopped. The dank, sweet smell of moss was overpowering. I yanked myself up. Pieces of yellow plastic trickled to the ground. Bloody hell! Ripping free the ear plugs, I wrenched the broken casing off my belt and hucked the rotten machine into a Douglas fir. Bits of gold and silver showered the base of the tree.

Waytago, Riley.

Spitting pine needles, I brushed off my sweater and carefully took a couple of steps. I cleared a few inches in front of and behind the ball. Ignoring the thump-thump in my wrist, I imagined the Walkman at my feet and let the little sucker have it.

A green streak whistled up through the brush, shot past the tree tops into the light and dropped. I trudged out of the rough to see it smack the flagstick and bounce back hard, leaving Candy with a difficult uphill 14-foot putt. "Too bad," I said aloud in my sweetest voice, "losing a beauty like that."

Things were looking up. Maybe another stroke. I turned and just caught a glimpse of lemon again as the morning light struggled through the thick branches. Looked like a jacket. Better pick it up, I thought, some member's sure to rummage through the Lost and Found for it.

I paid more attention to my feet than to the jacket, so was practically on top of it before I knew it. My heart skipped. I blinked in the hazy light. It wasn't a jacket. It was a man's golf shirt. And the man was still in it.

For a second, I had a wild hope that the guy-sprawled face down, head cocked right-was sleeping. The flies nipping at his staring eye burst that bubble. The dark pants and exposed ear were familiar. My head started to spin and suddenly, the air took a hike.

Gasping, I glanced up the small hill at the familiar balcony. It was a good twenty feet up...a long drop. All was quiet. I could hear my heart pounding, could feel the dampness sneaking into the hole in my left shoe but I couldn't hear the man breathing. A crow screeched and I jumped back, shielding my face with the sand wedge.

Pull yourself together! Swearing softly, I whiffed the wedge at the flies, took a deep breath and knelt. Reaching down, I felt hard for the carotid artery in his neck. I waited a long time. Way too long.

Rocking onto my heels, I sucked at oxygen. The dead man was Pitts. In disbelief, I looked around. Far ahead of me, above gently rolling hills, perched the glass and wood clubhouse. Funny, I never noticed how toy-like it looked. All around were the sounds of early morning on a golf course; birds squawking, lawnmowers burring, golf carts sputtering, staggered *cracks* followed by faint cries of *Fore!*

These sounds of comfort have measured my life. Each and every day included miles of walking, hours of practice and instruction, minutes of putting, seconds of satisfaction. For what? To end up entering my third decade, a pro has-been scratching for dough as a instructor *cum* caddie. It was supposed to have been different. But that was before the du Maurier, before Michael, practically before Christ.

Stupidly, I tried Pitts's wrist. It was cold and damp. Nothing would ever pulse in it again. I checked his watch. 7:35 by the oyster dial. I glanced at mine: 7:42. Imagine, Halliday had dished out 15,000 bucks for a special design and the bloody watch was slow! I leaned forward and sniffed his mouth, immediately wrinkling my nose, alcohol mixed with vomit.

Though it was a crisp morning, sweat trickled down my back. I stood up, gulping an urge to scream. O'Brien had taught me well, but I only followed part of the routine. As a coroner, I knew I shouldn't, but as a friend, I had to try. I knelt again to close Pitts's exposed eye. The lid was too stiff; the muscles in his face were rigid-an early sign of rigor mortis. I didn't touch anything else, nor did I move his body, but there was no way I was going to back out the way I had come. I couldn't leave him alone.

Wiping my mouth, I pulled out my keys. Attached to the chain is a pink whistle-a gift from my brother. Ideal for blowing the daylights out of ignorant drivers while rollerblading. I swallowed, put it to my lips and let loose three blasts. The whistle is one of those new pea-less wonders, the pitch so powerful, your ears ring like you're at the Queen's coronation. Its use is not limited to the streets of Vancouver Island. I frequently blow it to grab the attention of an about-to-be-clocked golfer. The screech carries a whole lot further than shouting fore! With some of the jokers I teach, I need it.

Head pounding and ears clanging, I slumped down. It was impossible, but my best friend was dead.

Ten

Within a couple of minutes, I heard someone crashing through the woods. "Hey!" a male voice shouted. "Hey! In there, somethin' wrong?"

I called out and the plump figure of Sandy, a groundskeeper, appeared.

"Don't come any closer!" I commanded.

The young man stopped, eyes riveted on Pitts. "OhmyGod!" he exclaimed, his plump face blanching. "Is he...?"

"Yes," I replied curtly. "Now, listen. I'm a coroner. Go back to the clubhouse as fast as you can and call the RCMP. Tell 'em you're calling for me, Riley Quinn."

"But," he stammered, "I thought you were..."

"Shut up and listen! Tell 'em a man's dead, they'll need an ambulance. Then come right back here and don't talk to anyone else. Got that?"

His head bobbed and he looked as though he might faint.

"Sandy!" I snapped at him. "Getta grip! I need you."

My bluntness worked. He gulped air and whipped his tongue across his lips. "Who...who is it?"

I stared at him. His blue eyes widened. "Guess you'll know soon enough. It's Pitts Wyndamere."

A wild look flashed across his pimply face. He started to babble. "Pitts Wyndamere," he whispered in horror. He scratched his neck furiously. "I...I..."

I cut him off. "For heaven's sake, get outta here and phone!"

Three hours later I watched in disbelief as the two attendants gently loaded Pitts's body-shrouded in black plastic-into the ambulance. Robert

O'Brien, chief coroner, spoke briefly to the driver then approached me. Pale eyes, magnified to egg-yolk size by tripled glazed glasses, studied me for a long time. I recognized the look and waited for the wisdom. It came with a light touch on my shoulder. "Emily Dickinson said, 'Dying is a wild night-a new road.' Let's hope she was right."

I might think about that line later, right now it was impossible.

He took a deep breath. "Well, we've done all we can, for now." He turned his wrinkled face and squinted down at the view. "It's a nice spot."

"Yes, he liked looking at the Georgia Strait." I sighed and looked into O'Brien's huge eyes. "We used to argue over who had the best view." I shook my head. "How stupid."

I glanced around. Everything-look, feel, smell-was slightly off, as though one of my contacts was the wrong strength. Rubbing my eyes didn't make any difference. Sea Blush would never be the same; its verdant tones were forever stained.

Walt had arrived within twenty minutes of Sandy's call. Constable Dickson is the guy innocent folks love to see and the guilty love to see the back of. Everything about him is extra large except his uniform. It may be XL, perhaps even XXL, but it looks more like paint than cotton. Razor-short yellow hair sharpens the angularity of his wide face.

The big guy held me tightly, crushing my chest, and muttered, "I'm so sorry." I was embarrassed but touched. I whispered into his thick shoulder that I was okay.

He backed off and gave me one of the looks I've seen him lace on a suspected drunken driver. My face must have passed inspection for he eventually turned and began sealing off the scene with thick yellow police tape. When finished, Walt flicked me a glance and marched over to Sandy.

The kid didn't have much to say. Leaning as far away from Pitts's body as possible, he whispered his responses. The more Walt tilted forward to hear, the steeper Sandy's angle got, until I thought the youth would pitch over backwards. At the last second, Walt grabbed his shoulder and pulled the dark-haired kid upright. He thanked him then told him to beat it. Sandy flew through the woods, falling at least twice by the sounds of it. Walt shook his head, tucked his notebook into his pocket then headed back up the slope to mark off the balcony.

O'Brien and the ambulance arrived together five minutes later and parked above, outside Pitts's condo. With Walt's help, the attendants slid down the sled. I stood and waited for O'Brien.

"My dear child, I'm so sorry," he said in his slow, careful way. He ducked under the tape then reached across and gave me a quick squeeze. O'Brien smelled of blueberry tobacco. A vision of my father curled across my mind as quickly as rising pipe smoke.

I stepped back, trying hard to keep my official part-time coroner's face. "Thanks, doctor," I said, my voice cracking. I stopped, swallowed hard and continued, "I found him face down about 7:40. Looks like he's been dead several hours, possibly more. Rigor's in the eyes, probably all over. He must have died in this position because lividity's in his face. I checked neck and wrist for pulse but that's about it."

O'Brien's voice deepened with authority. We were back to a working relationship, thank God. "When did you last see him?"

"Lunch, yesterday."

"Was he upset? Drinking?"

Walt looked up.

I nodded. "We, we had an argument. He was upset about my sister. She wants a divorce." My voice trailed off as I realized our last words had been angry.

"Right, then," O'Brien barked, "I'll handle the rest, shall I?"

I nodded, knowing I couldn't investigate the death of a member of my family. Looking relieved that I understood, he pulled on rubber gloves and immediately turned to business. Dr. O'Brien peered carefully at the area around the body, then, following my outstretched hand, walked to Pitts, stepping meticulously in my tracks.

O'Brien conducted an efficient and thorough examination of the body -funny how I already thought of it as such. I was glad it was O'Brien and not me or one of the other part-timers. His fingers are nimble and quick. Their touch and control had impressed me mightily the first time I watched them move over a body. No one could be gentler.

Finding no obvious causes of death, O'Brien called to Walt who now waited silently at my side. "Rigor's almost fully established."

So Pitts had been dead for almost twelve hours. When studying the phenomena of rigor mortis, the stiffening of the body following death, students learn of the so-called Rule of Twelve: rigor begins to show two hours after death, takes twelve hours to peak, lasts twelve hours and then takes twelve hours to leave. It starts with the head and upper limbs and moves downward. Passes off in the same order. But because everything-ambient temperature, activity of the deceased before death, location-can affect the onset of rigor, students learn not to blindly trust the Rule of Twelve.

"Vomit smells of alcohol," he said flatly. "No sign of struggle nor a weapon. You can forget that bloody suit." Walt nodded and shoved the white gown and booties back into their bag.

Walt took pictures of the body from both sides, top and bottom. Then together they awkwardly pulled it-frozen into a sprawled position-face up. Poor Pitts! So grotesque! Walt's camera whirred. They conferred quietly for a moment, then Walt carefully surveyed the ground around Pitts.

We three traced the body's skid pattern down the slope. Walt plucked a couple of chunks of glass off the grass and tucked them into a sealable, plastic baggy. "Not much to see up top. He must'a fallen off the balcony and tumbled down. Helluva drop." We clambered up the steep steps.

The sliding glass door which leads out onto the large deck stood open, horizontal blinds swaying slightly. We ducked under more police tape and walked up the balcony steps, sticking to the side. The wooden planks were dotted with thick glass shards. Walt collected them and, giving the largest one a sniff, said, "Alcohol." He took a quick look inside and whistled. O'Brien's hand on his shoulder stopped him in mid note, and Walt coloured slightly and went back to shard picking.

O'Brien and I entered the three bedroom condominium. I blinked back tears. Everything in the bright red living room looked normal. As though Pitts would trundle down any second, bellowing for more ice.

Every second unit has the same 900 square foot, two-storey floor plan with terraces front and back. The alternating ones were slightly smaller, two bedrooms instead of three.

Both levels are square. Once in the front door, which is actually on the side, you get a curious sensation of being outdoors. The wall on your right is virtually all glass displaying a panoramic view of the Strait of Georgia. Open dining and living areas encompass half the main floor with a stone fireplace filling the wall opposite the entrance. The remaining space includes a half-bath, a sliding glass door to the back balcony that overlooks the sixteenth fairway, a den and a kitchen, with the walls cut to bar height-Pitts's own idea to increase the view. An open staircase leads to the second floor. Pitts never ate at home so he dispensed with dining room furniture. Instead, the 16 by 40 foot room was filled with cream-coloured leather love seats and chairs and bright blue stone coffee and end tables. The look was stark. No sign of life except a dark blue suit jacket thrown over one of the chairs. "The maid was in yesterday," I said, walking to the antique roll-top desk in a corner. The oak surface was clean, not a paper in sight. I rolled back the top. Inside, the little wooden slots were stuffed with run-of-the-mill desk stuff: envelopes, papers, pens, a calculator, personal phone book, chequebook and bank books.

O'Brien rumbled from the kitchen. "Scotch. Lots of Scotch." He tugged open the fridge. "Didn't the man eat?"

"Only at restaurants. Didn't believe in cooking. Don't forget, he just got back from three weeks in Japan."

He nodded and ducked into the bathroom. I heard the squeak of the medicine cabinet's glass door. O'Brien returned, holding a pill bottle. "Were you aware that he had anti-depressants?"

I took the bottle. The prescription, dated June 2, 1992, was for Pitts and read *Amitriptyline Hydrochloride; take one tablet daily or as required; 30 (75mg) tablets.* A bright red sticker said: *May cause*

DROWSINESS; ALCOHOL may intensify this effect; USE CARE when operating a car or dangerous machinery. I nodded. "He was using 'em to help deal with his separation." I met his puzzled look. "My sister left him about eight months ago." I unscrewed the cap. There were about five white tablets left. "He couldn't accept it."

O'Brien nodded. I knew what was going through his mind. It should have been front and centre in mine, yet I kept it shoved way back. I couldn't believe it. Not Pitts. But I knew one of us had to say it, so I saved O'Brien the agony. "You think maybe he accidentally OD'd?"

He looked at me sadly. "It's a strong possibility, my dear. Have a good gander. Anything look odd or out of place?"

It was a standard question. The cleanliness bothered me a little -Pitts was a bit of a piglet-but the maid's presence would explain that. "No. Can't say there is."

Walt shouted. We stepped out onto the balcony. "He threw up down there." I looked over the waist-high railing and saw the scattered vomit. My knees shook, like I'd roller bladed for three hours.

"I figure he was standing about here, leaning against the railing," Walt's huge hand indicated a spot near the steps. "Got sick, maybe a little dizzy and dropped his glass here. See?" A large finger pointed to a slight dent. "It hit there and shattered."

He turned to me. "I'm sorry. Looks like he just fell. What'd you think, doc?"

O'Brien grimaced, deepening his wrinkles. He hated being called doc but hated confrontation worse. He and Walt had worked together for years, both respectful of the other's expertise. He nodded and said, "Most likely, I should say, but I would like to know what he drank, whether he had consumed any of the anti-depressants. An autopsy will tell us more. That all right with you, my dear?"

The doctor was being polite. As coroner, once he accepts a case, it's his body. No one touches it or moves it, even to turn it over, without his consent. His job is to determine if the death was due to natural causes. If not, or there are any suspicious or unusual circumstances involved, an autopsy must be ordered.

"Yes," I replied, agreeing to the minute dissection of my brother-in-law.

Eleven

Again I sat behind Pitts's desk and looked at the photograph. Pitts smiled at me beneath heavy eyebrows. Two days before, I'd hated that picture. Now, it mesmorized me.

"Riley, what's wrong?" Juet Wyndamere asked. "Y'look sick."

I tore my eyes from the photo and forced them onto Juet's heart-shaped face. She looked so young, so unaware of the horrible news waiting for her. We'd known each other for ages, but only casually, as she lived with her mother in Vancouver and Hal and I had spent most of our time touring. When her mother died unexpectedly two years ago, Juet came to live with her father. Almost immediately, she met and fell in love with Thomas Kent. A year later, they had wed. Now she was an orphan.

Speaking to the next of kin was part of my coroner training. O'Brien had taught me to be polite to the point of deference, to listen and carefully watch people's reactions. That was a whole lot easier when dealing with strangers. This was the first time with someone I knew.

"I've got some bad news..."

Her black eyes widened and a hand flew to her mouth. "Thomas?"

I shook my head. "No, he's fine. It's your father." She froze. I stood up and came around the desk. Taking both her shoulders in my hands, I said softly, "I'm so sorry but he's dead."

Shock blanketed her face, a sprinkling of freckles stood out on her cheeks and nose. She stared at me, unblinking. "No!" Suddenly tears erupted from her eyes and she flew into my arms.

Such sobbing! Such grief!

Eyes burning, I hung onto Pitts's only daughter with all my might. After a while, she slumped against my shoulder. I gently lowered her into the chair and handed her some tissues. She blew her nose then raised glassy eyes to me. "What happened?" She hiccuped. "H-h-heart attack?"

"We don't really know." I told her as briefly as possible about discovering Pitts's body. Juet gasped then bawled again. "We'll talk some more. Right now, I think you should go home. I'll go and call Thomas to come and get you."

She shuddered. "Don't leave me."

I gave her hand a squeeze and moved quickly behind the desk to dial Thomas Kent's office. With Juet's coal-black eyes staring out from an ashen face, I told Thomas that his father-in-law was dead. Juet flinched.

"What?" Thomas's voice was thin, a little high, sounding not at all like an experienced estate lawyer. I suddenly remembered that he was young-still in his twenties-and I wondered if this was the first death to affect him personally. "I don't unders...when? Does Juet know?"

"She's with me."

"Can I talk to her?"

"She's a little shaken. I want you to come and take her home."

At the mention of Juet's reaction, Thomas regained his composure. "I understand," he said in a deeper voice. "I'll be right there."

I was about to hang up when I heard his voice. "Riley?"

"Yes?"

"Uh, what about the Classic?"

"What about it?"

"Sorry. Don't mean to be cold. It's just that...well, we have to decide."

"Decide?"

"Whether it goes on or not. There's not much time."

I bit my lip. "You're right." I glanced down at Juet's bowed head. "I suppose we'll have to get the members of the board together." Juet looked up. I tried to smile.

"I can call 'em," Thomas said. "What time?"

I screwed up my eyes. "Tomorrow?"

"Should be sooner. Once the media gets hold of this, the event could be in trouble."

"Okay, okay," I sighed. "Tonight. Here."

"Right. I'll make the calls from home. Tell Juet I'm on my way."

"My Dad's dead and you're worrying about the bloody Classic!" She shook her dark hair. "I can't believe it! I thought you cared about him!"

I felt like a heel. "'Course I did! You know that. Look, I'm sorry if I sounded cold. It's business...I don't know what to say."

"Business! Don't talk to me about business. It's ruining us." She dropped her head into her hands. "Oh, Riley, what'm I going to do? Daddy can't be...it's just not possible."

"I know, I know," I said softly. "I feel the same." I took a deep breath. "It'll take time. But you'll be all right, you'll see. You're not alone. You've still got Thomas, Hal and me."

"Hal?" she snorted. "She's never been anything to me. You know that."

"She cares about you. We all do." I didn't know what else to say. Pitts's remarriage had hurt Juet deeply. From day one, Halliday never felt comfortable with Pitts's daughter. Hal told me she had no role to play, she wasn't Juet's mother and the kid wouldn't accept her as a stepmother. They weren't even friends. It was easier for me to develop a relationship with Juet, I hadn't stolen her father from her mother. At least, that's how Juet felt. It wasn't true, of course. Pitts had left his first wife before meeting Halliday, but to a young and bitter daughter, someone had to pay. And it wasn't going to be her mother.

Half an hour later, most of the staff was crowded into the dark green office waiting for me to speak. Thomas had taken a subdued Juet home. He and I had exchanged a glance and would talk later. I looked around the room at all the different faces. I knew what to say-the same words that had just broken Juet's heart-but now my mouth was dry. I didn't know if I could handle their reactions.

Believing Pitts was dead seemed impossible. A few of the older staff looked at me kindly, nodding their heads in support. Carrie, Pitts's secretary, sat directly in front, her eyes on her shoes, front teeth biting her lower lip. Dai, standing to my left, took a hesitant step closer. His aftershave overwhelmed me. I tried to draw a deep breath but my muscles were so tight, I puffed like an asthmatic.

"Viv, come in?" The voice on the walkie talkie burst into the room.

I sat upright, jolted from my thoughts. Several of the staff cried out in surprise.

Vivian snatched the black box and snapped back, "I'm in a meeting. Call later."

"Viv, it's Jake. I'm sorry to interrupt but this's important."

Vivian frowned and looked at me. I nodded, trying to push my shoulders down to where they belong. "It had better be."

"I'm down here at the trailer. There're four re-porters staring at me-I told you to get that thing outta my mouth!-sorry, Viv but what do I Tell 'em?"

"Tell 'em to hold on to their precious pants for a couple 'a minutes, I'll be down."

"Right," Jake replied, voice filled with relief. "Over."

Everyone stared at me. "Are we fired?" Carrie asked.

Shocked, I stared at her. "What? Where'd you get that...no!" I lowered my voice. "It's not that..." I took a deep breath and opened my mouth. Suddenly, Riley-the-coroner spoke. "Thanks for coming. There's no easy way to say this, so I'll just say it straight out, Pitts Wyndamere is dead."

There was a gasp and Carrie began to sob. I tugged a couple of tissues from the box in front of me and passed them to her. She looked up at me with overly-bright hazel eyes. "We're not sure what happened. I found him early this morning."

My voice seemed distant, rawer than ever. I cleared my throat but it still felt like sandpaper. "We'll know more in a day or so. We'll all miss him..." Carrie blew her nose. "But we've got a job to do, a tournament to carry off. The Board of Directors is meeting this evening. In the interim, we've got to carry on. That's what he'd want, so," I stood up, barely feeling my legs, and forced a small smile, "let's get on with it, okay?"

There were a few murmurs then, one by one, the staff approached me and shook my hand, whispering condolences. I held myself rigid, like a wall, and let their emotions bounce off. Dai held my hand, then clapped his left hand on top and squeezed. He smiled but it didn't reach his eyes. Viv, too, gave me a sad smile and surprised me by quickly leaning and brushing my cheek. Young Carrie was last. We stared at each other for a moment, then collapsed into a hug. I whispered that everything would be all right. She sniffled, blinked her huge eyes a couple of times and left Vivian and Dai alone with me.

"I'm glad that's over," I said. They nodded. We sat quietly for a couple of minutes.

Finally, Dai asked softly, "You found him?"

"Yes."

He leaned forward in his chair. "I'm so sorry."

I nodded and tapped the photograph. "Such a stupid accident. It's just hard to believe, you know?" I looked up.

Dai smiled slightly and said, "I think that's natural."

"Of course," Vivian said. "A tragic accident. It's a great shock for everyone." She paused, then continued, "I don't mean to be unsympathetic but I've got to go talk to those reporters."

"It's all right." I looked at her, trying to focus. "What're you going to say?"

"Not much, it's best that way. At least for now. Any idea what'll happen at the meeting?"

"Zippo. Hopefully go ahead, but I'm not sure who's in charge. I guess the Board'll have to pick a new chair." I hesitated. "So many things...I'll have to talk to his lawyer and..." realizing this for the first time, I added, "Halliday."

She nodded her braids and stood up, smoothing her skirt. "Any idea what happened?"

I shook my head. She hesitated briefly, then said, "Right. Well, I'm off to keep those wolves from the door. We'll talk later."

We watched her thin figure leave.

"You all right?" Dai asked.

"Yeah," I sighed, fingering the photograph. "There goes all the fun."

Twelve

"Halliday Quinn, right. Tell 'er it's urgent." I repeated my phone number. "Uh-huh, that's in Canada. Thank you." I hung up. Michael Harrigan-Pitts's lawyer-was next on my list. I dialled, got put on hold for two minutes, then transferred to his secretary. Finally Michael's baritone was in my ear.

"Riley? Oh my God, Riley, I just found out. Is it true?"

"Yes," I replied, a little taken aback. "How'd you know?"

"One of our tax guys was playing there this morning." His voice softened. "I'm awfully sorry. You okay?"

"I'm fine," I replied in my coroner's voice. "Look, can you come today? Sea Blush's Board of Directors are meeting tonight to decide whether to hold the Classic. You should be there. Autopsy's tomorrow. Not sure 'bout the funeral."

"Autopsy? What for? Stevenson-the guy who told me-said it was an accident."

"Nobody knows what happened yet. I'll explain it to you when you get here."

"Okay. I've got a couple of calls to make then I've got to... you know, get the papers." He hesitated. I could see him on the other end, thinking, rubbing the right side of his nose. He'd broken it playing university basketball and its lopsided alignment just keeps his rugged face from being too attractive.

Early in our relationship, I had once sat transfixed in the courtroom watching the man I love to call my Perry Mason. He used to love it, too. He had been defending a thin, dirty man accused of a vicious rape. Sitting there, draped in black, red curls shimmering under the harsh lights, I thought Michael Neil Harrigan was drop-dead gorgeous. Witnesses popped in and out of the box, one after another stabbing a finger toward his client.

The defendant kept fidgeting, black eyes everywhere but on the witness stand, running stubby fingers through his long, stringy hair. Michael sat calmly beside him, leaning over occasionally to quietly whisper. He listened intently as evidence was given, rarely displaying emotion. Sometimes he'd frown and stroke his nose. Then suddenly, loudly, Michael would erupt from his chair to complain.

The green eyes remained bright but my Perry Mason paled when the guilty verdict was announced. I saw him stoop over the defendant and shake his hand, murmuring soothingly. Then as the guards cuffed and led his client away, he turned to me and grinned. It was a while later that I experienced his unique ability to care one moment and not the next.

Michael's voice jerked me back to reality. He was rattling on, "...it's 1:50 already. Look, how 'bout I try and catch the five o'clock ferry? We'll talk then."

"All right," I said, ashamed at the instant tingle in my stomach, "I'll pick you up."

My next call was also to Vancouver, to the University of British Columbia. This one was fruitless as Katie, the archaeology department's secretary, shouted happily that my brother, Professor St. John Quinn, was, "Out playing inna sand, like all 'em digs' guys," and that yes, she had a number but wasn't supposed to call and no, they weren't scheduled to return for over three weeks.

Of course. SinJin had told me about this expedition. "Much to do about Cheops," he'd called it.

I waited for a few minutes, wondering whether to call and tell him. Of course he'd leave Egypt immediately, but what was the point? He hardly knew Pitts, having met him only a couple of times during Christmas holidays. I sighed and decided to let Halliday make that decision.

I sat for a moment, trying to organize my thoughts. The door burst open. Joel strode in.

"Is it true?" he said, with a touch of excitement. I nodded.

"Well, I'll be damned." He collapsed into the chair previously occupied by Carrie. "Heart attack?"

"Don't know. Coroner's investigating."

"Coroner?" His too-good-to-be-blue eyes narrowed. "But I thought you were the coroner."

"I am-part-time. Dr. O'Brien's the full-time regional coroner. Anyway, I can't be involved in this investigation." Joel looked puzzled. "Coroner's got to be impartial. I'm considered a next of kin so it'd be a conflict of interest."

He nodded then hesitated. "Told Halliday yet?"

"Got a call in, expecting her to call back anytime."

"Where is she this week. U.S. Open?"

I shook my head. "That's the week after Sea Blush. She's in New York. JAL Big Apple."

The phone rang. "That'll be Hal. I told them not to put any other calls through..." I let it ring again, waiting.

Joel's eyes opened wide. "Oh! Of course!" He stood up. "Talk to you later," he said, taking a couple of long strides toward the door. "Riley? Tell Hal I'm sorry, okay?"

For a second, I wondered why I didn't think he was sincere. I nodded, waited for him to walk out, then picked up the phone.

"Hal?"

"It's me," she replied, her voice tight. "They pulled me off the course. Is everything all right?"

I hesitated. This was going to be ugly. I've learned that it's good initially to say as little as possible until you can gage the effect. There's a lot to be said for being an outsider and not knowing what to expect, but I knew my sister. She hadn't cried when Bambi's mother died because she wouldn't even go to the theatre.

"Riley, something's wrong. Is it SinJin?"

"No, no, he's fine." I closed my eyes and swallowed. "It's Pitts. It's going to be a shock, Hal, but he died this morning."

There was a couple of seconds of silence then Halliday screamed, "No! Not Pitts, he...he can't be, no, Riley, it's a mistake, it must be a mistake..." her voice rose hysterically and she started to hyperventilate.

"Halliday!" I said sharply. "Slow down, breathe. Come on! You can do it. Deep breaths. That's right."

It took a couple of minutes but her staggered breathing slowed and the sobs subsided. Then I heard a muffled word, a cry from Halliday, then a familiar voice was in my ear. "Riley?"

One word and I recognized that accent. It was my old caddie, Pat Good. "Goodie! Am I glad to hear your voice."

"Same here, kid. I was carrying the bag for Hal." Her voice dropped. "What's up? She's crying an..."

"I know. Look, do you think you could stay with her a while? You see, I, I just told her that Pitts is dead."

"No!" she replied in horrified whisper. Her voice faded for a moment and I heard her say, "Oh, Hal, honey, I'm so sorry." The southern accent spoke again in my ear. "'Course, I'll stay with her. Don't you worry. I'll take good care of her."

"I don't know how to thank you, Goodie, but I'm so glad you're there. It's a bad shock and you know how sensitive Hal is. Tell her to call me back later when she feels like it."

I gave her my number, thanked her again and hung up. I'd exceeded my quota as the harbinger of death. Desperately needing fresh air, I headed downstairs. The clubhouse was unusually quiet; staff and guests were huddled, whispering. Before the salt wind could ease my lungs, my eyes burned with the vision of more tear-stained faces than I had ever seen at a screening of Bambi.

"Thank you, Mrs. Roulston. You're very kind." I glanced at my appointment book. Her lessons were the last I had to cancel. "We'll reschedule those two soon as possible, 'kay?" I listened for a couple of minutes. "Yes, it's a shock. You're right. He was a wonderful man. Yes, well, thank you again, Mrs. Roulston. I'll be in touch."

I replaced the receiver. I should have made one more call but I didn't have the heart to cancel Fred Willcock's lesson for Sunday.

Brenda popped her head in. Her eyes were red and she gripped a tissue in her hand. "I've got Constable Dickson on the line."

I nodded. She waited.

"Something wrong?"

Brenda started to shake her head then stopped.

"Come on. You can tell me."

"It's just..." She took a deep breath and the words fell out. "Some of the staff are concerned about their jobs. They're worried the club'll be sold. That they'll be let go."

I rocked back in my chair. "That's ridiculous! Where do they get these ideas? You tell 'em not to panic. Nobody's going to lose their job. Board's meeting tonight. I'm sure we'll have something to tell 'em tomorrow." I looked at the phone receiver in my hand. "Okay?"

Brenda nodded slightly. "I'll transfer the call." She turned and in a few seconds, my phone rang. I picked it up in the middle of the first ring. Walt and I exchanged greetings, then he hesitated. "It's okay. I've still got to get stuff done. You're calling about BioAction, right?"

"Yeah, but I feel badly, you know, talking about work so soon."

"No, go ahead."

"Well, not too much to report. They're an environmental group based in Vancouver. We don't have much, but from the sounds of it, they're pretty small. You know the type, fly-by-night, grab a hot issue, milk it for money then move on to the next. We've got hundreds like 'em on file. Most are pretty harmless, a little overzealous perhaps, but harmless."

"Any criminal record?"

"Nothing of consequence. A few members were arrested during the protest on the Charlottes, but so were lots of others."

"I remember." The widely-publicized protest against logging on the Queen Charlotte Islands, located north of Vancouver Island, had caused a fury of governmental conciliation and compromise. Round one ended with Environmentalists 1; lumber firms a big goose egg. The good guys gained a national park, the bad guys lost logging rights.

"Looks like a crank case to me, Ril, but my contact in Vancouver said she'd let me know if anything came up."

I thanked him and jotted down BioAction's address. I might check it out. You never know, a craving for Patty's cookies in Vancouver's West End could strike at any moment.

Karatsu found me a half-hour later watching the guys setting up the huge media tent. We stood silently as the last of the support poles were screwed together and erected. Heavy white rolls of canvas were unravelled then yanked and coaxed to span the perimeter. The bottom of one side was mostly clear plastic lined with arched windows.

Finally he said politely, "Please accept my deepest condolences on the loss of your brother-in-law."

I thanked him and watched the roof being stretched into place. The tent was fancier than any used in a circus.

"Will the event continue?"

I looked down into his small, dark eyes. They looked back intently. "I think so, but it's not really my decision."

"Oh? And whose is it?" he said.

"Why d'you want to know?"

A light flickered briefly in his eyes, then died. He pulled himself straight and replied haughtily, "I have a large investment in this event. I want to be sure it will not be wasted."

"It won't be," I replied and told him about the board meeting. I could see that he wanted to attend but I didn't invite him.

A sudden beeping punctuated the air, loud as gunfire. Startled, we turned and stepped out of the way of a delivery van backing toward us. The truck stopped and a young guy in jeans jumped down and yanked up the back doors. Two partially wrapped photocopiers waited inside.

"Pitts said he would talk to Halliday about using my clubs. Did he?"

I watched the young guy inch the first copier

onto the hydraulic lift. He jumped down, punched a button and the lift descended. "I don't know. You can talk to her yourself. She'll be here for the funeral on Thursday."

While the photocopier was rolled into the tent, I could hear the guys inside hammering at the supports. Someone to my left yelled "Fore!" Both the delivery guy and Karatsu ducked.

Pitts was dead, but Sea Blush lived on.

Thirteen

I stared at the spectacular scene from the front veranda of Pitts's condo. I couldn't get myself to venture out onto the back balcony. While at Lamar University in Texas, my golf schedule had rivaled that of a major league baseball player's. Desperate to find a Mickey Mouse course I could ace with little commitment, I had signed up for fine arts.

That's where I met Alma Winter, so aptly named, as her thin face bore the scars of howling winds and snapping cold. Her eyes, though the colour of an old iceberg, glowed with passion and within minutes the sixty plus woman had converted our little group of finger painters.

During our first semester, Winter immersed us in a study of composition. It started with long walks 'round campus analyzing nature and ended weeks later strolling about in museums analyzing humankind. She called it a study in contrasts: natural form versus artificial shape. Within weeks, I had changed my major from commerce to fine arts.

The first time I had felt the condo's deck creak under my feet and the rough rail scratch my hands, I was struck by the view's holistic beauty. Mrs. Winter would have been proud of the perfectly aligned fore, middle and back grounds.

Today, the sun glittered diamond chips off the choppy blue Georgia Strait. In the middle ground, looming in grey and green shadows, floated the small island of Lasqueti and its larger neighbour Texada. Tucked away in back peeked the snow-draped mountains of the mainland.

Taking a deep hit of moss scented air, I turned back to the condo and, shoving aside images of Pitts's face, entered the living room for the second time in twelve hours.

The air was heavy. I went to turn the air conditioner on and then, with my hand at the control, thought what the hell for? No fifty-five year old ex-Floridian, ex-Golden Gloves Champion, ex-husband of Halliday Quinn, and ex-brother-in-law and best friend of Riley Quinn was going to return later, stiff and sore from hundreds of golf swings, eager to escape July's sudden heat with a cool home and a cooler drink.

The answering machine winked at me. "Forget it," I said out loud and shuffled up the carpeted stairs. I turned left at the landing and went into Pitts's number one bedroom. Like Lewis Carrol's messy but cunning characters who munched from place setting to place setting at the Mad Hatter's tea party, Pitts used all three bedrooms, each for a week, then he'd start over. At first, I couldn't believe he slept on such a merry-go-round, especially since all three beds were identical.

"But that's just the point, my dear pro," he had said, with a slight glimmer in his eyes. "I gain a change of scene, a feeling of accomplishment yet sleep soundly every night. It does wonders to prepare yourself for travel." He pursed his thick lips. "Of course, the beds are different but I'm never thrown off by a new sleeping environment."

"The cleaning lady must love you," I had replied.

The duvet on the queen-sized bed in the first room was thrown half off, revealing a dark green bottom sheet. Although Pitts had only been home for a couple of days, little piles of discarded socks and shirts popped up all over. This was more like the guy. The cleaning lady had strict instructions not to alter clothes piles.

The sliding door to the walk-in closet was open.

As I approached it, the hairs on the back of my neck tingled. I whipped around but the room was empty. I strode to the top of the stairs and yelled below, "Anyone there?" An echo was my reply.

Rubbing the back of my neck, I returned to the closet where Pitts's suits and casual clothes fought for space. What would he want to wear for his own funeral? I'd never thought of it, but now, staring at the muted colours, I know exactly what I want to wear when they shove me in my box into the hopefully final inferno of cremation, my soft, baggy grey shorts, all three souvenir shirts from my winning events and my old, pale blue sweatshirt inscribed with William Blake's brilliant ode, *The Tyger*.

Some decision; what to wear for all eternity?

Finally I chose a dark blue suit with a narrow red pinstripe-Pitts was ultimately a business man-and a crisp white shirt. I hesitated over the tie then shagged convention and chose the one I had given him for his last birthday. I remember his eyes shone when he fingered it and his voice wavered when he thanked me. "It's beautiful, my dear pro," he'd said, ruffling my hair. "Where'd you find it? It looks just like one of my water-colours!" I nodded, thrilled that he'd recognized the style.

I carefully wrapped the tie over the suit's hanger, gathered the rest of the stuff and headed downstairs. From the antique desk, I took the safety deposit key and bank books. I was locking up when something nagged at me. Something I had forgotten.

There was a click as the fridge turned on. Of course. Someone had to toss the contents. Hanging the suit in the small hall closet, I stepped into the kitchen and pulled the door handle.

Shelves upon gleaming white shelves stared at

me. All empty except the one on the bottom right. There stood a bottle of soda water, half empty. That was it. Scotch bottles lined the counter to my right. The fridge shelves started to waver and it took me several seconds to understand why. Tears streamed down my face and a sudden, overpowering feeling of anger rose up inside me. I slammed the door. A thud bounced off the dark green shelves.

Damn you, Pitts Wyndamere!

Forty-five minutes later, I was nearing Nanaimo, having made a brief stop in Parksville, a one traffic light tourist town located a few kilometres to the north. Ken Lasher, the funeral director in the little seashore community, had been disgustingly kind. He'd gazed at me sadly, eyes slightly downcast and took the clothes carefully, as though his long fingers might tear the cloth. Ken mentioned that Thomas had called regarding the meeting of the Board. For a moment, I stared at his thin face. I'd forgotten he was a member. We chatted briefly. The air inside the small Georgian building was stuffy, our conversation muted. It had taken all my composure not to bolt. When he finally took my hand and shook it gently, I made my move. I raced down the green carpeted steps, glad to feel the outside heat slap my cheeks. Emily's wheels chirped as I peeled off, anxious to put mega distance between myself and the dead.

Thank heaven Nanaimo was filled with life, cars rolling, couples strolling and old men lolling on park benches.

O'Brien and Walt were waiting for me so I parleyed vite, vite with Louise, thanked her for the message about the autopsy and marched into the haze of the doctor's office.

"Riley!" O'Brien's saucer eyes widened. "Come

in, my dear. Come in." He dropped his pipe and moved as though to approach me when I stopped him with an upraised palm.

"I'm all right," I said, sitting in the wooden chair beside Walt." I flicked a quick glance at my police friend. He was poured into his uniform again. I'm used to seeing his huge figure bursting from multi-coloured golf shirts and checked shorts. "Really, I'm fine." I swivelled back to O'Brien. "What have you discovered?"

"Not much," Walt replied. "The condo was pretty clean, no sign of a struggle, not even of another person. 'Course, I didn't fingerprint the place..."

"No need for that," O'Brien cut in. "We've gone over it several times but haven't come up with anything new. Tomorrow's autopsy will tell us more." His expression softened for a second as he sucked gently on the pipe. "You received the message? Capital. I thought you would like have the funeral as soon as possible..." His voice died.

"Yeah," Walt jumped in, looking at me anxiously, "you know, so, so..."

I nodded. "It's okay. The Board of Directors are meeting tonight to decide. I'm pretty sure the tournament'll go on." They both smiled slightly with relief. "Thank you," I said to O'Brien, "for scheduling so quickly. I know it's not easy." I hesitated for a second. "May I attend?"

Surprise briefly released the wrinkles on his face. He tapped the smoking pipe on a clean ashtray. "Course not," he replied, removing his glasses. Peering myopically, he blew into a lens, yanked free his handkerchief and started rubbing it vigorously. "Please," I whispered. When he completed the same routine with the other lens and had squinted through both a couple of times. O'Brien carefully put them back on. "Really shouldn't." The huge eyes stared at me again. "I'll be doing it m'self."

Tears slid into the edges of my eyes. "Thank you," I whispered, knowing how few procedures O'Brien choose to participate in. Though a forensic pathologist, he usually let the local pathologist conduct autopsies. Unless the case was extremely intriguing or, now it seemed, personal.

Walt handed me a tissue and the men waited silently while I plugged the flow of tears. Finally, I stood up. "Good," I said, "Wake's tomorrow, from seven 'til nine. I'll try to organize the funeral for Thursday morning. You'll both come?" The two men nodded. I glanced at the Lady's hands. Not much time. "I'm picking up Michael-Pitts's lawyer. I'd better go."

"Tomorrow, then," O'Brien said. "Nine sharp. And Riley? Let's take you off duty for a week or two, all right?"

I nodded.

"I'll walk you out," Walt said, pulling himself up. I thought for a second his brown pants might split.

We nodded to Louise and were soon trotting down the entrance steps. "Is this *the* Michael?" Walt asked, his voice a shade higher than normal.

"Yes," I said, opening my car door. "Why?"

Walt tugged his cap a little lower, pinching his pale razor-short hair. "Just curious," he said, closing the door after me. Clapping me on the shoulder with a hand the size of a oven mitt, he cleared his throat and looked over my head. "Anything you need, just call me. Right?"

I touched his hand. "Thanks." He released me and I rolled off.

Though Michael's arms held me closely and my breath was filled with his soft scent, everything was wrong. He tentatively touched my hand and kissed me on the cheek instead of the lips. The embrace felt as awkward as our first. I backed off quickly and stood looking up at him.

Michael Harrigan hadn't changed in the four weeks, three days and two hours since I'd last seen him. We had stood at this very place, him leaving, me staying, no one talking. Today, with his short-cropped, copper hair, brilliant green eyes and lean face, he still looked like my Mr. Right. The only difference was that I was now assessing him as a stranger, not as a lover.

He looked at me in exactly the same way.

"Come on," I said, grabbing his briefcase. "We'll talk in the car."

But we didn't. My guess is the drive took the usual twenty-five minutes and the scenery was the same as it's been for centuries but I couldn't swear to it. In fact, if someone asked me later about the trip, I doubt I could recall one significant thing other than a pervasive sense of loss.

By the time I pulled into the parking lot of Tigh-Na-Mara, one of the best resorts in Parksville, I couldn't stand the silence a second longer. "So, Perry Mason," I said, forcing a light tone and yanking up the emergency brake. "What gives?"

Michael stared straight through the windshield. "It's not a good time. We've got enough to deal with."

His cold response shocked me. I'd hoped my question would break the ice but it deepened it instead. Now, I was really scared.

"Okay," I said, with just as much ice. "What're my official responsibilities?"

The green eyes met mine, professional, too professional. "As co-executors, we're responsible for probating the will."

"Right. What's that mean?"

"For most deaths, it's usually fairly simple; handle the funeral, find the will—if there is one—and make sure all the beneficiaries are contacted. safeguard any valuables, such as jewels or fine art, advise all creditors—I'll do that, prepare an inventory of all assets and liabilities-we can do that together—and prepare a financial statement. Then we apply for probate. A lot of steps to close the file."

"Okay. Then what?"

"Once probate's approved, we make sure all requests and bequeaths are honoured and tidy up all personal and financial affairs. Usually takes a few weeks, maybe months. Probating Pitts's will might be a little more complicated due to his investments." He tapped his silver, hard-shelled briefcase. "I've got most of his papers here, and the last will from the office. There might be others at his condo, I don't know."

I shook my head. "Uh-uh, I went through his desk this morning, found bank books, receipts, stuff like that, not much else."

"Well, we'll have to meet and go through it."

"Before I forget...there's a meeting of the Board of Directors tonight, eight o'clock at the Clubhouse. Wanna ride?"

He fumbled with his briefcase. "Thanks but I've a few things to do. I'll meet you there." He neatly changed the subject. "You didn't find a new will?"

"Nope." I looked out to the sea. "I knew what he wanted for the funeral, so I've already made the arrangements." Surprised, Michael looked at me. "Pitts told me when he asked me to be an executrix." Michael nodded. I closed my eyes and leaned back, letting the sun console my face. "No church funeral-he didn't believe in attending something when dead that he wouldn't have when alive-closed coffin, big wake, lots of flowers..." I stopped and clenched my eyes. "Lots of booze."

Michael opened the car door. "Sounds like Pitts Wyndamere, all right."

Fourteen

I stood on the club's front steps. Most of the Board of Directors were already inside, sipping coffee and sizing one another up. Though not a member myself, Pitts always invited me. "Your name may not be on any shares, my dear pro," he once said, "but it's on every blade of grass of this course and on the lips of every member. You're always welcome." With his support, I generally felt comfortable. It seems strange now, to watch the others interact without him. So many things were different.

A cab pulled up. I glanced inside. Thomas Kent and Kim Karatsu were in the back seat, their discussion so intense, they didn't see me. As usual, Thomas was very animated, nodding and gesticulating. Finally, the two shook hands and Thomas clambered out.

Karatsu saw me first. He smiled slightly and bowed from the neck. I nodded. Thomas looked up as he started to trot up the stairs, met my eyes and stopped cold.

"Oh. Hi, Riley," he said obviously embarrassed. I returned the greeting. "Juet here?" he asked, trying hard to be casual. Karatsu's cab drove away. The effort of not turning to watch showed on Thomas' young face.

"She's inside. You're the last. Come on, we'd better go in."

He took the steps in two strides and held the door open for me. The others were milling about the small conference room. I smiled briefly at Juet and moved against a wall to watch. Fishbowling's a great way to dissect people.

Thomas looked around, met Joel's eyes and nodded. Then he immediately strode over to his wife who was chatting quietly with Ken Lasher. The only member of the Board of Directors who didn't hold any shares, Ken had changed out of his dark suit into casual clothes and looked more like a dentist than a mortician. He'd known my brother-in-law a long time and I know Pitts had valued his objectivity.

Juet glanced up at Thomas but when he bent to kiss her, she turned. Thomas's lips brushed her cheek. He flushed but shook the hand offered by Ken.

Vivian, Michael and Joel hovered near the coffee pot. Vivian was talking. I didn't like the way Michael seemed to be lapping it up. I wandered over.

"...gotta go ahead," Vivian was saying, her voice rising. "I've worked..." She stopped and had the decency to flush slightly. "...well, everyone's worked too hard. There's too much at stake."

"You know it!" Joel said. "Reputation of the club's too valuable to play with. We've gotta think how potential investors will feel."

"Investors?" I asked. "I didn't know Sea Blush was for sale."

"It isn't," Joel replied quickly. "Just examining all the options." He quickly changed the subject. "Mike tells us you're in charge tonight?"

Mike? I looked at Michael. No one calls him by that name. His green eyes widened. I shrugged. "I thought Ken should do it, but he declined. He thought it should be an executor."

"That's pretty standard," Michael said. "Seemed to me that Riley was a better choice, seeing how she knows everybody."

"Well, I guess I'd better rattle the ol' gavel." I walked over to one end of the oval table and rapped my knuckles on its glossy surface.

One by one, they took a place around the table. On my right were Juet, Thomas and Ken;

around the other side sat Joel, Vivian, and Michael. I was disappointed that Michael didn't sit by my side and shot him a look to prove it.

"Okay. We all know why we're here, but Michael and I thought we should just review the decisions that need to be made tonight." Several people nodded.

"Sounds good to me," Joel said.

"You all realize that these decisions are interim ones only?" Michael asked.

Thomas looked a little surprised. Joel's blue eyes narrowed. "Why?" Juet asked.

"Well, things might change after the reading of the will and probate. Ownership in Pitts's affairs has yet to be determined. We're not sure of all the ramifications. I just wanted it clear that the decisions you make tonight aren't final."

"The hell they're not!" Joel snapped. "We're the Board of Directors; we make the decisions. We can't have them second-guessed a few days from now. If we decide the Classic goes on as planned, then it goes on. You can't change that kind of decision next week."

"I fully understand that, Joel," Michael said smoothly. "Of course decisions like that can be made as final. However, other decisions may change."

"Such as?" Thomas asked.

Michael shrugged. "Could be a number of 'em. Let's see..." he took a sip of coffee. "...for example, nominating the new director. That'll have to be done on an interim basis, pending probate."

"We can keep the Classic going?" Thomas asked.

"Yes." It seemed that a huge sigh fell around the table. "Probate'll take a while."

"That's fine, then," Joel said. "Let's make some decisions."

"Right," I said, grabbing control. "I've explained to Michael about the voting arrangements. He and I will vote Pitts's shares. Okay, first order of business is to appoint an interim club manager. Suggestions?"

"I nominate Juet," Thomas said, holding his wife's hand. "She's already the assistant, there wouldn't be much of a transition."

"Seconded," Joel said.

"Fine. All those in favour?"

Five hands went up. We all turned to Juet, whose hands stayed on the table.

"Don't I get a say in this?" she said.

"Course you do," I said. "Go ahead."

"I don't care about the club..." Someone gasped. "...or about the bloody Classic."

"Juet, honey," Thomas jumped in.

"Don't 'Juet, honey' me," she snapped, pulling her hand free of his. Her black eyes flashed around the table, boring into the surprised faces. "I care about my father." Her voice trembled. "About his memory. He just died and none of you seem to care. All you want to talk about is Sea Blush." She stood up. "Who gives a damn about Sea Blush? It's just a golf course. You..." her hand shot out in Joel's direction, "...all you ever think about is yourself. You tried to ruin my father!"

"Juet!" Thomas' voice broke in ahead of Joel's. "You're upset. You're not thinking..."

She whirled and stared down at her husband. "How dare you talk to me like that! You're in enough trouble as i..."

"D'you think we could cut the histrionics and get back to business?" Vivian shouted. Everyone paused to stare at Viv. She stood and looked across at Juet. "Look, honey, we're sorry Pitts is dead. But we're involved in something important.

Some of us've spent our lives...it's something that can't wait."

"Now, wait a min..." Thomas cut in, leaping up.

I slapped the table with my fist. The echo boomed against the walls. "Let's just start over, shall we?" I motioned to Juet, Vivian and Thomas. Reluctantly, they sat, Thomas slumping back in his chair.

"May I make a suggestion?" Ken asked.

"Please do," I said.

He stood. "Juet's right." There were angry murmurs. "But so're the rest of you. I deal with people and death every day. It's not easy. On the one hand, the family wants their loved one to somehow remain alive. It's as if talking about things that the deceased will not be involved in is tantamount to betraying their memory. On the other hand, life goes on." He turned to Juet with an understanding smile. "Decisions have to be made; the clock keeps ticking. You'll never forget your father..." Juet blew her nose. "...nor'll his friends. Arguing like this would only upset him. Don't you see?"

She nodded. Thomas gave her a quick hug.

"Perhaps being the manager won't be so bad," Ken said. "You'd be following your father's footsteps."

"That's right, honey," Thomas said. "What d'you say?"

"Okay," Juet whispered.

"That's fine," Ken said, sitting down.

"That's decided. Thank you, Juet," I said. "Now, the next question is whether we cancel the Classic?"

"I say no," Joel said. "Gone too far."

"I agree," Vivian said. "Pitts'd want it anyway."

We all looked at Juet. She smiled slightly. "I

know he would."

"Good, then," I said. "We're all agreed?" Everyone nodded. "Fine," I hesitated. "There's one thing I'd like to say."

All eyes were on me.

"Several of the staff have expressed concern over their jobs. Do I have your assurances that nothing about the ownership of Sea Blush will be done until probate's over?"

"Well, really, Riley," Michael said. "Nothing could be done." He smiled. "Legally, that is."

"We don't know who owns Pitts's shares, do we?" Ken asked.

"Surely Juet..." Thomas broke in.

"The will'll be read after the funeral," Michael said. "Halliday'll be here."

"Halliday," Thomas said softly.

"So," I asked, "you're agreed nothing'll be done 'bout the staff 'til later?"

Absently, they all nodded, thoughts of slicing the pie wetting their whistles.

The rollerblades hummed along the uneven pavement sending tiny vibrations along my feet and up my shins. My face felt dirty and sweat collected beneath the back of my helmet. I'd been skating for almost two hours and my legs felt leaden, my lungs dense. If only my mind was as exhausted.

With each ankle's push off, I kept thinking; *Everyone I've cared for is dead.* Hard stride left; *First, my mother.* Shove right; *My father.* Another left; *Pitts.* Harder right; *Mom's dead*; left again, *Dad's dead*; right, *Pitts's dead.*

A stone caught the front wheel on my left blade. Lurching forward, I grabbed air for balance. My left foot scooted ahead wildly, out of control. I spotted an embankment on the right and before my nose was rudely introduced to the pavement, I bailed out.

My wheels and head took turns touching the sky until finally I lurched to a skidding stop in a bramble thicket. So loudly was my heart pounding, I thought it would burst my chest. I lay huddled, limbs aching and bleeding.

After what seemed an eon, I slowly unlatched my helmet. Pulling its mangled white shell to my chest, I curled into a ball and burst into tears.

Halliday's not the only sensitive one in the family.

At home an hour later, curled up on my dark blue leather couch, I ripped open Pitts's present. Before I took another breath, I hoovered three peach chocolates the size of hockey pucks into my mouth. I stared at the lights of West Bay Estates. Chocolate euphoria is good-it doesn't let you think.

Fifteen

Scalpel glinting in his right hand, Dr. O'Brien prepared to make the first cut of the standard Y-incision. He glanced across at his attendant and began slicing into the flesh on Pitts's right shoulder. My head began to whirl. My heart leapt up into my throat. Someone began to make a horrible gagging noise.

It took me a second to realize the gagger was me. O'Brien stopped and turned my way. His head and mouth were covered in a mask, only his eyes were visible. In the harsh light, they were pale, full moons. Sitting on a stool located near the low cabinets lining one one side of the room, Walt Dickson dropped his notebook. A thump reverberated off the stainless steel counter.

I turned, burst through the double doors and bolted down the corridor. Heart pounding, I stopped and leaned against the hard concrete wall. Its coolness felt good against my wet back. Suddenly, Walt was beside me, urging me to breathe. Gasping, I slid down the wall.

"It's okay, Riley. It's okay," Walt's deep voice whispered. A huge hand gently patted my hair. "Just keep breathing, everything'll be fine."

The double doors whined open and O'Brien's capped head poked out. "Everything all right?"

I groaned and kept my face to the floor. It had been bad enough while O'Brien carefully undressed the body. His fingers moved so slowly, with such care, that I was lulled into a sense of comfort. Then, as I began to consciously accept that the body was Pitts's, that it was without life, that it was rotting before my eyes, I panicked.

"It's fine, doc," Walt called to him. "Don't worry.

Keep on. I'll just be a minute."

The doors creaked again and O'Brien was gone. "You okay?"

I nodded. Now that my head and heart were back to normal, my stomach lurched with shame. "Some coroner," I muttered at the floor. "Can't even make it through an autopsy."

"Hey!" Walt's voice boomed. "Come on. Don't be so hard on yourself! I've seen you watch lots of 'em." His voice dropped. "It's not the same when you know the person." He squeezed my hand. "You gonna be all right?"

Head bowed, I nodded.

"I've gotta go back. We'll talk when it's over, okay?"

I listened as his heavy shoes clicked away down the corridor. The steel doors opened and closed once again. I was alone.

The next hour I spent tramping up and down the corridor, desperately trying to force the crystal clear images of human dissection out of my mind. That failed, so I tried to dissociate myself from the body and let the images flicker freely. Every time the winking scalpel made a new incision, like the one from the pit of the stomach to the pubic bone, Pitts's face snuck in and my stomach pitched. Hoping air and humanity would assuage me, I flung a last glance down the hall and escaped into the brilliant morning sun.

Ninety minutes later, I retreated from the refreshing insanity of downtown Nanaimo and reluctantly climbed the steps of number 16, Church Street. My legs and right hip were stiff from last night's fall. A delicious reminder of life.

O'Brien was sitting behind his desk, making notes. Walt stood, thumbs locked in his belt loops, staring outside. I knocked shyly. O'Brien looked up and gave me a warm smile. "Come in, my dear," he commanded, standing up. He waved me to a chair. Walt turned and quickly strode to me, held my chair then dropped heavily into the one beside it. Only then did Dr. O'Brien return to his worn leather seat.

"I'm very sorry..."

"Nonsense!" He cut me off. "Nothing to apologize for. Perfectly natural. My mistake. Shouldn't have allowed you in the first place."

"No, it..."

"Let's just forget it, shall we?"

Relieved, I nodded.

"Now," he said, brusquely looking down at his notes. "Let me see. Right." He looked up at me. "Your brother-in-law probably just stopped breathing. There was a strong smell of alcohol—whiskey's my guess—and a whitish powder in the stomach-possibly the anti-depressants. You were correct, given the advanced rigor and stomach contents, he died about ten to twelve hours before you arrived." He looked up. "That makes it between 7:45 and 9:45, Monday evening."

"Did he die where I found him?"

"Possibly. At least, he died in that position. Lividity was in the face and front of the body. As to where..." He glanced at Walt. "We'll need a bit more information."

He tapped his pen for a couple of seconds. "It's a bit early for the test results-I've ordered both blood and urine toxicology reports for alcohol and the anti-depressants, of course-should get the alcohol results this afternoon."

I waited.

"Were you aware that he had heart disease?"

I shook my head. "I knew his blood pressure wasn't great but..."

"And his liver was scarred, some cirrhosis." He

sighed and straightened his glasses. Walt turned to look at me. "Overall, he wasn't all that healthy. I'm sorry, Riley, but it looks like your brother-in-law lived a little too high too often."

"Any conclusion?"

"It's a might early without the tests but...probably accidental."

Accidental? It wasn't a surprise. I stared at the beige carpet. All the medical and physical evidence fit, but how could Pitts have been that stupid?

"Anything wrong?" Walt asked.

I shook my head. "No. Guess not." I wanted to tell him how much it hurt, how one part of me still refused to believe. But I couldn't. Not in front of O'Brien.

"Wake's at seven?" O'Brien asked.

I nodded, pushing aside my doubts. "Lasher and Waterman's."

"Right, I'll make the, uh, transfer arrangements."

Dr. O'Brien walked us out of his office. We stood at the exit, face to face. Walt marched on ahead. Directly behind O'Brien, I could see Louise watching me closely, shaking her head. "Well, my child," O'Brien said in his slow speech, "remember, the Gods conceal from men the happiness of death, that they may endure life." Louise's eyes widened but she didn't smile.

Neither did I. "Thanks. I'll see you this evening?"

He nodded and watched me leave.

"Where're you going?" Walt asked once we were outside.

"Ferry-picking up Hal."

He nodded, shortening his stride to match mine. "Ril?"

"Yeah?"

"You, you look so worried. Sure you're okay?"

I stopped beneath an arbutus tree and looked up into his rugged face. "I'm not sure," I whispered. "It seems kinda stupid but..."

"But what?"

I leaned against the tree trunk. "Some things just don't add up. See, Pitts promised me he wouldn't drink alone. Yet we found that he'd been drinking. He told me he was meeting someone. So who was it?"

"I dunno. What's it matter? You said so yourself, he was upset, already drinking in the afternoon."

I shook my head slowly.

Walt towered over me. "I'm sure he didn't mean to...probably too upset to realize..." He stopped lamely.

I flung away tears. "Yeah," I said, turning away. "What's a stupid promise worth, anyway?"

For the third time in four days, I waited for the ferry to dock. I couldn't face the glass enclosure, so stood outside, thinking. In about five minutes, Halliday Quinn blasted through the door and kept right on coming. She held me tightly, sobbing in my ear. Angry as I was at her, I was shaken by the obvious aura of pain enveloping her plump figure and squeezed hard. After a few minutes, I gently pushed her away. "You look terrible!" I said truthfully. My older sister tugged self-consciously at her auburn hair-it looked as though she'd given up on combing-and dragged a scrunched tissue across puffy eyelids. No makeup foundation could cover the dark smudges beneath her eyes and in the newly hollowed cheeks.

"Well, thanks a lot," she replied, mustering some indignation. "You don't look any hell yourself."

I started to complain but was stopped cold by

the tears filling her yellow-green eyes. "Oh, Riley," she whispered. "I can't believe he's really dead."

"I know," I replied softly, as we walked to the car under a pale blue sky.

"Don't tell me. This tiny thing's yours?"

I nodded. She smiled thinly.

"Of course, you wouldn't like it. It's not a Porshe."

Halliday ran her hand along the car's short butt. "I don't know, it's kinda cute." She tried to smile at me. "It suits you." Her face darkened. "Riley?"

"Uh-huh."

"Did he suffer?"

"I don't think so."

"How, how'd it happen?"

An image of Pitts's body sprawled face down in the grass flashed into my mind. "It looks like he fell." I shoved her golf bag in the trunk and stuffed the other bags behind the seats.

"Fell?" she asked, hand on the door handle. "From where?" I jumped over my door and pushed my feet to the floor. "His balcony," I said, starting the engine.

Her hand dropped from the handle. She looked down at me with oh-so-wise eyes. "He'd been drinking, hadn't he." It was a statement.

"Yeah," I replied, revving the motor. "Get in."

We drove along the highway without a word but at the first stop light outside of the city's outskirts, Halliday said in a voice deader than Pitts, "He was an alcoholic, too."

"No, he wasn't!" I snapped, glaring at her. "I'm warning you. Don't start with that alcoholism crap!"

The light changed and I jammed down the gas pedal. Emily shot forward with a squeal.

"Well," Halliday shouted, hanging on to the dash, "if he wasn't, he was damn close."

I hit the brakes, slamming us both back in our seats. I yanked the wheel and the little convertible skipped off the highway and slid along the shoulder, spitting gravel. "What is it with you?" I yelled, banging the steering wheel as we ground to a stop. "Why's it always alcohol?"

"For heaven's sake, Riley!" she said, wide-eyed. "What're you trying to do, kill us?"

"Of course not!" I screamed, even angrier, now that I realized what a dangerous thing I had done. "What're you whining about? At least we didn't get hit."

Her whole body snapped back, as though whiplashed. I closed my eyes to avoid looking at the pain in her eyes. I took a deep breath and listened to the cars whizzing by.

My eyes opened. Halliday had her head in her hands. "I'm sorry. Forget I said that, okay?"

She didn't move. I edged the car further over on the shoulder. "It's just that the last time I saw you, we argued about alcoholism and now, fifteen minutes after you arrive, we're doing it again!"

Halliday fumbled in her purse, pulled out a tissue and blew her nose. Then she slowly looked at me and, in her older-sister-knows-better voice, said, "I told you at Daddy's funeral, this's something you've got to accept." Her eyes bored into mine. "Obviously, you haven't."

I looked away and watched an eagle soaring. "I'm not going to discuss Dad. We were talking 'bout Pitts."

She shook her head with a wry smile, "Dad, Pitts. Doesn't matter. Don't you see? It always ends the same. They drink: they die."

Finally, a statement I couldn't dispute. I did a

shoulder check and carefully rolled us back on to the highway.

Welcome home, Big Sister.

"Is everything, you know, organized?" Halliday asked tentatively.

We'd dropped her stuff off at my place and were sitting in a small cafe in Parksville, still hours before the wake.

I stopped chewing my burger and nodded. When I'd swallowed, I continued, "He told me what he wanted and I completed the arrangements early this morning."

"You're sure I did the right thing, not calling SinJin?" she asked.

"Yeah. Anyway, he's so disorganized, he probably wouldn't have made it here until after the funeral."

Halliday half smiled and sipped her coffee. Then she shivered. "Let's talk about something else..." her eyes fell on my left wrist. I pulled it below the table. Her face dropped. "...anything," she finished lamely.

"Okay," I replied. I couldn't bear to ask her about the win at Phar-Mor, but golf was all we had in common these days. Gossip's always hot and cheap so I jumped on it. "Tell me, is Kath still seeing that idiot Ron or has she come to her senses?"

Halliday actually grinned. "Still fighting like cats and dogs on the course and boinking like rabbits off." She shook her head and jammed a French fry in her mouth. Still chewing, she continued, "'Course, I haven't actually seen the boinking."

"Amazing! The guy's a jerk and a crummy caddie to boot. Man, I used him once, he misclubbed me all day, blew sprinklers like there's no tomorrow. Despite all that, I was playing well and there he was standing behind, slamming things..."

"I know what you mean!" Hal leapt in, eyes shining. "You're in between clubs all day, pulling your hair out and the guy can't read a marked sprinkler!"

We started to laugh. Then, between bites, we launched into a quick succession of stories upon horror stories, trying to one-up each other. It felt good, laughing with Hal. I couldn't remember the last time.

Her face became serious. "Gotta tell you, I'm getting a little worried out there."

I took a sip of Diet Coke. "Worried?"

She pushed her plate away, most of her fries still kicking. Very unusual. "There's a whole new crop of young ones, skipped right by college, and they're burning up the course. Melinda's what: 19?, 20?, Michelle's maybe 22?" She slammed down a powerful wrist. "Why even Meg's considered old now and she's barely 30!"

"What's that got to do with you?"

She raked her fingers through her mane. "It's been a bad year..." She stopped, seeing my reaction. "Uh-huh, Phar-Mor was a fluke. I hadn't had a top ten finish all year." She paused. "It's getting old. I'm tired of travelling and people I know are passing me by." She yanked at her hair. "Pressure's greater than ever before, every bloody tournament they hound me about the Hall."

She lifted her voice an octave and spoke in a sing song. "How's it feel, Halliday, to be so close to the Hall of Fame? Is this the big tournament? And when I don't win," she gripped a hand around her neck. "I'm a choker!"

I carefully squirted ketchup on a fry, too envious to say anything.

"By the gods! I feel like shoving the damn microphone down their throats. What'm I, psychic?"

Sixteen

People are so awkward at a funeral home. They try to avoid facing the casket but can't help be drawn to it, as though magnetized. I've personally survived those small, windowless rooms and the hours of whispered thanks to friends and relatives-some of whom you haven't seen since the last visit of Halley's comet-on two other occasions in my life. That makes Pitts's wake the lucky third.

It doesn't get any easier. In fact, as you get older, it gets worse. When I was thirteen, I stood ramrod-straight, dry-eyed-as far away from the shiny brown box as possible-and watched the grownups cry. The first night of visiting hours, Halliday took one pie-eyed glance at the coffin and fled the room screaming. My older sister knew what took me months to comprehend, that my mother was permanently gone, never ever to kiss me goodnight nor come to another golf practice.

So, here we were, the Quinn sisters. Death had united us once again.

By a quarter to eight, the room was overflowing with mourners dressed in dark colours and their conversations, in turn, quickly overflowed with the free booze. I was surprised at how many of the same businessmen who had grieved for my father, grieved, too, for Pitts. I guess it doesn't matter in a small town if you're a forester or a developer, the circle is small.

According to Pitts's wishes, I'd arranged to have yellow daisies poking from vases everywhere and big band music playing on the overhead speakers. He had wanted the place to rock, but Ken Lasher had nixed that idea in deference to two other, normal, sombre wakes going on. Ken only allowed the alcohol because he was a Board member and a good friend of Pitts's. There were huge floral arrangements-one all of yellow daisies. I glanced at the card, curious to know who knew Pitts so well. The card was signed simply, *Never forget, L.T.R.*.

Juet stood next to the coffin. Thomas was at her side, rocking on his heels. In one hand, Juet held an empty glass, in the other the framed picture of Pitts that had been on the coffin. The poor kid's face was ashen. Thomas looked uncomfortable, a trapped humming-bird. He gave me a tight smile and swirled his drink frantically. They seemed worlds apart but I was glad they at least were together.

We hadn't had much chance to talk so I wandered over. The three of us shuffled uncomfortably, watching the other mourners. Finally, I asked if either of them had seen Pitts on Monday night.

Juet just burst into tears, almost dropping the glass. Thomas grabbed it and gently handed her his handkerchief. She flashed him a look of gratitude.

"Why'd you want to know?" he asked, eyes on Juet.

"Just curious. Did you?"

"No reason to," he said. "If you'll excuse me, I need a drink. Honey?" Juet shook her bowed head. He raised his eyebrows at me.

"No, thanks."

"I'll be right back," Thomas said, squeezing Juet's hand.

I watched as Thomas whispered to Halliday. She shook her head and he continued to the table. Karatsu pushed his way across the room to join him.

"You okay?" I asked Juet.

Her face pinched but she remained silent.

"Anything I can do?"

She shook her head. I glanced down. The

knuckles on her right hand were white. I thought the glass would shatter so I reached down and gently pried it free. Still, she refused to speak.

I turned and eyed Hal. My sister was surprisingly calm, wearing what I call her final round face. When Halliday Quinn's in contention during the last day of a tournament, she's still emotional, still entertaining, but if you look carefully, you'll sense an underlying coolness, a mantle of overwhelming control. It's one of the main reasons for her success. After years of playing golf with crowds breathing over my shoulder, I too, had ways to tighten my own screws. And now I had the additional protection of my coroner's smile.

I had shaken what felt like the thousandth hand when I spotted Walt's blond head slicing above the crowd. Murmuring apologies, I wormed my way toward him. Following in his wake was O'Brien. Walt and I hugged; O'Brien took my hand. I said, "I'm so glad it's you two. If one more person asks me if it's true, I'll scream."

"Is what true?" O'Brien asked.

I answered automatically, "Yes, I am a coroner: yes, it was an accident: yes, the poor man had been drinking and, yes, what a tragedy."

They both gawked.

"It's okay," I said, trying to keep the tremor from my voice. "It's just been a long day." I changed the subject. "Any results?"

O'Brien nodded, silver hair gleaming in the artificial light. "Maybe you'd rather talk later..."

"No! No, now's as good a time as any."

He peered at me through the thick glasses. "Right. He'd had a lot to drink all right-300 mils."

300 milligrams percent per litre of blood equaled four times the legal limit allowed for driving. Many many glasses of the demon drink. I shook my head.

Damn him! What a stupid way to die.

"Awfully sorry, my dear, though it's not unexpected?"

"No," I replied bluntly.

"How's your sister taking it?"

"Seems okay. Wait a sec, I want you to meet her."

Halliday was leaning against the wall directly opposite the flower-covered casket, whispering intensely to Michael. Feeling my gaze, he looked up and gave me an embarrassed smile. My stomach fluttered. The scent of flowers was overwhelming. I motioned to Halliday. She glanced up at Michael and walked over.

"Hal, you remember, Walt?" I asked.

"'Course, she does," Walt replied, enveloping Halliday in a bear hug. "Good to see you again," he said, his voice booming. The murmurs around us stopped. Walt flushed to the roots but Halliday held his hand and smiled. Whispers began anew and Walt blushed a shade deeper. Hal looked extremely elegant and comfortable in a black dress, loosely tied at the waist. I, on the other hand, felt out of place in my silk slacks and shirt. I shoved my hands in my pockets.

They chatted about old times for a minute then I interrupted, introducing her to O'Brien.

He shook her hand, peering down with gentle eyes. "I'm terribly sorry, Mrs. Wyndamere," he said, softly.

Halliday thanked him perfunctorily, her eyes suddenly glued to the entrance. I looked. Face shining from sweat, Joel Sanderson slowly edged his way to us. O'Brien and Walt drifted away to the refreshment table. Without a word, Hal made a beeline to Joel.

I stood for a moment, watching, when I felt

pressure on my elbow. "Oh, oh," Michael's voice, a wee bit slurred, was in my ear. "Trouble."

"What?" I glanced at Michael. "What do you mean? Joel and Pitts were partners."

He looked at me in astonishment. "You don't know?"

"Know what?" I asked, as snippets of Halliday's voice, oddly sharp, began darting in our direction.

Michael pulled me around to face him. I could smell alcohol and backed off. "They were partners in name only, since the affair."

I shook my head.

"Oh!" Michael said. "Of course. You were on Tour when it happened."

"When what..."

I was interrupted by Halliday. She was whispering loudly, angrily jabbing at Joel's suit jacket. His handsome face darkened and he glanced around the room. Yes, Joel, I thought, you definitely have an audience.

Halliday's voice ripped free of whispering. "No! I'll never forgive you. Get out, damn you!" The room was suddenly silent. "Get out! You're nothing but a fraud. You drove Pitts to this!"

Joel's face was distorted with rage. He looked wildly about; all faces stared at him. "I came here for you, but you'd better watch what you say," he snapped. "Your drunk of a husband betrayed me!"

Someone gasped. Joel suddenly looked like a deer frozen in headlights. He bolted, shoving through a small group blocking the door. Halliday looked around, her eyes too bright. She burst out sobbing.

For a second, no one moved. Then Michael and Walt hot-footed it to her side. Gratefully, she sniffed into Walt's handkerchief and leaned against his massive shoulder. I watched as though pinned to the floor. Someone arrived with a glass of water.

Halliday drank, coughed and attempted to smile.

The noise level increased dramatically, as did the traffic to the booze. A couple of minutes, three handkerchiefs and new-drinks-all-around later, Halliday finally calmed down. Ever the proper hostess, I turned and braced for some more hand shaking.

Sometimes people leave you alone on these occasions. For a few minutes, I stood quietly, listening to the ever louder snatches of conversation.

"Poor old bugger!" This from an old guy I didn't know, who was gently touching the casket.

"Been drinking, what I heard." I twisted my head to look at the speaker. It was Doug Carlisle. He saw me and almost choked on his beer.

"Yes, Mr. Carlisle. That's true."

I thought his wife was going to faint. Carlisle's Adam's apple and jaw moved in tandem. "I'm sorry," he said, stiffly. "Please forgive me."

"It's all right, " I said smoothly. "Have another drink. Pitts would want you to."

Ten minutes later, Vivian and Dai arrived together. Vivian was dressed in a plain, dark blue dress, her blond hair pulled into a severe bun. She'd obviously tried to tone down and I was grateful. Male eyes still followed but only briefly.

Dai hesitated, looking embarrassed so I saved him the trouble.

"Yes, it was an accident and Pitts had been drinking."

His eyes widened. "Pardon? I...you thought... No! How can you think..." He stopped, still staring. "I, I've never been to a real wake before," he finally whispered, gesturing to the open bottles.

"Is that all?" I said. Now, I felt foolish. "Sorry. Been asked a lot. For some reason everyone remembers that I work for the coroner's office." I glanced around. The liquor was flowing freely, the noise level ascending and the social niceties were disappearing. "It looks kinda brutal, but it's what Pitts wanted."

They both vehemently refused a drink so we chatted inanely a little longer while Dai tried not to look at the coffin. The assistant course superintendent came over, gave me his condolences then pulled his boss aside, leaving me with Vivian.

"So, it was an accident," she said, eyeing me closely. "What a waste." She stopped. "Oh! I'm so sorry, I..."

"It's all right."

We stood and watched the coffin for a few moments.

"I'm going to miss him."

I looked at her. Her gold eyes gazed back sincerely.

"I never knew you liked him."

Vivian looked at me strangely. "He may have been my boss, but we got along. I admired his guts, his dream of the Classic." She stopped and again looked at the coffin. "He gave me my chance."

I looked at her.

She nodded, bronze eyes glowing. "I was in Japan, doing event work. My parents are originally from the U.S. Getting to work in the States is all I've ever wanted." She smiled and said softly, "You know, the big time."

I smiled.

"Over there, never thought I'd get the chance. But Pitts...he," she hesitated, "liked me. I don't know, saw my potential?" Vivian laughed suddenly. "Anyway, when he offered me the job as Tournament Director, I couldn't pack fast enough." She glanced at the coffin. "I want this tournament as bad as he did."

"So do I. Viv?"

"Yes?"

"Did you see Pitts the night he died?"

She looked surprised. "No! Why do you ask?"

"No real reason. It's just that he said he was seeing someone. I thought it might have been you. You know, tournament stuff."

"Not me," she said, looking me squarely in the eyes. "I was with someone."

"Oh?"

She just stared.

I got the hint. "Of course, it's none of my business."

She reached over and patted my arm. "Are you going to be okay? Still have doubts about, you know, the accident?"

"Yeah. Guess I always will. No reason for it." I shoved my hands in my pockets. "It's just hard to believe, that's all."

"And Hal?"

I looked around to find her. Karatsu had her cornered, his pale face moving animatedly. I groaned, unable to believe he'd choose this place, this time, to ask her to use his clubs.

"You all right?"

"Huh?" I jerked back to find Vivian peering up at me. "Oh, yeah. Sorry."

"Well, I just wanted to say...I mean, I know we've never been close but..." she fumbled in her bag. "I want you to have this." I took the business card. "It's my private number. I don't usually give it out but, I thought, well, in case you ever, you know, need to talk."

I looked at her in surprise. She smiled. "Thanks. That's very thoughtful," I said, stuffing the card in my pocket.

I glanced back at Halliday and saw her shake her head and point in my direction. The fat little man bounced his chest against several people until he finally reached me. Vivian gave him a curt nod and left.

Karatsu bowed ever so slightly then pulled out a white handkerchief and wiped his forehead. His black hair and eyes gleamed. "I apologize for disturbing you," he started politely. "But I am looking for something of value."

I raised my eyebrows at him.

"I asked Mrs. Wyndamere but she said you were handling the..." he paused and blew his nose. "The estate."

"I'm a co-executor, yes."

"Co?" he replied, obviously surprised. "May I ask who...?"

I nodded toward Michael. "The guy over there, with the red hair. He's Michael Harrigan, Pitts's lawyer."

"I see."

I didn't. "You said you were looking for something?"

"Yes," Karatsu lowered his voice. I could hardly hear his reply. "I'm looking for some personal items Mr. Wyndamere borrowed."

"No problem. Tell me what they are and I'll take a look."

He started shuffling toward the door. "Photographs."

"Photographs?" I walked along with him. "Anything special?"

"No," he hesitated. "Just some family pictures." We stopped at the room's edge.

"Oh, okay. How would I know 'em?

"They were in an envelope." He paused and straightened his tie. "I appreciate your assistance.

They're of great sentimental value."

"I was at Pitts's condo yesterday, I didn't see any photos. I'll look again, but I can't guarantee I'll get to it before the funeral."

"No?" His eyes narrowed briefly. "Not before Thursday, then? I understand. Thank you."

"Tell me," I asked. "Did you see Pitts on Monday night?"

"Monday?" His pale brow wrinkled. "The night he...no!"

My concentration was interrupted by the funeral director standing in the hall. Ken glanced at his wrist. Karatsu bowed quickly and was gone. I looked around. The room was empty except for Thomas, Juet and Halliday, who hovered silently in a small circle.

And, of course, the coffin.

"I don't wanna discuss it!" Hal shouted. "Just leave me alone!" She stormed off to her room.

I looked out the back window. The bald eagle was atop his tree. We both stared at Nanoose Bay-the eagle patiently waiting for a sign of prey, me waiting for God-knows-what.

Ten minutes later, the eagle's white head flashed. For a couple of seconds, a huge silhouetted wing-span flapped across the horizon. Then, the mature bird dove out of sight.

I padded to the kitchen to hit the lights and noticed there were messages on my answering machine. I punched the play button and slumped onto a stool.

The first two messages were for lessons. I poured water into the tea kettle, barely hearing them. I'd call them later. I pushed the plug into the socket. The next voice shocked me so much that my hand reared back as though electrocuted.

"Riley," Pitts said quietly, "look, I'm sorry about this afternoon. Didn't mean anything. It's just that Halliday's arrival's got me spooked." He paused and took a deep breath. "I know I drank too much, but I haven't had any since you left. I'm keeping my promise, my dear pro. Let me prove it to you tomorrow at breakfast, okay? You'll see, no hangover. Call me. Okay?"

His voice stopped. The machine clicked; the metallic voice said that the call had been received at 6:21 p.m., Monday, July 20.

I stood there, plug in my hand, and started to shake. As violent emotions, anguish and anger have a lot more in common than just the first three letters. I wanted to tell Pitts I was sorry. That it wasn't all his fault about the break-up with Halliday. That I trusted him. That I loved him. At the same time, I was so damned angry at Pitts for dying that I almost hated him. I played his message again.

When the emotional battle waned, I stopped weeping. Pushing away the kettle, I went into the living room. Sitting on the couch, gazing at the tree tops and gentle blue waves, one thought kept running through my mind. If Pitts didn't drink alone, who had he been with?

Seveteen

I wriggled the key I'd found earlier in Pitts's desk into the first hole, turned it and stepped back. The young, dark-haired bank manager gave me a thin smile and followed suit with his master key.

"Poor Mr. Wyndamere," Mr. Samuel said in a high voice, "he was just here on Monday..." He tugged the long, plastic box free and handed it to me. "Yes, I'm certain it was Monday. You see," the manager told Michael with pride, "I always dealt with Mr. Wyndamere personally. He liked that."

Michael shot me a quick grin as Samuel led us out of the tiny room, carefully closing the barred door behind us. "Well, actually he insisted on it," he continued, narrowing his dark eyes at me. "Very fussy, he was, about his business affairs."

"Yes," Michael said. "Pitts did things his way."

Samuel nodded and opened the door to a small office. I walked in and sat beside a small table. "You'll have some privacy here. I'll be back in a few moments with the final bank statements."

He hovered for a moment while Michael joined me, then solemnly closed the door.

I shook my head.

"Isn't this your bank?" Michael asked, setting himself in a hard chair across from me.

"Uh-huh, but," I said with a grin, "I insist on dealing with the instant teller."

"Don't blame you," Michael said, pulling up the long flap which covered the safety deposit box.

The narrow, thin cavity was stuffed with papers and envelopes. Michael drew them out, one by one, and read them aloud. I noted their contents on a sheet of paper and started to put them in bundles. By the time Mr. Samuel knocked, I had made heaps of paper-bonds, stocks and shares, Guaranteed Investment Certificates, Limited Partnership Certificates, a note from his stock broker in Vancouver listing investments in a self-directed Registered Retirement Savings Plan and five deeds to property-three on the Island, one in Florida and one in Japan. My brain tired of counting assets after the first million.

There was one odd piece of paper. On it, Pitts had written, *V.G.-$-Japan?* It made no sense to either of us. I shoved it into the growing don't-know-what-to-do-with-it pile.

"Come in!" Michael sang, digging Pitts's passport out of the box.

Samuel entered and handed Michael two crisp bank books. "Oh, by the way, did you find the envelope?"

"Envelope?" Michael asked glancing in one of the bank books. He raised a brow and handed it to me.

"Yes, Mr. Wyndamere took something from the safety deposit box on Monday. I gave him a bank envelope to carry it home."

"Right," I said. "Must have been the letters I asked for." Michael looked at me. I shook my head. I didn't want to discuss BioAction in front of the manager. "I didn't see any envelope but I'll look again, thanks," I replied checking the passbook. SAVINGS was stamped on the front and inside were pages of entries, mostly deposits. The total was underlined at the bottom of the third page: $59,112.49.

Mr. Samuel nodded rapidly. "Mr. Wyndamere was very shrewd. He never kept much more than the sixty-thousand insurable limit."

Michael said, "Typical," and handed me the other. It was stamped *Chequing* and had two pages of entries with a final total of $5,321.89.

Michael unrolled the last two papers and I jotted down the names and numbers of the insurance companies and policies. The three of us looked at the uneven piles.

"So," I said, "this's the measure of a man's life." I felt tears burning the edges of my eyes. "Doesn't seem to amount to much, does it?"

Michael reached across to touch my hand, then hesitated. Mr. Samuel coughed, then squeaked, "If it's any consolation, Ms. Quinn, Mr. Wyndamere was a very rich man. His family—your sister and his daughter—will be well provided for."

"We don't want his money," I said quietly. "We want him." There was an awkward silence.

"Yes. Thank you, Mr. Samuel," Michael said, standing. He extended a hand. "You've been most helpful."

Samuel shook the hand then turned to me. "Oh. One other thing. Mr. Wyndamere was looking into his daughter's trust fund."

"Yes?"

"Since her husband is trustee, I thought it a bit odd. He said something about a birthday."

"Makes sense," I said. "She's twenty-five next month."

"Must have been the reason. Once again, I am very sorry for your loss. If there is anything that I or the bank can do, please, just give me a call."

The funeral was like all funerals; sad; sadder; sadder still. Little brown box in a hole. Showers of tears. Good bye, Pitts.

Enough said.

The five of us were standing on the balcony of Pitts's condo when Walter Dickson finally arrived.

The view remained the same, thank God, some things never change. Still clad in our funeral black with cemetery mud clinging to our shoes, we shuffled about impatiently under a darkening sky.

Walt bounded up the stairs and tipped his hat to Halliday and Juet. Thomas and Michael spoke to him but he stomped directly over to me. "When'd it happen?"

"Maid was in early this morning. My guess is during the funeral."

He nodded. "Typical. Damn those bastards!" He flushed quickly then glanced at Halliday. "Sorry, ladies." He turned back to me. "I should'a told you not to put the time in the paper."

"Yeah, not such a good idea. Also, Walt..." I hesitated.

"Yeah?"

"We've, well, we've been inside."

"What!" his voice boomed. "Riley, you know..."

"It's not her fault," Halliday snapped. "Those two idiots did it."

Walt stomped across. "You guys," he said curtly. "You're both lawyers, right?" They nodded. "Thought so." Thomas and Michael stared back, trying not to be threatened by the bulky figure glaring at them.

"Well," Walt said finally, adjusting his belt, "can't be helped now. Okay, Riley, let's take a look. You," he pointed to the other four, "stay here and don't touch anything!"

The place looked untouched. If not for the broken glass, you wouldn't have realized that anyone had been inside. Nevertheless, something twigged at me, but I couldn't put a finger on it.

"What's missing?" Walt asked as we headed back down the stairs.

"From first glance, I'd say just the VCR and

CD player..." I stuck my head into the kitchen. Though unplugged, the microwave was still there.

"Probably got scared and left." Walt said.

I nodded. "I'll have a better idea later." The green light on the answering machine winked at me. I reached for the playback button but Walt touched my hand. "It'll have to wait 'til we're finished."

We went out onto the balcony. Thomas was pacing back and forth. "Any idea who did it?" he asked impatiently.

"Nah, pretty hard to tell. We'll check for prints, but I doubt we'll get anything."

"Thomas!" Halliday snapped. "For God's sake, stand still a second." Thomas flushed but obeyed. "Thank you. Now, Walt, you said earlier that this was typical, what do you mean?"

Walt snugged up his tight pants and hooked his thumbs in his belt. "Well, this's a typical MO, uh, modus operandi, for some groups. The guys look through the obit columns regularly. It's a pretty safe bet that no one'll be in the house of the dead person at the time of the funeral."

"So you know that happened here?" Michael asked.

Walt turned to Michael. "No, sir but it's an educated guess. The stuff they stole's typical, electronic's are a snap to sell." He swivelled back to me. "We're going to have to check this place out. Take an hour or so." He touched his cap and headed to his car.

"Right, well..." I looked at the others. "What'll we do?"

Halliday took a deep breath and looked toward Lasqueti Island. "Why not stay out here?" She looked at Michael. "How long's it going to take?"

He shrugged. "It's not a very long will, maybe

ten minutes?"

"Why not? Pitts'd love it." I looked at Juet. Her face looked a little deflated but she nodded hesitantly. "Okay, Mr. Mason. Go for it."

Michael shot me a hard glance which softened when it ricocheted onto my sister. "It's a little irregular but," he snapped open his brief case and pulled out a long document, "if that's what you want." Halliday nodded, then turned back to the Georgia Strait.

Michael cleared his throat. Thomas stayed still and watched Juet who was intently studying Michael.

"I'll skip the preamble, it's just a formality." He murmured to himself, green eyes darting back and forth. "Yes, yes, here it is. The distribution of the estate is as follows, a donation of $15,000 to the World Wildlife Fund."

Halliday looked at me wide-eyed. "World Wildlife Fund?" She smiled slightly. "Your idea, perhaps?"

"No, but I'm glad he did."

"So am I."

"Oh, forget the bloody charities," Thomas snapped. "Get on with it.

Michael raised his eyebrows. "All right, there're other minor dispositions, but I'll go straight to the heart." He looked at Juet. "To my darling daughter Juet twenty-five percent of my estate."

"Twenty-five?" Thomas said in disbelief. "Izzat all? Who gets the rest?"

Juet blew her nose and stared down at the wooden slats. Michael glared at her husband. "If you'll allow me. To Riley, my dear pro, ten percent."

I was stunned. Ten percent! I hadn't expected a penny.

"And the bulk of my estate," Michael continued, "goes to my dearest wife, Halliday. This includes outright ownership of my shares in the Sea Blush Golf Club."

"What!" Thomas screamed, almost jumping in the air. "This's outrageous! What's he giving it to her for? They're separated, for God's sake."

"Enough!" Michael snapped. "These are Peter Wyndamere's last wishes." He took a step toward Thomas. "And you'll bloody well respect them."

I looked at Halliday. Her face was white, her eyes, though sunken, burned brightly. She shook her head slowly, whispering, "No, Pitts. No."

Thomas was shouting, "We're going to fight it, you understand? Juet's his only daughter, she deserves more. A whole lot more."

"Stopitstopitstopit!" Juet screamed. All eyes locked onto her ashen face. "For God's sake, Thomas, shut up! He's dead. Don't you see? Daddy's dead." She started to cry and then stumbled blindly down the stairs, tripping on the last step and falling straight into Walt's chest. Startled, Juet pushed free and limped towards her car.

Thomas shouted after her but Juet keep going. "You'll be hearing from us Harrigan," he growled.

Michael jabbed the will at Thomas' chest. Thomas' thin face twisted into a sneer. He whipped a glance down at Constable Dickson who was picking up pieces of equipment that Juet had dislodged and then flicked back to Michael. Raising his eyebrows at me, he spun on his heel and sprinted after his wife.

"Nice guy," Walt said, coming up the stairs.

"Just a little young," I replied.

Walt laid his fingerprint kit on the deck.

"Can you dust the answering machine first? I want to get the messages."

"Sure," he said as he headed through the glass

door.

"You're heading back this afternoon?" I asked Michael.

He nodded.

"Good, I'll go with you."

Michael's jaw tightened but he didn't say anything. "What?" Halliday exclaimed. "But Ril, the tournament..."

I looked at my sister. "Don't worry, I wouldn't miss it for the world. I'll be back Sunday afternoon. Why don't you just get some rest, play a round or two if you're up for it."

She stretched. Both Walt and Michael watched silently. "Maybe you're right, it's been a bad couple a days. I'll just hang about, watch that incredible view you've got."

"That's the attitude..."

"Riley?" Walt's voice boomed from inside. "You can get the messages now."

I left Halliday and Michael and went inside to punch the playback button on Pitts's telephone answering machine. Three people had left messages; one left his number, two others just their names. I wrote the information down on a paper Walt handed to me.

"Now, Michael," I said, stepping back onto the balcony, "we should get going."

Halliday and Michael moved apart. Michael nodded.

"Good chance to finish some of this executor stuff," I continued. "Walt?" I shouted.

His blond head and huge shoulders appeared through the broken window.

"Can you handle this—you know, lock up and stuff?" I asked. "I'm going to Vancouver."

"No sweat. See you, Sunday. Oh, and Ril?"

"Yeah?"

"Where're you gonna be, in case I need to get in touch with you?"

I looked at Michael. He avoided my eyes. "At my brother's," I said flatly. "O'Brien's got the number."

The last time Michael Harrigan and I sailed to Vancouver aboard one of the province's chunky white ferries, we were as close as a five and six iron stuffed in a golf bag. I'd had less than my share of men—I like to think it was because I was choosy, but the reality is probably a whole lot less appealing. Michael was the first in a long time to tingle my toes with a kiss. On this drizzly summer evening, we leaned on the railing, an ever so polite distance apart.

The deck was practically deserted; most passengers snuggled inside, faces pressed up against the thick glass, watching the rain ping off the glistening white railings and grey decks.

The massive ship cut through snarling waves and my stomach lurched with its increasing pitch and roll motion.

I touched Michael's arm. "Tell me what's going on."

He swivelled to face me and red hair peeked from below the Holt of his kangaroo sweatshirt. My Perry Mason answered quietly. "We've been through all this before. I don't know what to say."

I wanted to cry out. *Say you still love me* but I'm not a complete fool. "I know there's a problem," I said instead, grabbing the slick railing with both hands, "but," I waited for the wave to break, "I thought we could work it out. Just tell me what it is. I know we can fix it."

Rain drove down harder and suddenly I was looking at Michael through a waterfall. He shook his head, the Holt now plastered against him like plastic wrap. The rain drilled along the deck. The boat pitched and I grabbed at him. We clung together for an instant, the boat levelled and Michael Harrigan stared through me with glittering eyes. "It's over, Riley," he shouted above the din. "Can't you understand? I've tried to be nice, not to hurt you, but it's over."

I stared at him, my vision partially blocked by my Blue Jays cap. "I love you!" I shouted, unable to bite it back.

He shook his head, then wiped his eyes and mouthed, "It's over."

I couldn't hear the words but the message was blindingly clear through the chasm of torrents between us. Stuffing his hands in the shirt's pouch, Michael Harrigan turned and walked away.

I yanked off the ballcap and stood, face up, curls pasted on my forehead and let the poetry of William Blake wash my Perry Mason from my soul.

When the stars threw down their spears,
And water'd heaven with their tears,
Did he smile his work to see?
Did he who made the Lamb make thee?
The Tyger, William Blake

Still shivering in our wet clothes, we silently struggled into a cab, Michael in the front, me in the back. As I sat down, the old plastic-covered benchseat sighed and bits of yellow stuffing poked through. Perfect.

The driver asked us where to? Michael gave him the address of his apartment in Kitsilano, Vancouver's yuppie terraced haven. Then Michael glanced at me and I called out my brother's address in the West End.

The drive into Vancouver was long and traffic was heavy. The highway from Horseshoe Bay cuts along the coast and usually I eagerly anticipate glimpses of the jagged skyline, cross cut by bridges and clumps of forest. The lights still sparkled across the Lion's Gate Bridge and twinkling office towers streaked the black sky, but everything was muted by the rain. That suited me just fine.

In front of my brother's pink and blue building on Gilford, I thanked the driver, grabbed my bags and scrambled out, desperate for air and privacy. Michael rolled down the window a few inches. "Tomorrow, my office at 10:00," he said in a professional tone.

I nodded, thankful that the rain hid my tears. The window rolled up and the taxi sloshed off. Then I did what any self-respecting jilted lover would do in the same circumstances, I hollered after the cab, "Damn you, you sonofabitch!"

It was the great detective himself who unlocked my memory. I lay, feet up, on my brother's old corduroy couch and watched my favourite television program *Sherlock Holmes' Mysteries*. While watching Holmes enthrall his buddy Watson, I had been going through Pitts's condominium in my mind. Something hadn't been right.

"Is there any other point to which you would wish to draw my attention?" one of the characters asked.

"To the curious incident of the dog in the night-time," Holmes replied.

"The dog did nothing in the night-time."

"That was the curious incident," remarked Sherlock Holmes.

I snapped my fingers. "Elementary, my dear

Watson," I said aloud while chewing a chocolate. In my mind I could see the surface of Pitts's writing desk. It was clear.

"So," I said to the television, "where was the envelope?

Eighteen
7:43 a.m., Friday, July 24

Vancouver, British Columbia, is Canada's most marvelous major city for three reasons: location, location, location. Greater metro Van is home to over 1.6 million inhabitants and is a future retirement mecca for millions more. B.C., Canada's most western province, is one of super natural beauty, indeed, except for warm tropics, Lotus Land-as jealous easterners call it —has been bestowed with practically every natural biome known to humankind.

Within the Vancouver area, one can trot under the shadow of towering forests, crane a neck mountain peeking, edge across a pedestrian rope bridge spanning a yawning chasm, be deafened by the drumming of bird wings, poke toes into spouting breathing holes for clams, be yanked off balance by a hooked salmon or watch a cygnet snuffle up and under a parent's pearl white wing.

If it weren't for the lineups on the bridges, it'd be heaven.

A gander barreled towards me, wings up, beak out. I danced to the right. His neck streaked forward, thick beak missing my calf by a nostril. Victorious, I spun around, jogging backwards, and waggled a finger at him. Up went the wings, forward drove the neck, twist went my ankles and I shot ahead, safe from all but his spitting hiss.

Within seconds, I pounded down the underpass and sprinted up the entrance to Stanley Park. This is the only place I run; the only place to run. If you can imagine the map of Vancouver as the torso and head of a grey whale, then Stanley Park would be its right flipper. Sea Island, home of the International Airport, would be its left limb. I'm not habitually interested in slamming my shins in my endless drive for an endorphin—high, but even Riley Quinn makes an exception for this 400 hectare nature reserve. One minor complaint, I'm not keen on the aquarium zoo, never could decide if kids' laughter was worth sentencing a killer whale to life in an oversized bath tub. Thank heavens the aquarium staff are making major adjustments to their stable of captivity.

Of course, you can do what the tourists do and walk, run, bike or even rollerblade 'round the park's sea edge, but you'll miss the magic. It's hiding in the forest's core. If you're not careful, you'll quickly find yourself lost, stumbling along spongy dirt trails carpeted in pine needles and moss. You might spot one of the mounted police patrollers, but I've been there hundreds of times and never even glimpsed one. But that's just the time you'll pause and, with heaving chest, discover that you can step inside a hollow tree or bend to tie a shoe lace and look up to find a secret lily-covered beaver pond.

The park's wondrous, dappled light and rich, chewy air cleanse your senses and release your mind. For the first time since Pitts's death, I felt capable of calm, sentient thought. As the endorphins began to circulate, I prodded my memory. Yes, Pitts was a drinker, maybe—God forbid—an alcoholic, but my brother-in-law was no fool. I just couldn't imagine that he would drink himself senseless. I thought about his promise and about his phone message to me Monday night. There were only two reasons Pitts would have taken a drink, if someone drank with him or if someone upset him, maybe even by phone?

So, dodging a fir bough, I asked myself again, what really happened to Pitts Wyndamere between 5:00 p.m. and 11:00 p.m., Monday, July 20th?

I trotted on. Other minor mysteries jabbed my thoughts like the pine needles poking at my arms and neck. What was in the bank envelope? Where was it now? Where were Karatsu's photographs? I burst into a sprint, letting the questions whirl freely in my mind. With my head spinning and my heart hammering, I vowed to the park's pantheistic gods to answer those questions and, most importantly, to prove that Peter Wyndamere did not go into that good night alone.

I heard a whinny and slowed to a walk. Through the spiky trees to my left, I glimpsed a black horse. Its rider, a Vancouver officer, glanced my way and tipped her hat. I grinned and watched the gleaming horse pick its way slowly along the overgrown path. What'd I tell you? Stanley Park's magic is always there.

"As far as I can tell," Michael said, in reply to my question, "nothing's missing from Pitts's business affairs. I haven't a clue what else could be in that envelope. Can't be very important or someone'd know."

I nodded. A few months ago, I would have told him the questions nagging me about Pitts's death. We would have mulled them over, solved them together. Not now. Not ever. Instead, I asked him about Joel.

"It was a simple case of two guys, neither good nor bad, facing prosecution for contravening a basic legal requirement of full disclosure." Michael raised both hands as an illustration. "Joel," right hand extended, "fought the conviction in court and lost. Fined $37,000. Pitts," left hand extended, "admitted guilt immediately and was fined $27,000."

"I don't get it. Full disclosure of what?" I asked,

leaning forward in the deep leather chair.

Michael sighed. "It's really kind of complicated."

"So, make it easy. I want to know." I steeled myself and locked onto his eyes. "As co-executor, I've a right."

It was twenty after ten, we were in his office overlooking West Georgia. Neither of us had spoken about last night, I doubt we ever would again. Our relationship was now strictly business. I was damned if Michael Harrigan was going to discover just how I hard I had to work to keep my emotions in check.

"Of course," he replied briskly, playing his business role with ease. "Coffee?" He buzzed his phone.

"Tea, please, with cream." I replied.

"Of course," he said, colouring faintly.

A woman's voice asked, "Yes, Mr. Harrigan?"

"A coffee and a tea with cream, please, Deb." He leaned back and put his feet on the edge of his desk. "All right, a brief history of their partnership. About ten years ago, they pooled their resources and got a line of credit. Both were keen on real estate and thought they could make themselves and others some money by setting up Limited Partnerships." He raised a copper eyebrow. I shook my head.

"Limited Partnerships are a common vehicle that allow a group of investors to buy into a large investment, say a building or even a horse. They buy units or pieces of the investment, giving them a chance to be involved in something that would normally be completely out of their range. The partnership is put together by someone, often a company. That group's called The General Partners. They run the show. In our scenario, Joel and Pitts were the general partners."

"Got you so far."

He stroked his nose. I looked at the soles of his glowing black shoes. "You have to be licensed by the Securities Commission to sell limited partnerships. So, Joel got a licence. They bought a small, commercial building in Vancouver and set up their first partnership valued at about two hundred thousand dollars. Sold it out in eight weeks. Next one was worth double and so on. Soon they had several offices and over forty salespeople. I think in the end they were involved in about twenty or so partnerships."

His feet dropped to the floor. "Then, in 1990, Joel had an argument with one of his sales staff." The green eyes narrowed. "You may know him, Doug Carlisle?"

I snorted. There was a knock on the door.

"Come in!" Michael called.

A young, dark-haired woman walked in, carefully carrying two matching cups and saucers. She smiled and handed one set to me.

"Ah, thank you!" Michael said, standing and taking the other.

Deborah left quietly.

"Well," Michael said, cautious sipping, "it seems that Carlisle tried to cheat on some expenses, something like that." His lean body dropped back into the chair. "Joel found out, fired him on the spot. Carlisle went straight to the Securities Commission."

I blew on the steam rising from the cup. "What for?"

"He told 'em that Joel and Pitts hadn't fully disclosed the details of the fee structure for the last partnership."

"Fee structure?"

"Here, let me show you." Michael stood up and went to a tall, maroon filing cabinet. I watched his back arch under the grey pin striped suit as he shuffled through papers in the top drawer. He pulled out a thick book, about writing paper size. He handed it to me and returned to his chair. "A Limited Partnership can only be sold with one of those, it's called a prospectus. "

I put my cup and saucer on his desk and looked at the heavy white bonded cover. At the top, it read, *Prospectus, February, 1992.* The title was followed by an inch deep paragraph of tiny fonted gobbledygook. Below, in thick black lettering, read, *$2,650,000 (maximum offering), 212 Limited Partnership Units in Turner Estates (Canadian 92-2), Limited Partnership.* Under that followed two chock-a-block paragraphs, then in big black print, *Price: $12,500 per Unit.* The rest of the page was covered in paragraphs that required my birding binoculars to read.

"The prospectus outlines all kinds of information, most of it required by law, details of the partnership, management, financial reporting, tax consequences, risk factors to name a few."

I flipped through the hundred or so pages, each as full as an old fashioned newspaper. "Inside somewhere," he said, "there's information on expense and syndication fees." I started to read the table of contents. "These fees, sometimes called soft costs, are setup costs..."

I interrupted. "Soft costs?"

He nodded. "Development, administration, legal, that sort of thing. Well, the last partnership was sold for seventeen million dollars, which included fifteen million for actual purchase price and two million in fees. Since Joel had three appraisals at seventeen million, nobody questioned the offering price."

He leaned forward. "Carlisle told the Securities Commission that the two million in fees was actually a one million dollar payment each to Joel and Pitts."

I looked up. "One million!" I dropped the prospectus in my lap.

"Yes, now taking the actual money wasn't wrong. But not disclosing exactly what the fees were for and to whom they were paid, that was wrong."

Grabbing the cup, I took a sip. Swallowing, I shook my head. "Pitts would never do anything illegal."

He nodded, hair glinting in the morning light. "I think you're right. From what Pitts told me and what I've heard, he didn't know enough of the rules to realize they were contravening the law. The poor guy was devastated. As I said, he immediately pled guilty and paid his fine. Joel, on the other hand, fought it all the way, never admitting he'd done anything wrong. Of course, when he was found guilty of fraud, he lost his sales license. It was a huge scandal, you know, articles in the paper, police investigation. I think the poor bugger's still being sued by some of the investors."

So that was what Carlisle had meant when he accosted Joel during the Charity Pro-Am. "So they stopped doing business together."

"Yeah, Joel went back east to get away for a while." Michael hesitated.

"What else?" I asked, sipping.

He just looked at me.

"Come on! There's more, let's have it."

He pursed his lips and exhaled. "You asked. Pitts testified against Joel."

"He what!" I jerked and a couple of drops of tea sloshed onto the grey carpet. "Shit!" I said, peering at the darkening spots. "I'm sorry."

"Forget it," Michael said harshly. "Riley?" I looked up. His eyes darkened. "Pitts helped the prosecution to get a lower fine. I doubt Joel ever forgave him."

I listened to the sounds of the morning traffic. They were muted, far away, unclear.

As was my vision of Pitts Wyndamere.

Nineteen

At a phone booth on Waters Street, I made a quick call to the Capilano Golf Club. My friend and assistant pro at the North Vancouver Club wasn't in. I said I'd call later and hung up. I ambled a couple of blocks, absorbed in trying to understand how Pitts could have betrayed his business partner. Something terrible must have happened, for I'd always found my brother-in-law to be loyal. I shook my head. Nothing seemed right any more.

Glancing around, I realized that I'd passed number 21 so back I trucked. Walt's note said Suite 205. I looked up. A small sticker of a green and blue globe on the second floor window beckoned me. I nipped around the side and clambered up a flight of wrought-iron stairs. The door at the landing stood open so I plunged into BioAction headquarters.

The sounds of hunt and peck typing, a ringing phone and a girlish voice wafted toward me. I stood unnoticed inside a narrow room open the full width of the building. Sunlight struggled to get through the dirty windows.

A pimply-faced teenaged male was scowling at a typewriter that belonged in the Canadian Museum of Science and Technology. A young woman nodded vigorously into the phone and two others, a man and a woman barely in their twenties, stood chatting against a round fridge. The electricity between them sparkled and it was obvious from their locked gaze that they wished more than smoke from their cigarettes could mingle.

I tapped my knuckles on a nearby desk.

The lovers jumped back. The long haired male, caught in the middle of a powerful drag of his cigarette, started choking. The woman turned huge blue eyes on me. "Yeah?" she asked, ignoring her now sputtering partner.

"Hi," I replied, with my best smile. "Name's Riley Quinn. I'm looking for some membership information."

"I'm Sue," she replied with a megawatt smile. She took a drag. "New?"

"Excuse me?" Then I realized she thought I meant I wanted to become a member. I was about to correct her when I thought that jumping on the green bandwagon might not be a bad way to get some information. "Uh-huh. How much?"

Sue told me and gave me a photocopied sheet to fill in. The little globe logo was in the upper left corner. Fifty bucks didn't seem too much to save the world. I handed over a cheque. She eyed it carefully then shoved it at the pimply typist. He carefully punched my name and address onto a small card and handed both to her. Sue gave me the card and pulled out one of the desk drawers and stuffed the cheque into a small black tin box.

"Great," she said, meaning it, "I'll just get you some basic info." She walked over to a large filing cabinet and started riffling through papers. The others took no notice of me so I gazed about. On the desk where the young woman slouched, still yapping on the phone, lay a thick blue binder: one word scribbled along its spine, *membership*.

Sue came back, cigarette dangling from rose lips, arms filled with papers. She dropped them gracelessly on the desk and took another long drag. "This'll get you started. Give you an idea of what we're all about, you know, that sort of stuff."

I nodded, pulling the papers into a neater pile.

"You'll get more stuff in the mail. By the way, how'd you find out about us?"

I wasn't sure how to answer. So I lied. "Some friends of mine on the Island are members, they told me about it."

"That's great," Sue said, squishing her cigarette butt in an overflowing ashtray. "Word'a mouth's always the best."

"Would you mind if I looked them up?" I asked, nodding at the membership book.

Sue's blue eyes watched me for a second, then she shook her mane. "Sorry. List's confidential."

"I understand," I said, hurriedly. "Tell me, d'you recognize this?"

She took the BioAction letter from me and immediately nodded. Then her forehead wrinkled as she read it. "What's this?" Her eyes flew open. "We never wrote nothing like this."

The other three looked up at the sound of her raised voice.

"But," I reached across and took it out of her hand, "it's your letterhead, right?"

"Yeah but..."

"What's goin' on?" The deep voice belonged to the boyfriend. He glared at me and walked quickly to Sue's side.

"Nothing. This letter was sent to a friend of mine. I'm checking it out for him."

"What's wrong with your friend?" the boyfriend asked, lighting another cigarette.

I looked into his insolent little eyes. "He's dead." The punk's pupils dilated but he didn't reply.

"Paul's gotta see this," Sue said. "You'll have to talk to him."

"Who's Paul?"

"The president."

"Okay. Where'll I find him?"

"He's at a MacBlo demo."

I thought about that for a few seconds. "Which

plant's he at?"

The boyfriend hooted, showing yellow stained teeth.

Sue smiled. "No. It's at MacBlo's Headquarters."

"Oh!"

The boyfriend grinned at me while Sue told me what Paul Dunlop looked like and then carefully wrote down the address of MacMillan Bloedel.

I thanked her, grabbed my propaganda and got the hell out.

The lumber giant's top executives curry favours from a penthouse on Howe Street. Reading the street address was unnecessary, as the protesters' shenanigans were visible from two blocks away. The hairs on the back of my neck stood at attention. I watched uncomfortably from the side as thirty or so environmentalists trooped about happily in a circle, hoisting signs and blocking the entrance to the cream-colored stone building. Some of the placard slogans read, *Trees not Stumps, Mac-Blow!*, and *Bears not Bare!*

It wasn't hard to spot Paul Dunlop. Sue said that he was tall, blond and bearded, and a good-looking character matching that description danced in the middle and shouted into a megaphone. Passersby slowed and gawked at the commotion, but nobody stopped. Some, in fact, shook their heads and one guy in a hard hat gave Dunlop the finger. He grinned and bellowed louder.

I'd seen plenty of picket lines in my day, as my father had worked at MacBlo, but never such an orderly demonstration. Nobody had wanted to walk our lines, they meant a strike. And strikes meant lost wages, hot tempers and often vicious actions never forgiven. My father had had to cross them.

His silver pinkie ring with its tree stamp symbol-
ized a biologist, and biologists are management.
But the little ring had been no suit of armour. After a few weeks in the rain, the men, increasingly
more desperate each day, had shouted louder and
pushed harder when my father and others struggled to get through.

Finally I caught Dunlop's eye and waved at him.
He handed the megaphone to a chunky woman
and trotted over.

"Hi, Riley Quinn," I said, extending my hand.

"Paul Dunlop," he replied, with a firm shake.

He was younger than I had thought—must be
the beard—but his hazel eyes seemed very deep.
He wore a plaid shirt with the sleeves rolled up
and jeans, faded in all the right places.

"I was hoping I could talk to you."

"That depends," Dunlop said, with a charm-
ing grin, "on what it's about."

I actually found myself wishing he didn't have
a beard. "It's something serious. I'd rather not discuss it here."

He rubbed the beard and gave me the once
over. "Okay," he said, "I'll bite. How long's it going
to take?"

"Don't know. Maybe a few minutes, maybe half
an hour."

"Well," he said, glancing at his watch. "We're
going to be here for another hour or so, then I've
got some people to talk to." The hazel eyes locked
onto mine. "How 'bout a drink, say sixish?"

I smiled. "That'd be great. You name the place,
I'm from the Island."

"Too bad. Where're you staying?"

"West end, near English Bay."

"Perfect, that's where I live. Look, there's a place
right on the Bay, the Milestones—you know it?"

"No, but I'll find it."

"Okay, Riley Quinn. I'll see you later." He sprinted off, then stopped abruptly and shouted back to me. "What do you do?"

"I'm a golf pro."

"Oh," he said, obviously disappointed. "You look like an athlete."

Back at SinJin's, I made a quick call to the Capilano Pro Shop and made arrangements to have brunch the next day with Christina Turner, another ex-LPGA player turned teaching professional. I felt badly 'cause Sunday's a bread and butter day, but Chris happily agreed to postpone a few lessons.

It was obvious she hadn't heard about Pitts but I kept silent, wanting to tell her face to face.

I had a couple of minutes so decided to wash up the few dishes I'd used. SinJin's fridge was practically empty. I put it down to three things; his being a bachelor, his going out of the country for three months, and his living within one block of every possible culinary convenience. But, as I poked about in the cupboards looking for soap and a dish rack, I noticed a low cupboard full of empty liquor bottles. Rapidly, I pulled open one door after another. All nearly bare except one. It was lined with bottles of alcohol, several opened.

This was something I definitely didn't want to think about. I slammed the cupboard shut and took a shower.

Twenty

"It's crazy. Don't know anything about it."

"But it's your letterhead, right?"

We were sitting at a small window table, the rolling waves of English Bay not fifty feet away.

"Yeah," Paul Dunlop replied, scowling at the page, "but we're not the League of Animal Protection, y'know. BioAction's serious. We don't threaten people." He flashed two rows of pearly whites. "Don't need to. The public's too aware. We've got groups like MacBlo by the balls." Dunlop tapped the paper. "Who's this Pitts guy, anyway?"

"My brother-in-law."

"Oh. Why would some nut threaten him?"

"I was hoping you could tell me that." I looked directly into his eyes. "Does BioAction target golf courses?"

His chips of hazel didn't budge. "Should be, but you can't fight 'em all at the same time. Right now we're targeting the Khutzeymateen."

"The what?"

He shook his pale head. "That's part of the fight. Not enough people have heard of it." He sighed then took a slug of beer. Carefully wiping his beard, Dunlop continued, speaking to me as though I were a child. "Khutz is a valley near Prince Rupert. Grizzly habitat. For decades, groups have been campaigning to preserve it."

"Griz —oh, the bear!"

Dunlop nodded like a tired parent. "About fifty of 'em. The government, in its infinite wisdom—i period, e period, pressure from pulp mills—decided logging was okay." He swore. "More logging! Did you know that sixty percent of B.C.'s ancient forests have been cut?"

His eyes flashed and his voice slid up. "We howled and as a token response, the gov agreed to finance a three-year bear habitat study. And, most importantly, to incorporate the results into timber-harvesting plans. Well, the study's done. Results show conclusively that logging'd pose an unacceptable risk to the bears. But pressure to harvest's increasing. We can't let the bad guys browbeat the gov. We've got the proof that Khutz must be protected." Dunlop clenched a fist. "A little more green pressure and the bears might win."

"That's great," I said, feeling both enlightened and embarrassed. This guy must be seven, eight years younger, yet I felt like I'd been lectured by someone who'd walked more than golf courses and pondered more than endorsements. "Got to admit, I don't know a lot about stuff like that."

He nodded, leaned back and gave me a lazy stare. "What do you know about?"

I played with my empty glass. "Golf." For the first time, my voice didn't glow with pride.

"Right." He looked at me as if I were the CEO of MacMillan Bloedel. "The environmental disaster of the '90's."

"What? Come on! Don't you think that's a little extreme?"

"You think a hundred gallons of pesticide a year, per course, isn't?"

I frowned. "I don't know." I looked up hesitantly. "Is that a lot?"

"Shit, Riley, that'd sure straighten your curls." He sat back in his chair. "What do you think gives you those perfect greens and weedless fairways? Or did you even think about it."

"I've thought about it, Paul Dunlop," I replied angrily. "What kind of name is that for a treehugger, anyway? Don't you know the combustible danger of tires?"

He started to speak but I ran over his words. "You're not the only one concerned about the environment. I may not wave signs in the air but I'm interested. I try to do my part."

"Whoa!" he said, flashing palms in mock protest. "There's life in the ol' gal yet."

"Damned right there is! Where do you get off insulting me and what I do? I worked all my life to play professional golf and I'm friggin' proud of it!"

The couple at the table next to us glanced over accusingly.

"Okay, okay!" Paul replied hurriedly. "I didn't mean to insult you personally, but golf course development's pretty bad shit, you know. The chemicals leach into ground water; wetlands are destroyed. For what? So some rich bozos can whack a little white ball around to prove their manhood?"

"Come on! That's not what golf's about." I could feel my speech quickening. "Okay. Maybe there're environmental considerations, but I think on the whole, the sport's a good thing. Gives people fresh air, exercise—you should see the change in self-esteem in some of my students, especially older women, when they realize they can play the game. That's positive. Besides, golf raises more money for charities than any other sport—millions each year."

"Maybe, but pesticides still kill. If they'll do a squirrel, they'll do your old ladies."

We both looked out the window. Several tankers dotted the horizon. I yearned for their stillness, their strong anchor.

"Look, I don't mean to lecture," Paul continued. "It's just that most people aren't aware. Canadians get up on their high horses and complain about Brazil. One acre of Brazilian forest is clear

cut every nine seconds." I stared. "Pretty shock-
ing, huh? Well, the Maple Leaf's not much better.
One acre every 12 seconds. In 15 years, all com-
mercially attractive trees in B.C.'ll be gone."

"No way!" I exclaimed, envisioning the thousands of forested acres throughout the province.

Paul nodded. "It gets worse. 13 billion dollars
has been committed in the rest of Canada to pulp-
mill development. It's all going too fast. The public
doesn't understand we're permanently losing a
great heritage."

He stopped and turned the hazel peepers on
me. "Do you have any plans tonight?" I shook my
head. "I'm starved. How 'bout dinner?"

I laughed. "I thought you'd never ask."

Paul waved for menus and we spent the next
few minutes comparing the house specialties.

While we waited for cheese burgers and salads, Paul said, "You don't look like a golfer."

I smiled coolly. "Oh? And what's a golfer look
like?"

He scratched his beard. He wasn't smiling but
there was a light in his eyes. "Dunno. Let's see,
chunky, blond, not athletic looking." He gave me
a once over. "Certainly not in the shape you're in."

I blushed. "There's a lot of golfers in shape."

"Maybe so. I've got to admit, my impression
comes from the news. I've never been to a wom-
en's tournament. Once, as part of a protest, we
crashed an event at Capilano. I wasn't impressed.
The men all had beer bellies and wore polyester
pants."

"Well, next week's your chance. The Tour's
coming to my club in Nanoose. You should come."

He stared at me for a long minute. I felt heat in
my cheeks. "Maybe I will."

The waitress interrupted. After she dropped the

plates with huge, steaming burgers and overflowing salads, Paul continued, "You said you were a pro. Does that mean on the Tour or what?"

I forked a hunk of cucumber in my mouth and chewed. "I was on the Tour for seven years. Left it about eighteen months ago. Now I teach at Sea Blush, a course owned by my brother-in-law."

"The guy who got the threat?"

"Yeah. That reminds me. Any idea who sent it?"

Paul finished chomping at his burger. "None. Don't know how they got the letterhead. We keep it in a locked filing cabinet."

"I thought of that. Maybe one of your members used it from a letter you sent. When I joined today, Sue gave me at least three pieces with a letterhead. I figure someone could photocopy it and the copy'd look original."

He nodded. Between chews, he said, "You joined today?"

"Yeah, told you I do my part."

We both grinned and attacked romaine.

When I'd polished off my plate, I asked, "Would you give me the names of your members in the Nanaimo area?"

"Well," Paul said, pushing his empty plate away, "membership's supposed to be confidential. What's the big deal, anyway? You really expect something to happen on the twenty-ninth?"

"Don't know." I worked a bacon bit out of my back tooth. "That's the day of the Pro-Am. Lot of influential people'll be there."

"What's this guy Pitts think?"

I hesitated. "He's, uh, dead. Died last Tuesday."

Paul's eyes widened. "Jeez, I'm sorry. Were you close?"

"He was my best friend."

He nodded then frowned. "But, I thought you

said he was your brother-in-law?"

"He is, er, was. He and my sister were separated," I explained. "When I had to leave the Tour, he gave me a job, a great job, back home." My voice started to shake. "We became very close the last year or so."

He leaned across the table. "Hey, you look like you could use some fresh air. Let's get outta here."

Paul quickly paid the bill—I was too upset to argue—and we stepped out into the warm, salt wind.

English Bay is a large blue hunk, bounded by fashion-crazed inhabitants of Kitsilano to the west and the green thatch of Stanley Park to the east. A recreational path runs along the Bay, eventually becoming the sea wall 'round the park.

This six-foot ribbon is Vancouver's answer to the Champs Élysée, the place to see and, more importantly, to be seen. Slouching on one of the many benches—usually donated in memory of a deceased loved one—the world may not pass you by but certainly every tourist and Vancouverite does.

Cut off from the rest of Canadians by the Rocky Mountains, British Columbians dress in the latest high-tech, waterproof, blindingly-coloured casual clothes while revelling in an earlier, gentler time. Priorities here are physical and social activities, family, and a bit of work. One look at the hundreds of babes, both male and female, striking poses along the rec path would convince aliens that they'd stumbled into Shangri-La.

Twilight bled across the sky as we walked and chatted-dodging joggers, rollerbladers, bicyclists and dogs. The chilly sea air forced me to throw on a kangaroo jacket, but my bare legs enjoyed its tickle. Paul wore jeans and pulled on an old University of Victoria sweatshirt.

"You went to UVIC?"

"Yeah, took biology. You?"

"Lamar University." He looked puzzled. "It's in Texas."

"Well, excuuse me! School in the States, pretty heavy duty."

His sarcasm wasn't unexpected. Most Canadians are intimidated by one of their own hitting the books south of the border.

"Not really. Golf's better, but that's just climate."

"Scholarship?"

I nodded. "Four years. A lotta fun, a lotta hard work."

"Yeah, right. Majoring in putting must'a put a real strain on the brain."

Again, not an unexpected response. I kept my voice neutral. "Actually, I majored in fine art."

We strolled along the water, cut inland and came upon one of my favourite places, Lost Lagoon. The lagoon is a large pond circled by an asphalt and cinder path. It's the place where the birds, not the babes, hang out. We sidestepped a dozen Canada geese, heads tucked under wings, balancing on one foot. Can't believe they sleep like that. Out in the pond were dozens of ducks and a handful of white swans.

"Wood ducks're my favourite," I said, watching the harlequin-coloured characters streaking along the surface.

Paul's eyes widened in surprise. "You know ducks?"

"Course." I pointed to our left. "Those two're Mallards, the three over there are Coots—they're a riot; make sounds like little farts. Alongside the fountain's a couple of Black ducks, a bunch more Mallards and one female merganser, Red-Breasted, I think."

Paul Dunlop's lower jaw sagged. "I'm impressed! Where'd you learn all this?"

"Golfers are not tantamount to idiots, y'know. In fact, it's because I golf that I know birds. Audubon's Field Guide is in my junk drawer— that's what I call the pocket in my golf bag where I stuff, well, you know, all kinds of junk. I spend a lot of time in..." I hesitated then smiled, "in what, before today, I would've called natural habitats." Paul grinned. I was beginning to get used to the beard. "You see all kinds of birds and animals on a golf course."

Paul kicked at bird droppings. A snoozing Canada goose popped open a yellow eye.

"What's the most difficult thing about the Tour?"

I shoved my hands into the kangaroo pouch. It was getting dark and I could no longer see the Merganser. "That's a tough one. I really enjoyed it, but I'd have to say the travelling logistics, getting from a to b, finding out where to stay. It's easier after the first couple 'a years 'cause most tournaments are at the same courses, year after year."

I looked across the causeway that separates Lost Lagoon from the Park. The lights from the automobiles glanced off the lagoon, splinters of light raked against the black outline of trees. The ducks chatted quietly among themselves. I inhaled the moist, thick air.

"I'm five minutes from my brother's apartment. I think I'll call it a night."

"Sure," Paul replied, pale hair glinting in the headlights. "I'll walk you."

We headed up the small incline out of the lagoon and into the most densely populated area of Vancouver. The streets hummed with tires, couples strolled, hand in hand, and a woman's laughter floated on the soft breeze.

I thought young Mr. Dunlop might sneak a kiss but instead he stood quietly, staring into my face. "I'll look into the list for you."

"Thanks. I'm heading back Sunday."

He leaned closer. I waited. "Take care, Riley Quinn," he said, suddenly shy. "G'night.

I watched his muscular butt disappear into the dark and tried to gage my disappointment.

Outta ten, six, maybe seven.

Twenty-One

The tiny tugboat-shaped seabus slapped against the hanging tires. I scrambled aboard with seven other shoppers and gave the young woman at the helm a Loonie and a quarter.

Under a blazing sun, we chugged across about three hundred feet of the calm waters of False Creek to Granville Island. Formerly a terminus and works yard for the railway, the mushroom-shaped peninsula is home to a huge public market, restaurant, theatres, an art school and hosts an eclectic huddle of artists and galleries. Chris and I had agreed to meet around noon at the pier so I had an hour to browse.

On Saturday, if you're not burning up the trails in Stanley Park, then you're jostling for bing cherries on Granville. As I watched the fields of shoppers, I figured there were more folks on this tiny spit of land than in all of Nanoose. It's kind of fun to get lost in a crowd—once in a while.

Munching a banana, I dodged strollers in the narrow streets and old ladies darting about the market aisles. Fixated on a young guy spreading soon-to-be chocolate fudge across a huge marble-topped table, I gawked for ten minutes. Finally, I couldn't stand the smell any longer and dragged myself away, clutching an enormous hunk of Rocky Road. Nothing like fresh produce!

Back out in the fresh air, a gallery window caught my eye. A small watercolour glowed from its easel perch. I glanced at the lower right corner. Though not as darkly coloured as the huge work Pitts had recently bought for the Clubhouse walls, the signature was that of the same Salish artist. I stared at it for a long time then ducked inside.

Ten minutes later, I met Christina, the carefully wrapped objet d'art tucked under my arm. We hugged, I told her about the painting and we nipped into a nearby restaurant. We hadn't seen each other for months so spent a bit of time chatting about our lives, both professional and private, though there's not a lot of distinction when you're a golf pro. She finally asked what had brought me to the big city. I gulped air and told her about Pitts. Chris was shocked, then a little upset. Though she never made it to the Tour, like most Canadian teaching pros, she had played the mini-tours in Florida and California.

From late November to early March, golf professionals from all over the great white north drag their bags south to do the thing they most love but rarely have time for, playing golf daily. When I was starting out, Chris and I had roomed together and Pitts had often arrived unexpectedly and hauled us from course to course in his old Bentley.

"Oh, Riley, I'm so sorry," Chris said, taking the tissue I offered. "How's Hal?"

"You know Hal. She went a bit overboard at first but I think she'll be okay."

"Pitts is dead," Chris said, as though trying out the words. "It's so hard to believe." She stopped. Her thin, freckled face broke into a hesitant smile. "Remember Harbour Hills?"

I, too, smiled. "Which time?"

She drew her fingers through her shoulder length hair. "You remember, Ril. That time you were two strokes ahead and you three-putted the eighteenth? Man," she laughed, "I didn't know who was angrier, you or Pitts. But when he tied your putter to the back of the Bentley..."

I howled. "That's right! Jeez. He was hoppin'!"

Tears streamed down Chris's face. "Yeah," she

gasped, "poor putter must'a bin dragged fifteen miles!"

We roared. My cheeks hurt. We stopped reluctantly, dragging the sound out as long as possible. Then we sat quietly and fishbowled, tear stained faces sorting through the crowds.

"How'd it happen?"

I told her. Then I added, "I'm not sure, but something's just not right."

"What d'you mean?"

"Well...it's just that no one admits to seeing him, you know, on the last night, yet he told me he was seeing somebody."

"Does it matter?"

"To me. I need to know what he was doing. I'm finding things out about 'im. Strange things, but...I've got to know. The main thing is, there's no way he'd of gotten so drunk alone."

Chris started to speak, then stopped.

"What is it?"

"I really don't like to do this, 'specially after the guy's dead, but," she lowered her voice, "did ya know he'd been having an affair?"

"What!? You sure?"

She shrugged. "I heard it a few times, a few years back."

"Who?"

"Don't know, somebody on the Tour."

I shook my head. First betraying Joel, now this. Pitts I hardly knew ye!

Chris touched my hand. "You won't tell Halliday, will you? I'd hate for her to know. It doesn't matter now."

"No," I said, my mind racing, "I won't tell her." I looked up at the steel scaffolding shoring up the Granville Bridge looming overhead.

Chris was wrong. It bloody well did matter.

At a quarter after seven that evening, I slouched

on my brother's old leather couch and stared at the boob tube. My housecoated figure reflected back at me from the black screen. Just washed hair dripping, I lay back, stretching, enjoying my enervation. My leg muscles twitched but I was pleased. The run had gone well. With my body exhausted, I felt the freedom to open my mind.

Chomping on a whole wheat bagel, I got up and ferreted out paper and pen from my brother's untidy desk. I dropped down on the couch again and stabbed at my salad.

Between bites and heavy pulls at a Diet Coke can, I jotted down some questions and comments:

1)What was Pitts doing on the evening of Monday, July 20, between 5:00 and 11:00 p.m.?

2)Who visited him? (The mysterious golfer? Check with Vivian.)

3)Where're Karatsu's photographs?

4)Where's the bank envelope with the BioAction letters?

5)Who sent the threatening letters? (From what Walt told me and the look on Paul Dunlop's face, it doesn't seem to have been BioAction.)

6)What else was in the bank envelope? (Probably business—Joel or Thomas might know?)

7)Who was Pitts having an affair with? (Ask Michael and golfing buddies.)

I sat back and read the seven questions aloud. There was no way that I was close to answering any of them, but staring at the words gave me some comfort. If you can write it down, you can usually solve it. At least, that was the line of my high school math teacher.

I tried not to think of the low marks which frequently adorned my calculus homework. Stuffing a dark chocolate chip cookie in my mouth, I flipped on the boob tube.

Twenty-Two

I saw a pod of killer whales from the top deck of the ferry, sun gleaming blue against their dorsal fins. White and black bodies rolled silently through the choppy water. The breeze was salty against my tongue and ruffled my hair. It was good to be alive. Good to be going home.

The little car hummed along the pavement; the sun warmed my face. I had hung around SinJin's apartment all morning waiting for Paul Dunlop to call, but the man from BioAction let me down. That meant not having enough time to nip home and check my messages—someday I'll get around to buying a machine which allows you to receive your messages from a remote location. C'est la vie, as Louise would say. Fred Willcock's lesson was at three-thirty. Though a bit rushed, I was looking forward to it. The old prairie dog really enjoyed golfing and chatting. Weaving my way around tractor trailers, delivery trucks and golf carts, I pulled into my spot. The Rolex's hands read 3:10.

Golf courses are known for serenity, whispered voices and gentile attitude, especially on the Lord's day. This Sunday, however, the Sea Blush Golf Club looked and sounded like it would soon be hosting the Rolling Stones, not the LPGA As of six p.m., Sea Blush would be officially in the hands of the tournament organizers. However, it already looked like a fait accompli.

A couple of male members smiled glumly at me as they loaded golf clubs into their trunks. Their locker room would be transformed in a couple of hours by the ladies of the Hospitality Committee. Several volunteers hung about the transportation trailer, watching and chatting, proudly sporting their new tournament wear. About 10 months ago, Pitts and I had chosen pale cranberry golf shirts with teal blue waves splashing around from the middle of the back across the front. The Sea Blush Classic logo, also in teal, adorned the single breast pocket. If I do say so myself, they looked mighty sharp.

I leapt out and ducked under a moving piece of scaffolding, giving the volunteers a wolf whistle. The chairwoman of the transportation committee curtsied; the others just laughed. One shouted after me, "A guy with the last shipment of jackets is waiting in the Hut!"

I waved thanks and trotted in that direction. On the way, I dodged two preoccupied electricians and crushed a bunch of pink Impatience. "Sorry!."

The young woman who was on her knees looked up. "Don't worry 'bout it," she said under a floppy hat. "There's 5,000 more where those came from."

"All for the Classic?"

She nodded wearily and bent to her task.

The Hut was cool and quiet. Brenda was diving into a huge box and pulling out cranberry and teal wind jackets. The delivery guy stood by, clipboard ready for signing.

"Everything okay?" I asked.

She showed her great teeth. "Riley! You're back." Then she hesitated, and as though remembering last week, added, "You okay?"

"Fine, just fine," I replied, clapping her on the back. "This the last shipment?"

She nodded then pulled one out of its plastic bag. "Pretty neat, huh?"

"Put it on."

She shrugged into the jacket, smiling shyly.

"Dynamite! Everyone's going to wish they had volunteered. Look, Bren, can you handle this? I've got a lesson with Mr. Willcock."

She hesitated. "No problem," she said, unconvincingly. "Everything else's in, I've checked it against the master list."

"What's wrong?"

Brenda paled. "Nothing."

"Come on, kid. I know you better'n that. Give."

"I feel so stupid but..."

"Go ahead."

"Am I going to lose my job?"

I stared. "Excuse me? What're you talking about?"

She started to remove the coat. "It's just, well, everyone's talking about the club being sold. Is it?"

"News to me, kid. Anyway, why'd you think you'd lose your job?"

She folded the coat carefully and said in a small voice. "Everyone says that Japanese guy's going to buy Sea Blush and hire only Japanese."

I grabbed her by the shoulders. "Listen! Nobody's selling Sea Blush. Got that?" She nodded. "Nobody's gonna lose their job, okay? Jeez, Bren. It's just gossip! Don't listen to 'em."

She smiled briefly. "Thanks. You'd better go, Fred's out there, waiting for you."

"Right. We'll talk some more later." I dumped some stuff on my small desk, grabbed a tennis ball from my top drawer then hot footed it over to the range. Several of the leader boards were up and the main sponsor signs were being hammered into place on the eighteenth green. Charlie Gregg waved from the fairway. His cart sat idle while two guys from Tournament Services loaded a huge spool of yellow rope onto another golf cart. Roping and staking the course would begin any minute.

Fred Willcock walked slowly over to greet me. His thin hands enveloped mine and, in seconds, he gripped me in a surprisingly strong hug. "My God," he said gruffly, light eyes hiding under a Saskatchewan Wheat Pool ball cap. "I'm awful sorry about Pitts."

"Thanks." I hugged him back. "It's been a tough week."

"A fine man, Pitts. Was just talkin' to Eileen 'bout 'im. By the way, she sends her regards."

"Please thank her for me. How's she doing?"

"Just fine," Fred replied. He smiled bravely but his eyes remained dull.

So that's how it is, I thought sadly. I knew he'd worked in Saskatchewan as a teacher for 35 years and this was only his second summer of retirement. I was afraid his dear Eileen wouldn't be with him to enjoy the third.

"Last time you promised to show me somethin' 'bout an underhanded pitch?"

I smiled. Fred Willcock was a great pupil. Not because of athletic ability or hand-eye coordination, no, Fred was great because he loved to learn. If half of my younger jocks and jockettes listened and practised like Freddie, they'd easily surpass 95 percent of golfers and break 100. Fred never will, but then he doesn't care.

"Righto. Drop the club, Fred. Today we're going to forget about the mechanics of the golf swing. Instead, we're going to play catch."

"Catch?"

"Yup." I showed him the tennis ball. "Ever play softball as a kid?" He nodded, his eyes getting brighter. "Great! You're already half way there. I'm going to show you a little drill my friend Jenny Wyatt, taught me. She's still playing on the Tour, you'll see her out there this week."

Taking a couple of steps backward, I said, "Watch me for a sec."

I stood perpendicular to Fred, no longer facing him. "You see, the golf swing's very similar to throwing a ball underhanded. Lookit my stance, feet are wide apart; weight's on the balls of my feet, not my toes, knees slightly bent, arms hanging naturally. No tension at all."

I tossed him the ball. As I tossed, my body turned to face him. Fred caught the yellow orb cleanly. "Now you try it. That's right. Don't think about it, just throw it."

He did.

"Great! You're a natural!"

His long face beamed.

"Now, a couple more times." We played catch and I watched his body. "See how your body turns automatically towards me?"

He nodded.

"That's just the way it should be after hitting the golf ball. Keep throwing."

"Ever bin to Saskatchewan?"

"Once, as a junior. There was a golf tournament at—is it the Wascana Lake Club? In Regina, anyway." I grinned. "It was strange, so flat. Kinda eerie, but beautiful in its own way."

"Don't know about the club," Fred replied, "I'm from Swift Current. But you're right, flat as a pancake." He looked across to the mainland mountains. "You know somethin'?"

"What?"

"Sometimes out here I feel closed in, like a penned dog." He slid off the Wheat Pool cap and wiped his forehead. "Weather's sure nice, though. Just the ticket for Eileen."

We both stood there thinking, I'm certain, the same thing. Eileen was the only one not benefiting.

"Tell me somethin'?"

"If I can," I replied.

"Rumour has it the club's gonna be sold. That so?"

What was going on? "Not as far as I know. Where'd you hear that?"

"Oh, everyone's talkin' 'bout it. Nobody's very happy. Some foreigner lookin' ta buy." He squinted at me. "Meebe you outta find out."

"Don't you worry, I will."

With a few minutes to spare in the lesson, I had Fred swing an iron with the same underhand motion. His swing, though a little restricted due both to age and a late start, flowed fairly smoothly.

He knew because, with each stroke, the grin on his face grew. I felt good, watching his gangly figure in motion. For a couple of seconds at least, Fred Willcock felt pride in his ability. Maybe, during that brief but brilliant smile, he wasn't worried about Eileen. I hoped so.

"Going to be at the Walker inquest all week," O'Brien said in his slow, deliberate way.

"That's the crib death?"

"Yes. Absolutely horrible thing for the parents but there's enough suspicion to warrant it. Children sweeten labours, but they make misfortune more bitter." I could hear his sigh over the phone. "Going to be a long one, lots of bloody lawyers."

I sympathized. The very first time I had met Dr. Robert O'Brien he opened our interview with, 'No offense, young lady, but I hate people.'" My jaw had reached my chest before I managed to pull it up. "That's why I became a pathologist and later a coroner," he had continued, puffing a thick pipe. "What's your reason?"

For a minute I was speechless. Then I heard

myself stammer, "I, I like people."

That unwrinkled his face. Then he laughed, showing yellow stained teeth. "Sit down, sit down, my dear. Talk to me."

We hadn't had an auspicious beginning but it was slowly getting better.

So I knew O'Brien would hate every minute he had to preside over the inquest. All those eyes, some sad, some curious, watching him.

"Wish I could go but..."

"No matter, there'll be others." I heard him sip at his pipe. "At least the wife's coming. For some bloody reason, she enjoys them. Must admit I get a big kick out of it because it's the only time she has to stand up when I come into the room."

I laughed. "I was hoping you could make it out here sometime this week."

"Like to, my dear. Perhaps Sunday. By the way, hear the club's being sold?"

Even O'Brien had heard the rumour! I was getting worried. What if Karatsu had an Oriental head pro in the wings? "Not that I know of. Seems to be gossip." I changed the subject. "Where'd you get that quote?"

"Bacon." He hesitated.

I wanted to tell him about my questions but thought better of it. Like all physicians, O'Brien dealt in facts. And I, like all athletes, dealt in feel. Then he surprised me.

"Walt tells me you're concerned about the circumstances surrounding your brother-in-law's death."

Damn the man! I almost choked, managing only to sputter a weak, "A little."

"A little what? Have you proof of foul play?"

"Well...not exactly."

O'Brien drew on his pipe. "What exactly do you

have?"

I swallowed, thinking, *I'm gonna get that idiot for making me look like a fool.* "It's...it's just that some things don't add up."

"Oh?" The accent hardened. "Your addition's different than mine?"

"It's not that I think you're wrong. Well, maybe I do." I exhaled then words tumbled out. "I'm sorry, Dr. O'Brien. Walt shouldn't have told you. It's nothing concrete...just a feeling"

"Usually, coroners deal in facts, my dear."

"I know, I know."

"Have you new information?"

I had to say no. Not the kind that counts. No matter, I'd get the facts.

"Are you dissatisfied with this office's investigation?"

I was, but only because I knew Pitts. At least I thought I had. So I was diplomatic. "Of course not."

"Capital. I don't need to remind you that you're not to be running 'round half-cocked. You're off this case. Any information, you give to me...straight away. That clear?"

"Yes, doctor."

"It's settled then." He hung up.

I dialled Walt's number and a female voice politely told me that Constable Dickson was out on duty. I didn't leave a message. I wanted to bawl the big guy out in person.

Twenty-Three

Twenty minutes later, I was trundling up and down the sixteenth fairway valleys watching the assembly of a television tower. The assemblers looked like monkeys as they climbed the scaffolding, pulling the next level into place and tightening screws.

A golf cart beeped behind me. I turned as Vivian rolled to a stop beside me.

"Wanna ride? I'm just tootling about, checking things out."

"Sure." I jumped in. The cart moved forward.

"What're they doing building a TV tower here? I thought the front and back nines were going to be switched for television."

She shook her head, long braid bopping across her back. "Changed their minds. It was really only a couple of holes they didn't like, the last few are going to look great on TV. Did y'know that there's going to be over 250 media reps?"

I whistled.

"So, how's the big city?"

"Crowded and frustrating."

"I know what you mean. I used to live in Japan, remember?"

"Don't know how you stood it. Nanaimo's busy enough for me, thank you very much."

"I hated it. Couldn't wait to get out." We slowed to a stop near the green. "Never felt at home, always a foreigner. Then I come here, prove myself and I'm still considered foreign."

The bitterness in her voice took me aback. "Gee, sorry. I never realized..."

"Forget it," she said eyeing two T.S.O. employees who were struggling to erect a leaderboard. Vivian hopped out and peered critically. "You sure this's the right size?"

One of the guys answered, "Yup. 10 by 12 like all the others."

"Looks smaller. What about the eighteenth?"

"That one's bigger: 20 by 20."

She stared a bit longer. "Sure that's level?"

The guy finally looked at her. "As level as water."

"It better be, or it'll cost you your job," Vivian said, stepping back into the cart. "I'll be back later to check 'em so make sure they're right."

As we drove away, I looked back. Both guys scowled at us.

"Little hard on them, don't you think?"

Vivian turned to me, her small face registering surprise. "Hard? Don't think so. Don't worry, Ril, I've done this before. Scare 'em up front and they'll do it right the first time. Let's go to the Hospitality Tent."

I remained silent, thanking the wind gods that she wasn't my employer.

"Vivian, come in?" the walkie talkie spat.

Vivian grabbed it. "Viv, here."

"It's Jake. We've got a problem."

She looked at me and rolled her eyes. "What kind of problem?"

"You're not going to believe this but we got a call from RayLynne Hogarth."

"That's nice."

"No, you don't understand. She's stuck in Customs in Toronto. They won't let her in."

"What do you mean, won't let her in?"

"Just that. She's only got a driver's licence and the Customs guy doesn't believe she's coming to Canada to play golf."

Vivian swore. "It's hard enough to get the Tour here. Jake, get right on the phone to that Customs idiot and tell 'im she's legit. And call me when you're finished."

"Okee dokee."

Vivian slammed the walkie talkie into the slot designed for canned drinks. It squawked again, as though injured. "And I thought you all Canadians were right friendly."

Vivian grabbed the black box. "Of course, we are, Charlie. How do you think you got in?"

His laughter crackled at us. "Like you say up here, toosh."

"That's touché, you idiot. Viv out." She turned to me, gold eyes sparkling. "Can you believe that? Talk about Mickey Mouse! In Japan, no one would question a professional golfer, more likely give 'em an escort."

"That's Toronto for you," I said of Canada's largest city. "Anything going on in the West's considered a joke. Always has been."

We jerked forward again. In a couple of minutes, a huge hunk of white canvas fluttered ahead like an untied mainsail. Several guys were grappling with the metal interior shell while a few others yanked and pulled the rest of the tent off a truck. Lots of swearing and sweaty faces. Vivian looked grim, ready to snap. I decided I'd had enough behind the scenes, waved good bye and left them struggling with the canvas Taj Mahal.

I hoofed it to the ring road and followed it east along the ocean until thirty minutes later I arrived at Pitts's place. Inside was darker than usual. I couldn't understand it until I realized that the sliding glass door was now a couple of stationary pieces of plywood. The area around the frame had been swept. I made a mental note to thank Walt for doing such a good job. Then I decided not to. Serve 'im right.

For some reason the place gave me the heebie jeebies. Maybe it was the dimness or the musty smell. Smothering my anxiety, I pulled up the desk's roll top and poked around. No sign of an envelope or Karatsu's photographs. I checked other likely spots, kitchen drawers, telephone stand— no messages on the answering machine—and the three bedroom night tables.

Still no luck. I thought I'd ask the maid when I realized I hadn't told her about Pitts. Her number was in Pitts's phone book so I'd have to wait and call her later.

I locked the door and embraced the sunshine.

"Okay. There're three kind of groups where we get involved; first, all deaths that aren't natural. That means every homicide, suicide and accident. Second group's generally called institution deaths—people dying in nursing homes or while in police custody, that sort of thing. The third group's a hodgepodge of everything, mainly result-ing from a few lines in the Coroner's Act—what my regional coroner calls delightful catch all phrases—any death which is sudden and unex-pected and any case which may require further investigation."

My former Tour buddies stared at me, liquid first courses untouched in front of them. I guess an Italian restaurant in Nanaimo isn't conducive to a discussion of death.

I smiled. "Well, you asked."

"Luvely," Alison Weld muttered in her Austral-ian twang. The rookie from Cairns took a swig of beer. "You really are a bloody coroner."

"Of course. What'd you think?"

"Dunno. Thought it might be some sort'a sick joke."

"No joke. As a matter of fact, I really like it." They stared at me. "No, really. When I came back here, I needed to find a hobby—something totally out of golf. I heard about the area needing a part-time coroner and thought, why not? You meet interesting people, pay's decent and the power's phenomenal."

Jennifer Wyatt shivered. "I thought you had to be a doctor?"

"In some places, you do. You see, there're two coroner systems in existence, ours, which has evolved from English law where a non-expert, often a doctor or a lawyer or even a professional golfer, sits back and objectively investigates, and the so-called Quincy System in California—also in Canada in Alberta—where they've combined the duties of the coroner who investigates with the pathologist who examines the body."

"But what do you know about dead bodies or causes of death?" Jenny asked.

"More'n you think. Obviously I didn't before, but I've had some extensive training. Anyway, the coroner's not required to determine the cause of death but to determine whether the death was due to natural causes. We've got pathologists to do autopsies and lab technicians to do tests and stuff. Dr. O'Brien—he's the regional coroner and the guy in charge, I'm just part-time—says we're conductors of an orchestra. We have to know how every instrument'll sound but not necessarily how to play 'em. I get help from all kinds of experts; doctors, cops, dentists."

"I guess it's not as bad as it sounds. But there must be some sort of qualifications?"

"Oh, there are. Dr. O'Brien looks for four things: energy, availability, intelligence, and a suspicious mind."

"Don't know 'bout the others, but the last one's you all right!" Ali said, with a grin. "More like nosy."

I grinned. "Yeah, always have been a bit of a snoop." I turned to Jennifer. "Nuff 'bout me. I haven't seen you since the big win." After four years on the Tour, Jenny had won her first tournament, the Crestar Classic in Chesapeake, Virginia. I knew what an incredible high that was. "So," I said, grabbing her left wrist, "you've got the Rolex." I shoved mine beside hers. "Not bad for a couple of Canucks, eh, Ali?"

Jenny blushed to the roots of her short, brown hair.

"Too ryght!"

"Wish you could'a been there, Ril."

"Me, too."

Her face beamed. "It was fantastic! I've never been so excited. Suddenly everybody wants you, starts treating you different. It took a while to settle in."

"I know what you mean. First time I won, I kept looking at the watch and saying to myself, It's an effin' Rolex! I'm wearing an effin' Rolex!

We laughed.

"Yeah, and five years exemption from qualifying!" Jenny ran her fingers through her hair. "What a relief! Now I might even take a few weeks off and not worry about the money list."

I nodded. Players automatically earn the right to compete on the Tour, therefore avoiding qualifying school, either by remaining in the top 90 positions on the money list or by winning a tournament.

"Heck of a year for Canadians," Jennifer said, her hazel eyes shining. "After Nora won, making it two in a row for us, she told me my turn was next. And then, two weeks ago, Halliday."

"Yeah," Ali said, "isn't she right close to the

Hall of Fame?"

My shoulders tensed but I nodded.

"One more win," Jenny said softly, "imagine! In four years, I've won once and in what?—twenty?—Hal's won almost 30 times."

"All right, already," Ali said. "Some of us 'aven't even won once."

I grinned at her tanned young face. "Don't worry 'bout it. It'll be the Aussies' turn next."

"I'll drink to that," Ali said, raising her glass. We joined in and clinked glasses all around.

"So," Ali said with a twinkle in her pale blue eyes, "who do ya think's suddenly too good for the softball team?"

Jennifer reddened.

I hooted. "I get it, now that you're a winner, you can't afford an injury."

"It's not just that," Jenny said hotly. "You know what it's like, any sort of injury would cost too much."

"It's all right, Jenny," Ali said. "I was only foolin'."

"Don't worry about it," I said. "You've done the right thing. Believe me, you don't want to have to quit because of injury."

"Riley, I'm sorry! I didn't..."

"It's all right. I know you didn't."

There was an uncomfortable silence as we all stared into our drinks.

"Let's order, okay?"

My buds agreed enthusiastically. We ordered and when the food finally arrived, Jenny asked, "Know what's really weird?"

Ali and I stopped munching to look up.

"There're people who've talked to me since I won that before wouldn't give me two seconds."

"I know," I said. "How's it make you feel?"

She took a long swig. "I don't feel mad or resentful. I just feel bad. I feel sorry for them having that attitude. We're fellow workers and when you do a job well, they respect and praise you for it but if you don't do your job well, they don't talk to you." She stopped and smiled shyly. "Thank God, I've got friends like you who treat me the same no matter what."

"What'd you mean?" Ali piped in. "You're paying!" We burst out laughing.

We spent the rest of the evening reminiscing and gossiping. I'd only been out of it for a little over one season and already I felt uncomfortable. No longer looking from within, yet I hadn't made the break to looking from the outside. I listened and laughed but all the while experienced an odd sensation, as though I were in a car pulling away. It was the same impression I had had when we rolled out of the cemetery after my mother's funeral. I had looked back and the reddish mound of earth grew smaller and smaller.

Soon the Tour would disappear from my view. And with it, my friends, my past, my psyche.

Twenty-Four

"To think that I'm the newest member in the Hall of Fame is incredible!" Sam Brennan said, her round face brightened by a huge smile.

"You're not kidding! Congratulations!!"

We hugged. Under a canopy of blue, players and caddies lined the driving range. The huge tree-bound area resounded with spurts of laughter, cracks of cleanly hit golf balls and the excited buzz of fans. Several players yelled greetings at me, others waved. It was like old home week, except now as a caddie, my place on the driving line was behind or to the right of the player. I shouted back, dodged a jab from Goodie, then turned to Pat.

"Come on! Let's see the hardware."

Beaming, she slipped the gold clip off her navy shorts and handed it to me on a gloved palm. Though I'd seen others', I made the appropriate oohs and ahs.

A Tour player's most prized possession is her contestant's credential clip. The LPGA uses several of these pieces of jewellery, designed like a money clip, for subtle identification. There are different clips for players, officials, founder/charter members, sponsors, media, spouse/VIP and Hall of Famers.

It's the job of the volunteer security folk to quickly spot and recognize the clip, if not the face, and allow authorized personnel to enter restricted areas. Many's the time I'd smiled at a nervous guard and was rewarded with nothing more than a direct stare at my pants. Gets a little unnerving sometimes. So much so, some players prefer to flash the clip in their hand. Not that I blame the guards. Often they are faced with a bunch of golfers trooping into the locker room, tired and fed up after a long day. No one wants to be accosted by security, but heaven help the poor sod if someone unauthorized gets in.

For us mere mortals, the contestant's clip is a green and gold square, with the player's name engraved in black along the bottom, and is worn with casual pride on one's shorts or pants. The centre of all the clips is dominated by the LPGA logo. If you offered, I might consider trading mine—today stuffed safely in my pocket—for all of Vancouver Island, but I'd have to get back to you.

The Hall of Famers' clip is special in three ways: it's gold—surprise, surprise—oblong-shaped, and has Hall of Fame written across it.

Sam was rattling on. "You know, it feels real good. I was strong enough to set my goal and to accomplish it and did not deviate from losing that thought or that goal, no matter what I did or how long I was out there."

"It's beautiful," I said. "You sure deserve it."

"Hey, Riley!"

I looked down the line of golfers. Caroline Robbin grinned at me from 30 feet away.

"Caroline!" I shouted and turned to go.

"Riley?"

I looked back at Sam Brennan.

"The clip?"

"Oh, right!" I said, feeling its coldness in my left hand. "Sorry."

She reclaimed her precious reward and I shot a glance at Halliday. My older sister, dressed for the cool morning in a gold sweater and dark green stirrup pants, was still signing autographs. A dozen fans leaned over the yellow rope which stretched the length of the range, dividing the spectators from the players. I hustled over and hugged Caroline.

Caroline's a tall, large athlete with an open face and smiling brown eyes. When she swings a golf club, she reminds me of a modern-day baseball player swatting a bat as though it were a stake. I reached up and yanked the white Panama hat from her head and dropped it on mine. It fit like a bucket. For a second, I was blinded. Then with a laugh, Caroline pulled it off and shoved it back where it belonged.

"Good to see you," she said with a brilliant smile. "Tour's not the same without you."

"Thanks. Same here."

"You caddieing for Hal?"

"Yup, just like the old days."

"Oh, yeah?"

"Used to carry her bag when I was a kid." I stopped for a second then whispered something I hadn't thought of in years. "Halli, Halli, hit the ball. Hit it further than them all."

"What's that? Sounds like a song."

I blushed. "It's just something—forget it. Rose here?"

Rose, one of Caroline's sisters, had caddied occasionally for her while I was on Tour. Watching them smiling and marching, stride for stride, down the fairway, many fans thought they were twins.

"No. Hasn't been able to caddie much this year. I've been kinda in between. Now I'm trying out a few guys for next season." She nodded to a young, blond man who quietly leaned on her bright red and white golf bag.

She waved him over. "Riley, this's Ned. He's caddieing for me this week."

We shook hands. Ned's face was awfully young, but his eyes were intelligent. Over his shoulder, I noticed that Halliday was now standing at the line, chatting to Jenny. She gave me a look that said,

Now!

"Hal's waiting, gotta go. See you tonight?"

"Sure thing."

I ran over to the spot where I'd left Halliday's clubs, grabbed the pink and teal bag and trotted to her side. On the way, I snagged free her pitching wedge and handed it to her before she could speak. Fortunately, one of the volunteers came by at that moment and dumped a wire basket full of balls at her feet. I dashed back to the water bucket, dunked half of my towel and raced back.

Hal held the club at either end and began swinging it side to side and over her shoulders, slowly stretching. Some of the young kids just gripped the club and let the ball have it, but, even at my age, warmup was important. For Hal, it was essential. Not only for her forty-year old muscles but for her mind. Where I'm a thinker, she's instinctive. She starts developing the game groove on the driving range, sharpens it while practice putting, then hones it out on the course, hole after hole.

Jennifer was already onto her five iron, four clubs ahead of us. She was using a trick I often share with my students, placing an iron parallel to her feet, and snuggling her toes up against it. A lot of pros and players find this guide a great method of keeping their feet straight. I watched Jen's slow, rhythmic backswing. She swung with ease, all the while chatting to her caddie, Rita.

Hal shuffled a little to her left, a not so subtle attempt at distancing. I pulled the bag further back and began wiping the grips of the other clubs. Rita darted in and whispered to Jenny. Jen glanced at me with a smile and kept on chatting and swinging.

Hal started her routine of hitting ten balls per

odd-numbered club. I stood for a while, watching the players with what I began to realize were completely new eyes. I still desperately wanted to play, but something was different. During my genesis on the Tour, I initially watched the others with awe, then envy, years later with satisfaction, and finally with a smidgen of conceit. Now, Candy Lorenzo's slow backswing seemed to be just that. Deliberate, even hesitant. Big deal.

I let my eyes roam the swinging figures until they landed on Melinda Barton, one of the long-hitting young stars. Melinda's stocky and her game is power. I watched several of her drives land beyond the 250 range. Again, big deal.

Golf is played in the head, not on the grass. Yet some argue that stupid people make better golfers than intelligent people. I'm a thinking golfer and I think simple people make the best golfers. To them it's more instinct, less thought. Making the game simple is Halliday's style. And, I believe, that of Lorenzo and Brennan, two of the greatest. A thinker like me is their antithesis. Sometimes, when I'd be out there beating myself up over a shot, Hal or Candy would step in and just hit it. Good shot or not, they'd move on and hit the next one. No obvious angst. Once, when I was playing with Pat, I shot 70—two under par, a pretty good round. Pat was playing poorly but because she's such a good chipper and putter, she continued to score-shooting, to my amazement, 68.

Something to be said for instinct, for being a natural. Can't be taught; can't be lost.

I pulled back and began to concentrate on the natural in our family. After all, the golfer motioning to me for her nine iron was footing this week's bill.

"Halliday, tell me," the guy from a local television station said with a mean smile, "feel up to hitting with these youngsters out here?"

If Hal noticed the slight, she gave no indication. Smiling brightly, she responded smoothly, looking directly into the camera. "Certainly the long hitters will have an advantage out here, but it always comes down to putting. I think over the last couple of decades that I have proven to be a pretty good putter."

Many of the heads in the small crowd gathered in front of the putting green nodded. A few hands clapped. Halliday glanced at them and smiled. Other spectators hanging about the roped-off perimeter rushed over. Vivian was off to our left, chatting up a couple of players whose names just happened to be near the top of the money list.

"Indeed you have. Tell me, what d'you think of Sea Blush?"

"It's a great course, very challenging."

"What d'you think it'll take to win?"

"Besides four great playing days, I think it'll come down to course management. You've gotta court this type of course. Winner's gonna need patience and a sense of humour. Hopefully, this old gal'll fit the bill."

Vivian was moving, working the players on the green the way she works men at a party. Though her style and dress is opposite to most of the players, she somehow manages to strike up a conversation with almost everyone. The more golfers she flattered, the better chance for recognition later. Who knew? A golfer can influence tournament organizers. She might land her American dream yet.

"You're awfully confident," the mike jockey continued. "What's your secret?"

The little crowd nudged forward. I watched with anticipation as Vivian neared Muffin Spencer-

Devlin. Muffin's a unique individual and could easily match Vivian word for word. Of course, Muffy might mention one of her interests. Let's say, reincarnation. Usually the conversation takes a one-sided spin. Muffin was talking earnestly. Vivian's eyes were growing wide and her mouth small just as I heard my sister say, "She's standing right over there."

The interviewer, the camera man and the little crowd turned my way.

"Of course," the interviewer said excitedly, "it's our own Riley Quinn. Come on over, Riley! Say hi to the folks." He dragged me by the hand and pushed me against Halliday.

I smiled like an idiot, tongue glued to the top of my mouth. An older woman peered around the camera man and snapped a picture. Nowadays, the LPGA provides training in communications for new players. They didn't in my early days. Give me an audience, an individual, even a room full of kids and the words'll slide off my tongue. They'd be heading out the door and the letters would pound them on the back. Shove a little black television lens in front of my nose and this Quinn's tongue tied.

"With Riley's knowledge and skill as both professional golfer and teacher," I heard my sister-the-savior say, "we're going to be a tough family to beat."

"That's right," I blurted, knowing full well that my face spelled relief.

"Well, good luck to both of you. We'll be watching."

The interviewer thanked us and left for other prey. Seconds later he was smiling with Nora Ray, so obviously he was on a hunt for Canadians. Several people in the crowd asked for pictures so we stood there and, if you believe some aboriginal legends, had our souls ripped repeatedly from our bodies.

Twenty-Five
11:00 a.m., Monday, July 27

"Y'know what they say," my sister said as we walked down the third fairway during the first practice round, "the twenties are for learning to win, the thirties are for winning, and the forties are for remembering. Since there's no senior women's Tour, there's no waiting for the fifties like the guys do."

"You're only thirty nine," I said, as we stopped at her ball. I dropped the heavy bag on the ground and we both pulled out our copies of The Yardage Book.

When we received authorization for an LPGA event, Pitts had immediately called Gerald Lake of Yardage Books, Inc. and asked if he would write the guide book on Sea Blush. Gorjus came with his laser-like machine, and using its infrared beam, painstakingly measured the yardages. Later, Gerald produced The Book, as he has done for virtually every tournament on the women's', men's' and seniors' tours.

I flipped open this week's bestseller and found the third hole. The little book reminds me of Walt's notebook, as it flips open upward, not across. Tucking the top blank page into my plastic cover, I walked over to the nearest sprinkler and checked the number written on it against those marked on the page.

Depending on the length of the hole, Gerald provides a one or two page simplified but to-scale drawing, highlighting sprinkler locations, yardages, and landmarks such as trees and hazards.

Caddies and pros stuff these accurate little gems into plastic covers, referring to them constantly during the tournament. All caddies will walk the course before or during practice rounds, familiarizing themselves and making notes for their player. Some players, like Jenny and Hal, accompany their caddie, grabbing the chance to play and study the course. Others, such as American Sandra Melbar or Spaniard Maria Vicarrio-Balley, prefer to let the caddies walk alone.

As the booklets can be used for men's' as well as women's' events, the yardages off the tees can be too long, and an LPGA caddie may have to pace off and mark their own distances to account for their player's shorter drives.

Every sprinkler head is visibly numbered. These usually correspond to the yardage from the sprinkler to the centre of the green, and therefore are only good for course members. For each sprinkler head drawn in The Book, that number is noted in brackets. Gerald measures the distance from each head to the front of the green. This measurement is also written in The Book, above the sprinkler number.

So, when I looked at the drawing of the third hole, I found the nearest sprinkler to Hal's 3 wood drive was Number 173. But upon looking in The Book, head 173 wasn't noted. Not all sprinkler heads were marked. Instead, sprinkler head 168 was highlighted with a distance of 151 yards to the front of the green. I paced off 7 yards from Hal's ball to head 168. That meant 151 plus 7 or a total of 158 yards to the front of the green.

"Thirty nine's not very old," I said finally. "Look at Cooper, Lorenzo, even Brennan. They're over forty—my God, Cooper's over fifty and going strong."

"Funny you should mention three Hall of Famers," she said, pulling out the hole sheet.

"For heaven's sake, you've only got one more win to go. It'll happen. Now, where's the hole?"

We studied the pin or flag placement sheet provided daily to every caddie and golfer. It's letter-size with 18 little circles drawn on it, six down and three across. Each is numbered and represents that hole's green. For example, hole number one's green was in the top left corner, number two's was one below it and so on. Each morning, when the Tour Official—Charlie Gregg this week—was out early with the groundskeepers, he marked the location for the next day's placement of the flagstick, pacing the distance in yards from the front and side of the green to the flag and marking it on the little circle for that hole.

Today, the circle for the third green was marked 6 from the front and twelve from the left. Adding 6 to 158 gave us 164 yards to the flagstick. For Hal, in this type of calm weather, that meant a five iron.

She swung easily and the ball dropped onto the shallow left side of the green. We walked along, stopping occasionally to measure and add extra sprinkler heads to the drawing. I sketched a few other tree groupings to complete the picture.

The ground rises to the large green, then starts to fall sharply toward the back. Kidney-shaped bunkers protect both the left front and side and the right back. Ignoring the ball, we walked the green, side to side, front to back.

"Quite a breaking slope back here," Hal said. "Better not charge it or it'll be tough to keep on the green."

"Agreed. Depending on where the pin is, I think we should aim right, avoid the double bunker."

She nodded while pacing the length of the green. We chatted some more, trying to decide where Charlie might put the pins. Then, tossing Hal a few balls, I placed a tee at one of those spots. She putted the balls at the tee, and we both noted how each one slid left.

"Can't seem to get comfortable," Hal said softly, tugging at her sweater.

I looked at her in surprise. Beneath the gold Panama, her eyes were dark.

"Nothing feels right, hasn't for a long time."

I rolled my eyes to the blue sky. "Not again! You're just imagining it," I said, a little harshly. "For heaven's sakes, what d'ya want? You won two weeks ago."

She put her head down and stroked the last ball. It rolled wide. "I told you before, that was a fluke." She looked up, her eyes suddenly glassy. "Something's wrong. I know it."

I scooped up the ball and walked over to the next spot. Pushing the tee in lightly, I said, "Okay, okay, maybe you're right. Give yourself a break, why don't you? It's been a tough year with Pitts and everything..."

Hal's shoulders started to shake. "Oh, Ril..."

"Fore!" a voice screamed.

We ducked. A ball plopped into the right side bunker. Jenny was marching up the fairway, waving her club, with little Rita hustling behind. Hal wiped her eyes and walked to the back of the green.

Rita Richardson reminds me of a turtle: jaw always snapping gum, thin neck thrust forward, petite body straining. A very good caddie is blond Rita, funny, quiet and loyal. We had never worked together though I often wanted to. Somehow, we had always been at cross purposes. I was looking for a caddie when she had just started carrying someone's bag or she was looking and I was taking a couple of weeks off.

"Hey, sorry about the shot," Jenny shouted. "Sun was in our eyes, didn't see you."

I smiled.

They trooped up the green. "Real thinking holes, aren't they?" Jenny said to me. "You're lucky, you know the course. What d'you think, Hal?"

"Yeah, real lucky," she replied quietly.

Jenny glanced at me; Rita snapped her gum. I raised my eyebrows. "Hal's feeling her age."

Jen stared at my sister. "Are you kidding? Look around you. The people peaking, playing their best, are thirty five and older."

Hal smiled slightly.

"Hey, look, don't let us interrupt you."

"That's okay. We were just leaving," Hal replied.

Then my big sister did just that.

I glanced at Jenny, hoisted the bag to my right shoulder and trudged after Halliday.

After a few holes, we slowly eased into the old rhythm; one we had used when Hal was a junior star and I proudly toted her bag. We used to talk, sing and laugh, sometimes even dance down the fairways. Most tournaments, Dad was behind the ropes, egging us on.

For only the second time in decades, the little Halli song slipped back into my mind. I tried to ignore it, concentrating on my pacing.

Then behind me, Hal started to whistle it.

I braked hard in the middle of a long stride, glad my face was hidden from her view. The whistling stopped just after I did. I kept on pacing and busied myself with drawing a particularly detailed sketch of a couple of gigantic pine trees positioned to split the thirteenth fairway, about seventy yards from the green.

Silently, we walked up the wide, two-tiered plateau. I found the yellow paint dot that Charlie squirts on the front of every green. Using the four-inch blot as a guide, I started pacing the depth. Hal just watched me. When I finished, she asked about my wrist.

"Fine," I replied. It was a bit of a lie as the bloody thing had ached since the seventh green. Using my right hand, I shoved a tee in a likely hole position.

My older sister looked at me carefully, her eyes yellow in the sun. "So," she said finally, putting two balls across to me, "we don't talk about that either." She reared up and surveyed the green.

I tossed the balls back. "If your drives are anything like today, we'll have to be careful on the second shot. You don't want to be forced to dodge those trees."

Hal looked down at the huge pines. "No problem. Junk I can see, I can handle. It's the hidden stuff that worries me." She tossed the balls into the right bunker and slid in with them.

I headed over to another spot and stuck the pin in. I knew I was part of her hidden stuff. It was going to be a long week.

The outlook didn't look much brighter when I ducked into my office for a wee break. Juet Wyndamere was sitting in my chair.

"Hello," I said, as we exchanged the customary cheek peck. "No, don't get up." I sat on the edge of the desk. "What's the scoop?"

Dark smudges underlined her heavily mascaraed eyes. Her plump face looked deflated. "It's...uhm," she started then stopped.

I waited.

She chewed her lip for a couple of seconds. "It's Thomas," she blurted. "Something's wrong."

I felt like saying: "No! Really?" But that was

unfair. Instead, I asked, "Like what?"

"We...we've been having a few problems." She flushed. "He's been getting strange phone calls, I don't know from who 'cause they hang up when I answer."

"Oh," I said, thinking: Shit! Not another affair! I kept my face straight. "What's so strange 'bout 'em?"

"You mean besides the fact they hang up when I answer?"

I grinned ruefully. "Yeah, that's a little odd."

"I, I thought he was seeing someone, but when I asked..."

"You asked him?"

Her dark eyes sprang open. "Of course."

I was impressed. Pitts's kid all right.

"When I asked, he denied it. Said I was crazy."

"I always got the impression he was crazy 'bout you."

Juet blushed. She looked a little healthier. "So I pressed him, but he wouldn't say."

"Well, it sounds a little weird but I don't know what I can do."

"That's not all."

"Yeah?"

"Later, when I told him after my birthday I wanted complete control of my estate, he blew up."

"He did?" I asked. Though hyper as an atom, Thomas was exceptionally patient with Juet. "Well, it seems a little out of character but..."

"You're Daddy's executor, right?"

"Technically co, with Michael, but yeah."

"Well, I don't know what's going on, but I saw Thomas talking to that Japanese creature..."

"Karatsu?"

"That's him. When I went over, they looked pretty guilty. That guy gives me the creeps. I don't want Thomas mixed up with him in anything." She paused and dropped her eyes. Oh oh. Here came the favour. "Thomas likes you. Anyway could you, I don't know, weasel your way in and find out what's going on?"

"Well, he's a grown man. I don't know what I can do."

"Just promise me you'll try. Okay?"

I agreed hesitantly, thinking how odd it was that her father had broken his promise to me and now, here I was promising his daughter.

Twenty-Six

I pulled the little scrap of paper from my shorts. A week ago, I had written on it the three messages from Pitts's answering machine. The first name I ignored, I had spoken to him yesterday.

I dialled the next number and, after a few secretaries and a persistent personal assistant, I finally spoke to Tony MacAdam, owner of two Nanaimo hardware stores. After I explained who I was and he politely offered condolences, I said, "May I ask what your call was about?"

MacAdam replied between puffs of a cigarette. "You're the executor, you said?"

"Yes, co, actually. The other's a lawyer in Vancouver."

"It's about Morningstar."

"Oh, yes, the French Creek development."

"You know about it?"

"A little. Pitts discussed his business with me."

MacAdam inhaled then exhaled. "Doesn't really surprise me, y'know. He talked a lot about you. Do y'know if he was planning to sell?"

"Morningstar? I don't know but he wasn't too happy with the set up. Seemed to think there were too many involved."

MacAdam laughed. It was a gritty sound. "That's no surprise, Ms. Quinn, considering what a maverick your brother-in-law was." He paused, then I heard the scratching sound of a match. He inhaled and continued, "Never quite sure why he got involved in the first place."

I imagined the smoke curling out of his mouth as we spoke, imagined the smell seeping out through my telephone into my face. I held the receiver back a touch.

"Doesn't matter really. It's just that a foreign fellow was out here, offering to buy. Said he knew Pitts Wyndamere, that Pitts was selling him Sea Blush."

"What fellow?" I asked, damned certain I knew.

"Name's Karat, something like that. Know anything about him?"

"Yes," I said, trying to keep my voice calm. "Pitts was discussing business with him but, I don't believe he was seriously considering selling Sea Blush."

"That's what I told the fellow! Pitts loved that place, I said, he wouldn't dream of selling." He paused, inhaled and exhaled. "Mind if I inquire about something?"

"Of course not," I replied a little hesitantly.

"You'll excuse me if I seem rather tactless but...who's the beneficiary? Is it Halliday?"

"Yes, at least most of it."

"I suppose he gave something to Juet."

I didn't answer.

"Tell me, Ms. Quinn, will Halliday sell, do you think?"

"I really don't know, Mr. MacAdam. It's a bit soon, but you may want to speak to her yourself."

"She's still here?" He puffed on his weed. Before I could speak, MacAdam answered his own question, "Of course, the tournament! She'll be here all week, then, won't she?"

"Yes."

"Perhaps I'll come. I've never seen her play. Would you tell her about our conversation?"

"Certainly."

We said our goodbyes and I hung up.

I glanced at the next name. Spence Deacon. I reached for the phone before realizing that Deacon hadn't left a number. Damn! I pulled out the Nanaimo and area phone book but there were no

Deacons listed with that first name or initial. I leaned back in my chair and plopped my running shoes on the desk. Where would I get the—of course! Pitts's phone book.

My phone rang. I stuffed the paper back in my pocket. Would have to drop by the condo later and pick the phone book up. I reached for the receiver.

"Riley? Riley Quinn?" an almost familiar voice asked.

"Speaking."

"Riley, it's Paul. Paul Dunlop."

"Hello, Tireman. How're you?"

"Would be a whole lot better if the cops weren't all over us. Jeez, what'd you do? Call in the troops?"

"What're you talking about?"

"The guys in blue who've visited our little abode three times in the last two days."

I laughed. Couldn't help it. Walt's doing, for sure.

"Go ahead laugh. You don't have 'em hanging around your business."

"I didn't have anything to do with this, really. Anyway, what's the big deal? BioAction done something wrong?"

"'Course not," Paul snapped. "They just give me the creeps. Got no right bugging us."

"Well, someone claiming to be BioAction threatened my brother-in-law," I snapped back. "That's not right, either."

"I told you, we had nothing to do with that." Paul drew a deep breath. "I'm sorry. Just a little edgy. Looks like the gov might allow logging on the Khutz. Anyway, I've got those names for you, only four in your area. If I give 'em to you, will you call off the cops?"

"I never called them on, but I'll see what I can do."

He sighed. "Okay, gotta pen? Good, here goes: Kevin Lalande, that's L, A, L, A, N, D, E, right?,

Post Office Box 17, Qualicum Beach. Next is Karen Potts, she's at 1238 Albert Street, Nanaimo, got it? Okay, then Alexander Graham, R.R. 2, Coombs, and the last is Dr. S. FitzGibbon, R.R. 1, Ladysmith. That's all she wrote."

"Thanks, Paul. I really appreciate it." I guess I should have said good-bye then, but neither of us did.

Finally, Paul said, "When's your tournament start?"

"First round's Thursday."

"You play 'til Sunday?"

"Not necessarily. There's a cut on Friday night. We might not make it."

"Well, if I happened to come to the Island, where is Sea Blush, anyway?"

I told him. "I'll leave a pass for you. When you get to the entrance, just have the security guard call the Operations Trailer. They'll let you in."

"Thanks. Where'll I find you?"

I laughed. "Haven't a clue. When you get here, check Hal's name on the pairings list, it'll tell you what time we tee off. You can find us on the course or at the practice areas. As a last resort, leave me a message in the Pro Shop."

"Okay. Don't count on me, though, this Khutz thing's getting out of hand."

"Hey, don't strain yourself. If you want to watch some great golf, come on over. I gotta go. Thanks again for the names." I hung up.

Will he or won't he? Do I care or don't I?

There weren't any answers on my desk.

Robin Holt, a five year veteran from Indiana, smiled into the cameras and accepted the two thousand dollar cheque from the publisher of *Golf for Women Magazine*. Vivian Graves stood on her other side, smiling beatifically. Last to swing, Robin had clocked the ball 260 feet.

Dai and I watched from beside the bleachers. The large audience cheered, having greatly enjoyed watching Holt and fourteen others compete in the Golf for Women's Longest Drive Contest. Of course, their applause was deafening for third-place finisher and British Columbia native, Lynn Joseph.

"Ever win?" Dai asked, shouting over the din.

"Nope. Came second twice."

Members of the audience scrambled down the bleachers and rushed over to the players, Sea Blush Classic programs and pens at the ready. I watched them huddle around Patty Sheehan, Lynn and Brenda Kirwan. The players smiled and chatted easily with the fans.

Something tugged my shirt.

I looked down. A small, pig-tailed girl gazed up at me with eyes that belonged on a calf. Dai grinned. A blond woman smiled, watching from a couple of feet away.

"Yes?"

A pudgy hand shoved a program in the vicinity of my waist.

"Gotta pen?"

The brown eyes clouded. The woman took a step toward us.

"I've got one," Dai said, offering it to me.

"What's your name?"

"Glynne," she replied in a tiny voice.

"Glynne!" Dai exclaimed. "That's Welsh." He looked down. "My name's Welsh, too."

The little face continued to stare at me.

"How d'you spell it?"

"G, l, y..."

I looked at Dai. He stopped talking and flushed. Still the little girl said nothing.

"Okay. G, l, y, n?" I said.

"Double n, e," Dai replied. The woman's lips mouthed the letters.

I wrote: "To Glynne, with the wonderful eyes. Good luck". I signed it and handed it back to the little girl.

"Thanks. You a golfer?"

But the kid was gone. Clutching the program tightly, she immediately raced over to Patty Sheehan, the fair-haired woman two steps behind.

"Oh, how fleeting is fame," Dai said softly, with a smile.

I hit him on the arm.

"Dai!"

We turned to see James, his freckled face white, loping toward us. Between gasps, Dai's assistant superintendent managed to blurt, "My key—one of the sprinkler masters—is missing!"

"What? You sure?"

James nodded his head, lank brown hair flapping. Dai reached into his pocket and pulled out a thick key ring jammed with keys, some quite small. I couldn't help noticing that a plastic Mickey Mouse dangled among them. He whipped through the jumble, stopping at a small gold key. "Still got mine. Where'd you lose it?"

"That's just it," the young man said. "I didn't." He pulled his own thicket of keys out of his pocket and thrust them at us. "It was on here yesterday, I swear."

Dai examined the key ring. "Looks sturdy enough. When did you use it last?"

James scratched his head for a moment. "Must'a been yesterday morning when we did the pressure test."

"Have you asked any of the crew?"

"No. Came straight here when I realized it."

"Okay, we'd better get right on it." Dai turned

to me. "Sorry, got to go."

"Wait a sec. What's the big deal? It's only a key and you've got the spare. Just make another one."

He pursed his lips. "I wish it were that simple but..."

"Dai! Hey, Dai, come in. This's Vivian."

Dai grabbed his walkie talkie. "Dai, here. What can I do for you?"

"You know the area we're using for the putting contest?

"Yeah, the patch next to the seventeenth?"

"So I understand." Her voice sounded metallic, really angry. "What happened to the spot on the ninth? We've got a big problem. Need you here—Now!"

"On my way. Over," Dai said, trotting to his golf cart. I jogged along beside him and jumped in. James climbed aboard, jamming me up against Dai.

We sped along to the seventeenth. Arms crossed, eyes flashing, Vivian stood outside the roped area. Jake was inside, shaking his head. We tumbled out of the cart.

"What's wrong?" Dai asked.

"Everything. Since when's this the putting area?"

Dai looked at Jake. Jake swallowed and stepped away from Vivian. "Don't you know?"

Vivian shook her head violently.

"Since this morning. James noticed that the patch on nine was wet, too wet for thirty putters. Charlie and I spent 40 minutes looking for another spot. This's it. It's not pretty, but it'll have to do."

"Oh, will it? Are you kidding, look at it. It's ridiculous!"

We all looked down. Nine new white holes glistened in the sun. The area roped off for the putting contest skirted the edge of the seventeenth's fairway. I didn't think the holes looked half bad, considering the short time Dai had had to create a green. An approach area to each had been roped off with tees and string, indicating each individual hole's boundaries. Any ball that rolled outside of the string resulted in a one-stroke penalty against the team. The final 10 pairs, consisting of one female and one male amateur golfer, would be teamed with one professional. All three would compete as a team.

"I'm sorry," Dai said quietly. "I didn't know you didn't know. Jake..."

"What about Jake?" she snapped, turning on her associate.

Jake flushed and backed off a step. "You weren't around. Charlie said that everybody's on level ground so what's it matter?"

"What's it matter!" She swore. "For crying out loud, Jake. This's professional golf!"

"Nothing we can do," Dai said. "It's a Tour decision. Jake's right, everyone's putting on the same grass."

"I just can't believe it."

"I know it's tough," Jake said, "but we're tied. There's nothing we can do."

"Well," Vivian said, storming off to her golf cart, "they might decide not to putt. That'd certainly shorten the field." She climbed into her golf cart. "I'm sure as hell not gonna be here when the pros complain. Jake! Get over here."

Jake looked at us with a smirk. "The ultimate putting challenge," he said. We laughed. "Coming, Viv!" he yelled and ran to the cart.

Neither Halliday nor any of my buddies were entered in the Putting Championship. So I headed off for a quick cycle before dinner. I figured that the 10 couples would enjoy competing with a pro whether I watched from the sidelines or not.

Twenty-Seven
6:45 p.m., Monday, July 24

"What d'you mean, you've levitated someone?" Jenny asked.

Alison grinned. "Too ryght. Do it in bars back 'ome all the time."

"No way," I said.

"Come on," Jenny said, grabbing my arm. "Let's try it. What do we do?"

"Here?" Alison said, looking around the hotel lobby. A dozen or so guests, including a few players and caddies, lounged in the sofas and chairs. Five of us hung around in a corner, sipping drinks, waiting for Caroline Robbin before heading out to dinner.

"Cool," Cherie, Lori West's caddie, piped in. She jumped up. "Let's do it."

"Awl ryght," Alison said. "Lori's in a chair, let's do 'er."

Lori West grinned. "Why not?"

"What's going on?" Caroline asked, plopping down beside me.

"Watch. These idiots think they're going to levitate Lori."

"Shuure," she replied, brown eyes focused on the idiots.

Under Ali's instruction, they split into two groups, Jenny and Tina Barrett—a rising star from Baltimore—on Lori's left and Ali and Cherie on her right.

"Follow me," Ali said, placing two fingers of one hand under Lori's elbows and two of the other under her knees. The others followed suit. "Naow, lift!"

They pulled and strained. Lori didn't budge, but she burst out laughing, showing large, white teeth. Several people began to watch us.

"Ryght!" Ali said, undisturbed. "Naow, follow me." She placed her left palm down and held it just above Lori's black curls. She motioned to the rest. Alternately, they dropped their hands one on top of the other, grinning self-consciously.

"Try it again," Ali commanded.

They did. To our absolute amazement Lori's body flew up into the air! Startled, they almost dropped her. She tumbled down. For a second, no one said anything. Then everyone erupted at once.

"Amazing!" Jenny and Tina said.

"Cool!" Cherie said.

"Scary," Lori said.

"Way scary," Caroline said.

"Luvley," Ali said.

"Let's get outta here," I said, catching a glimpse of a uniformed woman marching in our direction.

We blew that pop stand, as they say in Yellowknife, North West Territories. In seconds, we were hugging and laughing in the warm evening air.

"Sushi?" Lori asked.

"Yeah!" Cherie replied, black eyes glistening. "Sushirama."

"How 'bout it, Ril? Any sushi 'round here?"

I wrinkled my nose. I am regularly full to the gills on chocolate, but that's merely an expression. The real thing never touches my lips. "Maybe, but it'll be all the way into Nanaimo. It's a bit far. But there's a great pub a few kilometres from here. Lot of action."

"All right!"

Shortly afterward, we piled into a cab. Fifteen minutes later, we were jammed around a corner table in the Lantzville Pub. It was noisy and crowded, with big screen televisions flickering baseball in every corner. The Blue Jays scored and the noise level went atmospheric.

While we waited for our drinks, I decided to

cut to the chase and asked my friends if they knew of anyone who had been having an affair with Pitts. Jenny blanched, Ali fiddled with a serviette and Caroline asked me why I wanted to know.

"You guys know all about it, don't you! Why didn't anyone tell me?"

"Jeez, Ril," Jenny said. "We thought you knew."

"No, I didn't know. I don't even know if Halliday did. Who was it?"

They glanced at one another. Finally, Caroline said, "I, I think it's over, been over for a while."

"I don't care. Who is it?"

Tina looked at Caroline. "Go ahead, tell 'er."

"All right. It was Linda."

"Linda?" I could see the veteran player in my mind. About my age, maybe a little older. Slim, attractive, married. "Pitts was seeing Linda? You sure?"

They nodded. "A couple of people saw 'em together a few times," Tina said quietly.

A young man bearing a heavily-laden tray interrupted us, slapping down heavy mugs. "Ready to order, ladies?"

I nodded. "Your timing's perfect."

We ordered and then sat around, not talking. The inning ended. Jennifer pulled out a large envelope from her bag and shook the contents out. "Got something to show you, Ril." She picked a bunch of colour photographs and began handing them to me. "This's my new place in Sarasota."

I was watching Jennifer Wyatt tug free a photograph when it struck me. All along, I had been expecting to find Karatsu's snapshots in a an envelope matching their size.

"Something wrong?" Jenny asked.

"Huh? No! Nothing. So, let's see how the rich half lives," I said, absentmindedly reaching for the photos.

Maybe Karatsu's pictures were in a larger envelope? The grey one that Pitts had taken home from the bank? The one that was missing?

I had to get my car at the club so took my own cab in from Lantzville. As it was only a quarter to eleven, I drove along the coastal road and pulled up at Pitts's condo. I nipped inside, flipped on the hall light and dug his personal telephone book out of the antique desk. The little red light on his answering machine glowed steadily at me. Nobody loves him, I thought automatically.

"Idiot!" I snapped aloud, tears stinging my cheek. I picked up the phone, half thinking I should check in with Halliday. The 18 karat gold inlay down the centre of my Rolex glittered, the thin hands pointed to 11:05. Too late to call Hal.

As I started to put the phone down, I noticed a button that my older phone doesn't have: redial.

What the hay? I thought, punching it. The phone clicked quickly in my ear followed by a busy signal. Damn! I dropped the receiver back on its cradle and waited. Moonlight streaked across the living room floor.

I tried redial again. Still busy. Just as I hung up the phone, it rang. The harsh trill nearly yanked me outta my running shoes.

"Hullo?"

"Riley? Izzat you?"

"Yes, Hal. What—"

"Thank god! I've been calling everywhere. Jennifer said you were going to the condo."

"What's wrong?"

"We've been robbed!" Hal's voice was high, she was near tears.

"What?! You okay? Where are you?"

"I'm fine," she said, swallowing hard. "I'm at the McBrides'."

My neighbours. Good.

"I came home half an hour ago and someone had been inside the house!"

"Have you called the police?"

"Yes. Walt's on his way."

"I'm gone," I said and was.

"Steady!"

I swung. And missed. "Damn it, Riley! Watch where you're hitting!"

"Sorry, Walt. It's hard to reach."

He stared at me. "Somethin' else's wrong. Give."

I glanced over at Hal. "Later!" I hissed.

A couple of grunts and a few more blows and the cool night air stopped blowing into my living room.

"That outta hold it 'til morning," Walt said, eyeing the plywood. "Probably a coincidence, your being robbed, too. Sorry about your VCR. Looks like Hal scared 'em off or they'd have had the CD player, too."

Hal smiled. She was so white she looked ill. "Thanks," she said weakly. "Good of you to come when you're not even on duty."

"Yup," I said. "Good ol' Walt, into everything."

Walt stiffened, then shot me a blast of hazel eyes. "No problem," the big guy replied, turning back to my sister. "Sure you don't want help cleaning up?"

Hal and I looked around at the mess. "No, we'll deal with it later."

I walked him to the front door. He ran his fingers through his prickly yellow hair. "Okay. Out with it."

I glanced back toward the living room and lowered my voice. "I thought I could trust you."

His face opened in surprise. "'Course you can!

With your life, you know that." He took me by the shoulders.

"You made a fool of me in front of O'Brien."

His grip tightened. Eyes wide, he stammered, "Oh, that!" He flushed. "I'm really sorry, I was gonna tell you. We were talking 'bout you. You know, how hard it is to lose somebody. And...it just came out." He looked down at me. "I was worried 'bout you. Guess I shouldna said anything."

"Damned right, you shouldn't have! I told you 'cause I thought you'd understand. I've got no proof. You know that. Someone like O'Brien, you've gotta have proof."

His large face loomed closely. "Still friends?" he asked hesitantly.

I gave him a quick hug. "'Course, you big lug. Just use your head now and again. Okay?"

He smiled and opened the door. As I watched his broad back moving away, I shouted, "By the way, you can lay off of BioAction."

Walt turned, moonlight enveloping his face. "Sure thing." His teeth glinted. "Guess they didn't like the heat. G'night, Ril."

After he was gone, Halliday and I began to try to put a few bits back together. We worked without speaking, sweeping up the last glass shards, straightening the couches, restacking the books and compact disks. Colour slowly bled back into her cheeks and after we righted the love seat, I asked, "Tea?"

She smiled weakly and I padded to the kitchen.

"Riley?" Her voice floated at me, rolling over the gurgling steam. "Do y'think he was right?"

I unplugged the kettle and poked my head into the living room. Her eyes were bright. "Right about what?"

"That it was a coincidence, your being robbed

so soon after Pitts."

I hid my surprise by turning to open the fridge. I was plenty suspicious, given Pitts's death, the BioAction threats and the first robbery. But by the time I handed her a steaming mug, my voice sounded perfectly natural. "Sure. No reason to think otherwise."

We sat there, staring at the darkness that would soon evaporate and reveal the mud flats of Nanoose Bay.

This Quinn certainly thought otherwise. Now, maybe the other did.

Twenty-Eight

Watching players putt is the most intriguing spectacle in golf. Putting's a matter of feel; it's an art and a science. Ball striking's more a matter of mechanics; it's quick and there's no terrain to affect the ball's journey.

Putting is also excruciatingly slow, every nuance of personality seeps out of players as they stroke the ball. Everywhere I looked on the roped-off practice green, I saw art in the deftness of touch, science in the spins and personality in spades. I'm sure the gawking crowd would agree.

On the morning of the second practice round, Susie Mender's two-year-old son was practising with one of his mom's putters. John's so short that a foot of the shaft stuck up above his head. Susie, a cross-handed, or as they say in the trade, left hand low, putter, was concentrating on an eight footer while her husband hustled John off the green. Deb Beaulac's caddie shoved two golf pencils behind a hole. Dressed completely in black, Deb chipped from the collar. She once told me the pencils are good targets but as the ball bounces off them, they also act as miniature cricket wickets.

Deborah Mclaren, a yellow-haired tall drink of a player was discussing The Book with her pony-tailed caddie. In her olive drab shorts stretched over spotted spandex leggings, purple fleece jacket and a tie-dyed purple T-shirt, Mclaren looked more appropriately dressed for cycling. Judy Sonderson, a 14 year Tour veteran, leaned on her putter, eyeing her three-year old twin sons. Her caddie, joking with spectators, expertly lobbed her golf balls. The balls dropped a few feet in front of Judy, and spun forward. She stroked them toward another hole and sunk two by the time her caddie strolled over.

Michelle McGann was, as usual, holding court with a gaggle of spectators, many commenting verbally on her hat-of-the-day. It was a gold Stetson and as she stooped to putt, the sun bounced off it in glittering waves.

I waved at Jenny and Ali who were standing a little off the green. Ali was chipping in from the collar.

The weather was coolish but windless. The players were enjoying themselves, feeling a little more at home and soaking up the admiring glances and murmurs of the fans. Practice days are great fun. There's no game day pressure, it's a chance to show off, sign a few autographs, and to revel in a life that others would die for.

I ducked under the security rope and propped up Hal's bag. She was over on the left side, chatting with Karatsu. Karatsu looked up at her, speaking with more animation than I thought the doughboy could muster. I gave Hal a wave and went hunting in her bag for practice balls. She joined me in a minute.

"He still bugging you to use his clubs?"

My sister cleaned the head of her putter. She seemed strangely preoccupied. "We've talked, but I told him I couldn't change, at least not this week."

"Is that what got him so excited? Never seen him so interested."

Instead of answering, Hal took a couple of practice swings. I shrugged and dropped three balls. While swinging, Halliday said, "He wants to buy Sea Blush."

I looked up. "And?"

"Haven't decided yet. Thomas asked me to, as well."

"Thomas? When?"

Her eyes looked puzzled. "Didn't I tell you?"

I shook my head.

Her eyes flew open. "Of course! The robbery, in all the excitement I forgot. It's nothing really, he just dropped over on the weekend."

"What're..."

"Look, I don't feel like discussing it now, okay? Let's start short," she said, pointing to a hole about four feet away. Pissed that she could start and then stop talking about selling Sea Blush so abruptly, I marched over and turned to watch her stroke.

Halliday has an unusual way of addressing a putt. First she brings the putter to the back of the ball and then lines up her right foot. Only at that point will she bring in her left foot to stand traditionally over the ball. A long pause, a couple of glances to the hole and back, then she strokes.

The first three raced wide. I shook my head and tossed the balls back. The next bunch missed as well. I walked over. "What's going on?"

"Nothing," she said, heavily. "Let's try another."

Long stroke, ball catches the lip and flicks out. Hal narrowed her green eyes and tried again. This ball plopped into the hole. Same stroke, same roll, better result. She smiled faintly. We did the putt and toss for 25 minutes. All the time, Hal played unusually quietly, hardly speaking to the other players, sullenly signing autographs. I scooped and returned, one eye on her, the other on Karatsu.

Finally we had only five minutes to Hal's tee off time. I tapped my watch. She nodded and waited for me to walk over. Handing me the putter, she made a quick dash to the pit stop. I hoofed it over to Karatsu and poked him on the shoulder, rudely interrupting a conversation he was having with

Deb Beaulac.

"Excuse me, Deb. I need to talk to this guy." Deb gave me a brilliant smile of relief and happily moved off.

Karatsu's black eyes flicked up and down my face. "Yes?"

I wanted to tell 'im to get his dirty paws off Sea Blush, but figured any interest I showed would make him even more determined. "Tell me more about the envelope that held your photographs."

"What about it?"

"What'd it look like?"

He paused for a moment. "Letter size, not beige, maybe grey. Why? Have you found them?"

"No. I just..."

"Riley!" The voice was Hal's. Panicked, I looked around. Her clubs were where I'd left them. I looked at the crowd around the first tee. Hal's face peeked out at me, red with anger.

"Gotta go," I said, and ran to the clubs. Throwing them over my shoulder, I jogged over and pushed my way through the clapping crowd. Jennifer had just teed off.

Halliday yanked the driver out of the bag and stalked to the tee area. I glanced at Rita who hovered near the bench. Beneath the mirrored sunglasses, her freckled face remained calm but her small shoulders shook. It wasn't from the weight of the bag.

The absolutely worst thing a caddie can be is late. Way to go, Riley.

Halliday swung, the crowd cheered and we strolled down along the courtesy cut. It's an eight foot wide private sidewalk from the tee area down to the fairway that groundskeepers clip short. It saves the players from getting wet feet.

The small crowd marched along outside the

ropes. Several shouted at Jenny and Hal and when they turned, snapped dozens of photos. For the first time since I was a child, I felt invisible on a golf course. All lenses—eyes, binoculars, cameras—were focused on the players, and on Hal in particular. I heard a lady whisper, "That's Halliday Quinn. One more win and she'll be in the Hall of Fame."

I wanted to turn, yell into their wrinkled faces that Jennifer had also won this year, that Alison-thousands of miles from home-had come bloody close and that I-yes, *Riley* Quinn-had a few wins under my belt, too.

'Course, I said nothing. Soon, the game's rhythm eased my envy. The crowds blurred; my concentration sharpened on our game.

Hal and I focused on placing her drives. Good initial position is essential to playing under par, unless you're a garbage player and excel at scrambling all over the course.

The approach shot to the sixth is the trickiest on the front nine. A mid-length par 4, the fairway curves right around a large water hazard onto an elevated green. As the green has bunker trouble left and right, it's important to get your drive wide left, avoiding the water and giving you a straight shot onto the green.

Hal's play improved, but not her mood. She hit her tee shot perfectly, but the ball dropped soft and only rolled a few yards. We had a tough 135 yards to the pin.

"Nine'll do it," she said, holding out her hand.

I shook my head and paced to the nearest sprinkler. "Flag's deep, Hal. Going to add about 10. You'll be too short."

"If I use an eight, I'll airmail the green."

"Uh-uh. Take a bit off. That's the stick."

After a missed drive, Jennifer slapped a seven

iron hard and her ball struck green.

"Nine," Hal commanded.

I handed the club to her without a word. Hal swung hard, got lots of ball. It soared high but fell about 15 yards short.

"Don't say it!" she snapped, shoving the club in the bag. I kept my grin to myself and trotted behind. At least she wouldn't argue with me about clubs on Thursday.

After we bogeyed the hole, Jennifer and Alison politely scooted ahead. Hal and I trudged slowly toward the seventh tee.

"Tell me about Michael," Hal said.

Surprised, I asked her what she wanted to know.

"Still seeing him?"

I shifted the bag on my shoulder. "Why?"

Halliday's eyes flashed. "I have to have a reason to ask about my sister's life?"

I hesitated.

"Forget it!" she snapped, and stormed ahead.

We spoke only of distances and clubs for the next two holes.

On the ninth, Alison's drive scooted off into the trees. I moved to join her, Jennifer and their caddies in the hunt when Halliday touched my shoulder. Her face was pale, her eyes glistened with tears.

"For heaven's sake. What's wrong?"

"Oh, Ril. I...I feel so guilty. I shouldn't have Pitts's money."

"What're you talking about? It was in his will, he gave it to you." I could have immediately eased her pain by revealing what Pitts had told me a couple of months ago. I thought about it, but Halliday spoke first. After that it was too late.

"Yes, but..." She looked down and whispered,

"Did Pitts commit suicide?"

"For heaven's sake, Halliday! What's going on?" I dropped to a harsh whisper. "Of course, he didn't commit suicide! How could you even think that?"

"I don't know what to think!" she sobbed, tears streaming down her cheeks. "It's all my fault. I think I killed him."

I stared at her. The hunters shuffled about in the trees. I shook my sister by the shoulders. "Get a grip, Hal! You're talking nonsense, crazy..."

Jennifer's face poked out from the trees and immediately ducked back.

"Are you sure?" Her face opened with relief. "You know that as a coroner? I...I was afraid he was getting back at me, maybe..."

"Maybe, shmaybe. Don't flatter yourself. He loved you and yeah, you treated him like crap..." Hal's head snapped back as though struck. "...but, dammit, Pitts didn't kill himself!"

"He could've, if he were upset enough."

Her voice was so low, I barely caught the words. I looked straight into her yellow eyes. "What do you mean, upset enough? Did you talk to him? Did you guys fight?"

"No!" she said, turning quickly away. I tried to grab her shoulders, to see her eyes, but she shrugged me off and stormed into the woods.

"For crying out loud, Ali!" Halliday said a moment later. "The bloody thing's right here."

"Pretty high-tech stuff for grass."

Dai's eyes widened, the colour bleached grey from the harsh florescent light. "Pretty high-tech grass," he replied stuffily, sitting forward in his chair.

"Just kidding," I said with a laugh. I took another bite of my sandwich.

He hesitated for a second then his round face

opened in a smile.

We were huddled in his tiny office, located in the equipment garage. The office was an odd mixture of old and new. Old consisted of furniture; a pale green metal desk covered in grey gouges, a small, two drawer filing cabinet, a couple of shelves of books, his creaky chair, and a scratched wooden table. New items seemed to be two pieces of electronics, a large rectangular box with lots of little clocks which looked like gas meters for a whole sub-division that hung across one wall, and a computer, its blue screen humming and a printer perched on the table.

Over Dai's shoulder, lawn mowers-large and small, green and orange-were parked in neat lines. The open bay was quiet, as though the machines were having an afternoon siesta prior to the evening cutting rounds. The soft voices of a couple of groundskeepers floated in from outside.

"Pretty impressive, actually, all these clocks and stuff. What's it all about?"

Dai stopped chugging his milk, wiped his mouth with a grimy hand and grinned the grin of a fanatic. Then Course Superintendent Deugo launched into a spiel of turf industry facts. It was gibberish for the most part, but I twigged that he had computerized control of the course's irrigation and water pump systems-120 pounds pressure is normal, don't you know. Somehow the clocks were used to time specific tees, greens and fairways, thus he was able to evenly distribute pressure, water and wetting agents throughout the course.

"Wetting agents?" I asked, feeling that I should ask about something.

He nodded brightly. Good question, Riley.

"Wetting agents are sophisticated soaps," Dai said, ripping off a bit of a sandwich. "Detergents, really, that we use to help cure and fight against localized dry spots."

Oh, brother. "Dry spots?" I asked on cue.

"Yes, sandy soils in particular can become hydrophobic, unable to accept water. Researchers have figured that there's some sort of fatty substance that gets around each sand granule and once it starts to dry, it gets worse and worse."

I nodded politely and munched on a carrot.

"If you can re-wet it, then it'll hold for quite some time. You've got to keep the soil profile wet. It really works when you spray it on the grass. And the following day, there won't be any dew there. There'll be dew formation in an area right next to it, where it wasn't applied."

"I see," I said, not really seeing at all.

Dai swallowed half an egg sandwich in two gulps. "Anyway, the how's and why's of wetting agents are unimportant. Just think of them as making water wetter."

He unscrewed the cap on his thick thermos, looked at me inquiringly. I nodded. I prefer tea, but coffee'll go down my gullet just as easily. Dai carefully poured the steaming liquid into two chipped mugs. I took the one that said *Since I used all my sick days, I have to call in dead* and blew on the steam for a moment. "By the way, ever find that key?"

His round face seemed to close. "Sprinkler? Not yet. I've talked to the crew. No one admits to taking it. It's pretty maddening, there's no time to change all the locks on the sprinklers." He pinched his lips. "It's tough, we're on a pretty intensive watering and cutting program right now, fairways three times a day, greens and tees twice each morning." He slapped the desk. "Damn! He should've been more careful."

He looked so upset I decided to change the subject. "I wanted to ask you about pesticides."

Dai stopped in mid sip. "Pesticides? Sure, what about 'em?"

"Well, I met this guy on the weekend. He said that golf courses use 100 gallons of pesticide a year."

His eyes narrowed. "What environmental group's he with?"

"Who says he's from an environmental group?"

"Usually are." The light glistened red off his hair as he yanked it. "Years ago, I might'a just reached for the most convenient chemical on the shelf, but nowadays our industry is using Integrated Pest Management. In fact, we're heads above other industries. That's not to say IPM is the whole solution, it's just in your toolbag. Sometimes you've got to use pesticides."

"Then he's right."

"Maybe, but I'll tell you this. The way the government regulations are going, not just anybody can apply pesticides. You've got to be licensed. I can't buy chemicals for the course that you can buy for your back yard."

He bit into a carrot and crunched for a couple of seconds. "We follow the regulations; only James and myself are licensed and we apply the chemicals. We post signs in the areas sprayed that give the name of the chemical, when, and who to contact. We're also trying to educate the golfer to be a little more tolerant of conditions. That's hard when you pros demand the best."

He took a healthy sip. Emblazoned in red on his cup was, *You're only young once but you can be immature forever.* I tried not to smile.

"Personally, I'm more concerned with the pesticides used in my winter produce that comes in from countries over which we have no control. Ask your environmentalist about that."

"If I ever see him again, I will."

Dai paused for a moment then looked directly at me. "Heard your place was robbed."

"Yeah, came through a window at the back. Fortunately, nobody was home. They made a bloody mess of the place, but only took the VCR." I chomped the last bit of carrot. "Cops think they were scared off."

"Good thing, too. Could've cleaned you out." He poured us both a little more coffee. "Wasn't your brother-in-law's place broken into?"

"Yeah, during the funeral. Can you believe that?"

Dai sipped quietly for a few seconds. "It's a bit of a coincidence, don't you think?"

I stopped drinking in mid slurp. "I'm not sure. I thought about it, but it seems a little paranoid." I paused. "You know, Dai, there have been a few odd things happen since Pitts's death."

"What sorta things?"

"Well, the autopsy says he was very drunk, but he swore to me that very afternoon he'd never drink alone. I've talked to everyone and no one says they saw him. And then there's the envelope and fat K's photos."

"Fat K? The little Japanese guy?"

I nodded. Then it hit me. "Of course! The envelope!" I jumped out of my chair. "How could I've been so stupid!"

Dai's eyes widened. "What're you talking about?"

"The bank told me that Pitts took home something from his safety deposit box in a large grey envelope. I've looked everywhere but it's nowhere to be found. Pitts was hardly cold when Karatsu slid over to me and asked for some photos. Said they were in an envelope. Of course, I thought he meant a small envelope but I just asked him about it and do you know what the fat guy said?"

Dai shook his head.

"He told me the envelope was large and grey. The bastard lied! He visited Pitts the night he died and that envelope proves it."

Puzzled, Dai looked at me.

"It's simple. Pitts was given a large grey envelope at the bank on Monday afternoon. Karatsu saw that envelope, therefore, he must have seen Pitts after he left the bank."

Dai was on his feet. "Way to go, Riley!" He paused. "But why would Karatsu lie? Pitts died accidentally." His deep blue eyes burned into mine. "Didn't he?"

"I'm not sure. No real reason to think otherwise, but I don't like people saying Pitts died because he was a drunken fool. Somebody made him mad enough or got him drunk enough so that he mixed up his pills. If it was Karatsu, I'm going to find out why."

Dai was sitting again, his face serious.

"What's wrong?" I asked.

"I was just wondering about the photos. Did Karatsu tell you what they were?"

"Said they were family photos, sentimental value. Why?"

"Then why did Pitts keep 'em in a safety deposit box?"

"Dunno. Good point, Watson!" I clapped him on the shoulder. He grinned. "You know he's trying to buy Sea Blush from Hal?"

Dai looked up in surprise. "From Hal? But...oh,

I get it! She inherited."

I nodded.

"She going to sell?"

"Don't know. Hal's been acting a little strange since Pitts died. Haven't a clue what's going on in her head."

"Probably in shock."

"Guess so, but I'd hate her to sell it to that bastard. He gives me the creeps. Bet he'd sell his mother for a good deal..."

"What is it?"

"The bastard," I whispered. "I'll bet he did do it."

"Do what?"

"I think you're right. The break-in's weren't a coincidence. I'll bet you my Big Bertha Karatsu did them. That slime bucket was in my house!"

Dai whistled. "Those must be some photographs. We've got to check this guy out, Riley. Any ideas?"

I smiled faintly. "I know a good lawyer."

"Good. Ask him to look into Karatsu. Maybe we can find something to convince Halliday not to sell."

"Okay." I glanced at my watch. The date window seemed to jump up at me. "I almost forgot! Tomorrow's the twenty-ninth."

"That's right." He glanced down at one of the Sea Blush Classic brochures. "Pro-Am, isn't?"

"Right, the Pro-Am but it's also the day BioAction threatened..."

"Threatened? What're you talking about? Who threatened who?"

I exhaled heavily. "Long story. Probably nothing to worry about." I tossed my sandwich wrapping in the waste can. "Look, thanks for lunch. I've got to go. I'll call my lawyer later, but right now I'm looking for a lying, fat bastard."

Twenty-Nine

I found the lying, fat bastard in the Hospitality Village, stuffing back a bratwurst on whole wheat. Where else?

A village is not what Walt would call it. He'd name it-correctly-a bunch of circus tents surrounded by miniature picket fences.

Whatever you call it, it's the choice spot where corporations, such as Karatsu's 'Aku', fork over twenty grand to pitch a tent and sling a sales pitch. Only a few select, invited guests sporting the coveted gold VIP Badge are allowed to duck under the vine covered trellis and stroll the hallowed grass. Once in, guests are treated to all the beer and Bavarian sausage their corporate tummies can stomach.

I'd forgotten to wear my identification and was stiff armed at the entrance by a meaty looking volunteer. Surprised, I told him who I was and kept on moving.

The guy stepped in my way, crossed his arms and shook his head.

"Come on! I work here."

"Gotta badge?"

I pointed to his blue armband. "Just 'cause you have security written on your arm's no reason to be rude." I reached into my pocket. "This what you're looking for?"

He saw the VIP card, flushed and shuffled aside.

"Apology accepted."

I waved at a few of the guests, spotted Joel Sanderson and barged over. He was chatting to a couple of heavyweight sponsor reps. As I neared, I overheard one of the reps.

"...heard you were a little tight. Where're you

getting the capital?"

Joel put his arm around the rep's shoulder. "No problemo. Expect to receive some cash in the very near futu..." He saw me and his mouth stopped. As his arm dropped free, Mr. Business gave me an embarrassed smile. "Hullo, Riley!" Joel said with forced interest. "Come for a bit of corporate culture?"

Before I could answer, he quickly introduced me to the reps. As I shook their cash hungry palms, I wondered what *a little tight* meant-financially strapped?-and where did Joel expect the manna from heaven to come from-the sale of Sea Blush? Joel rattled on about my career. I was surprised he knew so much. He wouldn't let me wedge a word in, so after a couple of minutes in the spotlight, I sidled away.

I panned the little groupings of guests and found my quarry. There were several umbrellaed tables placed strategically near the fencing. Karatsu, wearing a Sea Blush Classic golf shirt and black pants, was sitting with Doug Carlisle at the far end. K was doing the Japanese proud, judging from the empty glasses and plates strewn in front of him. I nodded across to Carlisle and dropped into an empty lounge chair.

Carlisle lumbered up.

"Don't go on my account," I said innocently.

His jaw moved for a second, then he said stiffly, "I was just leaving." He turned to Karatsu. "A pleasure, sir."

Karatsu found his feet with ease. "Call me K", he said, with a slight nod. They shook hands and Carlisle hurried off. "Sit down," I said. "Sam Brennan's coming through."

Karatsu looked out into the seventeenth fairway which bordered the Village. We watched

Brennan wallop a fairway wood. As she turned to hand the club back to her caddie, she saw me and tipped her visor.

I shouted, "Not bad for an oldtimer!"

She grinned and shook her fist playfully.

"Amazing golfer!" I said.

"Yes," Karatsu replied, carefully wiping his mouth. "Very popular in my country. We offered her a contract but she's staying with Mazda."

"Now you're after Halliday."

His face looked grey under the shadow of the umbrella. He nodded. "There are only a few golfers who meet our requirements."

Would I have, I wondered? I decided I didn't want to know.

"Have you found my photographs?"

"Not yet. Tell me again about the envelope."

He tugged at his shirt, jiggling a large teal ball of blubber. "I've already told you-it was large, maybe grey. That's all I know."

"Well, that's really interesting."

His black currant eyes broadened. "Oh?"

"Very interesting," I said, leaning forward and locking my grey eyes onto his. "And you say you didn't see Pitts on the night he died?"

He blinked. "Correct."

"You're a liar!" I said, my voice rising. "You saw 'im Monday. The envelope proves it."

A woman at a nearby table flicked us a glance.

Karatsu licked his lips. "Keep your voice down!" he whispered.

"Tell me the truth, or I'll tell this whole bloody place that you're an effing liar!"

"Please!" he whispered urgently. He stood up so quickly the table rocked and his chair flipped backward. The woman stared. "Can we discuss this somewhere else?"

I stood up, righted a plastic cup and looked down at him. "Sure, let's take a walk."

Head low, Karatsu beetled out under the trellis. The security guy gave me a wide berth. After we passed a bank of porta-toilets, I commanded, "Okay. Out with it. When'd you see Pitts on Monday?"

He paused, black currants boring into my face. "How did you find out?"

"The envelope. He brought it home from the bank that afternoon."

Karatsu sucked one of his ample cheeks. Finally, he sighed. "All right. We had an appointment, to, er, discuss the sale of Sea Blush."

"What time?"

"Around five."

"What happened?"

"We talked. He hadn't made up his mind. I left about quarter to six."

I ran my fingers along the rope encircling the eighteenth fairway. "Where was the envelope?"

"On his desk."

"What was in it?"

"My photographs."

"Anything else?"

He shook his head.

"You're awfully keen on getting them back, aren't you?"

He stopped. "Yes, I told you. They have great sentimental value."

"Enough for Pitts to put 'em in a safety deposit box?"

A bead of sweat rolled down the bridge of his flattened nose. He moved forward. "I don't know. Perhaps."

I darted ahead and turned to face him. "Enough that you'd rob for 'em?"

A funny look swept across his eyes. "What are

you talking about?"

"During the funeral, some bastard broke into Pitts's condo. Last night someone broke into my home. Coincidence?"

"How should I know?" he snapped. "I was invited here as a guest of your brother-in-law and you accuse me of petty theft. You're crazy!" He paused, took a couple of breaths and regained control. "If you find the photographs, let me know. Otherwise, leave me alone." Karatsu turned and tramped off.

I shouted at his broad back, "It's my club, too, dammit. I'll leave you alone when I bloody well want to!"

"I know the guy gives you the creeps, but that doesn't justify checking up on him."

"I told you, the guy lied about seeing Pitts on the night he died. Coupled with the fact that he's bugging Hal to sell..."

"Hal?" For the first time, Michael's voice held interest. "Why's he bothering her? Pitts just died, for god's sake. Isn't it a little early?"

"That's right, too early. So, will you look into Karatsu or what?"

He sighed. "All right, it may take a day or two. I'll see what I can come up with. I'll call you." He hesitated. "Ril?"

"Yes?"

"Wish Halliday good luck for me? I won't be able to get over 'til the weekend."

"Sure. What about..."

The line went dead.

"...the caddie?" I finished weakly.

The ball rolled wide of the cup.

"Oh!" a fan yelled, "Saaam Breeennan!"

Bradley grinned sheepishly. Elaine Miller, her partner for the Aku Sea Blush Classic Shootout, strolled over and gave her a quick hug. The cameraman from a local Nanaimo station stopped filming, turned and jumped quickly into a golf cart.

Good. One more team down, two to go. The sea of about 500 fans struggling down the steep bank parted quickly to let the remaining players and caddies through.

Shootouts are a recipe for fast, exciting golf, both for players and fans. First you combine 10 players into random twosomes, then eliminate the twosome with the lowest score at every hole. Finally, the last surviving pair wins. Only the best are involved as the players are chosen from the top of the LPGA money list.

In my early touring days, desperately needing some cash, I was convinced that the bottom rung clingers should get the chance at a quick $1,000. Of course, the sponsor and the fans want household names, not unknowns whose total winnings average less than a servant's yearly salary. Eventually I got my chance at many a shootout, winning several times. Each cheque I sent to my brother, as part of a bursary for hungry athletic students.

By tee off at the third hole, three teams remained: Halliday and Meg Lenney (the good gals), Candy Lorenzo and Colleen Walker (the bad gals), and Cindy Foss-Reisner and Missie Donaldson (the other gals).

In a shootout, all teams tee off at the same time. Then, selecting the preferred drive, each team plays one ball, alternating shots for the remainder of the hole. The team shooting the single highest score will be eliminated. Ties are broken by a chip off, closest to the hole wins.

The par four, third hole is not long, only three

hundred and sixty five yards, but the narrow fairway begs for a three or five wood, maybe-for the gutsy-even a one iron. Meg agreed with me and rapped a five wood just over 200 yards. The crowd roared as the ball skirted the right bunker and rolled to safety. Candy followed suit with a three wood. Unfortunately, Missie wasn't as lucky; the roars softened into groans as her drive dive-bombed the bunker. I skipped down the courtesy cut.

Hundreds of pairs of eyes watched Cindy as she dug into the sand. Careful not to ground her club-which would have cost her team the hole and the match-she swung. Sand particles flew in an arc, spilling out onto the fairway. Something struck my face. As I reached up to brush it off, I realized it wasn't sand. It was water. The sprinklers were on!

Fans started to shriek and dart back to avoid the jet spray. The cameraman froze then frantically tried to shield his lens. Missie yelled and grabbed for her umbrella. I looked around to see Halliday and Meg churning down the fairway, a powerful white stream at their heels. I started to laugh and almost choked as a spray swung lazily by, hitting me across the face. Cindy charged out of the bunker, ducked under the rope and darted behind a large tree. 50 or so howling fans followed.

Charlie Gregg, safely snuggled under a canopied golf cart with Vivian, radioed frantically for Dai.

Thirty

3:30 p.m., Tuesday, July 28

In seconds, everyone near the third hole looked as though they'd stepped out of a huge, communal shower. A hundred fans stampeded across to the completely dry fourth fairway. Many were turning to leave, angrily wringing their shirts and polishing their sunglasses.

"I'm singing in the rain, just singing in the rain..."

The bellowing came from the middle of the spitting fairway. The crowd went silent, dripping eyelids staring, as my sister twirled her golf umbrella and cavorted across the green. Halliday's no Gene Kelly but she's got great legs and the lungs of a moose. Meg flashed a grin, tugged her umbrella free and joined in. Nanaimo Television started filming. Soon, Missie, Cindy-drawn from the safety of her tree-and we three caddies were lined up like bar room dancers, high-stepping, twirling and wailing.

Several fans dove under the ropes and joined in. In minutes, about 400 legs kicked and a couple of hundred voices roared into the spitting spray.

Chorus line à la Sea Blush.

"This was a nice start to the week," Meg Lenney said, freckled face beaming. "It makes a difference when it's not a practice round. It helps to be out there with the pressure on."

"That was pretty exciting, winning by a bunker playoff on the final hole!" the interviewer said. The crowd behind the camera cheered. "You two make quite a team."

Halliday nodded, pushing her now frizzy hair over her forehead. "Sure do. Meg's a good iron player, I knew she'd get us on the green. I was happy to be putting."

To their fans' delight, Hal and Meg exchanged a high five.

"I'd like to thank the course super and his staff," Hal said. "We wouldn't have been able to finish if it hadn't been for their quick recovery."

I'd heard enough. Halliday was 1500 dollars richer, 10 percent of which had my name on it. I slipped away from the putting green and headed for the locker room.

"Linda?" the Hospitality Committee Chair asked, interrupting her nail filing. She peered at sheet of paper. "She one of the ones who went fishing?"

"Fishing? When?"

The tiny lady smiled. "Monday, I think. She and a couple of other girls flew up to Comox." She ran a long, scarlet fingernail down the page. "Robinson?"

I tried to keep the excitement from my voice. Linda Robinson had been in British Columbia on the day Pitts died! "That's her. Could you see if she's still here?"

She looked up at me through thick lenses. "I don't know—oh! I know you, honey." She gave me a playful poke. "You're Riley Quinn." I nodded. "Well, why didn't you say? I'm Flo. Hang on a tic," she said and disappeared through the locker room door.

I waited, smiling brittley at the security guard. I could have flashed my LPGA clip and breezed through as planned. But when I had trooped down the stairs, a strange sensation had inched along my spine: I didn't belong.

Ridiculous! I'd tramped into hundreds of locker rooms across North America and I practically lived in this particular one. But with the bulky, unsmiling guard and unmistakable air of elitist sweat permeating from behind the open door, I backed off, shoving the clip deep into my shorts.

So I waited outside, like some kind of star struck fan. Flo returned, waving her nails. "Gone, honey. Seems she left a while ago. Wanna leave a message?"

"Uh, no. I'll catch her later. Thanks."

"Sure thing, hon," she said, nail file humming.

"You've got to let 'im go."

"What d'you mean, let 'im go? I know he's dead, I'm dealing with that. What scares me is how he died."

Walt shook his head. "We've been through this before. You've just got to..."

"No!" I snapped and stood up. "I'm not a child! In fact, I'm a bloody coroner and it's about time people treated me as though I wasn't crazy."

Walt scrambled to his feet. He placed his hands on my shoulders and looked down into my eyes. "Okay, okay. I'm sorry! I just hate to see you beat yourself up over this. Sit down. We'll start over, okay?"

I sighed and flopped down. We were on a small, grass embankment facing the volunteers' operations and food tent. Even at six p.m., the tent was buzzing with volunteers, most arriving for dinner break between the four and eight shift.

"How much time have you got?"

Walt didn't even glance at his watch. "Whatever you need." He reached up and peeled off the Velcroed band on his left bicep. He let it drop. The blue strip landed at my feet, the word SECURITY visible. "I'm all yours," he said, forcing a grin.

"It's...it's just that I can't seem to accept it was an accident."

"Any particular reason?"

I glanced sharply at him. His wide face was

thoughtful, hazel eyes intent. "Nothing substantive. Just a feeling." I tugged at the grass, threw a handful and watched the green slivers fall. "I can't reconcile it. I told you about the promise?" Walt nodded. "I know it sounds flimsy, but I really believed him. He wouldn't have drunk alone. On Monday night, he left a message on my machine. Hal and I heard it the day after he died. He asked me to have breakfast the next day, told me he'd be sober." I stopped and ran my thumb along suddenly wet eyes. "Did I tell you I found out that Fat K visited him the night he died?"

Walt stared. "What? Why that lying..."

I nodded. "Says they talked about selling Sea Blush. Says he left 'bout six. I don't know. Don't see why he'd lie about it, but then why lie in the first place?"

"Dunno. Sometimes people are skittish of, you know, death."

"Don't have to be a coroner for more'n five minutes to know that."

We sat for a while, watching the volunteers munch sandwiches and sip coffee.

"Riley?"

"Uh-huh."

"Did you and O'Brien ever discuss..." his voice faltered. He looked down.

"Suicide?" I whispered. The word crackled against the warm air, too ugly to survive the sunshine.

"Yeah," he said, still staring at grass.

I swallowed and nodded. "The coroner in me says it's plausible, the human says, God, I hope not."

"What does Hal think?"

"I don't know. We haven't talked much."

"So, what're you going to do? O'Brien's taken you off the case."

"Yeah, and thanks to you, he's really ticked." He started to apologize again. I cut him off. "It's okay, over and done with. You're gonna think I'm overreacting but...I owe it to Pitts to finish it off."

Instead of trying to talk me out of it, Walt asked, "Anything I can do?"

I smiled. "Yes, as a matter of fact." I pulled out the list of names that Paul Dunlop had given me. "Remember the threat Pitts got?"

"Uh-huh."

"These are names of BioAction members around here. Could you check 'em out? You know, criminal record, that sort'a stuff?"

"Sure but you don't think..."

"I don't know what to think other than fulfilling my promise to Pitts to look into it."

I reached down, grabbed the arm band and wrapped it around his muscular arm. "You'd better go. Thanks for your help."

Walt fingered the band. "Anytime." He pulled himself to his feet, brushed off his butt and started to walk away.

"Walt?"

He turned.

"You look great."

Glancing down at his volunteer golf shirt and black shorts, Constable Dickson blushed to the roots of his fair hair. "Thanks," he mumbled and loped away.

I waved goodbye to Halliday and the taxi rolled off down Sea Blush. I stared for a moment at my convertible. My sister hadn't asked for it, but I knew I should have offered. But I hadn't. She'd even tried to smile. Instead, I had called her a cab.

"Sure you won't come?" she had said, almost

meaning it.

I shook my head. "Pro-Am parties are for players, not caddies."

"But..."

A horn sounded outside. "There's the cab. You'd better go."

She went, without a backward glance.

I sighed and kicked at the stoop. A piece of paper sticking out of my bird house mailbox caught my eye. I had already taken the mail in so reached in half-heartedly, knowing I'd only find a pizza flyer destined for the recycling box.

When I saw the globe letterhead, I froze. I scanned about, breathing hard. No cars, no sounds other than the faint hum of the highway a couple of thousand metres down.

My 'hood is a quiet, residential area atop a low mountain. Sea Blush Drive picks up from where Summerland Road runs out, up from the highway, a steeply sloped hill to nowhere. A few short dead-end streets run off it. Only those of us who reside up here with the bald eagles or our visitors venture up the long climb. At least until the last hour or so.

I pulled back to the sheet. It was from BioAction or at least the same loonie who was pretending to be BioAction. The pasted words read:

Like today's rain?

Too bad you didn't listen.

Tomorrow you will pay.

I walked up to the road and looked north. The sun glistened off the tide reclaiming the red mud of Nanoose Bay. Near the water's edge, two eagles sat atop a dead fir tree, their great brown bodies silhouetted against an azure sky. Snow sparkled off the mainland mountains. I waved to Mr. McBride, my neighbour, as he backed out and drove away. Nothing overtly abnormal, except the crummy piece of paper in my hands.

I trotted around to the back yard and collapsed into one of the hammocks. Closing my eyes for a few minutes, I slowly inhaled the crisp air and moist forest scent.

Shoving a hand into my back pocket, I tugged free my list of questions. Right arm under my head, I began to read them aloud to the dropping sun, adding the bits that I'd learned.

1) What was Pitts doing on the evening of Monday, July 20 between 5:00 p.m. and 11:00 p.m.? So far, meeting with Karatsu, drinking and dying.

2) Who visited him? Karatsu. Anyone else? Linda, maybe?

3) Where're Karatsu's photos? In the missing bank envelope?

4) Where's the bank envelope with the BioAction letters?

5) Who sent the threatening letters? Who sent the latest to me?

6) What else was in the bank envelope?

At least I knew the answer to Number Seven, Linda Robinson had had an affair with Pitts.

Neither the orange sunball nor the fir trees had any answers. At least, none that I could hear. I chewed the moist air. I hadn't made much progress, unless you call receiving a threat progress. Mulling that over, I decided maybe it was. I must have been bugging someone to make them hand deliver a doomsday message.

I stretched and freed my consciousness. I might have swung there until Halliday came home after midnight, but just after a watercolour sunset, I heard a peach chocolate whining from the kitchen for attention.

I ducked inside to silence it.

Thirty-One

In page after alphabetical page of bits of Peter Wyndamere's crunched handwriting, the names, phone numbers, and sometimes addresses, of all the people he deemed important enough to keep were crammed into the small, green book. Most of the stuff meant the big zipper to me but every few pages a familiar name jumped out. I sighed and settled back against my kitchen chair.

A lot had happened in the last ten days. I shook my head. What a dweeb! I'd been worrying about weather and sponsors upsetting the event, instead fate had tested me with death, vandalism, even robbery. I felt like I was walking around with a bull's-eye painted on my forehead. What was next? I hadn't a clue, but my teeth were permanently on edge. One thing for sure, I'd never again curse a threatening sky. What's a little rain compared to your best friend's life?

This death business sure makes you think. One of my favourite movies is Frank Capra's *It's a Wonderful Life*. A little saccharine, perhaps, but glowing with the right stuff. James Stewart's long, innocent face and *aw-shucks!* voice often sneak into my thoughts, smothering my fears and despair. Especially during the endless Christmases which had followed my mother's death. Any great analogy-be it fairy tale, horror flick or campfire song-has at its root a basic human need. There're many, but some of the most powerful are to be loved, to be free, to belong.

Stewart's character, George-a perfect name for an average guy-finds all three in his own backyard. One blustery Christmas Eve, the measure of his middle-aged life tramps in the front door of his dilapidated home-the gentle folk of Bedford Falls.

I fingered Pitts's little book. Many of the people whose names were scratched inside had attended his wake. Unlike George or even the inimitable Huckleberry Finn, Pitts Wyndamere never witnessed the poigCandy of his friends' affection.

Pitts was no George, but then the earth is no silver screen. I wondered about the measure of my life. Golf strokes, certainly, perhaps chocolate chunks, but hopefully also bursts of laughter, moments of kindness, tastes of passion.

I sighed, yanked out the paper with the names of the three men who had left messages on Pitts's machine, and snatched the phone off its cradle. The last name, that of Spence Deacon, I found under the S's. Filed on a first name basis, he was probably not just a business associate. No wonder I couldn't find the guy in the Nanaimo telephone book, his number was for a firm of stockbrokers in Vancouver.

Fortunately, due to its time zone location, the Vancouver Stock Exchange opens early. I dialled the brokerage house. Mr. Deacon-not a broker but an account executive, don't you know, as I was told by a huffy Scotswoman-was on holiday. Not due back for several weeks. Well, excuuse me. I left a message to phone me. I began thumbing through the book, checking off the names I could put to faces of wake attendees. As executrix, I suddenly realized, I probably should inform every person listed. The obvious wouldn't-really-care types, like barber, tailor, etc., I crossed off lightly in pencil. In the end, there weren't too many unmarked names.

One name, I was told after a couple of rings, was for his dentist. The receptionist was most sympathetic, but the high-pitched whine of the drill freaked my molars. I had a vision of the dentist-face shrouded in a blue surgical mask-gouging Pitts's name from his client list. It made me shiver.

Inside the book's front cover, were two numbers; one bare-naked, the other adorned solely by the initials G.T.

In the middle of punching in the first, I stopped mid-poke and stared. Something looked odd. Twelve square, grey buttons gazed back. I frowned. The phone beeped. I hung up, grabbed the receiver and gawked again. Suddenly, I knew.

There was no re-dial button! Pitts's phone had a re-dial button and I had been waiting to punch it again when Halliday had interrupted with her we've-just-been-robbed call on Monday night.

The thought of Halliday gave me a jolt. I glanced at my watch. Good god-it was nearly eight! I stuffed Pitts's book in my windbreaker and raced to the car.

The practice green was a madhouse. Not unexpectedly. With 216 amateurs -some posin', most prayin'-54 slightly-bored professionals and god knows how many caddies trampling the short turf, it's a miracle the grass blades ever stood up again. Add hundreds of families and fans pounding the cinder track outside the ropes, and what do you get? What the military appropriately dubbs a SNAFU: Situation Normal, All F....d Up. That's the sitch early Pro-Am day, all right.

Still, the sight of hundreds of women and men swinging thin, metal clubs first thing in the morning is surreal. Forget the limp clock fixation, Salvador Dali; golf clubs and checkered shorts are mucho more evocative.

I looked through the blindingly coloured throng for my sister. No sign of her. Dropping Hal's bag, I waved at Jennifer and Caroline. Rita tossed me a knowing smirk. Typical caddie life, hurry up and wait.

A golf cart with Dai at the wheel roared by. The look on his face meant trouble, serious trouble. I shouted at Rita to look after the bag, sprinted across the green and caught Dai as he slowed to turn a corner. I was beside him before he knew it. He flashed me a scowl.

"What's wrong?" I said, hanging onto the dash. The cart flew over a hump. When our lower cheeks again touched the seat, Dai swore, then muttered, "Bad news."

Hanging on as we air-mailed another bump on the sixth fairway, I stared at him. What could be so bad that Dai Deugo would use the f-word?

Seconds later, we slid to a stop alongside a green. Three figures stood staring down; anger and frustration blanketed the crisp air. James, the assistant superintendent, a carrot-headed youth I didn't know, and Vivian turned blanched faces to us. Charlie Gregg rolled up on the other side of the hole and hopped out of a golf cart marked 'LPGA' The three started babbling.

Ignoring them, Dai ran to the green and dropped to his knees. I trotted after and peered down.

Three glistening black streaks cut across the sixth green.

"Get the sprinklers on it. Now!" Dai shouted, veins popping along his neck.

James sprinted to a nearby tree. He struggled for a few seconds with the key to the dark green metal box which contained the sprinkler clocks. The lid popped up. He fiddled, then a sprinkler just below us gurgled. We backtracked as the circular water spray burst out and blanketed the green.

Using the bunker rakes, Dai, James and the red-headed kid scratched desperately at the stains. The rest of us stood, shocked for a moment into silence.

Vivian began to babble. "We're ruined, ruined! The Pro-am participants will be coming through any minute." Her voice catapulted to hysteria. "Oh, my god! What'll the sponsors say? I'm finished. I can't even bear to think about tomorrow!"

I wished O'Brien was there. He would have thought of some pithy, appropriate line. Neither Charlie nor I found any.

"Could somebody calm her down?" Dai asked, head down in the shower.

"Come on, Viv," I said, awkwardly putting my arm around her shoulder. "It may not be too bad." I steered her away from the green. We sat on the bench and watched the guys sweat.

"It's been a nightmare, hasn't it?" she whispered, fumbling in her pocket. "All the pressure, never enough time. This was my big chance. It was going to be perfect!" She blew her nose and tossed the tissue toward the garbage.

Of course, she missed. As I stood up and went to pick it up, she continued to whine, going on and on about being ruined, about losing her only chance. Her voice was like a warped violin. I could tell from Dai's hunched back that this, he did not need. I tossed the tissue into the can and mumbled something about her not being the only one to have bad luck. Vivian sniffled, then turned dark eyes at me. "You're right," she said, her voice octaves lower. "I'm sorry." She tried a smile. "I tend to be a little self-centred." No kidding, I thought, but held my tongue. "So, let's talk about something else. You surviving?"

I shrugged and talked as a distraction. "Nightmare sums it up. Since Pitts died, everything seems different. Something's wrong, but I can't put my finger on it."

"Like what?"

"Not sure." I shook my head. "He...he wasn't the man I thought he was."

"Oh?" She watched the sprinkler over my shoulder for a few seconds. "In what way?"

"Many, it seems." She looked at me. I held her golden eyes with mine. "Did y'know he was having an affair?"

Her eyes widened but she shook her head. Then she stood up. I looked behind to see Dai and his rakers slosh off the green to stand beside Charlie. Viv and I joined them. Droplets rolling off their hair and faces, the three groundskeepers stared hopefully at the darkening grass.

The edges of the black streaks were softened as the oil began to slide down the green. The sprinkler hissed and spat.

"It's ruined, isn't it?" Vivian whispered. She turned to Dai and her voice rose. "How could you let this happen? I told Pitts he shouldn't have hired you..."

"Vivian!" Charlie's voice cut her's off. "For god's sake, woman! It's not his fault."

On my right, the young man dropped his head and started to edge back.

"It's mine," he mumbled, his face so colourless his freckles stood out in high relief.

James jumped in front of him. "No! Tell 'em what happened."

The boy's mouth worked, but no sound exited. Dai placed a hand on the young man's shoulder and said softly, "No one's blaming you, Nick. Just tell us what happened."

The flood gate ruptured. "I...I don't know. Everything seemed fine. I was cutting, front to back..." He stopped, gulped, and said miserably to Dai's boots. "I should'a paid more attention. On the third pass, I looked back..." His head jerked up, small mouth open. "There...there was a black trail. I couldn't believe it at first. I jumped down..."

"You left the mower on the green?" James snapped.

Nick's eyes flew open in renewed horror. He nodded. "I touched it. It was oil! Then I jumped back on the mower, lifted the blade and got the hell outta there."

His hazel eyes locked onto Dai's face. "I'm real sorry, Mr. Deugo. I don't know what happened."

"Neither do I, but I'm bloody well going to find out," Dai said, glancing over at the Toro greens cutter mower.

"What's going to happen?" I said.

Dai ran his fingers through his hair. "It'll die in a day or two. Turn brown."

"You mean it's not ruined?" Vivian asked.

"Shouldn't be," Charlie replied, tugging his mustache. "It'll look as ugly as a bullfrog. Might play a little rough, but I should be able to set the holes to minimize any problems." Dai nodded. "Don't worry, Viv," Charlie continued. "I've seen worse. Once, in San Diego, some idiot poured gasoline all over several greens. Nobody knew it 'til the morning. What a mess! The super jumped on it real good and washed it out but the greens were badly scarred. Fortunately, it was still puttable, so we lucked out."

Our little group watched the water slowly erode the oil tracks. "I suggest you cancel this hole for today," Charlie said to Vivian. "That'll give it some time."

She shook her head, reddish hair glinting in the

sun. "Going to screw everything up. A seventeen hole Pro-Am. The amateurs are going to kill me!"

"No way," I said. "They'll be happy just to play. Trust me. I know."

"Okay," she said dejectedly. "I'd better tell some people."

"One good thing," Charlie said.

"What's that?" Vivian asked as she stepped into the golf cart.

"At least this hole's not televised."

We all nodded, thankful that the money-generating deity of the small screen would not be offended.

Satisfied the green was thoroughly soaked, Dai switched the sprinkler off. Charlie and Vivian headed back to find and inform the first group. I sidled over to the mower and watched Dai's initial inspection. The Toro driving mower had three cutting swathes, one in the middle and one on either side. A tangle of black rubber hose and aluminum pipe crawled around the chassis like adders.

"Take it to the shed," Dai commanded his assistant. "Put it on the hoist and call in all the guys. I wanna see 'em now." James jumped on the mower. It roared to a start, jerked once then trundled off. "And you," Dai said, pointing to Nick. "Stay put. When marshals come by, tell 'em what happened. Tell 'em they're to keep everyone off the green. The players are to skip this hole and move on. Then, get your ass back to the shed." The kid's head bobbed. "And get those bunkers back in shape!"

Obviously relieved to be doing something, Nick grabbed a rake and began furiously scraping the wet sand in the right sand trap.

Dai looked at me, his brow wrinkled. "Aren't you caddieing?"

I glanced at my watch. "Still got a half hour or

so before tee off."

"Wanna come?"

I nodded. We rolled in silence to the maintenance shed, located at the back of the parking lot.

The maintenance area consists of one long, low building. Ignoring his office, Dai and I walked through one of the three open double garage doors. Rows of lawn mowers of all shapes, colours and sizes, filled the centres of the other garages. Tools hung on one wall; another was covered by lockers. The mower in question dangled sadly from the hoist, private parts exposed. The young staff crowded around a picnic table. I recognized a few, nodded, and edged into a corner.

James stepped forward. "Everyone's here except for Nick. Can I speak to you for a sec?"

Dai nodded and the two superintendents disappeared into Dai's office. I watched the crew. Several looked anxious and many shifted positions. A couple of minutes later, Dai and James returned. Splotches of white marred Dai's tan. A number of eyes widened.

"You all know what happened?"

Fifteen heads nodded. A tall kid in the back said, "How?"

"Don't know exactly," Dai replied in a deliberately level voice. "That's what we're hear to find out."

"Think it was deliberate?" the same kid asked.

"No idea, but coming on the heels of the sprinkler incident..." Several grimy faces smiled. "...I'm not sure." He walked over to the mower. "James found this," he said, shoving up a thick sheath of rubber, exposing silver metal beneath.

The heads craned forward. I scrutinized the faces. "Somebody's taken a hacksaw to this pipe," Dai's voice snapped like a whip. "And I'm going find out which one of you did it."

Some looked completely bewildered. A couple of expressions reminded me of the characters I had watched waiting for Walt at the police station. The look wasn't of guilt, but of unease. A familiar face flashed an expression that took my breath away. I stared at the plump cheeks, trying to remember.

"Dai?" I said weakly. "May I talk to you?"

Dai turned, upset at the interruption. He took one look at me, grabbed my elbow and steered me into his office.

"What's the matter? You look as if you'd seen a ghost?"

"I think I have," I whispered.

Thirty-Two

"What d'you know about Sandy?"

"Sandy?" Dai asked. "Oh-you mean Graham?"

I nodded automatically.

Dai shrugged. "Seems an okay kid, hired him at the beginning of the summer. Knows a lot about pesticides. Why?"

"Pesti..." I stopped. "Graham?" An image of Sandy's pimply face leapt into my mind. We had been standing over Pitts's body. "Alexander Graham," I said slowly. "Dai! Sandy's a nickname for Alexander!"

Dai nodded. "Guess so, but what's that mean?"

"Sandy was the first one to arrive when I found Pitts. He asked who it was and when I told 'im, an odd look flashed across his face. I'd forgotten it until just a couple a minutes ago. But in there, when you said one of them had tampered with the mower, that same expression crossed his face. It was a look of guilt and fear!"

"Okay, but I'm not quite sure how..."

I told him about the names Paul Dunlop had given me for BioAction members. "It's too much of a coincidence. We got threats from BioAction...hey, what day was yesterday? The twenty-eighth, right? That's the day BioAction threatened Pitts. The sprinklers came on! And today-the sixth green! It's gotta be him!"

"The little bastard!" Dai growled. "I'll teach him to mess with my equipment." He marched to the door and flung it open. "James!" he shouted. "Get Sandy in here!"

A few seconds later, Sandy's fair head poked through the door. "Tell everyone else to beat it," Dai said, closing the door on James' astonished face.

Sandy pressed his back against the door and picked at his neck.

"Your name Alexander Graham?"

The kid nodded.

"Ever heard of BioAction?" I asked.

Panic swept across his face, but he remained silent.

"I know all 'bout you," I said. "You sent Pitts and me threatening letters. You turned the sprinklers on and you wrecked the mower!"

The kid's pale eyes rolled like a frightened horse.

"Answer her!" Dai shouted. "You did it. Didn't you?"

Sandy shook his head.

"I've spoken to Paul Dunlop, he swears BioAction had nothing to do with this."

Paul's name touched a nerve. "That guy thinks he's God," Sandy snarled. "You know what he said when I told him about the pesticides? The jerk said that he knew, but BioAction was a single issue group. Single issue group! Can you believe that crap?" He sneered at Dai. "Guys like you're pouring poison all over the country and they don't want anything ta do with it." Suddenly realizing how much he'd spoken, Sandy shut up.

"Pois...that's bull an' you know it!" Dai exploded.

Sandy flashed a smug grin. "Can't prove anything," he said, gaining confidence.

"Maybe you won't tell us, but I bet I know what will," Dai said. "Get outta my way!"

"Why?"

"I bet your locker has a thing or t..."

"Locker!" Sandy swallowed hard. "No!"

"Too late for that," Dai said, storming out into the garage. "Hang onto 'im, Riley."

I grabbed the kid's chubby forearm and shoved him forward. Dai grabbed a tire iron and strode along the bank of lockers. Smashing the lock on the one marked Graham, he tugged the door open.

"Well, well, well," Dai said and reached inside, "what have we here?" In his right hand dangled a key ring. "The missing key to the sprinkler boxes. And what else?" Dai thrust some loose papers onto the picnic table. All with BioAction letterheads.

Dai handed me the key, then shoved Sandy down beside the papers, keeping his hands on the kid's thick shoulders. "Call the police."

"Wait!" Sandy yelped.

I stopped.

The kid chewed his lower lip. "Maybe we can do a deal."

"Deal shmeal," Dai said. "We've got you cold. Give me one good reason."

The kid stopped chewing, turned to me and smiled. "Heard you're wondering about Pitts's death."

Speechless, I stared at the youth.

"What makes you think that?" Dai asked, relaxing one hand.

Sandy shrugged. "People talk. A golf course's a small place. So..." He directed watery eyes at me, "...wanna know who visited your precious brother-in-law the night he died?"

"What?" I whispered. "You saw someone?" I took a deep breath, and dragged at my thoughts 'til they slowed enough for comprehension. "If it's Karatsu, forget it. I already know."

Sandy blinked. "Who?"

I flicked a glance at Dai, then turned back. "Okay, out with it."

"Uh-huh," the kid said. "Whadda I get?"

Dai leaned forward, breathing in the kid's

space. "You get that I don't rip your face off!"

Sandy tilted back. "Not good enough," he said, wiping his lips. Dai didn't move.

"Why you..."

"Dai! Wait! I want that name. Listen, punk. Tell me the truth and..." I peeked at Dai, "...we won't press charges."

"What?" Dai snapped, eyes wide-open. "Riley, wait! This bastard should be punished."

"I agree but..." I shot Dai a pleading look. "...he knows something about that night. I must know who was there. You understand, don't you?"

The Course Superintendent's dark eyes searched my face. For a second, I felt my defenses fade and he glimpsed my soul. "No," Dai said, softly, "but go ahead."

I smiled briefly then turned to Sandy. "One other thing, you're fired as of this minute, no severance. Deal?"

Alexander Graham shoved Dai's hands away and squirmed free. "Deal."

"Who was it?"

Graham hesitated.

"Tell 'er!" Dai commanded.

"Okay, okay!" the kid said. He looked at me. "A friend of yours. Thomas Kent."

"Thomas?" I whispered. "You're sure?"

"Look, lady, I see the guy practically every day. Married to Pitts's daughter, right? On that Monday, I was mowing the sixteenth green." He tossed a look at Dai. "You can look it up in the work schedule. Anyway, I had ta take a leak. Ducked into the woods. Heard voices. So I looked up and there they were, on the balcony."

"What time?"

"'Bout 7:15."

No one spoke for a couple of heartbeats.

"Well," Sandy said, grabbing a jacket and sneakers from his locker. "Gotta go." He hotfooted out the door.

"Sandy?" I said.

He turned.

"Why'd you threaten me?"

The fat face flushed. "I...I wouldn't have hurt ya. Just wanted to scare ya. Wanted someone to notice." Then he disappeared, the sound of his workboots clattering on the asphalt.

"Thomas," I said to the mower dangling from the hoist. "Why didn't he tell me?"

As I hopped out of Dai's golf cart, Halliday was putting. The ball missed the target and rolled to a stop a couple of inches beyond. No one picked it up. I ducked under the rope, sprinted around two players chatting over a cigarette, and snatched the ball from Halliday's outstretched hand.

Under a white Stetson, her chartreuse eyes stared at me. "Nice of you to visit," my sister said, taking the ball. She turned and looked for a new hole.

My head still reeled; too much was going on to think, much less deal with our problems. "Look, I'm sorry." I lowered my voice. "It's been a kinda weird morning."

Her eyelids flickered. "Oh?"

"Long story. Something's wrong with the sixth green."

She stared.

"Yeah, the groundskeeper spilled some oil."

"So what's that got to do with you?" She stroked the ball. White dimples flashed in the sun, then disappeared into the hole. I handed her another, one of two that I'd pulled from her previous target hole.

"It's got everything to do with me," I said, my

voice rising. "This's my club. My course."

Halliday stopped in mid-swing. She stared at me for a few seconds. I noticed for the first time a deepening web of lines around her eyes. "Riley," she said, wearily. "I don't care about your club responsibilities. I care about your caddieing responsibilities, which, so far, have been piss-poor." My sister approached me. "Look, I know you weren't thrilled in the first place. I told Pitts it was a bad idea, but he insisted." Halliday pushed the hat back on her head. Her voice was hard, brittle. I didn't know if she was going to shout or to cry. She surprised me and did neither, continuing instead to spit words. "Well, he's not here any more so let's just this one time be honest. You don't want to caddie for me." She threw down her putter. A couple of players glanced our way. "That's fine. I'll get somebody else."

I couldn't believe it. After all the crap I'd been through, this was too much. I suddenly ripped loose and swore at her. "You'll what? I told Pitts I'd bloody well caddie for you, I arranged my work schedule and I'm damn well gonna do it!"

Now even the fans began to gape. The Quinn sisters fighting were far more interesting than Michelle McGann's latest hat.

Hal's mouth opened. "No," I stopped her. Taking a deep breath, I stooped to pick up the club. Get a grip, Riley! "Can't you understand? I'm not just your caddie, I work here. It's important to me."

Halliday blinked. Tears welled in her eyes.

"Halliday Quinn and the Fulsome Foursome!" a man's voice shouted from the tenth tee.

I swore. "That's us." I gave my only sister a push. "Move!"

"A little to the right," Halliday shouted from

the back of the green. It had taken a few drives, but now with our Pro-Am round nearly over, she was revelling in her role as coach and cheerleader. Sitting cross-legged on her golf bag, she cheerfully lined up Fred Willcock's 30 foot putt. "Bit more. That's it, Freddie. That's the ticket!"

We'd have to be lucky; because of foot traffic, long putts are often tougher in the afternoon. Morning's better, as it usually has no wind, dew can sometimes deaden the ball, but the mower scrapes most of it off. Fred Willcock squinted up at the flag, nodded and stroked the yellow ball. It raced up the undulating seventh green.

"Go, baby, go!" the other amateur players urged.

Pushing thoughts of Thomas Kent from my mind, I yanked up the flagstick and back tracked. It seemed miraculous, but the ball looked like it was going to drop. At the last instant, the yellow streak slid past the hole!

A sigh slipped from the gallery. Halliday groaned and fell over backwards, kicking cleated shoes up in the air. The fans laughed. Fred shuffled up the green and helped her to her feet. My sister swatted Freddie's raised palm. "Almost, Freddie, my man! What a putt!" She curtsied and Fred bowed to the circle of spectators.

Halliday's turn. I handed the putter to her. She grabbed it without meeting my eyes. I shrugged, took a couple of quick steps back. Oblivious to the throb in my wrist, I slammed the flagstick back into the hole. Today, the sisters Quinn had the synchronicity of strangers.

Hovering over her ball, Hal looked up in my direction and gestured with her thumb. See what I mean? Normally, she wouldn't have to tell me, I would know. I yanked out the bloody stick and laid it on the collar.

Halliday placed the putter near the back of the ball, lining up her right foot. In stepped the left shoe. She paused, glancing back at the hole. The individuals behind her held their breath. The putter moved and the dimpled orb rolled over grass blades.

The ball three-sixtied the hole and ricocheted free. The crowd moaned. Hal shook her head slowly, scanning the spectators. Then she flipped the putter onto her left shoulder and, with her right arm, played it as though the boron-graphite shaft were a violin.

The fans roared and began clapping in time with her strokes. Finally, one of the players putted out and our little group wedged through the crowd to the eighth hole.

Thanks be to the great putter in the sky, only two more holes to go. I felt badly for the four guys who'd each paid a thousand bucks for this once-in-a-lifetime opportunity. At least Hal was entertaining. Her play stunk and I was so immersed in mentally juggling the circumstances of Pitts's death, I didn't care. It's hard to always be into it when you play one of these Pro-Ams every week, no matter what they say, personal lives can't be put on hold during 18 holes. I didn't even bother glancing at the board. If you're not leading, who gives a shit?

I equate Pro-Ams to hockey practices and actual events to hockey games. In practice, you don't push yourself. There's no rush of adrenaline to chase the puck into the corner, but in a game you're going flat out, excited, driving hard. We might get away with apathy on the links today. Tomorrow was a whole new round.

Winning's wonderful. The adrenaline rush as

you float down eighteen is orgasmic! There's a tremendous roar when you sink the winning putt. Everybody loves you. You love you. Your bank account gets a huge feed, people want you, talk to you...it's dizzying.

Then Monday comes, and you move on to arrive at the next tournament. Everyone knows you won last week and probably won't win this week. Your euphoria hangs in 'til Tuesday's practice round.

Wednesday you go into the Pro-Am in a preferred spot with selected amateur players. Everyone loves being with you, but you're only playing so so-you keep saying to yourself, it's only a Pro-Am. Spectators whisper behind your back, how'd she win last week? Reality hits you at Thursday morning's tee off and after the first few balls, you realize you're human. Bogey number three and suddenly the crap shoot is on. You're once again one of 144. Other players' names now grace the scoreboard, but you're trying just as hard.

As our group and our train of followers marched to the next tee, I stopped and adjusted the bag's two back straps. The bloody thing gets heavy after a few holes, even when you're not carrying rain gear.

A young guy on the fourth green stroked a fifteen foot putt that curled left and dropped. He let out a whoop that startled our entourage. Heads turned, binoculars focused. When the folks realized it wasn't a pro, their interest died.

Struggling back into the bag, I caught a glimpse of the guy's balding head as he ran a victory lap around a tiny tree. Glad someone's having a good time.

We finished a crummy eight under, seven off the pace. For once, I was glad to be just the caddie. While Halliday braved the post-play interviews and photo sessions, I glanced at the tee off times posted for Round One. We were up at 12:10 p.m.. Refusing a couple of friends' invitations for dinner, I hoofed it to my car.

Thirty-Three

The thin finger rapped against the bare desk. "I don't know what you're talking about."

"Oh, yeah? Come on, Thomas. Stop lying!" I slapped the arm of my leather chair. Startled, his eyebrows grabbed at the sky. "I know you were there. Someone saw you."

The eyebrows crashed down. "Who?" Thomas whispered quickly. Then he froze, realizing he had just blown it. "Must be some mistake."

I shook my head and settled back in the leather chair. "Better talk. Me now, or Walt later."

Thomas raked back a loose lock of black hair. "Okay. Okay! So I saw the guy. We talked: I left. What's the big deal?"

"You tell me. Obviously something big enough for you to lie about."

"It was nothing, I swear!"

"Then why lie?" I leaned forward. "Something happened that night that upset Pitts. He left me a message a little after six and he sounded fine. A few hours later, he died. Drunk. I wanna know why."

"Come on, Riley! The guy was my father-in-law!" His jaw twitched. "Give me a break, will you? I don't want Juet to know."

"Know what?"

He swivelled his chair and gazed out the twelfth story window. "We argued," he said, his voice muffled.

"'Bout what?"

The chair whirled back. "What d'ya think? Juet, of course."

"Was he drinking?"

Thomas sprung up and started pacing his small office. "A little."

"Drunk?"

He stopped. "Don't think so. It was only a bit before seven."

"So what was the problem about Juet?"

Thomas shoved his hands into the pockets of his perfectly creased, grey pants. "Same old stuff. Gave her the job as his assistant, but still treated her like a kid," he mumbled.

Somehow I knew that wasn't the whole story. I took a stab. "Money?"

He nodded slowly then started pacing. "You didn't really know 'im, you know. He was a mean sonofabitch when he wanted to be."

I held my tongue and waited.

"I just needed a little more time. But no! Pitts had to go nosing around. Juet's birthday's not for a couple of months."

A tiny, high voice whispered in my ear. "Oh, one other thing. Mr. Wyndamere was looking into his daughter's trust fund. Since her husband is the trustee, I thought it a bit odd." Thank you, Mr. Samuel! I might actually go in your bank one day. "The trust fund!"

Thomas' thin face flushed.

"You were fiddling with her trust fund and Pitts found out!"

His eyes flashed defiantly. "So what of it! It'll be ours in a couple of months. Dammit! You'd think I stole the crown jewels. Pitts, he's a developer. You'd think he'd understand. I'm going to pay it back, every cent. Including interest. But no, he got crazy, started calling me names." He stopped and slumped into his chair.

"What happened?"

Thomas shook his head.

"Thomas, for god's sakes, what happened!" An appalling thought struck me. "Did you fight?

Did..did he fall?"

He looked up in horror. "No! For god's sake, Riley, you've got to believe me! I told 'im I'd get the money. Juet would never know. I left around seven-thirty and he was still alive."

"Too bad you have no witnesses. So that's why you've been so buddy-buddy with Karatsu, huh? Thinking 'bout selling your shares in Sea Blush?"

Thomas' Adam's apple moved. "Wasn't much point before..."

"Before what?"

He looked scared.

"Before Pitts died?"

He nodded. "The bastard told me he'd decide when to sell Sea Blush." Thomas' face shone with anger. "Karatsu wants controlling interest, so my shares were useless." He hesitated then looked at me defiantly. "There's nothing more."

I nodded and stood up. "Well, the police will certainly be interested in hearing this."

Thomas dropped his head into his hands and groaned. "Please, Riley. Gimme a break. It'll kill Juet." He looked up, his face bright. "Hey! I got home about quarter to eight. Juet was there. She'll tell you."

"After she hears from the police, I doubt she'll be too keen on supporting you."

"Come on! She's been hurt enough. I know it was wrong, but," his voice faltered, then twisted off his tongue as though strangled, "you don't know what it's like, marrying money." I pitied him for the first time. So young, so driven. "I wanted to impress her, show 'er that I could take care of us."

I sighed. Juet had been through hell in the last couple of weeks. Who hadn't? But I knew what it was like to lose a father. Anyway, from our brief conversation a week ago, she was ready for the truth. "Tell you what I'm going to do. You go home right now and tell Juet everything..." The skin on his face lost colour. "...*everything*, and I'll consider not telling the police. But you'd better get that trust fund paid back, or else."

"Thank you," he whispered. "I will. Every penny."

"And, Thomas? Don't underestimate Juet. She's got a lot more brains than you give her credit for."

He wanted to know more, but I left him. He'd find out soon enough.

There was one more thing to do before I went home to Sea Blush. Twenty minutes later, I was inside Pitts's condo, poking the re-dial button.

This time, the phone rang. After the second ring, I heard a whir and an answering machine kicked in.

"Hey there. I'm Joel Sanderson and you're not. Leave a message."

Joel! The last phone call Pitts Wyndamere had made was to his old partner and new enemy! Another piece clicked into place. I didn't leave a message. I planned to visit Mr. Business in person.

I tried the number identified only by initials. It must have been my lucky day 'cause after the third ring, a male voice answered with a cheery hello. I told the voice who I was and that I was looking for someone whose initials were G.T.

"'Tis I," the voice replied. "Garnet Trainor at your service, but everyone calls me GT."

"Mr. Trainor, you knew Pitts Wyndamere?"

"Of course, how is th...excuse me, but did you say knew?"

"Yes, I'm sorry to tell you, but Pitts died last week."

"Dear god in heaven! The poor man! What happened?"

"I'm an executor of his estate. May I ask how you knew him?"

"Of course. Of course. My dear, what a shock! Real estate. We had that in common. You see, I sell real estate. Which Pitts loved to buy."

"When was the last time you spoke to him?"

"Let me see, must be over three months or more. I was meaning to call him. There's a new development in Comox."

"Well, thanks, Mr. Trainor."

"GT, please! Thank you for calling, Ms. Quinn. My condolences to you and your family."

I thanked him again and hung up.

Pushing my Irish luck, I dialled the bare-naked number. A lot of ringing but no answer.

I locked up. Then, sitting in Emily, I gazed at the setting sun and pondered my progress. I now knew that at least two people had seen Pitts on the night he died-Karatsu and Thomas, and that Joel had spoken to him on the phone. Add that to knowing that he was having an affair with Linda Robinson. The BioAction riddle was solved, but the bloody envelope, letters and photographs were still missing.

Damn! I hit the steering wheel. I had forgotten to ask Thomas about the envelope!

Thirty-Four

"So, that's it?" I asked, hoisting my feet up on my desk. "He's widowed, has two teenaged kids and is a respected business man? Sure you didn't investigate Ben Cartwright?"

"Very funny, Riley," Michael replied humourlessly. "*Bonanza's* been off the air for ages. Didn't he have three sons?"

"That's not the point."

"Well, what is the point? I told you what I found about Kim Karatsu and you don't believe it."

My feet slammed to the floor. "The guy's a sleeze, and you know it! Just looking at him gives me the heebie jeebies." I shuddered. "Look, you've got to do better or Halliday'll sell 'im Sea Blush."

"What do you suggest?" Michael asked in his officious courtroom voice. I felt like the old judge he used to call 'that fatuous ass'. "That I manufacture a minor business indiscretion?"

With an effort, I ignored his tone and doubled back. "If you want to be the one responsible for Hal making the biggest mistake of her life, then so be it." Then, having buried the arrow, I changed subjects to let the wound fester. "Found anything missing from Pitts's estate yet?"

"What? Uh, no. Everything seems to be accounted for." He paused for a moment. Obviously the arrow had found its mark, because he asked casually, "How is your sister, anyway?"

"Fine. So, by the way, is her caddie. Nice of you to ask."

He ignored my dig. "She seems awfully worried. Think she'll win?"

"Haven't a clue. The LPGA isn't like pro tennis, you know. The top five don't dominate. In golf, you're considered great if you win 10 percent of the time." I paused, realizing something. "How'd you know she's worried?" I gripped the receiver as though it would fall. "You've talked to her?"

"Well, yes, as a matter of fact."

"Oh, really?" I asked, quickly losing ground. "And what did the great Halliday Quinn have to say?"

"Don't talk about her like that!" Michael snapped. I waited, glancing at my white knuckles. "She...she's preoccupied. Under a lot of pressure."

I couldn't accept what I was hearing. I was losing Michael to Halliday. "My heart bleeds." I exhaled heavily. "She's still playing, that's the main thing."

"Still blame her, don't you?"

His voice oozed with pity. When I could breath again, I gasped, "I don't want to talk about it!"

"Oh, no you don't. You make a crack like that and think you can get away with it? No more, Riley Quinn. It's high time you dealt with reality."

"Oh? Pray tell," I spit out the words through clenched teeth, "what's reality?"

"You know damned well! For god's sake, Riley! I don't know you any more." *No?* I thought. *Likewise, Mister!* "One of the things I cared most about you was your kindness. Anyway, why shouldn't I talk to her? You'd never tell me about her, yet you've deliberately made your sister suffer for something that wasn't her fault!"

"Is that what she said?" I was shouting now, oblivious to the Pro Shop goings on on the other side of my office wall. "She said it wasn't her fault?"

"Well...she, she wouldn't say anything. Told me to ask you."

That threw me. "She said that?"

"Yes, but I got enough out of her to know. No way she could have anticipated that guy running a red light."

My ears roared as the glistening Quebec road filled my mind. We were laughing, singing along with some country and western, she-broke-my-heart-so-now-I'm-yours, whine. The Buick, given to Hal for the week by a grateful sponsor, hummed under her control, a little fast, maybe, for a wet, Friday night. Neither of us gave it a thought.

My sister's always loved two things in life, golf and speed. The colour of the traffic lights spilled across the highway, but even now I refuse to look closely enough to see whether the one in our direction was red or green. The last image I remember is Hal's profile, half lit by the lights of the oncoming traffic.

Eons later, somebody in a Holted oilskin smashed the driver's window and dragged us both free. A month passed before Walt, at my insistence, reluctantly showed me a facsimile copy of the police file photo; the Buick's passenger door touched the rearview mirror, the nose of the half ton nestled on my seat.

I still have the score sheet for Saturday, August 14. After three rounds in the prestigious duMaurier Ltd. Classic, played that year at the Montreal Golf and Country Club, the flowing calligraphy-a tradition since 1898-read: *H. Quinn-total 208*, and directly below, *R. Quinn-total 204*. In my final tournament, one of only four LPGA majors, I had led the field going into the fourth and final round.

"Riley? You still there?"

"Huh?" I blinked and again saw the walls of my office. "I've gotta go."

Despite his protestations, I gently put down the receiver. Ignoring the hot tears staining my cheeks, I concentrated on breathing and flexing my wrist.

"Hear 'bout Trish Johnson?" Goodie asked.

I pulled Halliday's nine iron from the water bucket. Scrubbing its face, I said, "No."

"Poor thing. Had ta withdraw this morn." Goodie shoved a seven into the water.

"Sick?"

"As a dog! Had to tee off first, can you believe it? Looked like a deer caught in headlights, but she managed ta drive." She raked pudgy fingers through spiky brown hair. "Pretty sad when a gal has to drag herself outta bed so that she can get credit for being in the tournie."

Shaking our heads, we strolled back to the driving line. It was the first round of the Sea Blush Classic, I was so hyped, my running shoes barely touched the grass.

"I know it sounds cruel, but she needs fifteen tournaments to stay on the Tour. Believe me, it's hell having to re-qualify."

Goodie nodded.

Halliday, dressed in cream shorts and an electric blue golf shirt, was already swinging her five iron. She glanced back at us from under a Toronto Blue Jays ball cap and gave Goodie a slight smile.

Goodie wished us luck, patted me on the shoulder then ambled down the line of swinging players. I glanced to make sure Halliday had enough golf balls at her feet then grabbed the seven iron that she had laid against her bag. I'd already counted the clubs to make sure we carried the requisite 14, so I twisted the wet end of a mid-size white towel over the grip. A couple of seconds later, I flipped the towel to the dry end and began rubbing. In my playing days, I'd watched caddies dry club grips so violently, I was certain I smelled burning rubber.

Halliday's spot today was near the middle of the driving range; a line of women wielding golf clubs stretched out on either side. Immediately behind the players, caddies stood beside huge golf bags, cleaning clubs and eyeing their employer. Though players and caddies joked, this was no practice or Pro-Am day; the hot air tingled with excited chatter.

Twenty-five feet behind a waist-high stretch of yellow twine, a couple of hundred aficionados strained to see the classic and not-so classic swings.

About four players down from us, a couple of dozen fans peered at Patty Sheehan, oohing and aahing at her every stroke.

"Would you look at that!" a man's incredulous voice said. "Five in a row, right down the middle."

I looked over, caught Patty's eye and grinned. She waved then handed her club to her caddie.

"Tremendous skill level these players possess!" the same voice said.

"Unbelievable," another voice, this time female, piped in.

I shoved the seven back in the bag and started on the fiver.

"These gals play a human game, somethin' you can relate to. In the men's show, they hit a driver 350 yards. I mean, who can relate to that?"

"Not me, that's for sure."

Me neither, I thought, drying the grip. Strength seems to be everything on the men's tour. Looking like a country squire in her trademark plus-fours, knickers and long socks, Patty strutted off. Her fans followed like a gaggle of shy geese. I wished her luck, but not too much. Like Halliday, she too needed only one more win to be a Hall of Famer.

Giving myself a wee treat, I focused on Sam Brennan warming-up. Despite being the most recent member inducted into the LPGA Hall of Fame, Sam's piercing blue eyes still stare each and every ball down with a rookie's intensity. Her golfing style echoes her demeanour: unquestioned authority. Once, when I asked her what made her successful, she'd tugged her visor deeper over short cinnamon-and-salt hair and replied, "I don't really consider myself having any weak points. I don't do a lot of things perfectly or outstandingly." She chewed her ubiquitous piece of gum, then flashed a smile, adding, "I think overall I do a lot of things right."

I watched Sam's short, cocked backswing and thought about the 30 times her mother had danced a jig to celebrate her daughter's wins. Wish my mother had been alive for any of my three.

I let my eyes wander and spotted Cherie, Lori West's caddie. Her tanned, young brow was bunched and she impatiently tapped the side of her golf bag. I sidled over.

"Hey, Cher. Something wrong?"

"Yeah, we're off at 11:50 and no sign of Lori." Her dark eyes searched the crowd. "Don't know how she does it."

"Does what?"

"Gets lost in the locker room." She sighed and began pulling on a pocket zipper. "Sometimes I think it's a maze or somethin'."

I laughed, wished her luck and headed back to Halliday.

"Got the tees?"

I rolled my eyes, shoved my hand into my left pocket and pulled out a fistful of extra-long, blue tees.

"Good," Hal said, deliberately taking off her watch and all rings except the emerald chunk that Pitts had given her. She placed them into my outstretched palm and watched intently as I stored them in a small drawstring pouch and shoved it in the junk drawer.

"Got enough dimes?"

Hal nodded.

"Right decade?"

"'Sixties.'"

I never understood this superstitious stuff. Yet Hal's not in the minority; golfers-in fact, many athletes-garnish their sporting lives with an inexhaustible array of charms, incantations and habits. A hoard of LPGAer's dress in certain colours or have favourite ball markers, such as pennies or dimes. One gal, if she birdies a hole early on, will always walk in the same direction to the next hole for the rest of the week. Some will never use a discarded tee, claiming that, if it was thrown away, it must have been due to a bad shot.

All our lucky talismans in place, I hoisted her bag onto my left shoulder. "After you," I said, and watched her wade through a thickening of fans, stopping every few feet to scribble an autograph. Most knew she was Canadian, many commented positively about the Maple Leaf emblazoned on her bag.

I once saw an interview with one of our Canadian guys on the men's tour. They asked him the question they ask all of us Canucks; What's it like being a Canadian? The twit's reply was a shock. He said he was tired of people coming up to him at tournaments and saying, 'I'm Canadian. Go Canada.' He said, "I'm out there, doing my job. I'm a professional golfer."

Well I think that stinks, and if I ever see the jerk again I'm going to tell him. There aren't many of us Canadians period, and not many are professional golfers. Grow up, bud. As my Dad taught us, every Canadian outside the country is an ambassador.

The crowd parted for me like the Red Sea and I trudged alone up the incline to the tenth tee. I used to love signing autographs, talk about satiating one's vanity! But when you lug a bag, I realized, no one pays attention to your face, only the name safety-pinned to the back of your caddie vest.

Thirty-Five

12:05 p.m., Thursday, July 30

"Brand new on the bag, huh?" Alison Weld's caddie asked me.

Standing off to his right, the small, fair-haired player from Queensland grinned.

"You're the one who's new," I replied, staring at the middle-aged man so thin, he'd probably fit in the golf bag he had slung over his shoulder.

"Don't worry 'bout her, Jim," Ali said. "She used to play."

Jim's cheeks, pitted by acne and alcohol, collapsed. "No shit! 'Pologies, ma'am."

"Accepted. And you?"

His thin lips tightened then he spat. "The Show."

The men's tour. Not too surprising, I thought, and winked at Alison. "What d'you think about the women?"

The guy spat again, a long, black stream. I had to restrain myself from backing off. "Not bad. Least the broads ask ya what ya think, let ya pull clubs. In The Show, we're just bag-totters." He showed yellow-stained teeth. "I like to be involved."

"Uh-huh," I said, scanning for Halliday.

Due to the number of players in preliminary rounds, you can either start on Number 1 or Number 10 on the first round; then start on the opposite on the second. Those teeing off from 10 will flop over after the eighteenth hole and finish their day with the front 9. After Friday night's cut, the surviving players tackle the course in order for the final two days.

Hal, along with Donna Gormley, was still inside the white starter's tent. The rectangular area around the tenth tee was lined with spectators, held back both by some of the 10 miles of rope strung by Tournament Services Operations and by five volunteer marshals. In the back corner, the standard bearer and scorer assigned to our threesome shuffled excitedly. I stood at the side with the other caddies, feeling the tingle of adrenaline tickle my toes.

Many players feel that starting on Number 10's an advantage. When the architect sets up the course, the first and tenth holes are usually easy par fours or fives, all the designer wants to do is get the players away from the clubhouse. Numbers 9 and 18 head back to the clubhouse.

The fact that the tenth will be used as a crossover hole in tournaments isn't generally considered in course development. Now, Tour players love par fives 'cause they can more easily birdie a par five than a four or three. Pitts and I, however, had anticipated crossovers so Sea Blush's tenth is a scanty par four with gaping bunker protection.

Hal and Donna ducked out of the tent. Murmurs of "That's Halliday Quinn," floated across the tee. I stepped over and handed Hal her ball, a Wilson 4, on which I had printed her initials with a blue marker. She gave me an apple, a couple of bananas and a plastic bottle of water. While I stuffed them into her bag, the three players conferred, discussing the ball brand and number that they were playing. Everyone was itchin' to be off on the first round of the Sea Blush Classic.

"Ladies and gentlemen," the starting marshal shouted and held up his white pith helmet. The other marshals followed suit. "From Witchita, Kansas; winner of one LPGA event, joined the Tour in 1987, Donna Gormley!"

Donna smiled and waved a slender arm. No one would guess from the megawatt smile that this was one of the Tour's holy terrors. With The Volcano, as we called her, you never knew, an explosion was always rumbling below the surface.

Several hands clapped. Then, with smooth, quick motions, Donna creamed her ball. It cracked off the tee and howled into the wind, bouncing past a huge bunker on the right side of the fairway. The fans applauded approvingly.

"Next, from Cains, Australia, joined the Tour in 1990, Alison Weld!"

Little Ali drove her ball a bit left of the fairway. Again, polite applause.

Hal stepped up and gazed down the fairway for a couple of seconds. The tenth's flat fairway curves left. Planning to fade the ball, Halliday shoved her blue tee into the grass on the right side of the tee box. Teeing off, you're always looking to place the ball in the spot with the largest margin of error.

"Finally, from Nanoose Bay, British Columbia," wild applause, "the winner of twenty-nine LPGA titles, including The Dinah Shore and The U.S. Open, riding a recent win at the Phar-Mor in Youngstown..." Cheers and whistles. "...and now only one win away from the Hall of Fame..." A tremendous roar. "Ladies and gentlemen, our very own, *Hal-Li-Day Quinn!*"

The applause was deafening. Even Donna and Alison clapped from the side, both grinning from ear to ear. Tears welled in Hal's eyes as she turned and waved. A shot of envy smacked me. I avoided my sister's quick glance by dropping my head and fumbling with my cranberry-coloured caddie's vest.

After a minute, Hal wiped her eyes and doffed her Jays' cap. The cheers slowed unevenly. She stood motionless over the ball and regained her composure. A silver arc shimmered, the ball whumped and soared into a sky pockmarked by clouds.

The gallery roared. Hal grabbed her tee and tossed it to a young fan nearby. The teenager held it tightly, puppy dog eyes glowing. Then, with a wave, Halliday strode down the courtesy cut. Donna, Ali and their caddies followed. The crowd rushed down the fairway, outside the yellow ropes. I yanked up the bag and hustled after the standard bearers. The black and white placard, hoisted proudly by the taller of the two, listed the players' last names and scores. As we had just started the tournament, a blue zero followed all three black-lettered surnames. After Hal's, and every other Canadian entered, was a tiny red maple leaf. Pitts's idea, and a nice touch. As my Dad would say, we were off like a bride's pyjamas.

A huge stand of arbutus shaded the right side of the gently curved fairway. On the left, small groupings of trees leaned inward, as though watching. Hal's ball had landed just beyond the first fir tree, at about 235 yards. Donna's shot was a good 15 yards further; Alison's snuggled just behind Hal's.

I found the nearest sprinkler head, number 127. The Book told me that this head was 111 yards to the front of the green. I marched off three strides from Hal's ball back to number 127. Since my stride equates to about a yard, I subtracted three from 111. I jotted down 108 yards to the front of the green. Hal checked the hole sheet.

"15 front, five left," she said.

"Right." So today's pin was 15 yards from the front and five yards in from the left. 15 added to 108 gave us 123 yards to the hole.

I pulled a club. "123; an eight'll do it."

Pea soup coloured eyes on the target, Hal merely nodded and held out her hand. I slapped the iron home as though handing a scalpel to a surgeon.

Ali was ready to swing so Hal and I moved a little to the left. I pulled a bit of grass and watched it swirl left down to the turf while Ali finessed an iron.

Halliday headed for her ball. Some players, like the very successful Maddie Woodlie, have their caddie stand behind them and help line up their shots. Not my sister. Hal plays from the soul and instinctively found her position. She swung, the ball arched high and dropped onto the left collar. A few spectators who hadn't already hustled down to the green applauded.

Donna's turn. The kid from Kansas used a wedge and pitched onto the green.

Hundreds of people surrounded the peanut-shaped green. Many, judging from their chairs and coolers, would obviously spend the day watching iron shots drop from the sky. The players treaded carefully, replacing their balls with markers. Halliday handed me hers for a wipe. Furthest away from the hole, she was up first. She walked from the left collar down the gently sloping green and strode beyond the hole. 30 feet was long enough, but coupled with the higher collar grass, her putt would be tricky, especially as inertia would tug the ball toward the front. The pink flag flapped lazily, its stick throwing a smudge of shadow just left of the hole.

I pulled the flag free and backed off the green. The other players and caddies already stood quietly along the right bunker. I raised my arm and the hole marshals lifted their hats. The crowd was silent.

Hal stroked the ball firmly. It fought gravity, holding its line straight to the pin. I leaned forward. The dimples bopped the back of the newly-painted cup and hopped left. The spectators let out a choked sigh. Hal grinned ruefully, nodded at the other players and putted out. Par.

She joined me, unzipped a banana and munched.

Ali, one of a quartet of Aussies on the Tour, lucked out with a fried egg in the right bunker. Cheerfully, she sank into the trap and carefully wedged her feet. With a long, upright swing, the Queenslander slid her sand wedge under the ball. It lobbed onto the green on a sand pillow and dashed towards the flag, rolling to a stop some eight feet past the pin. Polite applause.

Donna stroked a 25-foot uphill shot that curved right at the last minute. She frowned, kicked at the grass, then putted out for par.

Ali wasn't as fortunate, coming up short on her fourth stroke. She dropped the ball for a one over bogey.

The standard bearer's portable scoreboard read: Gormley-0; Weld-1 (in blue to denote over par), and Quinn-0.

On the short, claustrophobic eleventh hole, Halliday continued to putt well and finished with a birdie. Ali struggled with her irons but, along with Donna, managed a par.

Though we weren't really speaking to one another, Hal and I communicated as necessary, and Halliday parred the notorious number twelve. Ali's troubles continued, handing her a second bogey. Donna fought the tight fairway and grabbed a par.

Bolstered by a vocal crowd on thirteen, Hal outdid herself, reaching the green in two. Both she and Ali grabbed one-under-par birdies. Donna angrily settled for a par, after making a spectacular iron shot to dodge around the huge tree shading the three-quarter mark of the left fairway. The fans were still humming as we strode off to the second par five in a row.

The fourteenth's narrow green yielded three pars. The elder Quinn hung onto two under as we crunched along the cinder track to the fifteenth. She finished off the apple and made a basketball shot into the large garbage can.

Hal led off the short, par three with a five iron. Her shot soared above the tree-edged fairway and dropped right, 20 feet from the flag, then hopped back a couple of yards. The crowd nestled around the sloping green groaned.

As he had done for most holes on the first round, Charlie Gregg had placed the flagstick at the back of the green, near the exit gate. On the fifteenth, this meant 25 yards back and 15 left. With 144 golfers, an equal number of caddies, and bunches of officials trekking through the gate on the first day, the LPGA likes to get that hole location out of the way.

Donna swung toward the distant flag. The ball spun skyward, curved right and landed with an explosion in the huge, triangular bunker on the right. Seething, The Volcano threw the five iron against her blue and white bag and stalked off to the portable toilet. The fans clucked disapprovingly.

Halliday and I exchanged a glance. She shook her dark pony tail and checked her scorecard. During an event, each player keeps their own, unofficial score and tallies the official one for another. The scorecard, approximately 11" by 4", has room for signatures and two hole-by-hole score totals. Hal kept her score on the top one and Donna's on the main one. At round's end, Hal would tear her score off and align the strip with the card maintained by Ali. Though each player's score is kept by another, it is each individual's responsibility to ensure her score is accurate.

Ali's tee shot swung left and died 20 yards in front of the pin.

We marched down the wooded fairway, sharing a swig of water. The tree shadows were just beginning to grow.

I glanced up at the large scoreboard. As the Classic was inaugural, no former champion's name graced the white surface. Instead, as suggested by Pitts, the surnames of the top two Canadian money earners headed the list: H. Quinn and Nora Ray. Like on the smaller, portable scoreboards, a maple leaf followed their names.

There's room for 10 names; the last eight spots were filled by the top finishers of the morning round. I whistled. Betsy Flynn was hot! First round four-under-par 67. Lorenzo, Woodlie and my friend Caroline Robbin lagged one and two strokes behind respectively. Halliday searched the board for a couple of minutes. Neither of us said a word. At two under, we were two off the pace. But a lot can happen during 14 holes of play.

Hal and I examined the slim green, carefully noting the downward slope from back to front. Halliday's face slipped quickly into a mask of deliberation. The next three holes were tough, but a stroke gained here would put her alongside Robbin and the others tied for third.

Muttering quietly, Donna trudged down into the bunker. Her caddie stood by the flag and waited. Sand erupted. The ball popped free and chugged up the green. This morning, the shot might have been perfect, but now, nearing two o'clock on a hot afternoon, the steady sunshine had beaten the turf. Donna's ball rolled past the hole and dribbled onto the back collar. I held my breath.

The Volcano released a vocal warning burst. Her caddie dashed over and whispered calming words. Donna wasn't having any of it. She stormed out of the trap, kicking sand with each stride. The caddie stared after her hopelessly, then grabbed the rake and expertly resurfaced the bunker.

Ali began pacing, studying the green. Her 60 foot putt would mount a slight incline. Nothing to do but go for it. Ali's putter cracked the ball. It hopped and raced up the slope, fading within a couple of yards of the pin. The crowd cheered. The young Aussie ran her fingers through tousled sun-bleached hair and smiled shyly.

After Ali had marked and removed her ball, I took my position at the flag, careful to stand on the same side as its shadow, and sang across to Halliday, "Come on! You can do it." Hal took one last glance at the flag, I yanked it free and she putted. The ball trickled across 25 feet and seemed to rest on the lip of the cup. The spectators gasped and I held back a ferocious urge to stamp my foot. The ball tumbled and dropped from sight.

I let out a whoop which was immediately drowned by the roaring crowd. Hal leapt in the air, fist punching the sky. Birdie! Three under! She scooted across, scooped up the ball and tossed it to me.

Donna two-putted and stormed out the gate.

Ali quietly putted for a par.

The final three holes of the back nine are par fours. Though Halliday continued to strike the ball well, she misjudged the green on 17. Bogey.

We made the crossover to the front nine holes at two under. Ali found her rhythm and parred all three while Donna, erratic mood getting blacker, bogeyed twice.

Thirty-Six

Pitts liked to give the average golfer a jolt, so he had requested a long par five for Sea Blush's opening hole. Of course, that made it birdie heaven for the Tour's long hitters. Donna used her advantage and gained a stroke on Hal and Ali, both hanging on for pars.

Number two's par four is short and bald, but oh-so-mean. Beyond the raised tee, the fat fairway juts left around water, dips down then up onto a green practically blanketed by sand. The tee drops quickly, revealing a serpent stream that twists between the second and third fairways before trickling into the huge, bow-tie-shaped pond that dissects the middle of the third.

"Go for the outside elbow, 'bout 245. That's the shot."

Her last birdie had enthused Donna and she blasted her drive. The ball screamed into the sky, caught wind and hooked. The crowd moaned as the white dot hit blue. Donna howled and slammed her driver into the tee. I looked around for a Tour Official. The Volcano was lucky. When you need em, the little devils were never there, but man, start playing too slowly and their golf cart would suddenly sneak out from the trees.

Hal plucked a scruff of grass and let it fall. The blades swirled and scattered. I stared down the fairway at the water fountain. Droplets winked rainbows in the spray's mist. I licked my finger and stuck it in the air. The wind seemed to kiss it all over. She grimaced. "Wind's weird. Don't know 'bout 245."

She glanced at The Book and pointed to sprinkler head number 158. "That's 220. Better chance."

Everything a caddie says must be positive, so I bit hard and said, "You're striking well. Go for it."

"Okay," she said, taking the driver.

Hal launched a controlled fade. The ball curved gently from left to right and hopped, skipped and jumped its way to the elbow. She shook her head. About 10 yards short, but an excellent second shot position.

Ali's drive settled safely back of the crook and we trooped over the little bridge in a clatter of golf shoe spikes. A few seconds later, the security volunteer dropped the rope and hundreds of fans scrambled across and dashed ahead to the green.

While Ali set up, I dropped the bag and shrugged out of the caddie vest. The breeze was hot against my drenched back. Alison drilled a five iron that leap-frogged the trees but bounced off the edge of the left bunker and careened into a startled crowd.

I hustled into the vest and paced off the distance from Hal's Wilson to sprinkler 163. I was adding the 15 yards to the pin from the hole sheet, when she spoke softly.

"Ril?"

"Un-huh."

"Thanks for being here."

I stared at my sister for a couple of breaths. The sun skittered off her hair in reddish lightning bolts. Her eyes were narrowed, a lioness alert for game. I liked that look, it was the Halliday of my youth, confident and determined.

I smiled. "No problem."

"'Bout 160?" Hal asked, ball cap in her hand.

I nodded. "Seven?"

"Yup." Hal's second shot stayed right and collapsed in the right bunker.

"Shiit!" she whispered and blindly handed me

the club.

We trudged up the fairway, a ripple of applause our harbinger. Since the second and third fairways were only 30 yards apart, the spectators trotted from one to the next, especially when they spied a maple leaf.

By the time we arrived, an LPGA official was conferring with Donna. She nodded slowly, her thin face dark. Nobody likes to take a stroke. Under the official's watchful eye, she made a drop behind the hazard. I was impressed at how well she held back an explosion. Using a pitching wedge, Donna poked the ball. It sailed over the water and bunker and onto the left green. The ball sauntered slowly and died 20 yards back of the hole. Clapping was scarce as she marked her ball.

The official jumped back in her cart and rolled off quietly.

The yellow rope blocking deep left had been dropped and Ali stood beyond the green, jockeying for position among a curious throng. The marshal pushed the fans back, demanded silence and Ali chipped onto the turf to within 18 feet. More applause. Ali tossed her ball to Jim for a wipe.

Hal asked for the sand wedge and slid down into the bunker. Her view of the flag was obstructed by the trap's high edge and the sloping green, so she clambered out and back in, confirming distance. The wedge arched, the ball burst into view and plopped onto the green. It continued to roll downhill, banking hard left until, to the crowd's amazement, it stopped four feet from the hole. Betsy Flynn, look out, the fight was on! The spectators erupted. Hal dropped the dime. With a gigantic grin, she handed me the ball.

Donna stormed up and back. Finally, with her caddie's encouragement, she putted. The ball charged down the green, hip-hopped over the hole and died. The Volcano erupted, throwing the putter at her caddie. Shocked, the fans rocked back on their heels.

Donna was so incensed that she almost stepped in Ali's putting line, only a yelp from her shaking caddie just saved her. She wrenched the club from the poor guy and putted out. Then she marched out the gate, cleats kicking up turf. The scorer removed the little blue number two beside Gormley and slid in a blue three.

"For crying out loud!" Halliday said. "This crap's gotta stop."

"I know, but there's nothing you can do about it." I had to stop this quick or she was liable to get all tangled up. "You've got to keep playing your own game. Don't let her get to you. Come on, now, focus!"

"You're right. You're right," she said, taking deep breaths.

Even Ali's blue eyes were angry, but she made the putt and hung onto her score of one over.

Hal putted out for par. We strolled off to the third. The electrified crowd scrambled to keep up. First they had been following a Canadian star, now they had lucked into watching a player having a tantrum. In a game where calm demeanour and fair play is commonplace, it was a great break!

Our old cadence eased into life, ebbing and flowing like a tide. Halliday started talking, just course chit chat at first. I could see in her eyes that she was feeling me out, reaching then retreating.

The only way I could acquiesce was through golf, so I began chatting, urging her on.

All went well during the third and fourth holes. We grabbed par, just missing a birdie on four.

But after a mis-hit drive from the fifth tee

bounded into the rough, Hal began to lose ground. Boxed in by trees, she had no choice but to chip the ball with a sand wedge. Her backswing wasn't long enough but she kept the clubface to the sky and the ball burst free and found fairway. Not enough umph. I was afraid we were going to lose a stroke. It's that simple. One mistake, you start dwelling. It becomes two, maybe three and the poise slips away like sand through fingers. I kept the positive vibes humming.

"Concentrate, Hal. Just stay in the present. Think, Hal. Think *present!*" Golf's tough. There's too much time to reflect out there, too much opportunity to harp. Other sports are pure reaction, no time for thought, just rote muscle movements.

"I can't," she said in obvious despair.

"What d'you mean, can't?"

She shook her head and stalked out to the fairway. Ali and Donna were waiting at the green, having made excellent second shots.

I checked a sprinkler. We were still 230 yards from the front.

"Gonna have to drive it."

Suddenly, she turned on me, her eyes filled with tears. "Don't you think I know that!"

Shocked, I just stared.

Suddenly, her face crumpled. "You...you've got to tell me. I can't go on." Before I could answer, she blurted, "Pitts killed himself because of me, didn't he? *Didn't he*?!"

"Hal," I said, glancing around. "This isn't the plac..."

"I don't give a damn 'bout the place," she shouted. "I need to know, Riley, before I go crazy."

It could have been the searing sun on my neck or the hunger in my stomach but, truth be known, it was the rage ticking away in my head.

Talk about a volcano! Throwing down the bag, I locked eyes with Halliday and let the anger roar from my mind. "I can't believe you're asking me this! Whaddyawant? Absolution? Well, I can't give it. D'you hear me?! For God's sake, you know he was devastated when you left. He begged you to come back but you wouldn't. You wouldn't and now he's dead."

Tears glistened off her cheeks but I kept on, voice raspier than normal. "He loved you, Hal. You loved him. How could you treat him like crap?"

"Love?" she asked, wiping her eyes. She drew a breath and pulled her shoulders back. "What d'you know about love? You still believe Michael cares for you." She grabbed the driver, barely looked at the ball and swung viciously. I hadn't moved.

We walked mechanically up the fairway, a polite distance apart. From that moment on, I contributed nothing, save lugging the bag. By request, Hal did all yardages, pulled all clubs and played brilliantly. Her shots were aggressive, daring, successful. The crowds increased, numbering over 500 by the ninth green.

Without another word, the sisters Quinn finished the preliminary round at five under. Donna fought her temper and the spectators and lost, slipping to four over. Little Ali chugged along at one over par.

A local camera crew snagged Halliday as we exited the green. Normally, all media interviews are held in the Media Tent, but somehow this crew had gotten free. Under the shade of a huge Douglas fir, she impatiently answered their questions, cheeks and eyes burning.

"It was one of those days. No matter what I had in my hand, it was going to the hole."

"How'd you find the greens? You're the only

player in the afternoon to score well."

"Yeah. The greens got a little rough and hard, and the wind was inconsistent, but I was striking the ball real well off the tees, so I didn't have too many long putts. One way or another, the ball rolled real good. It's funny, the course seemed to play shorter than it is."

"As we know, your sister Riley Quinn is the club pro 'round here. What do you think about her course?"

Hal glanced at me. "It's good-I'm going to have to get used to hitting the three wood. There're a few holes out there where the landing area's pretty narrow for a driver."

As I walked away, a volunteer wedged in Halliday's final tally on the huge scoreboard. Flynn, Lorenzo and Robbin now trailed. Wyatt had sneaked onto the board. But Hal's red five was the best of the day.

Thirty-Seven

Goodie was sitting, head bowed, on her player's bag. I stopped for a moment, dropped Hal's bag and ducked under the rope.

"Hey, you okay?"

She looked up at me, eyes shielded by mirrored sunglasses. She shook her rooster-crowned head and smiled sadly. "Lynn's upset."

"Didn't play well?"

"That's just it!" The sun glanced off the glasses in purple jolts. "We were doin' real well, two under at 17. Then, I dunno, something happened and she bogeyed the last two to finish even. I wasn't worried. For Lynn, that's not too bad."

I nodded. MacGregor was a rookie.

"But she, like..." Goodie snapped her fingers, "yelled at me. Said players were saying that 15 under was gonna win. Some jerk told 'er you had to shoot two under to be even thinkin' about scaring the cut. Man! She hucked the putter at me and stormed off." She paused and rehung her head. "Damn," my old caddie whispered, "was never like this with you."

I grabbed her by the shoulders and yanked her head up. "Don't take it personally. You know how players get, gotta blame somebody else for their mistakes. Why, I betcha she's sitting in the locker room feeling pretty bad."

The glasses flickered. "Think so?"

"Definitely. Give 'er some time. She'll calm down."

Goodie sighed and slid off the bag. "Thanks," she said, standing. She pulled a pack of gum out of her pants and offered me a piece. Chewing vigorously, she asked, "Hey, how'd you guys do? Saw you on the board at 14: two under."

I stuffed the gum in my mouth. "Finished at five."

"Under?"

I nodded.

Goodie blew a pink bubble and let it burst. "Wow!"

"Do me a favour?"

"Anything."

"Hal'll be along any minute. She's being interviewed. Could you watch the bag and tell 'er I had to go? That I'll see her at home?"

The gum snapped. "Sure thing."

"Envelope? What envelope?"

"It should've been in Pitts's condo the day he died. Yet when we looked, it wasn't there."

"How do you know it was there in the first place?" Thomas asked.

"'Cause he took it home from the bank the afternoon he died. The manager remembered giving it to him to hold some papers. We haven't found them or the envelope."

I leaned forward in the leather chair. "Think! Did you see a grey envelope, 'bout legal size when you visited Pitts?"

Thomas screwed his eyes. They popped open. "What's this all about? You accusing me of stealing?"

I sighed. "I'm not accusing you of anything. I'm just asking. Are you going to help me or not?"

"Okay, okay!" He paused for a second. "Come to think of it...there was something on his desk."

"The roll-top?"

He nodded. "I probably wouldn't have noticed at all, 'cept when I came in, he shoved some stuff into it."

"What stuff?"

"Don't know," his smooth brow wrinkled, "papers, but something else."

I waited.

"Something shiny." He snapped his fingers. "Photos!" he said proudly. I nearly levitated from the chair. "Black and white photos!"

"You're sure?!"

"'Course I'm sure! I can see 'em now,-" He cocked his head to the left. "Kids, Oriental kids, I think. I only saw 'em for a couple of seconds, but yeah, they were photos, all right."

Well, I'll be damned! Another question solved, Thomas Kent had unearthed Kim Karatsu's bloody photographs.

I fought the excitement in my voice. "Anything else?" I asked. If my voice cracked more than normal, Thomas didn't seem to notice.

"Couple of papers, maybe. That was it."

I jumped up and pumped Thomas' thin hand. "By the way, how'd Juet take it?"

Thomas' eyes shied from mine.

I dropped his hand. "You haven't told her?!"

His narrow face drained of colour. "I was hoping..."

"Look, I appreciate the help you've given me, but you've got to talk to her. I'll give you another chance, but if you haven't done it by Saturday, I will."

As I drove to Joel's home in Qualicum Beach, a tiny sea-side community about 11 kilometres from Parksville and Thomas' office, I realized that I still didn't know where the envelope was, only some of what was in it. Could I trust Thomas' story? I only had his word that Pitts wasn't drunk, that he didn't take the envelope, and that Pitts was alive when he left. Why would he want Pitts dead? That was easy: money. With Pitts gone, Thomas might be able to sell his shares in Sea Blush and repay Juet's trust fund without her ever knowing he'd played with it. Was it enough to lie for? I feared it might just be.

The sun, a florescent orange ball, peeked out from behind trees and low clouds. Lasqueti Island hovered over my right shoulder, surrounded by choppy grey water. I slowed around a bend to avoid an elderly man and two small children sauntering along the shoulder. Their bronzed faces flashed up at me and I gave them a wave. Two pudgy palms fluttered at me while the old man held them close, grinning toothlessly.

Must be fun to have grandparents. I never knew mine, my mother's parents died in Europe and my father's in Florida before I was born. As kids, Halliday and SinJin had seen the Floridian grandparents a couple of times. They had told me about an old white house surrounded by orange trees. SinJin said you could smell the oranges, even in bed.

Suddenly Michael's voice entered my head. "...widowed, two teenaged kids, respected business man."

I drummed my fingers on the steering wheel. Something was wrong with that statement. I crunched it through my grey cells a couple of more times.

Then I had it, teenaged kids! Karatsu said the photos were of sentimental value, family pictures. But Thomas had seen Oriental children, not teenagers.

I saw the traffic light change to red, but it was too late. The little convertible chirped through the intersection to a chorus of squealing tires and honks.

I slowed and glanced in the rear view mirror. No accident, no cops. Whew!

Then I began questioning the sea air. Why would Karatsu have photographs of Oriental kids? He couldn't have grandchildren. So, who were they? And why would Pitts keep the photos in a safety deposit box?

I glanced down. The speedometer had crept over 110 kilometres an hour. Yanking my foot off the gas, I decelerated for downtown Qualicum, careful not to blink. It's too cute to miss.

"You didn't see him?"

Joel shook his head. We were sitting on his deck, watching the tide reclaim the beach.

"Nor talk to him?"

"Why are you asking me this stuff?" he said, s's hissing. "The guy's been dead for over two weeks. Face it, Riley. It's over."

"No, it isn't! It's not over 'til I say it's over."

The aquamarine eyes studied me. "You're speaking officially?"

"If need be, yes."

His tanned face tightened almost imperceptibly.

"So, let's try that question again, shall we? Did you talk to Pitts on the night he died?"

Joel studied his manicured nails.

I lost my patience. "No use denying it! He called you after 6:15."

"Oh?" The blue peepers widened in innocence. "You know that for a fact?"

"Un-huh. Last night, I punched the re-dial button on Pitts's phone." Joel's fingers tightened around the arms of his lawn chair. "Wanna know who answered?"

Joel waited. I peered down at the waves foaming along the beach and let him suffer.

"You did," I said, staring into his unreal eyes.

Surprise and shock jockeyed for position in Joel's attractive features. "I...I didn't answ..."

"Didn't have to." I glanced inside the patio door. "Your machine did it for you."

He sighed, jumped up from his chair and leaned over the railing. "So I talked to the guy. So what."

The whistling sound created by his speech was really irritating. I leapt up and punched his shoulder. "So what? The guy dies mysteriously and you lie about talking to him? How do you think that looks, huh?"

Joel shoved me back, none too gently. "I don't care how it looks! What's it to you, anyway? I didn't do anything to 'im."

"I want to know what happened to my brother-in-law the night he died. Someone was with him, made him angry, made him drink. That's the only reason he'd ever..." I hesitated.

"Be stupid enough to overdose? Is that what you mean?"

The words stung, but I kept on. "You hated him! You'd have done anything to hurt him!"

He raised his brow. Pale lines flashed beneath the tan. "Whoa! Pitts and I had our difficulties. There were times when I hated the two-timin' bastard, but that's over. I've come back and I don't want trouble."

"What did you talk about?"

"What we always talked about."

"Robie?"

He didn't answer.

"It must be tough, starting over. Money okay?"

He scratched his left eye. "I've got enough."

"Not what I hear. Been talking to Thomas Kent?"

Joel's face darkened.

"How about Kim Karatsu? Wants to buy Sea Blush. Probably give you a lot for your shares, thirty five percent, right? Solve a lot of problems."

"You're pissin' in the wind."

"Maybe. Maybe not." I changed subjects. "Know anything about a grey envelope?"

He pursed his lips. "No."

"Anybody with you that night?"

That surprised him. He hesitated. "No! Uh, I mean, yeah."

"Who?"

Two rows of perfect teeth glittered. "Can't say."

"Can't or won't?"

The house on Sea Blush was quiet when I let myself in just before 9:30. "Hal?" I whispered.

No answer. I tiptoed down the corridor. Light glowed beneath her bedroom door. I sneaked back to the kitchen. As quietly as possible, I cracked open a soft drink and leaned against the white counter. A sheet of paper attracted my eye. I took a swig and read.

Hal had neatly printed: *Vivian phoned at 9 to see how you're doing. Wants you to call back. Didn't leave a number.*

Great. I dug my wallet out of my jacket and fished free Vivian's card. Sipping slowly, I dialled.

The phone began to ring at the same time as a little bell rang in my head. Pitts's barenaked number and Vivian's were the same! Instinctively, I hung up.

"Busy?"

I was concentrating so hard, I nearly choked. Halliday actually came over and began slapping me on the back. Finally, I raised my hands and she stopped.

"You scared me!" I sputtered.

"Sorry. Heard the door."

"You've been crying?"

Hal nodded and her shoulders began to shake. My stomach flip-flopped.

"Hey. Hey!" I said, taking her by the arm and leading her into the living room. "It's gonna be all right."

Sobbing, she plopped down on my dark blue leather sofa.

"Look, let me make a cup of tea and we'll talk, okay?"

Her curls bobbed.

A few minutes later, I handed her a steaming mug. "What's wrong?" I asked hesitantly, knowing full well she might, with good reason, blame me.

"I just don't know any more." Halliday looked up, pale eyes glistening. "You and I, we, we used to be so close..." My grip tightened on my mug. "Now, everything's changed." She bit her lip. "First, I lost you, then Pitts." Hal dropped her head into her hands.

I didn't know what to say. It was the truth.

"Something I've got to tell you," she said, her voice muffled by her palms.

"Okay. Shoot."

Halliday pulled in a lot of air. "Please, don't be mad at me, but..."

I waited.

"I lied to you. Pitts was drunk the night he died."

"What? What're you talking about?" I jumped up. "You were there?"

She sobbed and shook her head. "No. I...we spoke on the phone." She blew her nose. "We argued. He..." She lifted her wheat-coloured eyes to mine. "He'd been drinking, a lot."

"But you told me..."

"I know! I was afraid! Oh, Riley!" she cried. "I think I killed him!"

I couldn't speak. Couldn't breathe. Couldn't move.

"Don't look at me like that! I didn't push him over the balcony."

When I found control of my body again, I whispered, "What did you do?"

"He was abusive! You don't know what he was like drunk-" I held my breath. I think I had a glimmer, but wasn't eager to peer closer. "He called me, oh..." she gulped, "horrible names." She paused, breathing so fast I feared she'd hyperventilate.

"Okay, okay. Calm down. Take deep, slow breaths. Come on, you can do it."

Slowly, she regained control. "I tried to reason with him, but he was too far gone. Finally I gave up. He just refused to accept that we were through. He swore at me as I hung up." Halliday looked down at the floor. "Those were the last words we spoke to one another."

"You did upset him!"

Hal stared at me, eyes wild.

"Dammit," I snapped, "you knew what he was going through." Hal looked at me as if we were strangers. Maybe at that moment, we were. I wasn't thinking straight. I was so angry with her for upsetting him, for divorcing him, but was angrier at Pitts for dying. Since he was no longer available for punishment, someone had to take the blame. "Couldn't you have given..."

"Given what?" my sister yelled. "I gave him every...oh, never mind! You won't listen to me, he always had you blinded. Well, I'm no longer tied to him. And you know what? I'm going to be free. I'm going to sell that bloody Sea Blush faster than you can wink." She gave me a defiant stare. "I've called an emergency meeting of the Board of Directors for tomorrow afternoon. Juet's organizing it. Of course, you're welcome."

I was stunned. When I finally found my voice, she cut me off.

"I won't discuss it again 'til then. I'm going to bed."

I sat on my couch and stared at the starry night sky. It had been a long couple of weeks. After Pitts's death, the one desire that had kept me sane was to prove that it wasn't his fault.

My own sister blew that one out of the water. And now, in a fit of anger and guilt, she was going to sell my beloved Sea Blush.

The fact that Pitts had Vivian's private number—the number she told me she only gave out to a select few—puzzled me. I should have pondered it, but with the weight of Hal's anger crushing my thoughts, I couldn't find the guts.

For once, chocolate held no appeal.

Thirty-Eight
8:05 a.m., Friday, July 31

Knees bent, right hand shoved behind her back, Halliday chipped the ball with her left hand. It hopped a couple of feet and slowed to a rest near the other two. Mind numbed by a night of worry, disbelief and denial, I automatically tossed them back. Again, Hal one-handed them.

I shivered, wanting to flap my arms for warmth. A cold start to the second round. Couldn't get Pitts out of my mind. It was all so stupid! My head hurt. I tried not to think about him lying at the bottom of the ravine and concentrated on the golf balls heading my way.

After the third ball trickled to my feet, I picked them up, dodged the cigarette Jody Cooperhad momentarily dropped, and trotted over to Hal.

"I'm freezing." I dug into the large side pocket of her bag. "Wanna windbreaker?"

Dressed in black stirrup pants, turtleneck and a light sweater, Halliday shook her head. Her face told me that I was not the only tormented Quinn. It also told me she wouldn't talk about it. "Told you not to wear shorts," she said curtly.

I looked around. The putting green was a jumble of players and caddies, all dressed in pants and sweaters or jackets. Leather golf bags of all colours and endorsements littered the perimeter; some with caddies mounted like jockeys. A couple of dozen fans stamped about, sipping coffee and dissecting strokes. Deborah McHaffrie, one of a handful of players who had picked up golf in her early twenties, wore a neon yellow toque pulled over her baseball cap. She knelt down to tie her low-cut, granny boot-like, black golf shoes and flashed me a smile.

I waved half-heartedly and pulled on my jacket. "It'll warm up," I said, shooting a glance at the heavy grey sky. Yeah, right. More likely increasing wind and rain. I hustled back to my spot.

Hal chipped a dozen more with her left hand, then switched to both hands. Finally, she nodded for the putter. I handed it to her and shoved the nine iron back into the bag. Light rain began to fall so I snapped on the bag's Holt to cover the clubs. Earlier, we'd dumped the four wood for the one iron. With this kind of weather, Hal might have to give golf's toughest club a shot. The wind whipped up, snapping at the Canadian flag atop the pole in the centre of the practice green.

Jenny and Caroline sauntered by, munching bananas. Both wore beige slacks, golf shirts and colourful sweaters. Rita stood nearby, carefully putting black dots under the name stamped on both sides of Jenny's golf balls.

I walked over and forced myself to look happy. "Congrats, both of you, on yesterday's round. Not half bad for a couple of duffers."

They feigned anger and pretended to attack me. We burst into laughter. It felt good to release some emotion. "Sorry, gals," I said finally. "Just kidding."

"Bloody well 'ope so," Alison piped in from the practice green. I shot her a grin and turned to the early leaders. "Weather's a bit of a bummer."

On cue, an invisible gush of air nearly snatched Caroline's Panama.

"I love it!" Jenny said, hazel eyes shining. She took a jacket from Rita's outstretched hand. "This's the day to move. The rain'll panic a lot of players."

"That's the attitude! I hope Hal can be a mudder if she has to." I wished them luck then dashed back to give Hal her jacket.

"A mudder?" Halliday asked, stroking a ten footer.

The ball twisted out of the cup. I tried to grin. As her sister, I was angry; as her caddie, I was worried. The fine lines on her face seemed pronounced, her eyes dull, energy level low. We hadn't spoken about last night; instead, we'd gone about the daily routine, deliberate in our avoidance. Needless to say, our sisterly synchronicity was nonexistent. Another day of fun on the links.

A rippling of applause rolled down from the first tee. Cleats crunched as the next group of players headed out. I glanced at my watch. We had 20 minutes. I flashed two open palms twice at Halliday. She nodded, waved at a further hole and began putting 25 footers. I tip-toed across the green, avoiding both Deborah's and Big Mama's putting lines. We played putt and toss for another five minutes then Halliday headed toward the locker room.

"How many towels you packin'?" Ali's caddie asked.

I slewed my eyes around my Holt and blinked free raindrops. A caddie's worst nightmare is rain. You've got to do a juggling act; the impossible task of keeping both golfer and clubs dry. Most caddies pack several towels. "Three. You?"

Yellow teeth glimmered. "I'm a one-towel man, meself."

I groaned. Another lecture from The Show.

Jim pushed the fisherman's hat up to his forehead. Rain streaked the dirty, grey canvas. Too bad, his hair could use a wash. "Once," he drawled, cheek bulging from tobacco, "my broad insisted on havin' eight towels. Can you believe it?" He snorted then spat. I winced and eyed Donna as she hit her second shot. "Felt like I was carrying a tonna bricks!"

Our turn.

At about the mid 200 yard range, the first fairway crooks left, then barrels straight approximately the same distance to a completely beached green. Any other hole, I'd recommend a driver for the second shot.

"3 wood," I suggested, double-checking the distance to the pin.

Hal pushed off her Holt and peered through steady rain. "Won't get there in two."

I nodded and poked a sprinkler head on The Book's open page. "You want to get just in front of this spruce, near the 94."

She frowned. "Then bump and run it in?"

"Right." I unsnapped the Holt and reached for the wood.

"One iron," she said.

A caddie has to be so cool. I wanted to scream that she was crazy, but she's the one who has to swing, not me. Scientifically, it was a logical choice; the one iron gives you more control. Of course, that's assuming you can handle the club. When Lee Trevino, one of the all-time greats, said that only God could hit a one iron, he wasn't kidding. A lot of male players never master it; only strong women even attempt to use it. So, I hesitated and decided to push just a little. "Sure?"

"Of course!" she snapped.

I yanked free the club and gave the handle a brisk rub with my first towel. Slapping the club into her hand, I edged back. I like to think Halliday slipped. In that rain, it was certainly possible. Whatever the reason, her swing was off by a couple of millimetres. The Wilson grabbed air, eventually falling, skipping across the slick fairway into the right rough.

Of course I didn't say it. Silently, I handed her the umbrella, grabbed the club and shoved the grip under my armpit, while wiping mud off the face. Giving the grip a good wipe, I stuffed the iron back into the bag and snapped shut the Holt. By the time I'd found and replaced the four-inch divot, Halliday was stalking about in the rough. Both Ali and Donna were sitting pretty, each with about 90 yards to the pin.

The wind shifted and the rain spat into our faces. With the flag 17 yards back and to the deep left, we had a 150 yards. In some ways, our position was easier than the others'. Their wedge shots would have a higher trajectory-and thus hostage to the wind-than our five iron.

A common error in this situation is not taking enough club. Under normal circumstances, a Tour player can hit a seven iron 150 yards, but whip up a little wind and the ball's held back. Golfers judge wind by the adjustment in club selection necessary to travel the required distance. So, a one-club headwind from a 150 yards out would be more like a two-clubber from 90. Hal would probably go up to a four iron while Ali and Donna might try an eight.

Hal swung the four iron and connected solidly. The ball buckled a little in the gusts and plummeted down below the stick.

Ali's eight iron winked. Buffeted by a sudden cross breeze, the ball dove left and plopped on the apron.

Severely under clubbed, Donna's third shot balked, dive-bombing the worm-shaped right bunker. Turning angrily at her caddie, she saw that he had the putter ready for the next shot. Donna screamed, "Sand wedge, you moron!" and stormed off to the trap. The poor caddie seemed to shrink in the rain. He had been caught doing exactly what he got paid for; anticipating his golfer's needs. The bag toter's supposed to have the putter ready after his player hits a shot to the green. But if by chance the player misses the shot, heaven help the caddie caught clutching a visible putter! Nothing annoys a golfer more.

A good caddie is someone who's 10 steps ahead of you, not just walking but in everything...like, it's starting to rain and she's got the umbrella ready; you're taking off your sweater and he's got the bag unzipped. It's terrible when you've got a caddie who's always fumbling. It's a tough job, not rocket science maybe, but a lot more than just carrying the bag. A good caddie's taken for granted; you don't even notice them. Goodie was the best I'd ever found. I don't know how Hal rated me. At this stage, I'd be afraid to ask.

Donna blasted out from the trap. The ball jumped, hit the turf with a tumbling spin and skidded off the green. The Volcano played soccer in the sand, without a ball, for several minutes. Lots of disenchanted muttering from the spectators swept along the winds.

Her caddie, white to the lips, hovered nearby and waited to clean up the mess.

"She's really pushing it!" Hal whispered angrily.

"I know. Nothing we can do. Just concentrate on this putt."

She trudged up the green to the flagstick. It sat at the apex, the hole cut evenly with the slope. Beyond, to the back, the turf slowly fell away.

"'Bout fifty," I said, telling her the distance in feet.

She nodded and stepped to the ball. It charged up the green but with each dimple catching water, the little sucker petered out. Discouraged, Halliday placed a dime behind the ball and handed it to me.

I dried every little dip while Donna stroked a 30 foot uphill attempt. It died too quickly and she angrily putted out for a bogey.

The showers eased as Ali two-putted for par. The crowd, resplendent in primary-coloured, breathable and rain proof fabrics, applauded vigorously. As much, I suspect, to warm their hands as well as Ali's heart.

Hal squatted. Shutting her left eye-she's right eye dominant, opposite to me-Hal held the putter between her right thumb and forefinger. Then, putter at arm's length, she plumbed the ball. A couple of smart alecks behind her shook their heads. By letting the club hang freely and squinting at the hole, you can tell whether the shaft is directly in line with the hole or on either side.

Satisfied, she stepped up and stroked. The ball disappeared into the hole like Alice's white rabbit. A hard-fought par. Hal turned and tugged her Holt at her armchair experts. They grinned sheepishly.

"That's why she's out there and you're not!" a lady yelled. Halliday and the fans laughed.

Our little train marched on, the caboose flashing: Gormley-3 over; Weld-1 over; and Quinn-5 under.

Thank the gods for raingear! It drizzled steadily until we teed off from the fourth. So much of the wet stuff had splashed down that the third fairway was beginning to resemble one huge water hazard. Parred two, bogeyed three. We didn't discuss it.

The fourth is a long par three, heavily wooded near the middle. The uneven green is guarded to the right by a large water hazard-the same spanking new river which threatened to submerge the third fairway.

Due to the winds, all three players drove with three irons, instead of the usual fours. Miraculously, all the balls struck near the green. Shoving back our headgear, we trooped happily up and down the uneven fairway. As we climbed a knoll near the green, my left foot slipped, my right arm grabbed air and Hal's bag pulled me to the ground. My left wrist and shoulder took the brunt. Shiit!

Several feet ahead as always, Hal turned. My sister took one look, slapped her slick knee and roared, face up into the mist. Ignoring the stabbing in my wrist, I rocked frantically like a flipped tortoise, and managed to slither sideways. I felt a strong hand on my shoulder, a pull and I was up. Jim's face, still dripping, loomed close. With an embarrassed grin, I shook his hand.

"Twern't nothin'," he said and slogged on.

The fans heading for the green stopped and applauded. There was nothing for it but to act like Halliday. I bowed as best I could under the weight and stumbled forward.

Golfers are not too hampered by the combination of rough terrain and slippery conditions. First, they're not carrying a 50 pound, slippery bag; second, they're sporting cleats.

But caddies are not allowed to wear cleats. On one hand, I guess it makes sense. I read somewhere that a golfer takes an average of 28 paces per green. Since each golfer has 24 spikes on her shoes, a player can leave over 12,000 impressions during one round. Take 144 pairs of stomping feet and that's 1,741,824 holes in one day!

On the other hand, slip-sliding like a beached walrus in front of hundreds of fans does nothing for one's vanity, much less one's backside.

The double collar of the fourth green caught two balls, Hal's at the back and Donna's to the right of the pin. Ali's snuggled 15 feet down and left. The flag hung, like a dirty shirt, 10 yards in from the front and six yards from the right.

It was a toss-up between the two apron shots for furthest away. Halliday's always anxious to play, so she stepped up. The green's slope is broken by a couple of soft humps near the back. With all the rain, it was tough to get a good read. Normally, by determining the green's nap or grain, a golfer can judge speed. A putt into the grain will be slower than one with it.

Studying green turf is a science in itself; grass will follow the green's slope, grow toward the southwest or toward water and run in the direction of strong prevailing winds. Then there's the type of grass: bent, bluegrass, Bermuda, or rye. They all have specific attributes; thin-bladed bent grass can be cut short, making speedier greens, and since Bermuda's the coarsest, it'll slow the ball.

When every blade, fat or thin, holds a few droplets of water, turf science is for the birds. Fortunately, Sea Blush's greens were bent grass, almost grain free.

A 30-foot downhill putt would've been challenge enough, but Hal's ball had to negotiate two humps while holding its line. Sweet dreams, baby.

"Going to have to charge it."

I nodded. Though downhill, the moisture would slow the ball enough to avoid running off the green. "Stroke normally, but use the toe or heel." Playing the ball off either end of the club softens the impact just a little as the club initially gives way to the ball. Toe or heel's a a personal preference; both give the same deadened feel for a fast downhiller.

"Okay," Halliday said, settling herself in position. Feet together, shoulders back, right arm behind my back, I grabbed the flag and waited.

The ball broke free, disappeared from my view as it dipped into the first hump, flew up and over the next one and chugged downhill. The last three feet are always the toughest 'cause that's when the conditions-grain, slope, wetness-start really kicking in as the ball begins to lag.

Hal's sparkling Titleist hugged its speed until the last 24 inches. Then suddenly, it broke right and rolled three feet beyond the pin.

"Good try," I said, taking the ball. "Tough putt."

Donna's luck was no better today. True, she was putting across three-quarter-into grain but she should have anticipated that this would not only slow down the ball but curve it left. A couple of seconds after the stroke, she knew. Her Spalding dribbled to an ugly death a good 15 feet from the target. She began swearing not-too-softly under her breath.

The Queenslander took full advantage of her straight, uphill putt and rolled her ball in for a birdie. For the first time since the Tournament started, Alison regained par. Both she and 50 or so water-logged fans were delighted.

Halliday's last putt barely made it, but she scooped out the ball for a par. She grabbed her opportunity to use the pottie while Ali waited with me by the exit gate.

Donna putted, pulling the ball from the get-go. I wiggled the fingers of my left hand and closed my eyes as it rolled wide. The Volcano stamped her foot several times.

I was getting pretty fed up. Her antics reminded me of a trained horse, so I said under my breath, "Come off it. We know you can count."

"What'd you say?" Donna glared at me.

I looked innocent. Out of the corner of my eye, Ali's cheeks quivered.

Donna took a couple of steps in my direction. "I've got enough problems without your interference!"

The fans nearly fell over the ropes, straining to hear.

I raised my palms. Talking would only make things worse.

"What's going on?" Halliday whispered.

"Your sister's bugging me!" Donna snapped.

Hal looked at me. I shook my head.

"Poor sport!" sang a voice behind Donna's back. Eyes blazing, she whirled. A dozen sopping fans stared back, a couple sporting grins. Donna seemed finally to realize how much of an ass she looked, for she spun, addressed the ball and dropped her bogey putt.

We played the fifth as though for the first time, both eager to forget yesterday's emotional Waterloo, and came out the other side with a par. As did the others.

A bogey on tricky number six dragged us down, but Halliday skirted the huge water hazard on seven and struggled for a par.

Donna's drive on the seventh struck an arbutus and fell, stymied, behind a thick fir. The Volcano exploded. She flung her driver as though it were a baseball bat and charged down to the unfortunate ball. Her caddie, veins splitting his neck, snatched up the club and stormed after her.

Reciting a litany of profanity, Donna grabbed the ball and hucked it out into the fairway! Stunned, an incredulous lady volunteer marshal told her in a strangled voice that she couldn't do that.

"Yeah?" yelled her poor caddie. He stooped and drilled the tiny sphere at a scorer. The poor man didn't know whether to catch it or duck. The ball buzzed by his shoulder and collapsed in a bunker.

Thirty-Nine

The eruption ended. Donna stalked off; her caddie, now horribly embarrassed, meekly followed a dozen steps behind.

To quit without penalty during an event, a player must be either sick or injured. I don't know what Donna was going to tell the Tour officials, but we were certainly sick and tired of her game!

That left Ali and Halliday to finish the round. Quietly, the two players watched Donna's backside disappear down the fairway then the veteran and the rookie returned to business.

Thank God. With the seismic activity squelched, Halliday might be able to regain her interest and survive the day. Friday's the hardest. The cut looms that evening, every player and caddie is scrambling for strokes, desperate to undercut what they guess to be the bottom-line score and snatch a chance to shoot for the big bucks on the weekend.

With its slight right dogleg and flat green, the eighth hole is birdie heaven. Great stands of trees loom along the right fairway and a small, triangular bunker notches the left side, at just the spot to catch an errant mid-range drive. A couple of drainage ditches play bookends at the front of the green.

Hal played a fade off the tee. The ball performed perfectly, curving slightly from left to right. It touched down beyond the last stand of trees at about 235 yards.

Ali's similar attempt fumbled as her ball was rocked by the increasing winds.

As I yanked on the second shoulder strap and trotted after Halliday, the clouds darkened, as though a sleepy angel had tugged down the blinds. The winds howled and for the first time, thunder rumbled.

We marched on, trying not to think about it. Golf courses, with their open terrain and tall trees, are a favourite playground for lightning. Ever since last year, when one fan had been killed and five others injured by a bolt at the Men's Open, golfers and spectators alike had tread carefully, ears tuned for the evacuation siren.

My heart sank when I saw Halliday's glistening white Titleist, dimples snuggling the tangled roots at the foot of a gigantic birch. Hal dropped to her knees but immediately realized the lie was unplayable. Even if she could manage a modified swing, the gnarled growth would deflect any club.

Under Rule 28 of The Rules of Golf, a player has three options once she has deemed the ball to be unplayable. We chose to drop the ball within two club-lengths of where it lay but no nearer the hole. Of course, that meant taking a penalty stroke.

With the pin 17 yards from the front, Hal wielded a seven iron and overshot the flag by a couple of dozen feet. Fortunately, the rain-softened green absorbed the ball on impact. Ali's ball charged in from the left, squirting to within 10 feet of the target.

Lightning split the sky, prickling the hair on the back of my neck. I was glad to be on the barren eighth green. Thunder roared almost instantaneously. Hal turned to me, pupils like golf balls.

Another brilliant fork slashed through the clouds, booming thunder on its heels. I looked around for a hideout. A concession tent billowed in the rain about 150 yards beyond the green. Already, fans from the ninth and fourth holes were scrambling to get in.

The siren split the air; play was suspended. Our spectators scattered.

Once the Tournament Official stops play, the Operations Manager's primary responsibility is player pick up. The thousands of spectators are left to survive on their own with nothing more than a bit of canvas for protection.

Tugging Ali by the arm, Jim shouted at us and slid down into one of the ditches. We dove in and, with the volunteer marshals and standard bearers at our heels, wormed down to the bottom.

Lightning sparkled again but the thunder was a couple of heartbeats behind. Huddled together, our little troop heaved a sigh of relief. Another jagged splinter was followed by distant rumbling. The storm was moving on.

There was nothing to do but slosh our feet in the ditch's runoff and wait. Another siren would reinitiate play.

The volunteers, suddenly realizing that they were practically breathing the players' air, scooted a short distance away. Ali and Jim began reviewing The Book.

Halliday bopped the putter against her knee. "I hate stoppages."

I nodded, eyes cast upward.

"Gives me too much time to think. When I'm playing, I don't think about him as much." She started to clean the grooves on the clubface. "You know, I've done a lot of thinking since he passed away." I reached inside the bag and pulled out the scraper. Hal ignored my outstretched hand. Instead, she took the small implement and began scrubbing. "I owe 'im everything. He believed in me, gave me the chance to be a pro."

She flicked a look at me. "I thought after Mom's

funeral I'd never get the chance." Her face brightened. "He changed that. I had such a crush on him!"

Her quick laugh startled me.

"He was sooo cool. I thought it was love. I really did. For the first time since Mom died, someone wanted to take care of me. You were at Lamar on scholarship, doing so good, all Dad talked about..." I could taste her bitterness. I thought about the scholarship she'd had to give up. "And I...I was stuck in Nanaimo with him. God, you don't know how badly I wanted out."

"I still needed you," I heard my voice say.

I think I looked as surprised as she. Across from me, Alison's face blanched and she tugged on Jim's sleeve. They quietly shuffled away.

"Needed me?" Halliday shook her head, hair beginning to dry and curl slightly. "Whatta 'bout my needs? You got babied; I got to do laundry. I got a chance and I grabbed it. So what if I used Pitts? I didn't mean to. It took a couple of years before I knew I'd made a mistake. By then, it was too late." Violently, she dug dirt off the club. "Gratitude's a powerful guilt trip."

I didn't know what to say. It didn't seem to matter; Halliday Quinn needed to talk.

"For fifteen years, I tried to stick it out. Did the best I could. We...we had some fun. Once I was winning, I tried to pay him back. He just laughed, wouldn't take anything. After a while, I found I couldn't fake it anymore. Other guys showed an interest." I leaned forward to hear her whisper. "I didn't do anything, but each time it got harder. I spent more time on Tour. Pitts was becoming possessive, drinking more, hitting more."

Her voice was flat, bereft of emotion.

"Hitting more?" I pushed the club out of the

way and pulled her shoulder so that I could see her face. "He hit you?!"

She nodded and ducked her chin into her jacket. Then she gulped and tears spilled down her cheeks. "Oh my God, Ril. I couldn't believe it. I'd done the unthinkable, married an alcoholic like my father!"

I couldn't keep my thoughts straight. Images of Pitts and my father darted in and out. I could smell the sweat and alcohol. Then SinJin's empty liquor bottles winked at me. I shuddered, holding my breath, unable to face that demon again.

"It, it made me sick. I couldn't breathe. I..." her voice dropped, "I had to leave."

The siren hooted. I blinked and saw the glistening slope across from me. Grabbing tissue from the junk drawer, I shoved a couple at Halliday. She blew her nose as I dragged the bag out of the ditch.

Hal bogeyed the hole. Alison made par. Silently, we shuffled on.

The shots were different on the ninth, but the scores the same.

We finished the first half one stroke below par. Within two and half hours, Halliday Quinn's name went from the top of the leaderboard to the dust below it, replaced by a four-under logjam shared by Americans Flynn, Sheehan, and Lorenzo, and Jones from Wales. At least, Alison had broken par. The vagaries of a life spent smacking a tiny white object!

The back nine is a blur. The clouds broke, the wind died and sun streamed thickly through the shining trees. Didn't help.

Somehow, Halliday managed to par the next three holes, despite a drive into the almond-shaped bunker on 11. Lost a stroke on 13 but regained it immediately on 14. The scoreboard read: Weld, one under; Quinn, one under.

The fans on 15 oohed with excitement as we approached the green but their enthusiasm waned when they saw Hal's score and died completely when her ball raced through the green. Another bogey. The standard bearer shook his head and shoved a blue goose egg beside Hal's name. The red one stayed beside Alison's.

We were slipping badly, about to disappear from view.

I pulled my sister aside. "Snap out of it!" I whispered urgently. "If you don't pick up your socks, we're dead."

She nodded, already resigned to failure.

"You can't quit now! All you have to do is hit fairways and greens. The birdies'll come."

"It's no use," she said, her eyes lifeless. "Why fight it? My life's a mess."

I whacked the golf bag. A couple of spectators leaned closer. I didn't care; it was all or nothing time. "Damn you, Halliday Quinn! You said yourself you owe Pitts everything. Is this how you repay 'im? He dies and you're gonna quit? For God's sake, what are you? Another Donna Gormley?"

Her pale green eyes glittered. "Don't you dare compare me to that slut! I could outshoot that bitch one-handed."

"Well, that's how it's gonna look. Second round of the Classic, both Gormley and Quinn, quitters!"

"Gimme the damn driver!" Halliday snapped. The fans began to clap.

Ali had already teed off and was sitting on a bench. Hal ripped into the ball. Had this been at the Aku Shootout, Robin Holt would've lost. I grinned and slammed the club in the bag. Four holes remaining and we needed two birdies.

Hal chipped like Lorenzo, putted like Sheehan and we had one birdie. Ali slipped back to one over.

Lost a birdie on 17 by half a foot. I crossed my fingers as we headed down the finishing hole. Both players chipped to below the steeply sloped green. Ali ran a 40-foot birdie putt to within three feet. The crowd cheered as she putted out for par.

Hal's third shot was a 30-footer, slightly across the green. The line was perfect but the speed insufficient. We ended the second round at one under.

I glanced at the huge scoreboard. The four under logjam had already broken, Flynn slipping to three under. I gave Hal a quick hug and walked her to the clubhouse. Before she disappeared, she reached beyond my shoulder and pulled out the putter. "Throw it in the trunk." she said. "I want it to suffer."

One of the players said the cut was two under, a nearby fan said three over. I tried not to panic. We'd know for certain in a couple of hours.

Linda Robinson was staring at the enormous scoreboard. I pushed over and found her name under the two day total of 150. Six over, no hope in Hades of playing Saturday.

We compared scores for a couple of minutes. Then I asked her if she'd known Pitts.

Linda nodded but her thin face tightened.

"I'm trying to find out who he was with the night he died. I understand you knew him quite well."

She played with her name clip for a couple of seconds.

I glanced about. No one within earshot, still, I lowered my voice. "In fact, I hear you two were quite close. That you had an affair."

The fingers stopped, her eyes widened. She looked around. "Hal's not here. This isn't for her, it's for me."

"It's true," she said in a soft voice. "But that ended months ago; his choice."

From her tone, I knew she wished it hadn't. "Where were you the night he died?"

She pinched the clip. Her name flashed in the sun: Linda T. Robinson. "Believe it or not, I went fishing. I came early, hoping to see him, but he had other plans. A couple of the girls had a trip up north organized so I went."

I was hardly listening, still staring at the clip. "The flowers! You're L.T.R., 'Never forget', right? You sent them to the funeral!"

She smiled thinly. "I wanted to go, but..." her eyes darkened. "Pitts always liked yellow daisies."

I nodded but my mind was somewhere else. If Linda Robinson hadn't visited Pitts on the night he died, then who had?

"Any idea why you broke up?"

She flushed. I felt like a creep, but kept my eyes on her face. She dropped her head. "I think there was someone else."

"You're certain?"

Linda's dark hair shook. Then she looked up and smiled sadly. "You can always tell, can't you?"

I didn't know what to say, so I left her rubbing the clip between her thumb and index finger. Another life buggered up by my brother-in-law.

So the question of who Pitts had been seeing wasn't solved. Since he died, I'd kept grabbing at a thread-that Pitts drank and maybe OD'd because someone had upset him. From the bare surface of his desk, he obviously hadn't been working that evening. Pitts Wyndamere did not waste time. Someone pretty interesting had to have been there after Thomas-if Thomas was telling the truth.

That could have been the woman Linda mentioned. But who was she?

Forty
5:40 p.m., Friday, July 31

"I want to thank Mrs. Wyndamere," Kim Karatsu said, "for giving me this opportunity to discuss my position." Halliday gave him a tight smile. "First, may I express my condolences to you all."

"Oh, just get on with it," Joel muttered.

Karatsu shot him an icy stare and continued, "As you may be aware, I represent a consortium that is interested in investing in Canada, specifically on the West Coast. Our goal is simple, to make a sound investment for the future." His sallow face beamed. "Sea Blush meets that goal."

"Look," Joel jumped in again, "could we get down to brass tacks?" His blue eyes raked the faces around the table. "We're all willing to sell. So, what's your offer?"

"No, we're not," Juet said before Karatsu could open his mouth.

"What?" Thomas almost shouted. The others stared at Pitts's only child.

"What d'you mean?" Joel asked.

"Just what I said," Juet replied firmly. "We're not selling. Not to this guy, not to anybody."

"But, honey, what're you..." Thomas started, only to be cut off by Joel.

"Now, wait a minute!" Joel said. "I don't know what you're talking about. You've got no say in this."

"Oh?" Juet replied, black eyes burning. "As Thomas' wife, I own half of his shares. They're not being sold."

Thomas' jaw dropped. "Juet, darling," he whispered, tugging at her arm, "don't be so hasty. Can't we just talk this over?" Juet pulled her arm free, refusing to look at him. He leaned over, voice hissing in her ear. The young lawyer had the gaunt look of a man running scared. I knew then that he hadn't told her about the trust fund money.

"Keep your bloody shares for all I care," Joel snapped. "We don't need 'em."

Karatsu stiffened and threw Halliday an icy stare. My sister bit her lower lip. "I'm afraid we do," she said quietly. Thomas stopped talking. All eyes focused on Hal's mouth. Hal looked at Ken Lasher who sat quietly to her right. He nodded.

"What d'you mean?" Vivian asked, speaking for the first time. As Tournament Director, she had been invited by Thomas and Joel, who felt she deserved to know what was going on as much as the Head Pro. Though neither Juet nor Halliday was thrilled with Viv's over-dressed presence, nothing had been said. I wanted to tell Vivian to take a hike. After all, I now owned 10 percent of Pitts's estate and was itching to flex my new-found muscle. Unfortunately, my percent didn't include Sea Blush shares.

"Mr. Karatsu's offer is for all or nothing," Halliday replied, eyeing her step-daughter. Juet defiantly stared across the table.

Karatsu's eyes glittered. Then everyone spoke, voices tumbling over one another for the foreground. Finally, Joel's was victorious. "This's outrageous!" he was saying. He raised his volume and shouted over the din, "Outrageous!"

The other voices fell away. Everyone watched Juet Wyndamere except Joel. His baby blues glared at her husband. "I suggest that Mr. and Mrs. Kent get their act together, pretty damn quick."

Thomas blushed an ugly red. "Or else?" I asked, tired of Joel's blustering.

His head snapped in my direction. "S'none of your business, Riley." He snorted. "Why don't ya go give somebody a lesson, or somethin'?"

That stung. Before I could reply, Halliday's voice cracked like a whip. "Don't you talk to her that way!"

Joel leapt to his feet. "I'm getting tired of you screamin' at me," he shouted at Hal. "I don't give a damn who you are, I'll say whatever I want to whoever I want." He leaned across the table on his beefy arms. "Got that?"

Juet murmured and Thomas shifted uncomfortably. Vivian beamed at Joel. My turn. I opened my jaw only to be cut off by the sound of Ken Lasher's fist against the tabletop. "Would everybody please be quiet!" he said firmly. Everyone was. Joel and I played chicken for a couple of seconds before he gave in and hunkered into his chair. I dropped into mine.

Ken took a deep breath and continued, "It's obvious that this issue isn't going to be resolved today."

"Maybe," Joel said, eyeing Karatsu. "Maybe not. What d'ya say, Kim? With Hal and my shares, you'll own 86 percent. What's the diff? You'll still have complete control."

"No!" Thomas said quickly. "I need..." Juet was staring at him. He hesitated then stopped.

Karatsu's face was alabaster; his voice brittle. "That is not good enough," he said, glancing at Halliday. "I was told our offer would be seriously considered; that all the principals were ready to sell." The man from the Far East stood. "There are many other investment possibilities. All or nothing, or the offer is withdrawn. You have one week." With a brief nod, he waddled out of the room.

"I'm not sure I understand. You told me that number was only given to close friends."

Vivian nodded, my reflection skittered up and down on her mirrored sunglasses. She reached for the door handle of the Ops trailer.

After Karatsu left, the meeting had dissolved into twosomes of intense discussion: Thomas and Juet side by side but fairways apart, Joel and Vivian murmuring and gesturing over coffee, and Ken and Halliday, pacing and chatting in fits and starts, silhouetted by the wall of windows. I felt like the fifteenth club on playing day so beat it. After marching around the course for thirty minutes, I saw Vivian waving good-bye to Joel and joined her in the parking lot. The others had long since flown the coop.

"Pitts was a close friend?"

"No. He..." Her arm stopped in mid-air. The denial was a tiny bit too quick. Then Vivian forced a smile, showing as many teeth as an alligator. "He was my boss." She twisted the knob, pulled open the door and ducked inside. I followed.

"With the tournament, sometimes he needed to get in touch with me after work." She tossed back her bronze braid and laughed. "After hours, what a joke! With this job," she said, gesturing around the trailer, "there aren't any." Though empty, the narrow space looked less like an office and more like a campground, cups and half eaten lunches were scattered about, boxes overturned, tables coated in paper, news clippings hunched in jumbled piles.

Vivian slid into her chair and yanked off the sunglasses. I watched her perfectly made-up face while she leafed through phone messages. There were enough to play cards. As the cinnamon eyes scanned, her expression varied from amusement to disgust, even to anger. Halfway through, she shook her head, stopped and glanced up at me.

"You outta know. Many times I've headed out and your's is the only car left in the lot."

I grinned. "Yeah. Guess so."

We fell silent, staring at the yellow messages. It seemed neither of us wanted to discuss the meeting.

"Awfully quiet in here, isn't it?"

"Yup," she replied, checking her face in a compact mirror. "Once the Tournament starts, the LPGA takes over and we get to do fun stuff, like return week-old phone calls. The only hairy minutes now come at the end of the day when we have to do the scorecards and the bios for the announcers tomorrow. Thank God that's done for today." Apparently satisfied with the artificial mask that hid her real face, Vivian dropped the compact back into a drawer. "Still, the volunteers keep you hoppin'." She glanced up, apparently hearing the whine in her voice. "Don't get me wrong. They're so generous. I mean, they've got huge hearts and they love women's golf, but the challenge is that you usually need 'em to be younger, stronger, faster. Here's the issue, you're a volunteer-55 plus-and I'm going to work you twelve hours a day?"

She shook her head. "Of course not, but it's what we need out there. This year we've got about a thousand. I think that eight hundred would be better, but we've got to learn to use 'em more. You know, delegate. Next year." She smiled. "They're really amazing. They're having a great time. And it's really ludicrous if you think of it, they pay us to be here, to work for us. And they work! They'll do anything to be a part. I've been walking 'round this week and people I don't even know, know my name. I'm famous." I grinned. "It's like having one huge extended family. Makes you realize that organizing a golf tournament isn't so stupid after all." She flushed slightly. "That was pretty wild back there, wasn't it?"

I nodded but didn't know what to say. It looked like the club was going to be sold, a lot of jobs would be lost-mine certainly-and I'd have to be the one to tell the staff. Vivian, on the other hand, was sitting pretty. With her in with Karatsu, her position was secure. I thought of Brenda's round face, the fear of unemployment shading her eyes. There was an awkward silence. Vivian changed the subject. "Let's talk golf. I heard today was kinda rough for you two."

I nodded. "Yeah. Hal struggled a little but I think we'll make the cut. Heard anything?"

"Not yet. Maybe by seven-thirty, eight. Takes 'em awhile to put all the scores into the computer." Vivian jumped up and wormed her way around a stack of boxes. "Drink?"

"Love one, thanks."

She handed me a cold can and returned to her chair. We cracked them open simultaneously.

I leaned forward and extended the can in my left hand. "To Sea Blush."

She grinned. "Sea Blush."

Our cans tapped and we swigged.

Vivian leaned forward. "To women's professional golf."

"I'll drink to that."

We both did.

"To Pitts Wyndamere," I said.

She raised her arm for another toast. "Pitts. Without him, neither of us'd be here."

I chugged the last couple of ounces.

"Riley?"

"Uh-huh," I said, crushing the soft aluminum can.

"Ever find out who he was seeing that night?"

I froze, arm ready to pitch the empty into a nearby basket.

"You said something at the funeral. I just wondered."

I let the can go. It clanged off the wall and dropped into the basket. Two points. "I've found out a lot of stuff about Pitts. Some of it, I wish I didn't know. You know, Viv," I turned back to face her, "none of us dies cleanly."

For a second, her face tightened. Then she laughed shrilly and said, "That's pretty morbid. What're you talking about?"

"I don't know. It's just that I didn't really know him but I thought I did. Know what I mean?"

Her eyes were slits. "Not sure," she said, her voice dropping.

"I don't want to get into all of it but...for example, he was having an affair and never told me."

Her eyes popped open. "An affair? With who?"

I shook my head. "Beats me. Hoped you might know. I thought he was my best friend...you know, married to my sister, gave me this job, yet the guy had secrets." I looked at Vivian. "You didn't know?"

She took a small sip. "If he was seeing someone, he didn't tell me."

"Well," I said, standing. "Join the club." A thought struck me. "Hey?"

"What?"

"You worked for Karatsu, right?"

"I'm not proud of it but yeah, I worked for the guy."

I shivered. "Ugh. Don't know how you stood it. He gives me the creeps. Anyway, Karatsu asked me, as executrix, about some stupid photographs. Said he gave 'em to Pitts. Know anything about 'em?"

Vivian shook her head.

"Well, thanks anyway." I stretched. "Gotta go. Feel the need for a long workout. À demain."

The wind. The sweat. The pain. What a relief! My Rollerblades hissed on the damp highway. I pushed beyond thought, beyond time-beyond hope?

The sun was low, its glow peeking through darkening clouds from behind a fringe of trees. Fat drops of rain splattered along the highway. I gritted my teeth and rolled on. Blading on a wet surface is tricky. True contact with the road is lost; one swerve and it's all over.

I slowed a little, concentrating on technique. The mixture of cloud, rain and diffused sunset mottled the air, making it hard to see.

I was too tired to hear. My ears roared with the sounds of my breathing, of my blades. It happened in a split second. I don't know what warned me, but I was dodging just as I was hit. A blow to my left hip and suddenly my blades touched air, not asphalt.

My helmet struck first, then my left shoulder, hip and then I tumbled. A whoosh filled the air, I saw water glistened off metallic paint, a splotch of colour and then nothing.

Forty-One

"Hey!" An arm tugged at my shoulder. I groaned. "You okay?"

Tasting blood, I pulled open my eyes. A man's face, his lank hair cascading in my eyes, was inches from mine. I don't know which pain I recognized first, pounding head, burning hip or shrieking wrist. The wrist quickly took centre stage.

"Maybe you shouldn't move," he said, fumbling with my helmet snap.

"I'm okay," a voice replied from far away.

I tried to move, groaned again and dropped against his shoulder.

"What happened?" the distant voice asked.

"Looks like you were forced off the road. I was about a hundred yards behind, just coming around the curve. Saw the car, saw you airborne." His teeth flashed. "A couple of seconds later and I would've missed you. Gone right by." He eased off the helmet.

"I think I can walk," the voice said. With the helmet off, I recognized the voice as mine.

Together we managed to remove the Rollerblades. I said forget 'em but the guy shoved them under one arm and helped me with the other.

I winced getting into his car, but then lay back, thankful to be alive.

"Where to? Hospital?"

"Parksville RCMP"

He turned to me. He was about fifty with dark hair and eyes, and he hadn't shaved since this morning. "I know someone there."

"Maybe we should go to the hospital first?"

I started to shake my head. Stopped when an internal hammer hit. "It's okay," I whispered, keeping very still. "Nothing's broken."

I must've dozed off, 'cause they had to nudge me awake. "Riley?" Black eyes searched my face. "Oh my God, Riley! Are you all right?" Walt's huge hands gently lifted me out of the car and carried me inside. My savior trotted behind, helmet tucked under an arm, a skate in each hand.

Walt carefully laid me on the old couch in his office and disappeared.

A week or a couple of minutes later, he returned holding a small first aid kit and two ice packs.

"Praught says you didn't break anything," he said, unscrewing the cap on a small bottle of iodine. "You sure?"

"Praught?"

He swabbed my lip. The big hand was shaking. "The guy that found you."

"Ouch! Yeah, nothing broken. Just sore." I tried to smile but my jaw hurt. "Friggin' sore."

"Where d'you want these?" he asked, holding up the ice.

"Everywhere." I held out my left wrist. He wrapped one pack onto my wrist with a frayed tensor bandage. I took the other and gingerly stuffed it down my wind pants, covering my left hip. I shivered. Walt pulled a blanket over me.

"Wanna couple?"

I looked at the proffered pills. "No, thanks. The pain reminds me that I'm alive."

"Sure you're all right?"

"Honest."

Walt peered at my face. "Try telling that to the mirror. So, what happened?"

I felt my left shoulder and winced. "Not sure, but I think someone deliberately ran me off the road."

Walt's blond head reared back. "What! The

Praught guy said it was an accident."

"He saw it?"

"Not the whole thing. Says he saw the tail of a car, then you." He grinned. "Said you were flying like a duck!" Laughing hurt.

His wide mouth shrank. "Sorry, you could've been killed."

"S'okay. Good to laugh."

Walt reached down and pulled up my helmet. One side had collapsed completely, the other was dented in a couple of spots. "Told you it's crazy to skate on the highway. Damned good thing you were wearing this."

We'd had this discussion mucho times before, but I was too tired and sore to argue. Anyway, the flattened helmet dangling from his over-sized paw seemed to prove his point.

"I'm not so sure it was an accident."

"Come on, Ril! You don't really think somebody intentionally drove you off the road?"

"S'possible. There was no traffic coming the other way. No reason for the car not to go around me."

"You know drivers can't judge distances, some of 'em almost kiss your butt and others go so wide they're in the other lane." He frowned. "Anyway, why would anyone wanna hurt you?"

"Don't know. It's just that it's been a bad couple a weeks, Pitts dying, house getting broken into and now I get pushed off the road." I gingerly shifted my hip. "Walt?" His hazel eyes stared at me. "I think I'm on to something."

"Like what?"

"Not sure, but maybe I was right and Halliday's wrong."

He shook his head. "Maybe the knock on your head was worse'en we thought."

"No, seriously. Do me a favour?"

"You know it. Anything. Anytime."

I smiled. "First, find me a pair of running shoes."

Walt looked blank for a second, then grinned at my stockinged feet. "Hang on a sec." He headed out the door.

I took stock of my bodily parts. Everything moved, albeit slowly and with some aggravation. The wrist was really bad, throbbing continuously. The ice was of little help.

Walt charged back in the room with sneakers. "These might fit ya."

I slipped on the right one. A little tight. I nodded to Walt and tried to lace it up. Ever laced a shoe one-handed? Practically impossible. Walt snorted and dropped to his knees. In a couple of seconds, the scuffed sneakers were bound to my feet.

"Next?"

"Can you check out a couple a guys' whereabouts at the time I was hit?"

Walt raised his pale eyebrows. "'Course." He pulled out his notepad. "Shoot."

"Kim Karatsu and Thomas Kent." Walt looked up from his little book. "Karatsu you might've seen at Pitts's funeral. Fat, Japanese guy. Staying at Sea Blush."

"Why would either of these guys run you off the road?"

"I'm not sure, but both saw Pitts the night he died and lied about it."

Walt's eyes were like granite. "They tell you this?"

"Yeah. It's a long story. I'll fill you in later but something's not right. Thomas has a couple of personal problems and Karatsu, well, I just don't trust the bastard."

"Okay, I'll have 'em checked. Whatever happened, the motorist should've stopped. Any idea about the car? Praught said he thought it might've been brown or maroon, but admits he was paying more attention to you."

"Could've been either. Darkish, square butt...maybe a bumper sticker. I just caught a glimpse as I fell." I shifted the ice on my hip. "Not much to go on."

"No, but we'll run with it anyway. Meanwhile," he said. "Gotta get you to a doctor."

"But..."

"Police orders," he said sternly. "We'll drop into Emerg on the wayda your place."

After 45 minutes cooling our heels, watching accident victims wheeled in and out, a doctor as young as Paul Dunlop told me what I already knew, scrapes and bruises only. It had sure hurt for him to find that out. He handed me a couple of sample packages of a pain killer and turned to his next patient.

"Hey! I almost forgot!" Walt said as we rolled up to Sea Blush. "You're in. Hal made the cut!"

"That's great," I replied without a lot of enthusiasm.

"What's wrong? Aren't you happy?"

"Of course." I said. "Just a little tired, that's all."

We pulled to a stop in my driveway. Walt jumped out, trotted around the car and opened my door. "She's off at 10:20. You gonna be able to caddie?"

I struggled out. "Hope so," I said, between my teeth. I tried to reach up and kiss his cheek but my muscles wouldn't go the distance. "Thanks," I said, squeezing his hand instead.

I stepped inside, waved and waited until the police car's headlights disappeared down the road. Then I let myself back out, locked the door and gingerly climbed into my convertible.

"Riley!" Joel said, opening his front door. "What a surprise!" He glanced over his shoulder and stepped outside. Obviously embarrassed, he started to pull the door shut behind him. "What happened to your face?"

Before I could answer, a familiar voice shouted from inside, "Who is it?"

Joel's tan turned brick red. "It's Riley," he shouted.

The bronze head was around the corner before it could be pulled back. "Oh. Hello, Riley," Vivian said, flashing an awkward smile. She walked toward us. "What brings you here?"

I glanced down the driveway. Two cars were parked, side by side. Both dark colours; both with bumper stickers. The brown Audi I knew belonged to Vivian. "That maroon car your's?" I asked Joel.

"What's this all about?" Joel replied.

I touched my sore cheek. "This."

They both stared at me blankly. "Somebody tried to run me over couple a hours ago. I wanna know who."

They both started to bluster.

I looked at Joel. "Where were you at about seven o'clock?"

He frowned. "You can't come here and accuse..."

"I can do anything I want!" I shouted. "Somebody driving a car like that yours tried to kill me! Are you going to tell me or do I have to bring the cops?"

"Hey!" The veins underneath the skin on his neck burst to attention. "Don't threaten me," Joel snapped, his voice as flat as his eyes. "I was here, all evening." Joel glanced at Vivian. "Didn't even drive the damned car."

"And you?" I asked, looking at Vivian.

She smiled grandly. "I drive the Audi, you know that." There was a slight spark of tension between them. Joel looked as though he was going to speak, but didn't.

"Where were you around seven?"

Vivian slipped her hand into Joel's. "Here. We'd just started making dinner."

I looked at Joel. He didn't look too sure but he nodded. I thought they were lying, but didn't know what else to do. I decided to end with a jab. "Didn't know you two were an item."

"It just started," Vivian said with a rush. She squeezed Joel's hand. "Trying to keep it quiet until after the tournament, aren't we, darling?"

'Darling' kept very still. The knuckles on her fingers were white.

"Well, congratulations! You must be very happy." They looked anything but. "So," I said to Vivian. "Guess Joel's the lucky guy you were with the night Pitts died?"

Both pairs of eyes flew open. Vivian's bored into mine; Joel's searched her pale face.

"That's right!" Vivian jumped in, only a couple of beats late.

"That's enough, Riley," Joel said, backing them both into the house. "You want to talk any more, talk to my lawyer."

Halliday practically pulled me through the front door. "Where've you been? I've been worried sick.

Walt called an hour ago and said you'd been in an accident! Said he dropped you off here." She stopped when she saw my face.

"It's not as bad as it looks, honest."

Suddenly, Halliday enveloped me in a fierce hug. I gasped for air. "Whoa! Please, it hurts!"

"Oh!" She backed off immediately. "I'm sorry!"

"It's all right, really. Lemme sit down and I'll tell you everything."

We sat; me with ice on my wrist and hip and Halliday with fear in her eyes. They shone with tears when I told her, describing it as an accident. "I'm all right, really. The doctor..."

"Doctor?" her voice leapt. "You needed a doctor?"

"No! Walt made me go to emergency. Just a precaution. It's only cuts and bruises, nothing serious." I nudged the ice. "What else did Walt say?"

"Said to tell you that he's got nothing yet." She looked at me quizzically. "That mean anything?"

I nodded.

"I was so worried when Walt said automobile accident." She dropped her eyes and studied her hands. "Every time I think about you...getting hurt..." She lost her breath, started to hyperventilate.

"Hal! I'm okay, really. Please, please don't get so upset."

"But I feel," she gulped, "so responsible."

"For what? It wasn't your fault. You weren't even there." Her shoulders started to shake. "Waita second. Why do I get the feeling we're not talking about tonight's accident?"

The floodgates opened. Halliday Quinn burst into tears. "I'm so sorry, Riley," she bawled. "I can't bear it any longer. I'd rather die than harm you!" She started to shudder, breath coming in gasps.

"If, if I could change places I would." She broke down sobbing.

As I watched the pain wrack my only sister, a vision of that night slammed down, blinding my view. I forced myself to look. The traffic light spilling along the highway toward us was green. Not red. I shut my eyes against it but the truth was still there. Our light had never been red. But I'd blamed Halliday anyway. Pitts was right. So was that damned Michael. I blamed my sister for my injured wrist, for my forced departure from the Tour. Shame burned my mind and my soul.

Through tears, I saw Halliday's eyes staring at me. "Riley? What happened? You, you said the light was green."

I blinked and hugged the anger for one last moment. Then I flung it from the far reaches of my psyche. "I'm sorry, Hal," I said, my voice a mere whisper. I held up my left wrist. "There was nothing you could've done. It wasn't your fault. It's about time I admitted that to myself-and you. When it happened, I was just so scared, scared that it'd be permanent." My voice caught. "S'nightmare, not being able to play...nothing's worse'n that." She nodded, eyes glistening. "I, I couldn't accept it, I hated everything and everybody. Had to blame someone..."

Halliday was beside me, hugging me before I swallowed my next breath. We sat silently for a long time and let the Quinn wounds begin to heal.

Finally, she whispered, "I'm not going to sell Sea Blush." I looked at her.

She smiled and shook her head. "I only said that 'cause it made you mad. I know how much the course means to you. It means a lot to me, too."

I hugged her as tightly as my sore muscles

could stand.

"I almost forgot! You'll be glad. Tomorrow we're on with Caroline and Jennifer."

"Great! We'll have some fun while we win."

We grinned like fools at each other. Then Halliday spoke, "Someday I'd like you to tell me about your life here." She swallowed then added shyly, "I've been a little jealous."

I sat back. "Jealous? Of me?"

Embarrassed, she nodded. "You survived leaving the Tour, seem to have found yourself. Everyone at the club raves about you, Walt thinks the world of you. So does that cute course super." Hal bit her lip. "I'm afraid without the Tour, there'd be no Halliday Quinn."

I stared at her. Here she was, my childhood and-I have to admit -adult idol, complimenting me! "Don't worry." I managed to sputter. "You'll do just fine."

The chartreuse eyes searched mine. "You'd help me?"

I smiled. "What're sisters for?"

Forty-Two

"Something came for you yesterday." A little flushed, Brenda deliberately folded the newspaper. "It's on your desk."

"Thanks, Bren. Everything all right?"

"Sure," she said, forcing a grin. "It's a gas, seeing all the players." Her freckles darkened and her fingers played on newsprint. "Sorry 'bout yesterday's round. Sister okay?"

"Fine. Today's a whole new ball game." I glanced down at her hands. "You've read the paper?"

Brenda's eyes were wide. "You saw it?"

"Uh-huh. Kinda rough on Hal, aren't they?"

Her head bobbed. "I didn't..."

"Don't worry. She's had bad press and pressure before. It'll be okay."

A small brown package sat in the middle of my desk. With my luck lately, I was hesitant to open it until I saw the return name and address, he'd written *Paul Dunlop, The REAL BioAction!!*

I grinned and ripped the brown wrapping. Inside were two paper bags filled with golf tees and a short, handwritten note.

Riley, seen any buffleheads lately? Thought you might enjoy using these, they're biodegradable! Made right here in B.C. from a bunch of natural stuff like corn and potato starches-totally ecofriendly! Once exposed to water, these little suckers turn to mush in a day. Did you know over 1.5 billion wooden tees are used in North America annually? That's lotsa trees. Chow.

I grinned and stuffed a bag in my shorts. Who knew? The way Hal was playing, she might go for a new charm.

Yesterday's cut had been 147; any player with

a two-day total of more than 147 strokes ate maca-
roni and cheese or MC'd-missed the cut. 72 players had made it into the money round.

While slowly stretching my back, I took a gander at the huge scoreboard near the practice green.
With half the field remaining, only four huge pan-
els were needed. Quinn, H. was on the third sheet
at 143, three strokes off the leaders' pace.

Though it was early, the activities of the television crews gained momentum. Cameras and mikes
were being checked, miles of cables double-
checked, interviews for the morning shows in
progress. The third round of the Classic was being broadcast at 2 p.m. Pacific Time on the sports
network across Canada and the United States. In
order to provide the armchair putter glimpses of
the day's leaders on the televised back nine, players teed off in pairings-groups of three, really-from
the highest to lowest scores. 24 groups, the dew
sweepers off at twenty after seven and the leaders
exactly four hours later.

10:20 tee off put us in group 19 with five pairings to follow. With a round lasting between four
and four and a half hours, the last groups would
trundle up 17 and 18 around 3:30. Perfect timing
for a broadcast scheduled to end at 4. If TV times
are later, tee off's are later. That's show biz.

By nine-fifteen, it was perfect golf weather. The
rain and clouds from the day before had headed
east to rankle the prairies. Sky clear, winds light,
temperature already 24 degrees Celsius.

The fans knew it was pro golf day. Hundreds
surrounded the driving range, generating a wave
of chatter broken only by the erratic clap of a hit
ball. If any player wasn't excited, this increasing
hum would cause every muscle in her body to fire

spontaneously. If I touched the back of my neck, I was sure I'd get a shock.

Saturday's a time for the zone and nothing else. Players and caddies still joke and laugh uneasily in the spotlight but now every single golfer had a fair chance to win. Each practised self-voyeurism, mesmerized by her body, by her thoughts, even by the air. How was the swing? The grip? The feel of the club? The shoes? Wearing too many clothes? Were the trick shots sticking? Thoughts flashed by as quickly as each swing. Players knew immediately where they were at in the scheme of their perfection. I hoped Halliday was close, but that was something you never asked. One superstition that I bought into.

I quickly downed two painkillers then rubbed the handles, scrubbed the clubfaces, marked the balls, counted the clubs, filled my pockets with pencils and prayed.

When Halliday finally took her right hand and ran her fingers against her throat-signaling *enough!*-I pocketed the last ball and, skirting the other players, headed to her side.

"I've got to talk to you," I said, cleaning the flatstick.

"Okay, but before you do, tell me something," Hal replied. She finished signing a couple of autographs.

"What?"

"You look really stiff and sore. Sure you're up to it?"

"I'm fine. It'll just take a while to warm up, that's all. Now, come on. It's important." I looked around the maze of players, caddies, fans and bags. "Follow me."

I hoisted up the bag and winced. Hal leaned forward to help. I shook her off, carefully adjusted the two straps and wormed my way through the spectators over to the caddies' tent. It was empty save a couple of volunteers. They grinned at me and offered us coffee.

We declined and sat at one of the picnic tables.

"So? We're off in 20 minutes. What's this all about?"

I looked at Halliday. Her face was pale, cheeks thinner, but life glowed from behind the slightly-puffy eyes. I'd been thinking about when to tell her. It was a risk, revealing it so close to a round, but I knew my sister. She rides emotion the way you and I ride a roller coaster. Joy could carry her through eighteen holes. "I should've told you this earlier..." Her eyes widened. "Much earlier, but I couldn't." I dropped my eyes and fiddled with my wrist. "I was so wrapped up in my own self-pity that I deliberately hurt you."

"What are you talking about?"

"It's about Pitts." I met the bitter green eyes. "Remember I told you you'd be letting him down if you quit? That you owed him something?"

Halliday nodded, lower lip quivering.

"Well," I sighed, "that was pretty hypocritical of me. I owe him a lot and I'm letting 'im down."

She stared, fear plucking at the wrinkles around her mouth and eyes.

It came out in a rush. "He really loved you, Hal." I smiled briefly. "He told me so many times. He was so proud of you..." The fear in her face melted. "He wanted you to have the money," I said fiercely. "Every bit of it. No matter what. You gave him happiness, youth and a sense of purpose." Tears streamed down Halliday's cheeks. Her eyes glistened in disbelief. My throat felt tight as a tourniquet, and I struggled to get the words out. "He knew you didn't love him as a lover, more as a friend and father but, in the end, he didn't care. Watching you, being with you-you gave him youth." Joy shone across her face like a floodlight. "He was happy," I continued, gulping, "He wanted you to be, too..."

The words died. We both drew deep breaths, sitting inches apart yet closer than we'd been in years. And, in some ways, farther still. You can't reveal deceit without pain; can't expect forgiveness without distrust. The Quinns of our youth belonged in the past; the sister competitors in yesterday. Today began a new and unknown family tradition.

I stood up, shouldered the bag, and walked away. When I glanced back, Hal's dark head lay in her hands, rocked rhythmically by shuddering shoulders.

"From *Vaaancouver*, graduate of Lamar University in Texas. Ranked as top player in Canada from 1985 to 87. Joined the LPGA Tour in 1988. Winner of the 1992 Crest-Star Farm-Fresh Classic. Representing Ping, *Jen-Ni-Fer Wyyatt!!*"

The crowd bellowed, "Jen-Ni-Fer! Jen-Ni-Fer!" John Stevenson, my Course Marshall and one of our standard bearers for the day, proudly shoved the scoreboard up and down. We exchanged grins.

Jenny's eyes lit up, oval face split by a cheek to cheek smile. The former provincial ice hockey star waved and punched a tee into the turf. The smile disappeared as she moved behind the ball and executed a smooth practice swing. Target in mind, Jenny stepped into position. Driver quivered, downswing delivered, ball airborne.

"Next," the marshal's voice cut into the applause, "from Port Angeles, Washington. Graduate of the University of Texas, 1983 NCAA individual champion. Joined the Tour in 1984,

Caroline *Robbin!*"

Caroline doffed her white Panama, a smile to warm a dentist's heart across her wide face. She loped to the first tee area, set her ball and took a couple of practice swings. Several fans gasped. It was like watching Casey at the bat. Caroline swung for real and the ball burst off the tee.

"Halli! Halli!" the crowd sang after her introduction, delighted to have two Canadians in the same group. Halliday stood in the centre and turned slowly, smiling briefly and saying "Thank you" to the circle of fans.

Her club arched, returned. The crowd's eyes moved, following the Wilson 4's huge crescent of descent.

Halliday handed me the driver. I stared into her face. Her eyes, though slightly swollen, calmly returned my gaze. Her colour was higher than I'd hoped, her movements a little quick. Still, her hand was steady. "Tell your friend I like his tees." I nodded. She turned and headed down the courtesy cut. Hoping I'd done the right thing, I wiped the club's head and shoved it in the bag.

No turning back.

All three players were charging the ball. Saturday is 'move day', you're either moving up or down or out of the tournament altogether. Nobody wins the tourney on Thursday or Friday; you go for fairways and greens and move into position. Unlike other sports, a golf score is fluid, changing every day. There's always a bunch of people coming down and a bundle going up. On Saturday, you hope to move up, hope the leaders falter, and boom! you're close. Sunday's the day to win or lose.

Jenny's third shot, from 95 yards, immediately set a dynamic tone. Her ball lay partially buried in light rough, left of the green. An excellent chipper,

Jenny widened her stance, hung back a little from the ball and hit a floppy wristed shot. Like a text-book illustration, her Titleist popped, grabbed at air then hit the neck of the fairway running. It scooted up and, to the overt dismay of the gallery, settled within four feet of the pin.

With the flag six yards in from the left, Halliday launched a 100 yarder. Though known more for guts than finesse, my sister can pull 'em outta the bag when challenged. The ball soared, dropped straight down and stuck -like a tumbler's dream, landing a hand's width from the hole.

The spectators went bonkers; Hal had her first birdie of the day. Caroline followed with a stunning 70 foot putt that burnt the hole. She grinned and dropped for birdie. Jennifer dug deep, stroked clean, and birdied the hole. Feathers all around! The three players exchanged high-fives and strolled to the next tee. I smiled as John Stevenson and his partner scrambled to change the scoreboard. Two under followed each name.

It might have been the adrenaline, but Caroline overclubbed the short par four. Her ball went skinny dipping in the large water hazard banking the left fairway. Halliday and Jenny dropped to three woods and both hit fairway. Though Caroline lost a stroke, Jenny just missed holing out her approach shot and settled for a birdie. Hal's first putt caught a little too much turf. She stroked again: par.

Number three also lacks distance. A good third of what little it has, is covered by H2O. What challenge it misses in length is recouped by an extremely narrow fairway. Fairways usually spread a good 30 to 40 yards and are bordered by eight to 10 feet of light or secondary rough. Beyond that grows primary rough, 60 inches in height and distance. Not so the skinny third.

Jenny wisely wielded a three wood and avoided the peanut-shaped bunker looming on the right. The crowd spilled beyond the tee, hugging yellow rope, mesmerized by their closeness to the players.

One after the other, Hal and Caroline swung three woods, both balls bounding 20 yards farther than Jenny's. With fans breathing over our shoulders, Halliday and I located the sprinkler labelled 115 hugging the left fairway's edge. Adding 15 for today's flagstick depth, we had a 130 yards to a rising green.

Halliday neatly poked a seven iron, not quite full strength, and the ball cleared the left bunker and bounced up the green. She took the flatstick from my hand and trotted after it. We were within a dozen feet of another birdie.

"Go Quinns!" a voice boomed.

We turned. Among the crowd, Walt's wide face smiled at us. He was wearing a volunteer's shirt and hat. Pointing to the security band around his arm, he saluted Halliday. She laughed and snapped one back. "How's the bod?" he yelled at me. I gave him a thumbs up. He nodded and waved me over.

"Sorry it took so long. Karatsu was alone in his condominium and Thomas was at the office-no alibi."

I gave his huge hand a squeeze and trotted after Halliday.

"Good luck!" he shouted.

Caroline hit her approach with a niner. The ball overshot the flagstick, dropped and caught the downward slope, its dimples finally stopped spinning near the front collar. The fans moaned.

After much toing and froing from sprinklers, Rita and Jenny agreed on a seven iron. Good choice, as the ball snapped down a fathom from the hole. Jennifer waved at the delighted crowd as Rita trotted ahead on divot duty.

Caroline's putt charged uphill. "Run it out! Run it out!" she urged, but it rolled wide. Shaking her head slightly, she marked the ball and handed it to Ned.

Halliday's line was across the green. Tough one to hold, as gravity and the natural slope would tug the little sucker wide right. At least there weren't too many spike marks. Hal walked beyond the flag and back, stooped to repair her ball mark, then moved into position. I stood behind, holding the flagstick upside down. The spectators inhaled. Halliday stroked. The ball curved, compensating for the slope, and as it slowed, broke the path. Accompanied by the crowd's desperate moan, the Wilson swung just under the hole and stopped, as though dotting an exclamation mark. Everyone took a breath: a disappointed sigh. Hal putted out for par. I handed the flagstick to Rita and backed off.

Jennifer pocketed a couple of dead leaves while she reviewed her line. Then, she softly directed the ball. It picked up speed, bobbled momentarily then dropped from view. Birdie!

Caroline popped one in for par and our entourage rolled on.

We birdied four. Though most caddies think of the player and themselves as a team, it's not uncommon to hear a caddie mutter, "We birdied 1, 3, 4 and 9 and she bogeyed 12 and 14." Halliday nearly gave the crowd a once in a lifetime experience, barely missing a hole-in-one when the Wilson hit the stick and dropped just wide of the four and one-quarter inch hole. That shot had 'em still buzzing as we trooped onto Number 6 and even after

Hal'd parred the long fifth.

Jennifer was on the move and on the score-board, now tied with Lorenzo and Jones at four under. Halliday and Sheehan joined Flynn at three under. Vicarrio-Balley-the first member of the L.P.G.A in the history of Spain-and Barrett rounded out the list at two under.

With the stiffness gone and the pain masked by drugs, I was feeling not too shabby. As her cleats crunched along the winding cinder path which curved behind the eighth tee and swung by the seventh green, Halliday hoovered an apple and a banana. By the time we ducked under a little forest and trudged up the railway ties to the raised tee at the sixth, she finished drinking and tossed a small bottle of spring water into the garbage.

"Feel better?" I asked.

She nodded. "You?"

"Uh-huh."

Slowly, her face was settling; its expression quietly shaping into calm determination. I felt a twinge of excitement.

"Pin's back on 14, but I still say three wood."

Halliday stared at the fairway. The flag was invisible, hidden around a sharp right curve created by the banks of a water hazard. "Okay," she said and took the offered wood.

Jenny's drive slid right and bounded down the flat fairway, just skirting the hazard. The fans sighed with relief. Hal's kicked left, bounced in a small depression and leapfrogged into the secondary rough.

"Distance's good," I said, taking the club. Halliday ripped off her glove.

Caroline's drive also veered left. It carried more umph!, however, and darted into the clump of bushes, scattering fans. I didn't look at her.

It took a couple of minutes until Ned found the Caroline's ball. It was holed up deep inside a fat bush, the only way out was with a rake or maybe a buzz saw, certainly not a golf club. The fans hung about, giving advice. Caroline trotted back behind and to the left of the bushes and climbed a little knoll. "I'm taking an unplayable!" she yelled at her caddie. The spectators' buzz increased.

Forty-Three

"Unplayable? What's that mean?" one woman asked.

"Ssh!" the man at her side whispered.

Ned looked up from the bushes. "So I pick up the ball?" he shouted.

Caroline nodded-as did several fans-then she waved at him to join her.

The Caroline had a tough shot. Down one stroke, she was now 50 yards back of where her first shot had landed. I wasn't sure she had enough clearance for a swing toward the pin but Caroline went for it. The ball soared, rattled through the tops of a couple of the trees, burst free and plunged to the centre of the fairway! The spectators cheered. As the Connecticut Yankee trotted down the slope, waving her hat, the applause rolled ahead.

Halliday connected solidly with her eight iron and the ball plopped within 13 feet of the hole. A few moments later, Jenny's ball dropped, hit a bump on the uneven green and rolled just beyond the target. Not to be outdone, Caroline chipped softly, earning herself a 10-footer.

The green, which rises from the front and slopes from side to side, is bisected by several soft undulations. Very tricky bent grass putting. Hal banked right, hoping to catch the slope into the hole. Her ball started obediently but forgot to stop and rolled a foot wide. I wasn't worried. A par on this sucker would be peachy.

Caroline's ball followed directions like a new cadet. She took the bogey with grace. Hal granted my wish and putted out. Smiling, Jen snatched another birdie.

All players avoided the mammoth water that

threatens to envelop the seventh fairway and green and tallied birdies. As he changed Halliday's score to four under, John Stevenson gave me a massive wink. The red number looked pretty good, though the six beside Jennifer's name really began drawing crowds.

Caroline, ever present smile dulled by her score of one under, clawed her way back. With a towering drive off 8, a snappy approach and swooping putt, she grabbed a birdie. Caroline grinned hugely as Ned congratulated her with a loud high five. Jenny's pace slowed to par, with Halliday joining in.

The ninth's dogleg left requires a well-placed draw, a soft left hook will just come short of the water hazard and give a lot of breathing room to the bunker-stocked right fairway. For the first time we were under the watchful eye of television, and all three drives struck fairway.

With a colour commentator whispering behind their backs, the players punched nine irons onto the green. Caroline was left with a back-to-front 15 footer; Jenny had a 'three-time zoner'-a good 40 feet away. A voice behind me whispered, "I've gone on holidays longer than that putt."

Though Halliday was faced with a 25 foot uphill attempt, I couldn't help chuckling.

The three bleachers were chock full. Spectators spilled over the sides and crouched along the front. High above, on skeleton scaffolding, a huge camera lens stared down, soaking it all in.

The sun was high and the pudgy shadow of the flag looked as though the pole was peering into one of those distorting mirrors instead of standing alone in the sunlight.

Jenny, using her putter as a Texas wedge, blasted her ball from the collar. Rita yanked the

flag and stepped back. The fans shouted encouragement and cheered as though the white orb was
in a race. The Titleist sprinted across the turf only
to fade and die a foot from the hole. A moan swelled
through the bleachers.

Halliday carefully checked her line and nodded to me to hold the flag because the rising green
blocked her view of the hole. Finally she stepped
in. The ball shot forward, climbing hard. Again,
cries of "Sit down!" and "Be the one!" from the
bleachers egged it on. I pulled the flag and moved
as the Wilson sputtered wide of the hole. Everyone shook their head. To the crowd's delight, Hal
held up her right thumb and index finger. Spreading them apart about two inches, she shouted to
the fans, "Missed it by that much!"

The bleachers rocked with laughter and pounding feet. Jenny and Caroline smiled.

I handed the flag to Ned, took the ball from
Hal and gave it a wipe. "Great putt! We'll get it
next time."

She tossed me a grin. Under the Panama's red
brim, her eyes were glowing yellow, like a cat ready
to pounce. This was turning out to be fun.

With fans practically lying across her shoes,
Caroline waited for the marshals to clear some
space.

"I've heard of kissing someone's feet," Hal
quipped, "but that's ridiculous."

The fans yanked back their legs as though
burnt. Caroline sniggered, then reached down
and shook a couple of hands. Faces flushed, the
spectators laughed hesitantly. Halliday marched
up and peered over the rope. "Hey! I was only
kidding!"

Everyone broke up.

After space had been meticulously arranged,

Caroline finessed the ball smack dab into the hole! With a *whoop!* she turned and gave one of the fans a hug.

Jenny and Halliday soft-touched for pars. As we rounded the turn to the back nine, I unloaded the bag to study the board. Wyatt was alone, on top at six under. Sheehan and Jones followed, edging up to five under. Lorenzo, Barrett and V-Balley were now joined by Halliday at four under. Robbin sneaked onto the bottom with her freshly potted three under. Flynn had dropped from sight.

"Riley!"

I looked around. Sitting in a golf cart marked 'Superintendent' sat Dai. Dragging the bag, I walked over and ducked under the fir boughs.

"You all right? You're moving like a sore turtle."

I smiled faintly. "That's just how I feel." His eyes darkened. "No. Really, I'm fine, just a little tired."

"You're doing great!"

"Yeah. Hal's coming along." I pulled up the bag and grimaced.

Dai leaned forward. "Sure you're okay?"

"Fine, thanks. I've gotta go."

He nodded. "Sure. Just wanted to wish you good luck. Ril?" I turned back. "I'll be watching."

We parred the next three holes. Jenny slipped on 12 and dropped one. Like a kid with a new toy, Caroline hung on to her score.

On the par four 14, all three drove off the tee, aiming for left centre. With a sharp right dogleg, there's no sign of the flag off the tee and every inch of the 445 yard hole is lined with thick clusters of trees. Today, the firs and arbutus were joined by a serpentine, sun-block layered gallery.

The balls hit on target, landing within 30 yards of one another. Then came the tough part; the entrance to the green is narrow and surrounded by a large stand of arbutus. Good course management demands laying up the second shot just below the fairway neck. The only other choice is to try and thread a three wood shot through the tight entrance. Those daring enough will probably splash down in one of the four bunkers protecting the rising, undulating green. Of course, on a par five, no one's too worried about playing in the sand.

With a little over 230 yards to the flag, Halliday and Jenny once again whacked drivers while Caroline belted a solid three wood, all with one goal in mind, to lay up 60 yards from the front.

Caroline's shot fell short, just skirting a small bunker near the 100 yard mark. Jenny's Titleist and Hal's Wilson nestled side by each, smack dab on target.

With the gallery moving around the green, Caroline trotted up, found the flag near the right back and sauntered back chatting with Ned. The marshals' hats glinted in the sun as she took her position. The pitching wedge flashed, the ball popped up and plopped down just above the flag. Caroline grinned as the fans cheered.

Halliday swung next, using a sand wedge. Her soft touch spun the ball back as it touched the top edge of the green. The Wilson dribbled and settled in a small depression. Wearing a grin, Halliday skewered the air with her club.

Jenny's shot caught a breeze and slid left. The ball plummeted into the figure-eight bunker on the lower left. The crowd moaned.

Jennifer stepped into the sand and wriggled into position. Without her club, she practised the swinging motion several times. Satisfied, she nodded to Rita who handed over the sand wedge. Jenny swung for real. The ball shot up in a spray of beige and pitched up and down the humps, spinning five feet wide of the flag.

Caroline strolled onto the putting surface, plucked a pebble off her line and stroked. The ball trickled. "Down, baby, down!" a fan shouted. Caroline clenched her wrist as the ball caught the lip of the hole, teetered like a drunken sailor then rolled back.

"Oh, nooo!" the gallery cried. Shaking her head, Caroline tapped it home for par.

Hal's turn. She rapped the ball. It scooted up and down, charged ahead then hopped over the hole! To excited applause, my sister slapped it home. Par.

Alone, Jennifer Wyatt stood on the emerald carpet. Oblivious to the 1,000 eyes upon her, the young Canadian settled in and stroked. The ball curved, slipped along a slight incline and plopped into the cup. Another par.

Despite shaky putting, Halliday parred 15 and 16. I tried to talk to her, but she shook her head and retreated inside her zone. I knew from the putting that she was losing the touch but I could do nothing but mumble encouraging words into her deaf ears. Caroline dug out of a bunker on 15 to save par but lost a stroke on the sixteenth green's slippery slope. Jennifer settled back into hitting fairways and greens, parring them both.

Wyatt still headed the scoreboard, followed closely by Davies. Sheehan dropped a stroke on 12 to join the four under knot of Lorenzo, Barrett, V-Bailey and Quinn. Caroline's slip on 16 cost her the bright lights: her name was replaced by Weld. The little Aussie had grabbed three birdies in a row to drop to three under.

17 and 18 are great par fours; middle to long distances, straight fairways providing terrific views

for spectators and finishing in huge sloping greens littered by bunkers and trees. Teeing off is fun: grab a driver and bang it.

Unfortunately, driving wasn't our problem. In the last few holes, 50 percent of Halliday's game had disappeared. Putting is all feel. Sure there are mechanics to the stroke, to holding the line and reading the break, but most of manoeuvring the flatstick happens somewhere between a neural synapse and a muscle twitch.

When Hal missed an easy six footer, a chink of ice nudged my heart. Her eyes were Holted, lips drawn, even the easy walk stilted. Halliday Quinn was fighting an untouchable opponent, the incapacitating fear known as the dreaded yips.

"It's okay," I whispered as she marked the ball. "It'll come back. Don't force it. Remember what Dad'd say..."

"...paralysis through analysis," Hal completed, dully.

"Right."

Jaw set, she nodded but I knew that every neuron inside was on fire, scrambling to find the right path. I'd felt it many times; a hopelessness gnawing at your stomach, fear trickling in your brain and lead numbing your movements. It's as though you held a golf club for the first time. Thanks be to the gods, we were on our final two holes.

Hal three-putted 17 for a bogey. Caroline and Jenny exuded confidence, both grabbing pars.

We walked up the last fairway as though in a nightmare, each step indescribably slow as we feared reaching the ball. With snatches of encouragement ringing in our ears, Halliday hung in and made it in two.

"Don't worry 'bout it," I said as we watched Jenny's 50 foot birdie attempt. The ball charged hard but sputtered a dozen feet too soon.

"Sure," Hal replied, her voice wooden. She took the club as though it were hot. I didn't want to leave her, but sprinted up and grabbed the flag from Rita. Hal moved mechanically and sent the Wilson up toward me. No need to pull the stick. She'd miss-hit from the get-go. The ball sputtered and rolled wide, 20 feet short. An uneasy murmur rippled through the gallery.

Caroline's 45-foot cross-green dribbled left and fell away.

I took the flag and watched Halliday, urging her on in my mind. Any one of the thousands of fans could have predicted the result. Another short one. I did my best to keep erect.

Jennifer stroked. Her Titleist raced up the green and dropped into the hole like a homesick gopher. Another par to finish in the lead, at five under. The bleachers rocked with cheers. I don't think Halliday even heard them.

Caroline dug deep and charged the hole. It surrendered. Two under for the young American. She grinned and waved to the crowd, but I knew that the three-putt on 16 dampened her enthusiasm.

"Okay, Hal," I said as calmly as I could. "You've made this shot a million times." She stared at me, eyes lifeless. I nodded. "Today you'll make it a million and one." I handed her the flatstick. "Don't think about it, just let 'er go."

And she did. The ball trickled to the hole, held its breath and dove into the four inch depth.

As the fans clapped, I grabbed Halliday and gave her a quick hug. "Waddago! You did it. Now, forget about it. Right?"

Dazed, she nodded.

"Are you okay to sign the card?" I asked, worried that she might not be able to concentrate. At the end of every round, each player must sign their scorecard, certifying its accuracy, in front of Tournament Officials.

Every couple of tournaments, a player, distracted by anguish or delight, signs an incorrect scorecard. If the score is higher than the player's actual score, the player remains in the tournament but must keep the higher score. If the score is lower, the player is immediately disqualified.

"I'm fine," Hal said, ripping off the piece of her scorecard where she'd kept her own count. The players exchanged completed cards and began lining up their scores with those tallied by the other player. The fans continued to applaud as the three disappeared into the scorers' tent.

With the bag on my shoulder, I struggled through the crowd.

"Riley! Riley Quinn!"

I looked up. Paul Dunlop's bearded face poked from behind a tree. I wriggled my way over.

"Thought you didn't like golf."

His hazel eyes twinkled. "Don't. But some of the players and maybe a caddie or two aren't bad."

I smiled. Though exhausted, the aches beginning to shriek, just standing near him I felt a twinge of excitement. "Thanks for the tees. Hal used 'em."

"BioAction's pleasure. By the way, ever find out who wrote the poison-pen letters?"

"Jeez, yes! I'm sorry, I should've called but it's been kinda busy."

Paul glanced around. "I can see that. Are you finished for the day?"

I shook my head. "Got some stuff I've got to do."

His face dropped.

"Look, how 'bout a quick lunch?"

He grinned. "That'd be great."

"Okay. Let me just dump these," I pointed over my shoulder to the clubs, "and I'll be right with you."

I left him, dropped the clubs off at storage and popped a couple more pills. I ran into Halliday on my way back. "Gonna grab some lunch then I've got a couple of things to do. You okay?"

"Fine," she replied wearily. "Think I'll have a long shower and get out of here for a while."

I nodded. "Good idea. I'll meet you at the house later. Maybe we can grab some dinner?"

"Don't know when I'll be there." Her eyes glistened. "I'll try. Give you a call, okay?"

I watched her disappear, eyes downcast, into the clubhouse.

"She all right?"

I spun to find Paul standing at my shoulder. "Yeah. Just a little discouraged."

"So, Riley Quinn. Tell me: what's the difference between a birdie and a bogey?"

I laughed and linked my arm in his. "Young man, you've got a lot to learn."

"Oh, yeah?" Paul replied, with a grin. "Know any good teachers?"

Forty-Four

I stared at my four-page list. All household goods and furnishings, every single personal possession, the Rolls, the Jeep and the sailboat, each piece of art, accompanied by an appraisal. It was all there, in blue and white, right down to the shoebox filled with baseball cards from my brother-in-law's youth.

It was already getting harder to recall his face and I accepted he would never burst through the front door again. Time stands still for no one, no matter how much you wish it would. Minutes and hours go by that the deceased do not experience. Very quickly, they are no longer a part of your life, merely of your past.

The answering machine blinked at me. When do you turn it off? Not yet, I guessed. Pitts Wyndamere was still receiving messages from the living. I poked it.

The machine whirred and clicked, then a man's voice, speaking very quickly, gave his name and number. I started hunting for a pen and paper as the machine's metallic voice gave the date and time of the call as Friday at 11:00 a.m.. I waited. The machine beeped three times. No more messages.

Pen ready, I punched the playback button. Nothing happened. I peered at the machine. Like mine, it had two other buttons: rewind and fast forward. I hit rewind. The machine hummed and stopped. I waited. Again, nothing. I pushed playback. The tape clicked but no message.

Shaking my head, I punched fast forward. After a couple of seconds of speeding tape, I poked playback. The same male voice broke the silence in the room. I jotted down his phone number but the tape hadn't rewound far enough back to get his name. I went through the routine again. I must have punched the wrong button because suddenly the room was filled with another voice.

"...be by on Monday evening. I want those photos." The voice stopped.

I froze in disbelief. The machine chirped that the message was received on Sunday, July 19. I dropped the pen, shoved my list into my pocket and ran out of the condo.

Suddenly, I had an appointment with a liar.

"Oh!"

"Surprised to see me?"

"What? No. Of course not! Come in."

I stepped through the door.

"See you're tied for third. Congrats! Hal had a great round."

"Thanks." I looked around. The place was empty. I closed the door.

"Look," Vivian Graves said. "I wasn't that understanding yesterday. I'm really sorry to hear about the accident." She shook her head. "Some of the corners on Dolphin Drive are wicked! You sure you're all right?"

"I'm fine," I said automatically.

"How'd it happen?" The doll-like face was a picture of curiosity.

I shrugged. "Some nut ran me off the road."

"Guess he didn't see you." Vivian Graves paused and ran her fingers through loose pale hair. "You see him?"

I shook my head. "Happened too fast."

I may have imagined it, but her body seemed to relax.

"So, what can I do for you?" she asked, leaning back in her chair. Though dressed in jeans

and a Sea Blush Classic golf shirt, Vivian managed an aura of elegance.

It hit me as I sat down. No one knew exactly
where the accident had happened except the police, Hal, my good Samaritan motorist and, of
course, the maniac who caused it. I looked across
the cluttered desk top. I was face-to-face with the
person who had tried to kill me! Struggling to keep
calm, I gazed into the golden eyes and lied. "I know
about Karatsu's photographs."

Fire engine red finger nails flew to her mouth.
She caught herself and coughed deliberately. "Oh.
Lucky you."

"He wants 'em back."

Vivian hooted. Scarlet lipstick stained a front
tooth. "No kidding! Well, they're mine. You can tell
that effing pedophile for me that he can suck air."
She leered at me. "Something he's not real used to
doing."

I almost bit my tongue trying to hide my surprise. Pedophile! No wonder Karatsu wanted the
photos back. No wonder Pitts had stashed them
in a safety deposit box.

"Pitts knew about 'em?"

She nodded. "Well before the Tournament I told
him not to deal with Karatsu, but he wouldn't listen. K's desperate to market his clubs in North
America. Paid Pitts a bundle to be part of the Classic. Even thought he could get your sister to use
them. Glad she turned him down. Aku," she
snorted, "pieces of crap! Pitts said we'd discuss it
when he got back from Japan. Finally I told him
the details over the phone, but he wouldn't believe
me. Demanded to see the photos. I gave 'em to
him Sunday, but I told him I wanted 'em right
back."

I was having a hard time concentrating. I wasn't

sure what I'd got myself into. One thing was certain, I didn't want Vivian to realize how little I knew. So I decided to stall, find out what I could. I changed subjects. "Maybe you can help me," I said slowly. "I'm trying to find out what really happened to Pitts the night he died."

The golden eyes watched me.

"Someone visited him-a woman." That was a guess. "I thought I knew who it was."

"Yes?" she said, nostrils flaring. Vivian Graves stood up.

My butt remained in place. "Linda Robinson," I said. Vivian stretched, then started leafing through some papers. I shook my head. "But she was out fishing. Someone else visited him." I took a deep breath. "You did." I kept my voice flat, tone matter-of-fact.

"No," she said quietly, eyes on the desk. She was very good but I didn't believe her. She knew it.

I waited and tried to keep calm. She went over and looked out the small window. When I felt my voice would be even, I asked, "Why'd you lie to me about Karatsu's photographs? You told me you'd never heard of 'em."

Vivian snorted. "Pretty obvious, don't you think?" She sat down and looked at me. "Not the kind of stuff you want to be involved with."

"But you were. You went to get them from Pitts the night he died." I leaned forward. "You lied about that, too."

The gold eyes flashed. She sat forward, slim back ramrod straight. "I don't know what you're talking about!" Vivian said. "Who d'you think you are, coming in here and calling me a liar!"

I smiled. "You don't have an answering machine, do you?"

Slightly thrown by the subject change, Vivian

nodded warily.

"They're really amazing. I always thought that once you rewound to the beginning, the old messages disappeared. Stupid, huh?"

Vivian's breath came faster, but she remained quiet. A car door slammed outside the trailer, startling us both. I glanced at my watch. 6:25. Play and practice for the day was over; most players and fans would be kicking up dust. Soon, Sea Blush would be deserted.

I smiled. "Funny thing is, those messages are there 'til another message overwrites them. If you happen to leave a message and it's, say the fifth or sixth one received that day, your message may not get erased for a long time."

The colour drained from her face.

"I see you're beginning to understand. I just came from Pitts's condo. Had a few things to do, one of 'em getting phone messages." I looked directly into her eyes. "Imagine! Phone messages for the dead."

"This's all very interesting," she said, casually examining her nails. "But I don't see what it has to do with me."

"No? Lemme explain. I just heard your voice on Pitts's answering machine, telling him that you would come to his place on Monday evening to pick up the photographs."

Vivian held her breath for a couple of seconds. "So what? I left a message. Doesn't prove anything."

"Oh, yes, it does. It proves you're a liar."

She watched for a minute then said, "I've got nothing to say." She sat back and folded her arms across her chest.

"You still say you didn't visit Pitts the night he died?"

"Told you before. I was with someone."

"Not good enough. Who?"

"Joel."

I shook my head. "Don't think so. At least, he's not too sure."

"That idi..." Vivian stopped abruptly. In a calm voice, she continued, "We were together all evening and all night."

I slammed my hand on the desk. "Cut out the crap! I know all 'bout you and Pitts." Her face told me the lucky shot had struck home. I bulldozed on. "You met the night he died. That's when you picked up the photos."

"So what if I did," she said quietly. "The man was my boss, after all."

I sat still, stunned at her confession and what I thought it entailed. Remembering that her private phone number was in Pitts's book, I suddenly realized that there aren't too many reasons someone would write down a number but no name, and I'd just thought of the best one. "You were having an affair." As I said it, it made perfect sense. She would have done anything to get out of Japan. Pitts was an easy passport.

She threw back her copper mane and laughed. "Gimme a break! The guy was old enough to be my father."

I kept staring.

"Okay, okay, so we did it a few times."

I held my breath.

"Didn't mean anything to me. I told 'im it was over." She shook her head. "He kept calling me Halliday, for God's sake. It was pathetic."

Somehow I thought Pitts hadn't received any of her pity. "He was drinking. You argued over Karatsu's photos."

She nodded. "Yeah, he was pretty looped. The phone call from Halliday made things worse-"

"You were there when she called?"

"Yes," she admittedly hesitantly. Hal was wrong when she thought Pitts was alone. Maybe my sister wasn't to blame for his death.

"He went crazy!" Vivian continued. "Started ranting. I didn't want any of it so I took the photos and left."

A mental light clicked on. Pitts's note from the safety deposit box, *V.G.-$-Japan?* "You were blackmailing Karatsu!"

Vivian Graves flashed a red-stained smile.

"Pitts wouldn't go for it."

The brilliant smile disappeared.

I knew I was right. I barged ahead, too many thoughts spinning to stop and think. "Something else happened before you left, didn't it?"

She watched me like Halliday watches a ball on the tee. "He fired you, didn't he? He wouldn't tolerate a blackmailer."

Vivian exploded. "Can you believe it? After the Classic," she snorted, "the SOB thought he could just get rid'a me!" Her eyes blazed. "After all I'd done! He wouldn't have had his precious tournament if it hadn't been for me. I, I..." She stopped, breathing hard, eyes on fire. "I left him," she continued lamely. "He was drunk."

I decided to play my card. "How'd you know where my accident happened?" I asked casually.

Vivian seemed relieved that we were no longer talking about Pitts. "Dunno." She shrugged thin shoulders. "Word gets around, you know how it is. You're all right. That's the main thing."

"Yeah, I'm peachy." I stood up and leaned over her cluttered desk.

"It's just that, besides the police, only three other people knew where it happened: the guy who picked me up, Halliday; and the bastard..." I stopped. Vivian's eyes were bright and her face suddenly tense, "or should I say bitch, who tried to run me over."

I didn't see her hands. The walkie talkie was airborne before I knew it. I ducked. It grazed my left cheekbone. Vivian Graves was on her feet as the pain hit me. She dashed around the desk and kicked at my chair. Her right foot hit my thigh. Ribs screaming, I tumbled over. She flung open the door. My head cracked against the tile floor.

The last thing I remember was the crunch of her footsteps.

Forty-Five

6:55 p.m., Saturday, August 1

I couldn't catch my breath. Every attempt breathed fire instead of oxygen into my chest. Outside, the engine of a car roared to life. I blinked. The walls and ceiling of the narrow trailer swung across my eyes. I tried to sit up, fell back gasping and whimpering. Pain lashed at my left wrist.

I shut my eyes for a couple of seconds and found a shallow but tolerable level of breathing. When I opened my peepers, the cluttered surroundings snapped into focus. Tires squealed. Horns blasted. The walkie talkie lay a couple of feet to my left. With a moan, I rolled. The fingers on my right hand tiptoed over to the black box. I tugged it back and punched the talk button.

"Security!" I croaked. "This's Riley Quinn. Stop Vivian Graves! She's heading out of the parking lot." I dropped the walkie talkie and shoved my hand down for support, took a deep breath and pulled myself onto my knees. A man's voice shouted outside.

The machine squawked. "Riley? Walt here. What's going on?"

I grabbed at the box. "Walt? Get someone to block the road! Got to stop Vivian! I'll explain later." The walkie talkie clattered to the floor. Another not-so-deep breath. Using the chair for support, I hauled myself upright. Walt's voice snapped, "On my way!" A couple of shaky steps and I was out the door.

A horn trumpeted. Somebody was shouting. As I ouched down the steps, I looked over at the entrance to the parking lot. A white delivery van blocked all passage. A grey-haired man at the wheel was screaming obscenities.

The brake lights on Vivian's Audi flickered as

it roared in reverse. With a screech, the little car slid back, its wheels spinning. The rubber grabbed and the hunk of steel leapt forward, swinging right. I caught a flash of Vivian's face as she spun the wheel. The auto charged up the mound alongside the road. It fishtailed violently, tires spitting grass and mud. The Audi spun across the turf, manoeuvred past the truck then humped down onto the road. Horn blaring, it shot off quickly out of sight.

"Get outta my way!" I screamed at the delivery guy and clambered into my convertible. The van sputtered to life and jerked forward. I shoved Emily into first gear and squirted 'round the van's square end.

I was in third gear in seconds. In the distance, I saw a flash of metal as the Audi swung right onto the main road. I geared down, glanced left and peeled around the corner of Dorcas Point Road. Out of the corner of my eye, I saw a red Firebird screaming down Sea Blush lane. Constable Dickson was on my heels!

The Audi was at least three cars ahead. I tried to pass the Toyota in front of me, but oncoming traffic was heavy. I gritted my teeth and stayed in fourth. The Firebird whined a couple of cars back.

At the intersection, Vivian burst through a red light and spun left onto Northwest Bay Road. A truck honked, slid into the intersection and missed the Audi's tail by inches.

The other drivers froze. The woman in the truck sat silently, rigidly staring through the windshield. The light changed. Eyes on the Audi's butt, I blasted Emily's horn. Finally, the trucker started her engine and the huge wheels lurched forward. By this time, the stoplight had changed back to red. I slammed my good palm against the steering wheel. When we finally rolled, the Audi was nowhere to be seen. I slid over to the shoulder, slowly got out and waited for Walt. Within seconds, the long red nose of his favourite lady was tucked behind Emily.

The big guy's mouth was working as I hurried over. "Don't talk. Just listen." He jaw closed. "Vivian's the one who tried to run me off the road. You've got to catch her! Call for help. I'll explain later."

Walt's eyes narrowed but he quickly snapped the button on his car radio and spat instructions. I looked up and down the highway. No Audis in sight.

"Okay," he said, slamming the radio into its socket. "That should stop 'er. Now, start talking. You look like you've been hit. What's going on?"

I ran a finger lightly over my left cheek. Tingle of pain. Over the din, I gave him a sketch of my run-in with Vivian.

"She admitted to running you off the road?"

I started to shake my head, thought better of it. "Not in so many words, but that's the only way she could have known about the accident."

"Makes sense." He glanced at his watch. "Not much we can do now. You look like you could use a little ice. What d'ya wanna do?"

My head was ringing, my chest aching and my wrist stiffening. "Go to my place."

Hal met us at the door. At first she seemed awkward, but that changed when she saw my face. "What happened?" she asked, hand reaching to my cheek. A movement over her shoulder made me step back. Michael Harrigan walked into the hallway.

"Are you all right?" he said, striding toward us. He glanced quickly at Halliday. "I came by to say hello, but you weren't here."

"I was sure you'd be home soon," Halliday said in a rush. "So I invited him in for a drink."

"That's just peachy."

We went inside. I left Hal to be hostess and ducked into the washroom. My left cheek was stained with blood. I gently cleaned it and examined the damage. Except for a horizontal gash, a spreading purple bruise and a little extra shine, my face looked pretty much the same. I downed some painkillers and took a quick shower. Pulling on jeans and a T-shirt, I grabbed ice packs and joined the others on the balcony. With ice on my left wrist and face and a cold drink in my free hand, I retold my tale. I wondered how Hal would take the news of Pitts's affairs.

She was dumbstruck. Michael's eyes flew back and forth from mine to Walt's.

"But why would Vivian try to kill you?" Halliday whispered finally.

"That's the million dollar question," I replied

"You're certain it was her?" Michael asked.

"Uh-huh. No one 'cept the police, the guy who picked me up and Halliday knew where it happened. You didn't tell anyone?" Hal shook her head. "See? The only way she could have known was to have been there."

"I think Riley's right," Walt said. "But Hal's got a point. Why?"

I stared out at Nanoose Bay. "I think she killed Pitts."

"What?!"

"Are you crazy?!"

I glanced back at them. "I know it sounds a little extreme, but something's not right about his death."

"For heaven's sake, Riley!" Michael exploded.

"Think of your sister! Just because you don't like to think the man overdosed is no reason to say he was murdered!"

"That's what you think!" I snapped. "It's been fishy all along-his call to me telling me he wasn't going to drink that evening, everyone lying about seeing him, Karatsu and his bloody photographs and then..." I removed the ice pack from my face for emphasis, "Vivian admits to having an affair with him." I hesitated. Halliday's face was pinched. "And practically admits to blackmailing Karatsu!"

Shaking her curls, Hal said, "If that's true, Pitts would've fired her."

"He did! On the spot. Only she got him before he got her."

"I think it's crazy," Michael said.

"Well, I don't!" Walt boomed. He stood up and rocked from heel to toe. "From the very beginning, Ril was upset. Didn't believe the official story." He hiked up his black shorts. "I'm sorry," he said to me. "I should'a listened."

The phone rang. Halliday ran into the kitchen. A couple of seconds later, she called for Walt. He disappeared inside. With nothing to say to one another, Michael and I stared at the sky. I couldn't imagine that we'd ever spent time here together. But we had-many glorious hours.

They came back a few minutes later. Halliday looked sick.

"Got her," Walt said with a grim smile. "At the airport. Almost made it." He strode across to my side. "She's at the station. I've gotta go. I'll call later." He leaned down and brushed my non-injured cheek. "Glad you're okay." He gave Hal a squeeze and shook Michael's hand.

Forty-Six
10:15 p.m., Saturday, August 1

Walt came by a little after ten. Michael had gone about an hour earlier and Halliday and I were still sitting on the balcony, in the dark, talking about our childhood.

"It's over," Walt said. "She confessed."

"No!" Halliday wailed and burst into tears.

Walt towered over her, shifting uncomfortably. "I'm sorry, I guess I..."

"It's all right," I said, trying hard to hold back my own tidal wave. "Just the shock. She'll be okay inna minute." I took a breath. "How 'bout making tea?"

He nodded and ducked inside.

"Come on, Hal," I said, gently. "Let's go in."

We did.

"At first, she was very quiet," Walt said, handing us each a steaming mug. "Wouldn't say anything 'til they found the letters in her trunk."

"Letters?" Hal asked, between bursts at blowing her nose.

"Blackmail, right?" I said, looking at Walt.

He nodded. "For years." He grimaced and sat down. "An ugly business. She'd got photos of Karatsu with young kids-pretty disgusting stuff. Used them to extort thousands. We've got Karatsu in for questioning. I think he'll be pretty cooperative given the chance to put it to Vivian."

"But what about Pitts?" Halliday asked.

Walt smiled thinly. "She told us all about it."

We stared.

"Uh-huh. We've got you to thank, Ril." I frowned. Even that hurt. "Vivian thought you knew everything. It all came out before she realized it. Then it was too late." He turned to Halliday. "I'm really sorry. Vivian says Pitts was on the phone with you as she came in." He glanced hesitantly at her. "It seems he was pretty upset." Halliday nodded, bitter green eyes glowing. "Vivian says he slammed down the phone and started drinking. Said something about being unable to trust the women in his life. Vivian didn't realize that he knew about the blackmail and tried to get the photos back. Pitts refused. They argued. He drank."

Walt put down his mug. "Seems he got pretty drunk, then violent. Told Vivian that he knew all about the blackmail. Told her he'd tell Joel."

"Pitts knew about Joel?" I asked.

Walt nodded. "Seems he'd had someone watching Vivian. Had her finances checked, found out about extra money coming in from a Japanese account." He took a sip. "Anyway, Pitts told her she was through and that Joel would dump 'er. Vivian said killing Pitts came to her suddenly, like a revelation. She sat there, staring at us with those golden eyes and said that Joel was the only man she'd ever loved. That she'd do anything for him. So she ducked into Pitts's bathroom and grabbed the pills."

Halliday shivered.

Walt looked at her, wide face full of concern.

"Go on," she said.

"Well, then she came out and found him on the balcony. He'd been sick. Perfect opportunity. She slipped a pile of anti-depressants into his glass, filled it with whisky and handed it over." Walt looked down uncomfortably.

"Go on," Halliday said for the second time.

"Well, he downed the drink. Vivian says she pretended to be sorry. Tried to talk Pitts out of calling Joel." He looked up at Halliday. "It was just a ruse to let the pills take effect. Finally, Pitts collapsed. Vivian walked about behind his place, making sure no one was looking. Then she," he coughed, "she pushed him over the railing. Grabbed the envelope with the letters and photos and rushed over to Joel's. She left Pitts to die."

There might have been tears running down Halliday's cheeks, but I couldn't see them for my own.

"I'm very sorry," Walt said finally.

No one said anything for a very long time. Finally, all seven of my questions were answered.

Being right is not all it's cracked up to be.

Forty-Seven

On the morning of the final round of the Sea Blush Classic, my sister and I stood on the first tee surrounded by hundreds of chanting fans. All my friends were there. With the exception of SinJin, my family, too. I was thrilled to be with them, to hear the laughter in their voices, to be enveloped by their love. Halliday and I had agreed that, no matter what happened at the end of today's round, we'd invite our friends back to Sea Blush. Win or lose, we had our lives to be thankful for.

Dr. O'Brien had called early to tell me that the toxicology tests for the level of anti-depressants in Pitts's body would take a couple of weeks. It was merely routine, anyway, as Vivian Graves had confessed. Walt phoned to say that Karatsu-hoping to win the court's favour-was being most cooperative, admitting to breaking into Pitts's condo and my apartment in a desperate search for the photographs.

Now, under the blazing summer sun, O'Brien stood, along with his wife and Walt, at our backs. Dai waved from the fairway. I heard someone shout my name and turned.

Paul Dunlop's smiling face poked out from the crowd. I walked over. "Little good luck charm," he said, shoving something into my hand. Then he was gone. I headed back to Halliday and opened my fist. Inside lay a BioAction sticker. Grinning, I peeled off the little circle and stuck it on my caddie vest.

Caroline's group had gone off 20 minutes earlier. Hal, paired with Alison Weld and Maria Vicarrio-Balley, was in the second-last bunch today. Waiting in the wings were Jennifer, Patty

Sheehan and Candy Lorenzo.

When Hal's name was finally announced, the gallery roared with applause. Tears tumbled down her cheeks as she walked around the rope, shaking hands and whispering thank-you's. With a grin, I handed her the driver. Instead of taking it, she stepped in and hugged me. It hurt but I hung in there. The noise was deafening.

"I love you," she shouted in my ear.

Squeezing her as hard as I could, I bellowed the chant from childhood, "Halli, Halli, hit the ball! Hit it further than them all!"

The fans picked it up. As my older sister approached her ball, the first tee resounded with cries of "Halli, Halli, hit the ball!"

Suddenly, silence. Not even a breath of wind. An eagle soared overhead. Halliday Quinn connected. The crowd cheered. I carefully pulled the golf bag over my shoulder. And, as I had done hundreds of times before, followed my big sister up the fairway.

The End

About The Author

Nicola Furlong was born in Edmonton, Alberta, and raised in Saskatchewan, Ontario and Prince Edward Island. The sixth of eight children, her passions are chocolate, athletics, reading and more chocolate. She graduated, with a combined degree in fine arts and psychology, from Carleton University. After over a decade working in federal public service in Ottawa, she recently moved to Sidney, a small town north of Victoria, British Columbia. In addition to fiction, Nicola writes personal experience essays and articles on environmental issues.

WATCH FOR THESE NEW COMMONWEALTH BOOKS

WATCH FOR THESE NEW COMMONWEALTH BOOKS

	ISBN #	U.S.	Can
☐ **DOUBLE INHERITANCE**, Winnie Bennett	1-55197-026-0	$4.99	$6.99
☐ **A CANADIAN TRAGEDY**, Joel Fletcher	1-55197-022-8	$4.99	$6.99
☐ **THE TEAKWOOD CROSS**, Harry Mileaf	1-55197-028-7	$4.99	$6.99
☐ **THE TWO GREAT PROPHETS**, E.V. Kemp	1-55197-030-9	$4.99	$6.99
☐ **THE CHRISTIAN'S CUSS BOOK**, M.S. Aue	1-55197-036-8	$4.99	$6.99
☐ **PRESCRIPTION: MURDER**, J.L. Evans	1-55197-001-5	$4.99	$6.99
☐ **PAIN GROWS A PLATINUM ROSE**, G. Martorano	1-55197-009-0	$4.99	$6.99
☐ **FALSE APOSTLE**, Michael E. Miller	1-55197-011-2	$4.99	$6.99
☐ **LIGHT ALL NIGHT**, Richard Robinson	1-55197-015-5	$4.99	$6.99
☐ **THE PROMISE**, Andrew R. Gault	1-55197-007-4	$4.99	$6.99
☐ **PLAYING AS ONE**, O'Neil/Saltonstall	1-55197-013-9	$4.99	$6.99
☐ **PIMPINELLA**, Ilse Kramer	1-55197-003-1	$4.99	$6.99
☐ **MADNESS IN THE STREETS**, Dana Landers	1-55197-005-8	$4.99	$6.99
☐ **A LITTLE GIRL LOST**, Isabel Sinclair	1-55197-040-6	$4.99	$6.99
☐ **THE RIVER RAN BETWEEN THEM**, James Allen Welch	1-55197-032-5	$4.99	$6.99
☐ **WESTERN THUNDER**, Freeda Brown	1-55197-027-9	$5.99	$7.99
☐ **ALONE WITHIN**, Dianna DeBlieux	1-55197-044-9	$4.99	$6.99
☐ **MEMORIES FOREVER**, Jody Lebroke	1-55197-017-1	$4.99	$6.99

Available at your local bookstore or use this page to order.

Send to: COMMONWEALTH PUBLICATIONS INC.
9764 - 45th Avenue
Edmonton, Alberta, CANADA T6E 5C5

Please send me the items I have checked above. I am enclosing
$_____ (please add $2.50 per book to cover postage and
handling). Send check or money order, no cash or C.O.D.'s, please.

Mr./Mrs./Ms._____

Address_____

City/State_____ Zip_____

Please allow four to six weeks for delivery.
Prices and availability subject to change without notice.

WATCH FOR THESE NEW COMMONWEALTH BOOKS

	ISBN #	U.S.	Can
❏ RIBBONS AND ROSES, D.B. Taylor	1-55197-088-0	$4.99	$6.99
❏ PRISON DREAMS, John O. Powers	1-55197-039-2	$4.99	$6.99
❏ A VOW OF CHASTITY, Marcia Jean Greenshields	1-55197-106-2	$4.99	$6.99
❏ LAVENDER'S BLUE, Janet Tyers	1-55197-058-9	$4.99	$6.99
❏ HINTS AND ALLEGATIONS, Kimberly A. Dascenzo	1-55197-073-2	$4.99	$6.99
❏ BROKEN BRIDGES, Elizabeth Gorlay	1-55197-119-4	$4.99	$6.99
❏ PAINTING THE WHITE HOUSE, Hal Marcovitz	1-55197-095-3	$4.99	$6.99
❏ THE KISS OF JUDAS, J.R. Thompson	1-55197-045-7	$4.99	$6.99
❏ BALLARD'S WAR, Tom Holzel	1-55197-112-7	$4.99	$6.99
❏ ROSES FOR SARAH, Anne Philips	1-55197-125-9	$4.99	$6.99
❏ THE TASKMASTER, Mary F. Murchison	1-55197-113-5	$4.99	$6.99
❏ SECOND TIME, Thomas E. Sprain	1-55197-135-6	$4.99	$6.99
❏ MY BROTHER'S TOWN, B.A. Stuart	1-55197-138-0	$4.99	$6.99
❏ MISSING PIECES, Carole W. Holden	1-55197-172-0	$4.99	$6.99
❏ DIARY OF A GHOST, Alice Richards Laule	1-55197-132-1	$4.99	$6.99

Available at your local bookstore or use this page to order.

Send to: COMMONWEALTH PUBLICATIONS INC.
9764 - 45th Avenue
Edmonton, Alberta, CANADA T6E 5C5

Please send me the items I have checked above. I am enclosing
$_____ (please add $2.50 per book to cover postage and
handling). Send check or money order, no cash or C.O.D.'s, please.

Mr./Mrs./Ms._____

Address_____

City/State_____ Zip_____

Please allow four to six weeks for delivery.
Prices and availability subject to change without notice.

WATCH FOR THESE NEW COMMONWEALTH BOOKS

	ISBN #	U.S.	Can
☐ PACHYDERMS, Danny Buoy	1-55197-130-5	$4.99	$6.99
☐ THE BRIDGE GAME, C.A. Thompson	1-55197-144-5	$4.99	$6.99
☐ SWEET PROMISES, Edith Bach Hall	1-55197-080-5	$4.99	$6.99
☐ SUMMER OF THE RED FERRARIE, E. Sanders	1-55197-198-8	$4.99	$6.99
☐ DISLOCATED, Billie Utterback, Jr.	1-55197-146-1	$5.99	$7.99
☐ THE ZACHARIAS SOLUTION, G.R. Humphries	1-55197-118-6	$4.99	$6.99
☐ HELL'S BELLS ARE RINGING, C.R. Dillon	1-55197-081-3	$5.99	$7.99
☐ C-NOTES: MY JOURNEY THROUGH BREAST CANCER, Patsy Paxton	1-55197-117-8	$11.95	$13.95
☐ TWO WORLDS ONE HEART, Tom Butler	1-55197-053-8	$4.99	$6.99
☐ PAYBACK, Jack Gatton	1-55197-094-5	$4.99	$6.99
☐ HELLESPONT PLANTATION, James Scott	1-55197-134-8	$4.99	$6.99
☐ ZERO SUM GAME, A.C. Aaron	1-55197-057-0	$4.99	$6.99
☐ NO MORE TOMORROW, Albert Lyon	1-55197-158-5	$4.99	$6.99
☐ THE RISE OF ELEVATORS, E. Radford	1-55197-127-5	$4.99	$6.99
☐ THE HESS PAPER, Daniel Wyatt	1-55197-156-9	$4.99	$6.99
☐ THE TIDES OF LOON ISLAND, M. Peterson	1-55197-123-2	$4.99	$6.99
☐ NEUROSYNTH, Diana Kemp-Jones	1-55197-124-0	$4.99	$6.99
☐ MATHILDA, Catherine M. Feldman	1-55197-089-9	$4.99	$6.99
☐ WRAITHS, Larry C. Gillies	1-55197-120-X	$5.99	$7.99
☐ HOPSCOTCH TO HELL, David S. Wagner	1-55197-148-8	$4.99	$6.99
☐ VAPOURS, Larry S. Milner	1-55197-109-7	$4.99	$6.99
☐ MILKMAN IN PIN STRIPES, Bob Weir	1-55197-150-X	$4.99	$6.99
☐ JOURNAL OF JOHN BRIGGS, C. Hotchkiss	1-55197-114-3	$4.99	$6.99
☐ RANGE RATS AT SEA, Dan Kovalchik	1-55197-128-3	$4.99	$6.99
☐ HONG KONG BLUES, Tom Page	1-55197-115-1	$4.99	$6.99
☐ THE CAT'S-PAW, Raymond J. Radner	1-55197-129-1	$4.99	$6.99

Available at your local bookstore or use this page to order.

Send to: COMMONWEALTH PUBLICATIONS INC.
9764 - 45th Avenue
Edmonton, Alberta, CANADA T6E 5C5

Please send me the items I have checked above. I am enclosing
$_____ (please add $2.50 per book to cover postage and
handling). Send check or money order, no cash or C.O.D.'s, please.

Mr./Mrs./Ms._____

Address_____

City/State_____ Zip_____

Please allow four to six weeks for delivery.
Prices and availability subject to change without notice.

Golf can be more dangerous than just dodging duffers' hooks and slices! Riley Quinn, a former LPGA star and now Sea Blush club pro, tees off an investigation to the death of her brother-in-law, the club owner. The jeopardizes her new part-time career as coroner on Vancouver Island. As the Sea Blush Classic, a professional women's golf event progresses, she finds herself sand-wedged by a villainous environmental group, a mysterious Japanese consortium and her estranged sister, Halliday, a tournament celebrity. Riley Quinn quickly discovers that not all bad lies are on the golf course.

Teed Off

by
Nicola Furlong